MARNIE

Winston Graham is the author of more than thirty novels, which include *Cordelia*, *Night Without Stars*, *The Walking Stick* and *Stephanie*, as well as the highly successful *Poldark* series. His novels have been translated into seventeen languages and six have been filmed. Two television series have been made of the *Poldark* novels and shown in twenty-two countries. *The Stranger From the Sea* has now also been televised. *Tremor*, Winston Graham's latest best-seller, is also available from Pan Books.

Winston Graham lives in Sussex. He is a fellow of the Royal Society of Literature and in 1983 was awarded the OBE.

D0582819

WINSTON GRAHAM

MARNIE

PAN BOOKS

First published 1961 by The Bodley Head Ltd

This edition published 1997 by Pan Books
an imprint of Macmillan Publishers Ltd
25 Eccleston Place, London SW1W 9NF
Basingstoke and Oxford
Associated companies throughout the world
www.macmillan.com

ISBN 0 330 33903 6

A CIP catalogue record for this book is available from
the British Library.

Typeset by CentraCet Limited, Cambridge
Printed by Mackays of Chatham plc, Chatham, Kent

CHAPTER ONE

'GOOD NIGHT, miss,' said the policeman as I came down the steps, and 'good night,' I answered, wondering if he would sound as friendly if he'd known what was in this attaché case.

But he didn't, and I took a taxi home. Throwing money away, because you could do it easily by bus, but this was a special day and you had to splash sometimes. I paid the taxi off at the end of the street and walked down to my two-roomed flat and let myself in. People might think it lonely living on my own nearly all the time, but I never found it lonely. I always had plenty to think about, and anyway maybe I'm not so good on people.

When I got in I took off my coat and shook out my hair and combed it in front of the mirror; then I poured out a half and half of gin and french as another part of the celebration. While I drank it I went over a few train times and emptied a couple of small drawers. Then I took a bath, my second that day. Somehow it always helped to wash something out of your system.

While I was still in it the telephone rang. I let it go on for a bit and then climbed out of the warm water

1

and draped a towel round myself and padded into the living-room.

'Marion?'

'Yes?'

'This is Ronnie.'

I might have guessed it. 'Oh, hello.'

'Do I detect a lack of enthusiasm in the voice?'

'Well, it's a bit inconvenient, dear. I was just in my bath.'

'What a delicious thought. How I regret this isn't television!'

Well, I mean, I might have expected that from Ronnie.

'Are you still set on going away on your own tomorrow?' he asked.

'But, Ronnie, I've said so at least six times.'

'You're a queer girl. Are you meeting another man?'

'No, of course not. I've told you. I'm spending the weekend with this school-friend in Swindon.'

'Then let me drive you down.'

'Ronnie, dear, can't you understand? We don't want a man. We just want to natter together about old times. I don't get much opportunity to see her.'

'They work you too hard at that office. I'll come and see old Pringle one of these days. But seriously . . .'

My thumb-nail had got caught on the office door and the varnish had chipped. Needed touching up.

'Seriously what?'

'Won't you give me your phone number?'

'I don't think she has one. But I'll try and ring you.'

'Promise. Tomorrow evening.'

'I can't *promise*. I'm not sure where the nearest box is. But I'll really promise to try.'

'What time? About nine?'

'Ronnie, I'm beginning to shiver. And there's a horrid stain on the carpet all round my feet.'

Even then he clung on like a cadger at a fair, taking as long as he could to say goodbye. When I could get the phone back I was nearly dry and the water had gone cold, so I dusted myself with talc and began to dress.

Everything I put on was new: brassiere, panties, shoes, nylons, frock. It wasn't just taking care; it was the way I'd come to like it. I suppose I have a funny mind or something, but everything has to be just as it should be; and I like it to be that way with people too. That was why the tie-up with Ronnie Oliver was something I'd be glad to be out of. Human beings . . . well, they just won't be ticked off, docketed, that's what's wrong with them; they spill over and spoil your plans – not because you are out in your estimates but because they are. Ronnie, of course, thought he was in love with me. Big passion. We'd only met a dozen times because I'd kept on putting him off, saying I'd other dates etc. Anyway it was the old old story.

My cast-offs were in my case, which would only just shut. You always seem to hoard up stuff even in a few months.

I went round the flat. I started in the kitchenette and went over it inch by inch. The only thing I saw in it was a cheap tea towel I'd bought just after Christmas, but I grabbed that and packed it with the rest. Then I went through the bathroom and lastly the bed-sitting-room.

I always reminded myself of the coat I'd left behind in Newcastle last year. Remembering that kept me on the alert; your eyes get to see something as part of the background and then you've left something behind and that's too bad because you can't come back for it.

I took down the calendar and packed that. Then I put on my coat and hat, picked up the suitcase and the attaché case and let myself out.

They were glad to see me at the Old Crown at Cirencester. 'Why, Miss Elmer, it's three months since you were here last, isn't it? Are you going to stay long this time? Yes, you can have your usual room. It's not been good hunting weather this month; but of course you don't hunt, do you; I'll have your cases sent up directly. Would you like some tea?'

I always grew an inch staying at the Old Crown. Often enough I got by as a lady nowadays – funny how easy it was; but this was nearly the only place where I could believe it myself. The chintzy bedroom looking on the courtyard, with this four-poster bed and the same servants, they never changed, they were part of the furniture, and every day out to Garrod's Farm to pick up Forio and ride for hours on end, stopping at some little pub for lunch and coming home in the failing light. It was life; and this time instead of staying two weeks I stayed four.

I didn't read the papers. Sometimes I thought of Crombie & Strutt, but in an idle sort of way as if working for them was something that had been done by another person. That always helped. Now and then I wondered how Mr Pringle would take it and if Ronnie Oliver was still waiting for his telephone call, but I didn't lose any sleep over it.

At the end of four weeks I went home for a couple of days, but said it was a flying visit and left on the Saturday. I dropped most of my personal things at the Old Crown and spent the night at Bath at the Fernley, signing in as Enid Thompson, last address the Grand Hotel, Swansea. In the morning I bought a new suitcase, a new spring outfit; then I had my hair tinted at one of the stores. When I came out I bought a pair of plain-glass spectacles, but I didn't put them on yet. When I got to the station that afternoon I took out of the left-luggage office the attaché case I'd left there nearly five weeks ago, and there was room for it inside the new suitcase I'd bought that morning. I bought a second-class ticket for Manchester – which seemed as good a place as anywhere, as I had never lived there – and a *Times*, which I thought might help me in picking out a new name.

Names are important. They have to be neither too ordinary nor too queer, just a name, like a face, that'll go along with the crowd. And I'd found from experience that the Christian name had to be like my own, which is Margaret – or usually Marnie – because otherwise I might not answer to it when called, and that can be awkward.

In the end I chose Mollie Jeffrey.

So at the end of March a Miss Jeffrey took rooms in Wilbraham Road and began to look for a job. I suppose you'd have seen her as a quiet girl, quietly dressed, with fair hair cut short round the head and horn-tipped spectacles. She wore frocks that were a bit too big for her and a bit too long. It was the best way she knew of looking slightly dowdy and of making her figure not noticed – because if she dressed properly men looked at her.

She got a job as usherette at the Gaumont Cinema in Oxford Street, and kept it until June. She was friendly enough with the other usherettes, but when they asked her to go places with them she made excuses. She looked after her invalid mother, she said. I expect they said to each other: poor object, she's one of those, and what a pity; you're only young once.

If they only knew it, I couldn't have agreed with them more. We only had different ideas what to do about it. Their idea was fooling around with long-faced pimply men, ice skating or jiving on their days off, two weeks at Blackpool or Rhyl, queuing for the Sales, Pop discs, and maybe hooking a man at the end of it, some clerk in an export office, then babies in a council house and pushing a pram with the other wives among the red-brick shops. Well, all right, I'm not saying they shouldn't, if that's what they want. Only I never did want that.

One day I tried for a job at the Roxy Cinema, close by the Gaumont, where they wanted an assistant in the box office. The manager of the Gaumont gave me a good reference and I got the job.

When I'd been there three months the staff arrangements worked out that I was due for a week's holiday, so for the first day or two I went home.

My mother lived in Lime Avenue, Torquay. It's one of a row of Victorian houses behind Belgrave Road, and it's easy for the shops and the sea front and the Pavilion. We had moved there from Plymouth about two and a half years ago, and we'd been lucky to get a house unfurnished. My mother was a cripple, or at least she got about fairly well but she'd had something wrong with one leg for about sixteen years. She always said she was the widow of a naval officer who was killed in the war, but in fact Dad hadn't ever got further than Leading Seaman when he was torpedoed. She also said she was a clergyman's daughter, and that wasn't true either, but I think Grandfather was a Lay Preacher, which is much the same thing, only you don't lose your amateur status.

Mother was fifty-six at this time, and living with her was a woman called Lucy Nye, a small, moth-eaten, untidy, dog-eared, superstitious, kindly creature with one eye bigger than the other. One thing I'll always say for Mother, you never saw her anything but carefully and properly got up. She always had a sense of what was right and proper and she lived for it. When I got in that day she was sitting in the front window watching, and as soon as I rapped on the door she was there, stick and all.

She was an odd person – she really was – I got to

realize it more as I grew older – and even though she kissed me and even though I knew I was the apple of her eye – God help me – I could still tell there was a sort of *reserve* in the welcome. She didn't let up, and even while she kissed you she kept you just that bit at a distance. You knew she'd been waiting at that window for hours to see you come down the street, but you wouldn't be popular if you let on.

She was a thin woman; I always remember her as extremely thin. Not like me because although I'm quite slight I'm well covered. I don't think she'd been like that even at twenty-two. She had a really good bone structure, like old pictures of Marlene Dietrich, but she'd never had enough flesh to cover it, and as she got older she got haggard.

That was the hard thing of living away from home. I should never have thought of her as haggard, not that word, if I'd stayed with her; it was going away and coming back that forced you to see things with new eyes. She was in a new black tailormade today.

'Bobby's, seven guineas,' she said, as soon as she saw me looking. 'I took it off the peg, one advantage of keeping your figure, isn't it? They know me there now. Hard to please, they say, but not hard to fit. Well, Marnie, you're looking a bit peaky, not like you should after being abroad. I hope Mr Pemberton hasn't been working you too hard.'

Mr Pemberton was my fiction man. I'd made him up three years ago, the year after I left home, and he'd worked like a charm ever since. He was a wealthy business executive who took trips abroad and took his secretary along; it explained me being away and not always able to leave an address; it explained me being flush when I came home. Sometimes I had nightmares that Mother would find out; because there'd be Hell to pay if she ever did.

'And I don't like your hair that colour,' she said. 'Blonde hair looks as if you're trying to attract the men.'

'Well, I'm not.'

'No, dear, you're sensible that way. I always said you'd got an old head on young shoulders. I always say so to Lucy.'

'How is Lucy?'

'I sent her for some scones. I know how you like scones for tea. But she's gettin' slower and slower. It tries me beyond human patience sometimes, what with this leg and seeing her *creep* about.'

We were in the kitchen by this time. It never changed in here; honestly it didn't; not any of the house really; it always struck me coming home like this; you moved homes and you stayed the same; *everything* moved with us; from Keyham, I suppose, to the bungalow at Sangerford, then back to Plymouth, and now here. The same cups and saucers even, laid out for tea on the plastic tablecloth, the framed colour print of *The Light of the World*, the rocking chair with the padded arms, the awful fretwork pipe-rack, the Welsh dresser with the woodworm, that clock. I don't know why I hated the thing. It was oblong, coffin-shaped with a glass front, and the lower half covering the weights and pendulum was painted with pink and green love-birds.

'Cold, dear?' Mother said. 'There's a fire laid in the

front, but it's a close day and I didn't put a match to it. Of course, this side of the street don't get the sun in the afternoon.'

I made tea while she sat there eyeing me up and down like a mother cat licking over its kitten. I'd bought presents for both of them, a fur for Ma and gloves for Lucy, but Mother always had to be got into the right mood first, she had to be talked round so that in the end it was as if she was doing you a favour by taking it. The only risk was getting her suspicious that you had too much money. She went word for word by the framed texts in her bedroom, and God help you if you didn't keep in step too. Yet I loved and thought more of her than anything else in the world because of her guts in the struggle she'd had and the way above everything else she'd kept up *appearances*. Appearances for her were the Holy Bible. I still remembered the terrible rows she gave me when I was ten and had been caught stealing; and I still admired her for acting like she did even though I hadn't enjoyed it at the time and even though I hadn't reformed the way she thought I had – only got smarter so she didn't find out.

She said suddenly, 'That's French silk isn't it, Marnie? It must have cost you a pretty bit of money.'

'Twelve guineas,' I said, when it was thirty. 'I got it in a sale. D'you like it?'

She didn't answer but put her stick down and fidgeted round in her chair. I could feel her eyes boring my back.

'Mr Pemberton all right?' she asked.

'Yes, fine.'

'He must be a man to work for. I often tell my friends, I say Marnie's private secretary to a millionaire and he treats her like his daughter. That's right, isn't it?'

I put the cosy on the tea and the caddy back on the mantelpiece. 'He hasn't got a daughter. He's generous, if that's what you mean.'

'But he's got a wife, hasn't he? I doubt she sees as much of him as you do, eh?'

I said: 'We've gone into this before, Mam. There's nothing wrong between us. I'm his secretary, that's all. We don't travel *alone*. I'm quite safe, don't you worry.'

'Well, I often think of my daughter knocking about the world the way you do. I worry about you sometimes. Men try to catch you unawares. You've got to be on the lookout, always.'

Just then Lucy Nye came in. She squeaked like a bat when she saw me and we kissed, and then I had to go about the business of giving them their presents. By the time this was over the tea was cold and Lucy stirred herself making some more. I knew of course what Mother meant about her; she moved round the scullery emptying the teapot like an engineer in a go-slow strike.

Mother stood in front of the mirror, fidgeting with her new fur. 'Do you like it under the chin or loose over the shoulders? Over the shoulders is more the thing, I shouldn't wonder. Marnie, you spend your money.'

'That's what it's for, isn't it?'

'Spent proper, spent right, yes. But saved too. You've got to think of that. The Bible says love of money is the root of all evil; I've told you so before.'

'Yes, Mam. And it says that money answereth all things.'

She looked at me sharply. 'Don't scoff, Marnie. I shouldn't want a daughter of mine to scoff at sacred words.'

'No, Mam, I'm not scoffing. Look.' I moved across and pulled the fur down at the back. 'That's the way I've seen them worn in Birmingham. It suits you that way.'

After a bit we all sat down to tea again.

'I had a letter from your Uncle Stephen last week. He's in Hong Kong. Some port job he's got, and with a good screw. *I* wouldn't like it among all those yellow people, but he was always one for something different. I'll find his letter for you later on. He sent his love.'

Uncle Stephen was Mother's brother. He was the one man I really cared about; and I never saw enough of him.

Mother said: 'What with my fur and one thing and another. Your father never give me anything so good.'

She did an act with a bit of scone, picking it up in her thumb and first finger as if it was breakable and putting it in her mouth and chewing as if she was afraid to bite. Then I noticed the knuckles of her hands were swollen, so I felt cheap for being critical.

'How's your rheumatism?'

'Not good. It's damp this side of the avenue, Marnie; we never get a gleam of sunshine after twelve; we never thought of that when we took it. Sometimes I feel we ought to move.'

'It would be a job to find anything as cheap.'

'Yes, well it depends, doesn't it. It depends what you like to see your mother in. There's a lovely little semi in Cuthbert Avenue, just down the hill from here. It's coming empty because the man who lived there has just died of pernicious anaemia. They say he was like paper before he went; he made no blood at all, and his spleen swelled up. It's two reception and a kitchen, three bed and one attic and the usual offices. It would just suit us, wouldn't it, Lucy?'

This bigger eye of Lucy Nye's looked at me over the top of her steaming cup but she didn't say anything.

'What's the rent? Is it to rent?' I asked.

'I b'lieve so, though we could inquire. Of course it would be more than this, but it gets all the sun, and it's the neighbourhood. This has gone down since we came. You remember Keyham, how it went down. But you won't remember. Lucy remembers, don't you Lucy?'

'I 'ad a dream last night,' Lucy Nye said. 'I dreamed Marnie was in trouble.'

It's queer. Being out and about in the world, especially the way I'd lived, was enough to knock the corners off you, to make you grown up. Yet the tone of Lucy's voice gave me a twinge just like I used to have when I used to sleep with her when I was twelve and she'd wake me up in the morning and say, 'I've 'ad a bad dream.' And something always seemed to happen that day or the next.

'What d'you mean, trouble?' Mother said sharply. She had stopped with a piece of scone half-way to her mouth.

'I don't know; I didn't get that far. But I dreamed she came in that door with her coat all torn and she was crying.'

'Probably fell down playing hopscotch,' I said.

'You and your silly dreams,' Mother said. 'As if you didn't ought to know better by your age. Sixty-six next birthday and you talk like a baby. "I had a dream last night!" Who wants to hear about your old woman's fancies!'

Lucy's lip quivered. She was always touchy about her age and to say it out loud was like treading on a corn.

'I only just said I'd 'ad a *dream*. You can't help what you see in your sleep. And it isn't always so silly. Remember I dreamt that last time before Frank came home—'

'Hold your tongue,' said Mother. 'This is a Christian household and—'

'Well,' I said, 'whatever else I came home for it wasn't to listen to you two rowing. Can I have another scone?'

The kitchen clock struck five. It was a funny note, loud and toneless, that I've never heard from any other clock, and the last note was always flat as if it was running down.

'But while we're talking of old times,' I said, 'why don't you throw that thing out?'

'What thing, dear?'

'That perishing clock,' I said, 'it gives me the creeps every time I hear it.'

'But why, Marnie, why? It was a wedding present to

14

your grannie. It's got the date on the bottom, 1898. She was real proud of it.'

'Well, I'm not,' I said. 'Give it away. I'll buy you another. Then maybe Lucy'll stop dreaming.'

The other girl in the box office of the Roxy Cinema was called Anne Wilson. She was about thirty, tall and skinny, and she was writing a play, hoping I suppose to be another Shelagh Delaney. We worked overlapping shifts so that there were always two of us in the box office in the busy hours – except Sunday, that was. Only one could take the money but the one not serving helped behind the scenes.

The box office was a glass and chromium kiosk in the centre of the marble foyer. The manager's office was to the left just past the entrance to one of the tunnels leading to the stalls. It was just out of sight of the box office but Mr King, the manager, prowled about between his office and the box office during the busy hours. He kept his eye on the staff; usually he would go up to the projection-room at least twice in every performance, and he was always at the doors to say good night to his patrons at the end of the show. Three times every day, at four and at eight and at nine-thirty, he would come to the kiosk, see we were all right for change and take away the money that had come in.

Every morning at ten he came to the cinema, unlocked his Chubb safe and carried last night's takings in a shabby attaché case two doors down the street to the Midland Bank.

Sometimes, of course, in spite of his care we would run short of change at the wrong moment, and then one of us would go across to his office for more. This happened in October soon after I got back, because the syndicate made a change in the price of seats and we found we needed a lot more coppers. One day Mr King was at a meeting and we ran short of change.

'Hang on,' said Anne Wilson, 'I'll go and get some.'

'You'll have to go upstairs,' I said. 'Mr King's in the café with the two directors.'

'I don't need to bother him,' Anne said. 'He keeps a spare key in the top drawer of the filing cabinet.'

Christmas came on. I wrote home and said I couldn't get home because Mr Pemberton would need me all through the holiday. In the second week of December we had the record-breaking *Santa Clara* booked and we were following the new fashion and running it for three weeks. It was my day on on the second Sunday.

On the Friday I told my landlady I was going to see my mother in Southport. On the Saturday after I got home from the Roxy I began my usual turn-out, and while I was doing this a strange thing happened. I was using an old newspaper as an inner wrapping and came across a paragraph about a girl I'd pretty nearly forgotten.

It was an old *Daily Express*, dated as far back as 21 February. 'Police in Birmingham are looking for pretty, mysterious Marion Holland who vanished without trace from her work and from her flat last Monday evening. They are also looking for one thousand one hundred pounds in cash which vanished at the same time from the safe of Messrs Crombie & Strutt, Turf Accountants, of Corporation Street, where Marion was employed as confidential clerk. "We didn't know much about her," forty-two-year-old balding branch manager George Pringle, admitted yesterday, "but she was a shy retiring girl and always most reliable. She came to us with a good character." "A very quiet one," is landlady Dyson's view. "Never had no friends but always polite and well spoken. Told me it was only her second job. I think she'd come down in the world." "It's like a nightmare to me," confessed twenty-eight-year-old Ronnie Oliver of PO Telephones, who has been dating Marion. "I can't help but feel there has been some terrible mistake."

'The police are not so sure about the mistake. General description and type of job are similar to those of Peggy Nicholson who disappeared from a position as secretary to a Newcastle business man last year with over seven hundred pounds in cash. They would like to interview both ladies and would not be at all surprised if they turned out to be one. General description. Age twenty to twenty-six, height five feet five inches, weight about eight stone, vital statistics to fit and a "taking" way with her. Susceptible personnel managers please note.'

It shook me coming on it like that. It shook me because I hadn't ever seen details like that before. And living my life in sort of separate compartments the way I do, it jolted me seeing it just then. Of course there was nothing connecting Marion Holland of Birmingham with Mollie Jeffrey of Manchester, still less with

Margaret Elmer who kept a thoroughbred horse at Garrod's Farm near Cirencester and had a strict old mother in Torquay. But it was a coincidence. It was a hell of a jarring, nasty little coincidence.

The only thing I liked about it was the bit about having 'come down in the world'. It just showed what elocution lessons would do.

For a while after reading the paper I sat on the bed wondering if I should go through with it or if this was a warning that this time I was going to be caught.

In the end I got over that nonsense. Really, once you start thinking, you're done. But I thought I wouldn't try this sort of job again. It was riskier than most.

I left on Sunday at twelve and took my suitcase with me. I took it to London Road Station and put it in the left-luggage office as usual. I had lunch in a cafeteria and was at the Roxy by ten to four.

The doors opened at four and the first film began at four-fifteen. I went with Mr King into his office and got twenty pounds in silver and five pounds in copper. He was in a good humour and said we'd had the best week's takings since 1956.

'Let me carry those for you,' he said as I picked up the bags.

'No, really, thanks. I can manage.' I smiled at him and straightened my spectacles. 'Thank you, Mr King.'

He followed me out. A small shabby-looking lot of people were waiting at the door of the cinema. It was two minutes to four.

I said: 'Er – have I time to get a glass of water? I want to take an aspirin.'

'Yes, of course. Hold them a minute, Martin.' This to the commissionaire. 'Nothing wrong, I hope?' he said when I got back.

'No, not really, thanks very much.' I smiled bravely. 'Go ahead. I'm fine now.'

By seven the cheaper seats were full, and there was a queue outside for the two and eightpennies. A trickle of people were still coming in and paying four and six so as not to wait. In five minutes the secondary film would be over, sixty or seventy people would come out and a ten-minute break for ice-creams would give the queue outside time to get in and be settled before *Santa Clara* came on for the last time.

I never remember being nervous when it comes to the point. My hands are always steady, my pulse beats like one of those musical things they have for keeping time.

As the last of the stragglers leaving the theatre went out and Martin moved to let in the first of the queue I called quietly to Mr King.

'What's the matter?' he said when he saw the look on my face.

'I'm – frightfully sorry. I feel awful! I think I'm going to be sick!'

'Oh, dear! Can you . . . Can I help you to—'

'No . . . I – I must see this queue through.'

'Can you?' he said. 'No, I see you can't.'

'No . . . I'm afraid I can't. Can you hold up the queue for a few minutes?'

'No, I'll take your place. Really. I'll call an usherette.'

I grabbed up my handbag and stumbled out of the box. 'I think if I lie down for about five minutes . . . You can manage?'

'Of course.' He climbed into the box as the first members of the queue came up to the window.

I stumbled off down the right-hand tunnel away from the manager's office. You passed the man who tears your tickets, went down the corridor, and just this side of the doors into the cinema proper, was the Ladies.

But instead of turning in at the Ladies I went through into the cinema. A girl flashed a light at me and then saw who I was.

'Where's Gladys?' I whispered.

'On the other door.'

As I went along the back of the cinema a big American face was telling the audience why the film he was appearing in at this cinema for seven days beginning next Sunday week was a unique event in motion picture history.

There was no Gladys at the other door because she was down flashing her light looking for vacant seats, so my excuse wasn't needed. I went out of the door and up the other tunnel until I was almost in the foyer again. Then I turned in at the manager's office.

The light was already on. I shut the door but didn't catch it. Then I pulled a chair forward and kicked off my shoes.

The filing cabinet, top drawer. The key wasn't in the back . . . I went all down the other five drawers. Nothing . . . The cabinet was high and I pulled a stool over and stood on it. The top drawer was full of publicity pamphlets, copies of *The Kine Weekly* etc. At the back was a pair of Mr King's gloves. The key was in one thumb.

Almost two minutes gone. At the safe I slid back the key guard; the key clicked nicely; but it was a real effort to pull the big door open.

There was nothing but papers in the three top compartments, but in the drawer beside the bags of change were piles of stacked notes. Not only today's takings but Saturday's as well.

You can get a lot of money in a medium-sized handbag if it's empty to begin with. I shut the safe, locked it and put the key back. Then I slid my shoes on and went to the door. I could hear the movement of people and the click and rattle of the change machine.

I went out without looking back towards the foyer and turned into the cinema again. This time Gladys was back.

'Full house?' I asked before she could speak.

'There's about two dozen four-and-sixes and some singles, that's all. You off duty now?'

'No, I'm coming back in a minute.' I went on down the side aisle.

'It's pretty tough leading the life I lead,' said the man on the screen, and he seemed to look at me.

'I don't like it but I can take it,' said the girl, 'if I'm with you.'

That stuff was as real as nothing. I got to the end of the cinema and let myself out by the exit door.

CHAPTER TWO

IT WAS the year after all this that I wrote for the job at John Rutland & Co. at Barnet.

I don't know; maybe there's such a thing as fate, as luck. If you walk under a ladder or spill the salt or cut your nails on a Friday. Well, I had no feelings before I wrote. I might just as well have picked out some other advertisement or opened another paper.

I'd been working in London since January at a firm called Kendalls who were Insurance Brokers but I'd soon found that the only thing I'd get there was a reference, so I'd worked on just for that and kept my eyes open to see what else was about.

The letter that came back was headed *John Rutland & Co. Ltd., Printers of Quality, established 1869* and it said: 'Dear Madam, Thank you for your letter replying to our advertisement for an assistant cashier. Would you kindly call to see us next Tuesday morning the 10th inst. at eleven o'clock. S. Ward (Manager).'

When I got there it was quite a big place, and after waiting in an outer office while another girl was interviewed I was shown into a small room with two men sitting behind a desk, and they asked me the usual things.

I said my name was Mary Taylor, and I'd been with Kendalls since January. I hadn't been employed before that. I'd married at twenty and had lived in Cardiff with my husband until he was killed in a motor accident in November last. Since then, although he'd left me a little money, I'd started to work for my living. After leaving school I had done shorthand and typing and also taken courses in bookkeeping and accountancy. I was a shorthand typist at Kendalls but was looking for a job with more prospects.

I had a good look at the two men. The manager, Mr Ward, was in his fifties, a sour dried-up man with gold-rimmed spectacles and a big wart on his cheek. He looked the sort who had worked his way up in forty years and God help anyone who tried to do it in thirty-nine. The other man was young, dark, with very thick hair that looked as if it needed a brush, and face so pale he might have been ill.

'Are you a Cardiff girl, Mrs Taylor?' the manager asked.

'No. I come from the East Coast. But my husband worked in Cardiff as a draughtsman.'

'Where did you go to school?'

'In Norwich, the High School there.'

'Are your parents there now?' this young man said. He was twisting a pencil.

'No, sir. They emigrated to Australia after I was married.'

Mr Ward shifted in his seat and put his tongue between his teeth and his cheek. 'Can you give us some other references apart from this one from Kendalls?'

'Well . . . no, not really. Of course, there's my bank in Cardiff. Lloyds Bank, Monmouth Street. I've been banking there since I went to live there.'

'Do you live in London now?'

'Yes. I have furnished rooms in Swiss Cottage.'

The young man said: 'I take it you haven't any family of your own – I mean children?'

I looked at him and turned on a smile. 'No, sir.'

Mr Ward grunted and began to ask me whether I understood PAYE and insurances and whether I'd ever worked an Anson adding machine. I said I had, which was a lie, but I knew I could get any machine taped quickly enough. I noticed that once he called the young man Mr Rutland, so I guessed he was one of the directors or something. I'd thought so from the minute I saw him, a younger son or something learning the business by starting at the top. I'd seen them before. But this one looked all right.

'Well, thank you, Mrs Taylor,' Mr Ward said about five minutes later, and something about the way he said it, even though he said it as if it hurt, told me I was in. I mean, it was as if he'd had a hidden sign from the young man.

Later when I went there I looked through the back files and saw they had written to the bank in Cardiff. The bank had said: 'We have known Mrs Mary Taylor only for three years since she first began to bank with us, but her account with us has always been in a satisfactory condition. Our personal contacts have been few, but we have been favourably impressed by her dealings and her personality.'

It isn't hard really to get a job these days. Very often you can build a background as you go along if you look far enough ahead. Some firms of course will ask for all sorts of references, and then you have to gracefully back out; but at least fifty per cent will be satisfied quite easily, and a few will even take you on sight, if you look respectable and honest.

Opening a bank account under a wrong name is a real pain in the neck. I'd managed this one as an experiment when I was working in Cardiff three years ago, in the name of Mary Taylor, but it had meant getting known under that name first, and I'd thought I wouldn't bother with another. PO Savings Accounts are easier, and they don't ask for any proof of who you are. I'd simply used this bank account to put money in from time to time, and once or twice I'd spoken to the bank manager about little things, and so I'd built up this background there. I hadn't used it as a reference before, because you can only do that sort of thing once, and they hadn't asked for it at Kendalls; but I gave it them here because I got the impression that this job might be worth sacrificing a background for.

The other minor problem is insurance cards, but that's not really too difficult to get around. I know a place in Plymouth where you can buy them; then all you do is fill in your name and a nice new National Insurance Number, and buy the stamps up to the date you want and stick them on and cancel them. Insurance cards run for twelve months, and of course nowadays they're 'staggered' so that they don't all have to be in at the same time. The important thing in starting a new

job is to start with a nearly new insurance card – it
saves you stamps and it gives you perhaps ten months
before the card has to be surrendered. The important
thing is never to stay in a job until the card has to be
surrendered.

I find it all interesting. I like tinkering with figures,
and lots of people are such fools with them. I've seen
one or two clever boys in my life, and some of them
were really clever, but once they've got the money they
haven't a notion. They're like children playing in the
sand: it just runs through their fingers. You've seen films
like *Grisbi* and *Rififi*. Honestly it's just like that.

I started at Rutland's the following Monday week.
Nearly as soon as I got there I had an interview with
Mr Christopher Holbrook, the managing director. He
was a fattish man of about sixty, with big-business
spectacles and a smile that he switched on and off like
an electric fire.

'We're a *family* firm, Mrs Taylor, and I'm pleased to
welcome you into it. I am a grandson of the founder
and my cousin, Mr Newton-Smith, is another grandson.
My son, Mr Terence Holbrook, is a director, as is Mr
Mark Rutland whom you have already met. We have
a staff now of ninety-seven and I don't hesitate to say
that we do not work merely as individuals but as a
unit, a family, everyone being concerned for the good
of all.'

He switched on the smile, which started slowly and
warmed up nicely; then just when it began to get really
good it switched off and you were left with his face

going cold like a two-watt element, and his eyes watching you to see the result.

'We are *expanding*, Mrs Taylor, and this year, as an experiment, we have opened a retail department which you will see if you look to your right through the window just across the street. This all means the engagement of new *staff*. For the moment, for a week or two, we want you to go over to the retail side, but ultimately we hope to have you here in the main building assisting Miss Clabon whom you have already met.'

He picked up the house telephone. 'Has Mr Terence come yet? . . . No? Well, ask him to come in, will you, as soon as he arrives.'

I said, 'You want me as cashier on the retail side, sir?'

'Temporarily, yes. But if our present plans go forward we shall bring in an assistant for you who will take over when you are transferred here. Miss Clabon is engaged to be married, and she may leave us within a year or two. Have you been in printing before?'

'No, sir.'

'I think you will find it interesting. We are high-class jobbing printers, as the saying is. We do all kinds of work from expensive illustrated catalogues to publicity posters for British Railways, from menu cards for City dinners to textbooks for schools. Rutland playing cards and diaries, Rutland writing papers, are, I don't hesitate to say, known all over England. I think you will find, Mrs Taylor, that ours is an *enterprising* firm and one that it will be rewarding to work for.'

He paused there, waiting for somebody to say 'hear, hear', so I said, 'Thank you, sir.'

'Later on this morning I believe Mr Ward will show you round or he will detail someone else to do so. I always believe that new members of my office staff should be given a general *overall* picture of the firm's activities at the earliest opportunity. I feel one can't afford merely to *employ* people, one must *interest* them.'

He switched on his smile as he got up, so I got up too and was going to leave when there was a tap at the door and a young man came in.

'Oh, this is my son, Mr Terence Holbrook. We have a new member of the staff, Terry, Mrs Mary Taylor, who is coming to us this morning as assistant cashier.'

This one shook hands with me. He looked older than the other young man – probably over thirty – and there was no likeness. He had fair hair, almost yellow and worn long, and a lower lip that stuck out, and beautiful clothes. His look took me in in four seconds flat.

'How d'you do. I hope you'll be very happy with us. You wanted to see me, Dad?'

Later I was shown round; but I didn't get much intake that first morning, except of noise and machinery and new faces and smells of paper and print. The building was on two floors, and the upper floor was where the office staff worked. I liked the look of the cashier's office, which was the last one before the stairs. It was divided off by a frosted-glass partition, and to reach it you had to pass through the next office where there was only the telephone switchboard, with one girl, and some filing cabinets. I mean, it could hardly have been better.

I've got the new-girl approach pretty well laid on by now, and I soon settled in. I thought Sam Ward the manager showed me the sarcastic side of his tongue sometimes, and Susan Clabon, the main girl cashier, took a bit of thawing; but as soon as I went over to the retail side and met Dawn Witherbie I had a friend for life who told me anything I wanted to know.

'Well, dear, it's like this. Mr George Rutland, Mark's father, was managing director when I came, but when he died Christopher Holbrook became MD and Mark Rutland came into the firm. Rex Newton-Smith – that's the fourth director – he's just a passenger, turns up four times a year for directors' meetings. Lives with his mother, even though he's fifty odd. D'you like sugar? One or two?

'Of course Christopher Holbrook, he booms away in his office, but it's the two younger ones and Sam Ward who do most of the work. Terry Holbrook and Mark don't get on – you noticed that yet? Sticks out like a sore thumb. Damn, this spoon's hot!

'Mark's made such a difference since he came – he's turned the place upside down. It's his idea, this retail side, and it's been making money ever since it opened. You coming to the staff dance? It's not until May. We usually have a good time. Didn't get home till five last year. *You* ought to have a good time with your looks. They all turn up, directors and all. Mark didn't come last year because he'd just lost his wife; but absolutely everyone else. Terry's great fun; really lets his hair down. But watch out for him. He's mustard. He talks rather sissy but that means nothing. Phew, only half eleven; how the mornings drag.'

'He lost his wife?'

'Who, Terry? No. He's married but they don't live together any more. It's Mark who lost his wife. A year last January. Kidneys or something odd. She was only twenty-six.'

'Perhaps that's why he looks so pale.'

'No, dear, that's natural. He looked just the same before. It's funny how they don't get on, Mark and Terry. I often consider. Why do two men hate each other? Usually it's a woman. But I don't see how it can be in their case.'

It did not worry me how they got on. I didn't expect to stay that long.

But it didn't pay to hurry. I opened an account at Lloyds Bank in Swiss Cottage and transferred to it the balance of my account in Cardiff. Then I told them to sell my few little investments and had the money paid into my Swiss Cottage account. Then I began to draw the money out in cash and pay it into my account under my own name at the National Provincial Bank in Swindon.

I didn't go down to see Mother during this time. She had an eye like a knitting needle, and sometimes being asked questions got on your nerves. It always surprised me she'd swallowed the Pemberton story so easily. Perhaps I'd cooked up so much about him that I almost believed in him myself. It's a great help with people like Mr Pemberton, to believe in them yourself.

One day when I'd been with Rutland's seven weeks I was called into a sort of summit conference and there they all were: Mr Ward, and the progress chaser, Mr Farman, and the sales manager, Mr Smitheram. Newton-Smith, the fourth director, was there too, an enormous great man with a moustache and a thin squeaky voice as if he'd just swallowed his kid brother.

Old Mr Holbrook did most of the talking, and as usual he made it sound like an election speech, but in the end I realized he was saying they were all pleased with the way I'd helped to rearrange the bookkeeping on the retail side, and now they wanted to ask my advice about reorganizing the cash system of the works itself. I was flattered in a way and a bit caught out of step, because the one they should have really asked first was Susan Clabon; and after a minute I suddenly looked up and saw Mark Rutland watching me and knew he was behind this, behind me being invited in like this.

I asked questions and listened, and soon saw there were two opinions about it on the board. Then I gave mine as well as I could, though I sided more than I wanted to with the stick-in-the-muds because on the whole the more machines you have the harder it is to cheat.

In spite of what Dawn Witherbie had said I was quite surprised at the polite nastiness there was under the skin at that board meeting. It seemed to be Mark Rutland against the Holbrooks and Sam Ward, with Rex Newton-Smith acting peacemaker and the other people trying to keep their feet dry.

Just as it was over the bell went for the dinner break

and there was the clatter of feet on the stairs coming up to the canteen. I thought as I left I'd walk through the printing shop while it was all stopped. Almost right off Terry Holbrook caught me up.

'Congratulations, Mrs Taylor.'

'What on?'

'Do I need to say, my dear? Not to an intelligent girl like you.'

I said: 'You should have asked Susan Clabon to come in as well as me. It wasn't really fair to her.'

'They did want to,' he said. 'But I wouldn't hear of it. I said you'd got better legs.'

I looked at him quickly then, like you turn and look suddenly at someone who's leaned on you suggestively in a bus.

He said: 'In twelve months you'll be chief cashier. Twelve months after that – who knows, my dear. You need sun blinkers to look steadily at your brilliant future with Rutland's.'

We walked down between the litho machines. There were several girls and men still lingering. By now I knew most of them by sight and a few by name.

'Hullo, June,' Terry said to one of the girls familiarly. 'Ready for the dance next week?'

She was one of the girls who worked a folding machine, and the three-sided plywood partition round her high chair was stuck with pictures of Pat Boone and Cliff Richard and Tommy Steele and Elvis Presley.

'You a jive expert?' Terry Holbrook asked me, looking where I was looking.

'I've done it,' I said. 'But a long time ago.'

'Blasé, that's what she is,' he said to the girl. 'Hullo, Tom. Back any winners on Saturday?'

'Yes, one,' said a young man who was wiping some yellow dye off his thumb. 'But it was Eagle Star at five to four on, so I didn't clear anythink by the end of the day.'

Eagle Star, I thought, as I walked on. I've seen him. A big brown horse with a spot on his nose. He was at Manchester and ran in the November Handicap . . . The way the posters were printed got me. The ink was brilliant and the machines printed one colour at a time, building up the poster until it was complete . . .

'Interested?' Terry Holbrook caught up with me. 'It's an Italian machine we bought a few years ago. An Aurelia. Does everything we want slightly better than any other, my dear.'

He wasn't really thinking what he was saying: he was eyeing me. The place was nearly empty now. I thought, This frock isn't dowdy enough.

'Why Italian?'

'Why not? It was the time of the credit squeeze over here, and the Italians offered us ten different variations of HP. This next one's a German – pre-war. It'll have to be replaced soon. Mark – the directors are keen on a new idea that's just come out . . . these two are English. Aren't you bored?'

'What with?'

'Looking at machines.'

'No, why?'

'It isn't girlish to be interested in machines.'

I looked at him out of the corners of my eyes, and

noticed for the first time that he'd got a rather bad birthmark on his neck. That was probably why he wore his hair long. He wasn't good looking anyway, with his jutting bottom lip. There was a sort of sly smiling wildness about him, though.

'We're the wrong way round,' he said. 'This is the typesetting room where all the work begins.'

'It doesn't matter,' I said. 'Anyway I have to get my lunch.'

'What do you think of the firm, my dear? I don't mean the work, I mean the people.'

We were there by ourselves in this room, and the whole building seemed suddenly quiet. I had a feeling he was going to do something, put his hand on me or something: so I moved away, went over and stared at a Linotype machine.

'One big happy family,' he said. 'That's Dad's line, isn't it?'

'What I've seen of the people so far I like.'

'The important thing is to choose your company. I wonder what sort of company you like, Mary.'

That was making his sordid thoughts rather plain.

'Of course,' I said, 'it's only a few months since I lost my husband.'

That held him. His look changed, but I couldn't make out what he was thinking. Then I caught sight again of the mark on his neck and for some reason or other I began to feel sorry for him. Feeling sorry for people is something I've been able to live without in my life. So far as I recollect no one has ever wept over me, so for me there's strictly no traffic either way.

But he was out of the run. I wondered if that mark had always pulled him down, if boys had jeered at him at school and teenage girls had sniggered, and maybe he had been let down and was on the wrong side of the fence too.

I went to the door of the composing room. I wondered if that was why he dressed the way he did: yellow waistcoat, chocolate-coloured trousers etc. I wondered what he was like inside and what he thought about me there in that comp room and what he would have said or done if I'd been the easy catch.

I wasn't the easy catch. I said: 'I must go and get my bag, Mr Holbrook.'

Every day when the retail department closed, the money taken during the day was carried across the street to the main building and locked away for the night, because there was no proper safe in the shop. This money was never banked because every Friday twelve or thirteen hundred pounds was paid out in wages, and the takings from the retail side went towards this. Takings on the retail side varied a lot; sometimes there was hardly a hundred in cash taken in a week, sometimes four or five, it depended what particular customers we had and how they paid.

On Thursdays before the bank closed the wage cheque was taken to the bank by two men and enough money drawn out to make up – together with what had built up on the retail side – the total wages to be paid on Friday morning. Susan Clabon and another girl then worked making out the pay envelopes. When the change was made I should be one of the two paying out the wages.

The safe was in the cashier's office, but of course the girls didn't have keys. Mr Ward kept one set and Mark Rutland another. The managing director, Christopher Holbrook, had a third.

One day Mark Rutland came on me in Mr Holbrook's office sniffing at the roses on his desk. I'd just got round to the right side of the desk in time. I blushed and said I'd brought the cheques for Mr Holbrook to sign and had got taken by the smell of the roses.

He said: 'They're the first of the season. My father was a great rose grower. In fact he was more interested in that than in printing.'

I licked my lips. 'The only one I ever had was that pink rambler with the white centre. It used to climb all over the gate of our bungalow in – in Norwich. What's this one called?'

'It looks like Etoile de Holland.' He put his sallow face down and sniffed it. 'Yes. I think it's still the best of the crimsons . . . Have you ever been to the National Rose Show?'

'No.'

'It's on next month. It's worth a visit if you're interested.'

'Thank you. I'll look out for it.'

As I got to the door he said: 'Oh, Mrs Taylor, we're having our annual dinner and dance next Friday. It's the usual thing for everyone to turn up, especially new people. But if you don't feel like it because of having lost your husband let me know, will you. Then I'll explain to my uncle.'

'Thank you, Mr Rutland,' I said, butter hardly melting. 'I'll let you know.'

that your knuckles for the nerves were white. The wall stupid to snigger [...]
"These things about me and I only just before I said [...]

CHAPTER THREE

I suppose I wasn't the sort of child anyone would ever hold up as an example to others. Ever since I was seven or eight I've found myself sharper than most. If I got in a mess I always managed to slide out of it, and most times I avoided the mess. So by the time I was nineteen I thought pretty well of myself.

The twice I'd been caught stealing, when I was ten, was because the other girl had suddenly gone un-brave and confessed all. It was a lesson about working with other people that I never forgot. And the fearful row Mother kicked up when the police came, and then all that stuff with the probation officer, had taught me a lot too. I don't mean I was a hardened criminal in my teens, or anything like that, but when I did anything I watched out I wasn't caught. And I wasn't either.

The second time I got into trouble when I was ten my mother had beaten me with a stick, and I still have one mark on my thigh where she dug a bit deep. I was scared out of my life, I really was, because I'd never seen her in such a rage before. She kept shouting, 'A thief for a daughter, that's what I've got, a thief for a daughter. Surely God have afflicted me enough without *this*.' *This* being a real old *wham* on my behind. 'What've you lacked, eh? What've you lacked? Fed, dressed, clean, respectable, that's how I've kept you, and now *this*!' Another *wham*. And so it went on. 'Disgrace! D'you hear me, child? The meanest, disgracefullest, sacrilege blasphemy! Stealing from the house of God!'

She'd gone on like that for what seemed like about six hours, while every now and then old Lucy had put her head round the door saying: 'Stop it, Edie, you'll kill the child!' 'Stop it; Edie, you'll have a stroke.' 'Stop it, Edie, give it a rest, you've done enough!'

I suppose, knowing her, I couldn't have done anything to tread on her corns so badly as break open the alms box in the chapel. And with the tears streaming down my face and bits of wet hair sticking to my cheeks, and my voice half plugged with pain – not remorse – I couldn't explain to her then, and never had got round to saying so afterwards, that I had really been doing it all for her.

Of course I wasn't hungry or down-at-heel; Mother saw to that; she went without things herself to do it. And that made it harder for me to take. Try being grateful when you're *expected* to be grateful; it mops you up. Lucy would even rate Mother sometimes. 'All on your back it goes,' she'd say. 'Better in your belly, Edie. It don't do no good to be well dressed in your coffin.' 'When it's our time to die we'll die for sure,' Mother would say. 'But not before. God's will be done.

Marnie, get on with your homework. And don't call it belly in this house!'

Breaking open those boxes had been the first shots in my own private war, as you might say.

There were all sorts of things at the root of it. When my Dad was killed in 1943 Mother was expecting her second baby. I was nearly six then, and first Mother got the shock of losing her husband, and then within a few weeks of that she was bombed out of her house in Keyham and we went to live in a tiny two-bedroomed bungalow in Sangerford, near Liskeard. I could just remember that.

When it came time for the baby to be born they sent for the doctor, but it was before National Health and he was busy with some more profitable cases, so Mother had the baby without anaesthetic and with only the district nurse to help. Something went wrong, the baby died, and ever afterwards Mother dragged her leg. There was a court case against the doctor, but nothing came of it and he got off scot free.

The year after that we went back to Plymouth, but the other end near the Barbican, and I went to school there till I was fourteen. When I left the headmistress wrote: 'Margaret is a girl of real ability and it is a great pity that she has to leave school so young. Had she been prepared to work I am certain she would have gone far and even achieved something special in Mathematics and Science. I am equally sure that her abilities are capable of misdirection, and in her last year she has given ample evidence of this. It is vitally important to her welfare that she should keep the right company. I wish her well in her future life and hope she will not fritter away her gifts.'

Well, I'd tried not to fritter away my gifts.

The annual dinner and dance of the firm was held at the Stag Hotel in the High Street. Mark Rutland's suggestion had let me out nicely, but at the last minute I decided I didn't want to be let out. You know how it is sometimes, you get the urge to see for yourself.

Everybody was there, all the printers and binders and setters and all their wives, and all the girls, with their husbands or boy friends. Old Mr Holbrook had brought his wife. Mr Newton-Smith was a bachelor, Mark Rutland a widower, and Terry Holbrook a divorcee.

Dawn Witherbie said: 'It makes you think, girls.'

When the dinner was over old Mr Holbrook made a speech, giving a review of the year's work; but it was a hot night and the windows had had to be opened on to the High Street, which still carried a lot of traffic.

He said: 'Ladies and Gentlemen. It gives me pleasure to rise for the fourth time at this our annual dinner and dance to propose to you . . .' Heavy lorry and four cars. '. . . on the whole a very satisfactory year. I won't hesitate to say that we suffered some uneasiness over the trading disputes of last June but happily . . .' Three motor bikes. '. . . so that we were not ultimately involved.' He turned on his smile. 'It is, as I have said before, a source of great comfort to me that we in this firm are something of a *family*. We are not so large . . .' Sports car overtaking two buses. '. . . also our order sheet gives rise to some satisfaction though naturally not to complacency. Compared with last year . . .' His smile died away as he compared this year with last year, but he switched it on again at the end to show that the figures pleased him. 'During the year we have had three marriages in the firm. Will the happy couples please stand up and take their medicine.' The happy couples stood up and were clapped. 'Six of our staff have for one reason or another left us, but we have taken on fifteen new members. We say to them . . .' Several cars both ways. '. . . up, please, so that we can see just who they are.'

The man next to me was squeezing my elbow. I moved it but he squeezed it again. 'You're new, Mrs Taylor. Stand up.'

So I stood up, the last of the few, and smiled vaguely and somehow caught Mark Rutland's eye and then quickly sat down.

After dinner I stayed out for quite a while, but as soon as I came back Terry Holbrook asked me to dance.

He was good, so he made it easy. I hadn't danced much these last few years but that wasn't because I didn't enjoy it. It was because I hadn't had time, and because going to a dance with a boy usually leads to necking. But I often dreamed of having lots of money and lovely clothes and a diamond necklace and going to a Ball where everything would be beautiful and gracious and softly lit and full of colour and music. One of the romantics, me.

Terry Holbrook said: 'Has anybody told you before what a pretty girl you are?'

'I don't remember.'

'Oh, modesty, my dear! Anyway, let's be impersonal and say that's a ravishing frock.'

I'd bought it yesterday, falling for it because it was expensively simple and thinking people here wouldn't realize. But this man knew all about women's clothes . . .

He did a few odd steps, and I thought last time, last time . . . It was in a dive called 'Sheba'; I'd gone in with a girl called Veronica; I couldn't remember her surname; she'd let herself go good and proper, shoes off, hair flying; I never could quite, something short; I'd stand back and look at myself and think, it's crazy to get that way over a dance. That fellow in the shirt striped like a wasp had come over; blue jeans so tight they creased the wrong way, Brando hair cut; hands were clammy and he smelt of sweat . . .

'You dance like a dream, Mary.'

'Thank you.'

'But a slightly dead-pan dream. Do tell me what you're thinking.'

'What a nice family party this is.'

'Please! How tactless!'

'Why? Isn't it?'

He looked me over, eyes drooping. 'Can you do Latin American?'

'Some.'

'Did you know Jive and Rock 'n' Roll were Latin American in origin?'

'No.'

'It's all essentially the same style of dance. The man

43

is only the central figure; all the real action is done by the woman. Don't you think that's as it should be?'

Again that feeling he was poking sly fun at me. His face would flare up at the corners of his mouth and eyes when he spoke.

Later we danced again, but half-way through the band started introducing stunt novelties that sent him into a temper.

I said: 'Well, if you don't like it, let's sit down.'

'My dear, you can if you like but I'm a director, I have to look as if I *enjoy* it.'

'Does Mr Rutland never dance?'

'Why don't you ask him, if you're interested.'

'I'm not specially, but you spoke as if the directors *have* to join in.'

'He doesn't, my dear, that's why he's unpopular.'

'*Is* he unpopular?'

'Ask your friends.'

'Hasn't he joined in any of the other dances before?'

'My dear, this is the first annual dinner he's ever condescended to attend since he condescended to join the firm.'

We didn't seem to be getting on very well, so for the next hour or so I wasn't surprised that he didn't ask me to dance. Not that I was short of partners. But about one, when a good bit of the top table was making a move, he came across and said:

'It's getting a fearful drag now. I'm asking a few people over to my place to finish off the evening. Care to come?'

'To dance?'

'No. For a few drinks and a chat and a gramophone. Quite *unambitious*.'

This was the time to slide out. I'd kept free of everything personal in Manchester, and it always paid off. But you don't always do the clever thing. I said: 'Thanks, I'd like to.'

'Divine. We'll meet at the door in about ten minutes. I think the MacDonalds will have room for you in their little car.'

Well, he only lived about ten minutes away. The MacDonalds were two of the firm's guests and were both as tall as cranes – the steam sort – but nice enough in their smart way. They were London smart, which means a bit phoney, but not as phoney as provincial smart. She was a blonde with that sort of urchin cut that makes you look like a drowned cat, and she was wearing a flowered grosgrain frock that showed too much leg and too much bosom. He wore his hair long and a dinner suit with blue velvet lapels. I shared the back seat of their Mark 9 Jaguar with Dawn Witherbie and a funny type called Walden. Alistair MacDonald drove like a madman, but Terry somehow got there first, so we all got out and went into his flat, which was three rooms done very modern; you know, bright purple carpet, orange and yellow walls, neon lights shaped like letter Zs, and a cocktail bar in one corner with the front made of padded and buttoned blue leather.

There were twelve of us and everybody talked and drank a lot. Not that *I* drank much because it didn't do to be talkative the way I lived. Somebody shouted, 'Put the tape on,' and then a sort of round-the-clock dance music started coming out of the radiogram, and two or three couples began to circle in one corner. But on the carpet it was hard work, and after a while Terry dragged a table forward and said, 'D'you play poker, Mary?'

'No. Do you mean gambling?' I said. 'No.'

He laughed. 'It's only fun. Not really gambling. I'll soon teach you.'

'No, thanks, I'll watch.'

'If you're as quick at learning this as you were the cha-cha . . . Two shilling maximum, Alistair?'

'Low limits kill bluffing, old boy, old boy,' Alistair MacDonald said. 'Anybody will see you if they can do it on the cheap.'

'Yes, dear boy, dear boy,' Terry said, mimicking him. He lowered his voice and did a little finicking wave towards the dancers. 'But we're a mixed bag this evening. I think we have to take a democratic view.'

Gail MacDonald pulled the shoulder strap of her frock up. 'Darling, don't be a bore,' she said to her husband. 'We're slumming tonight.' She glanced at me. 'Darling, I don't mean you. In that divine frock – is it Amies?' – she knew it wasn't – 'you look like an early Modigliani, that lovely warm skin . . . Of course we'll play for whatever you say, Terry, poppet.' She kissed him.

Some of them got round a low table which had a banquette on two sides. I wouldn't play at first but Terry insisted on teaching me. Somehow in the process one of his hands was always touching me somewhere; one minute it was round my waist, then it was on my shoulder – and always two or three fingers seemed to overlap on to the bare part – or he held my arm or my hand. I didn't like being pawed, and I was glad the MacDonalds had offered to take me home.

I pretended I hadn't any money, so Terry lent me two pounds, but I had no luck and when that was gone I said I was drawing out; this gave me the chance to slide away from him.

I began to watch the game. Terry was right, it was easy to learn – anyone could go through the motions in ten minutes – but it didn't stop there. It looked as if anybody with a bit of time and head exercise would be able to work out what chances of winning you had when you picked up a card and what chances you had of doing better by swapping your cards. For instance if you had four cards of the same suit and hoped to pick up a fifth, for a – what was it? – a flush, the odds against you, because there were four suits in the pack, were roughly four to one. But if you had three cards of the same number – three fives, for instance, and hoped to pick up a fourth, the odds against you must be forty-eight to one because there was only one more in the whole pack. No, twenty-four to one, because you had two chances.

When nobody was looking I grabbed up my bag and found some paper and began figuring.

About three o'clock, the Smitherams and Dawn and another couple went home, and we all had a drink and I thought it was going to break up; but two or three of the others shouted to go on, so they squatted down once more, and this time they made me play again. I took out a pound note of my own and sat down swearing I'd *walk* home when that was gone.

But it didn't go. I won. All the things I was quite good at came in then. For years I'd had to hide what I was thinking however I felt. Ever since I was ten I'd had to do it. Then the liking for mathematics and money. Then the fact that I'd been watching everybody and trying to guess whether they were bluffing.

Not that I got any fun out of it. Gambling has always scared me to death. The only time I ever put a pound on a horse I felt sick like seasick, and it was almost a relief when the race was over and the money was lost. I don't know why it is because I never much mind giving money away.

By five o'clock when it all broke up I had won twenty-two pounds. I felt clammy and awful and glad it was over. I wouldn't pick up the money at first.

'No,' I said, 'take it back. It's too much.'

'Taken in fair fight,' said Alistair MacDonald, patting my shoulder. He was the only other one who had won. 'But don't ever be ingenuous again or we won't believe you.'

'The candles burn their sockets, the blinds let in the day,' said his wife with a gaping yawn behind her spread-fingered hand. 'It's me instantly for bye-byes. Home, James.'

Terry wanted everyone to have farewell drinks, but nobody would, and we began to get coats and things out of the bedroom. I found I'd picked up a stain on the sleeve of my frock, and stayed dabbing at it, but I swear

I was only about five seconds longer than the others. When I came out all my winnings were still on the table and Terry was saying good-bye to the man Walden and two others, so I clutched up the notes and stuffed them in my bag.

I went to the door with my coat over my arm as Terry saw the others out. He looked at me half winking, with this odd lower-lipped smile of his, and then when he closed the door on the others I said:

'Thank you very much. It's been lovely. And I'm really awfully sorry about this money.'

'It was fair fight, as Alistair said. Stay a few minutes more, do.'

'I couldn't. I'm asleep. And the MacDonalds are waiting for me.'

'Oh, no, they've gone.'

'Gone?' That pressed the bell all right. 'D'you mean—'

'Don't look so *alarmed*. I'll run you home in a few minutes.'

'But they said they practically passed my door.'

'Did they? They must have forgotten.' He took my arm and led me back into the living-room. 'No, seriously, my dear, I told them you were staying a bit longer and I was going to drive you home. Really, I'd be enchanted.'

'And what did they think?' I asked.

'Think?' He snorted with laughter. 'Oh, really! Victoria's dead. Don't you know?'

'I'd heard,' I said.

49

He went across to the curtains and pulled them back. 'You see. It's half daybreak already. The sun will be up in a few minutes. Your honour's saved.'

I didn't answer. He came back and looked closely into my face. 'Look, sweetie, I thought it was a delicious idea. It's no *use* trying to go to sleep at this hour. We've got to be back in slavery in less than four hours. Besides, I'm raving hungry, and I expect you are. I thought we could have breakfast together; then I could drive you home, wait while you changed and bring you back to Barnet.'

I went across to the table and started gathering up the cards. There's a lot of things I know about, but this was a bit out of my league. I mean, I could handle the Ronnie Olivers of this world and get through without them laying a finger-nail on me. And I could deal with most of the numerous models that prop each other up at street corners and roam in espresso bars. But this one was different. For instance, his language. I wasn't even sure he meant any harm now. And he was my boss. If I wanted to stay with the firm I ought to try to keep in with him.

'What do you want for breakfast?'

He laughed. 'I knew you were a girl after my own heart. Bacon and eggs, d'you think?'

'All right. But please, I don't want to be driven home after. When we've had breakfast you can phone for a taxi. After all, I can afford it today.'

I went into the kitchen and began to put some bacon and eggs on the grill. He laid the table in the living-room while I cooked and did the toast. Then he came into the kitchen to make the coffee.

'But, my dear, you may spoil your delicious frock. I'll get you an apron.' He came back with a blue plastic one with flowers.

'Is it one of yours?' I said.

'Naughty. It belonged to my wife.'

'Where is your wife?'

'She lives in Ealing now. We didn't get on. Let me do it.'

I tried to take the apron off him but of course he had to put it round my waist and tie it. When he had finished it his arms got back round my waist.

'Did I tell you you were pretty?'

'. . . watch the toast.'

'Well it isn't true any more. Now you're beautiful.'

'Uh-huh.' I slid round the side of the stove.

'It's too true. Because now you're pale – and tired. It fines off the *shape* of your face, makes just the difference.' He kissed the back of my neck.

'Terry, if you do that I shall go home.'

'Why?'

I pulled the toast out, put it on the table and began to cut the crusts off. 'Have you made the coffee?'

'Why will you go home if I do that?'

'I just feel that way.'

He was still standing near by. A lot too near by. 'I don't think I'm exactly well acquainted with you yet, Mary. I don't at all know how you tick.'

'Just like anyone else. *Tick-tock-tick-tock.*'

'No, you're not like anyone else. I've – well, to put it in a genteel way, I've had my adventures. Girls, women, not to exaggerate, my dear, are not exactly a closed book to me. But you're not like them. Your mechanism's different.'

'I expect it's the hairspring. Could you turn off the grill, please.'

He reached back and switched it off without ever taking his eyes from me. 'Bury me deep if I lay claim to too much, my dear, but with most women I know – I'd know what they'd do or say if I made a pass at them – I'd know it before they knew themselves – I'd know if they were willing. Not you.'

'Here's your plate – careful, it's hot.'

We went back into the living-room and started in on breakfast. He was quite right about one thing; I was hungry. I ate like I was hungry in spite of feeling on a knife edge. He kept looking at me. Opposite me like this, his face was pear shaped. It wasn't a nice face but it was an interesting face. It was wild and sly and very, very alert. I felt scared, and a bit mad at being stared at. I wished I'd never come.

'Mary, can I say something very, very *rude*?'

'I can't stop you.'

'Well, you could slap my face.' He pushed out his lip. 'This is what I'm going to say, if I may. I know your husband has been dead for only a short time but . . . well, you don't look like a married woman.'

The light from the window had got brighter while this was going on, and the room with its card-table and

52

its empty glasses and its full ashtrays was a pretty ghastly sight. I got up.

'Well, I think that's a good cue for me to go home.'

He got up too and came round the table. 'I'm waiting.'

'What for?'

'This is the best side to slap. The other side is already well coloured behind the ear.'

It was the first time he'd mentioned his mark. I said: 'Why should I? It's only your opinion.'

'You could prove me so wrong.'

'I could but, thank you, I still think of Jim.'

His eyes were a sort of gum colour – that gum you get in grip-spreaders for office use. Only it wasn't thinking of offices that made them like that.

'I wish you'd slap my face.'

'Why?'

'D'you remember *Through the Looking Glass* and the Queen who cried *before* she pricked her finger?'

'I never read it.'

'Women usually slap men – if they feel that way – *after* they've been kissed. I thought you might like to try before. It would be a variation.'

My heart was going now. 'No, thank you. But will you ring for a taxi?'

I made to step away but he got his arms around me very expertly and nearly squeezed the breath out of me. Then as I jerked my face away he began to kiss my neck. I put my hands on his chest and when he felt the pressure he stopped and let me go to arm's length, but still held me round the waist. I nearly forgot my new voice then and let him hear the way I could really talk the Queen's English. But I had to get out of it nicely if I could.

'Consider yourself slapped.'

He said: 'Sorry, beautiful, but you really are enticing. And you bend like a wand. Like a wand. Shall I say something else?'

'Yes. Good night.'

'It's morning. And very early in the morning like this, after not having been in bed all night, is a delicious time to make love. You're tired and relaxed and your skin's cool and slightly damp, and there's nobody, nobody, *nobody* awake. Have you tried it?'

'I will sometime.'

'Nothing doing now?'

I tried to smile and shook my head. 'Nothing doing.'

'One kiss ere we part?'

Oh, well . . . he looked clean and healthy. 'And then you'll get a taxi?'

'Sure will.'

I turned my face up to his and he put his lips against mine. Then instead of it being just a kiss it grew and grew. His lips and tongue were wet and thrusting all over my lips and clenched teeth. I jerked my head away violently, trying not to be sick. I must have caught his nose with my cheek-bone because he let me go suddenly and I nearly fell down on the floor. I clutched hold of a chair and looked at him and he was rubbing his nose and looking at me in a way that put the fear of God into me. It really did. I saw my coat on the chair and grabbed it up and my bag beside it and walked to the door. I fumbled about with the catch, all fingers and thumbs, thinking he was just behind me. The door opened somehow and I was out and had slammed it shut. Then I beat it down the steps at full speed and got out into the cold morning air, rubbing my mouth with the back of my hand.

CHAPTER FOUR

I WONDERED if I ought to give in my notice and leave.
I wondered a lot about it. I expect it would be small
change to most women, just a kiss in a flat. But I didn't
like it at all. I felt sick every time I thought of it, and I
didn't want to meet him again.

He didn't turn up at the firm that Saturday at all.
Dawn said: 'Where did *you* get to last night; I thought
you was coming when we went?'

'No,' I said. 'The MacDonalds took me home.'

'Oh. Very *a la*. I didn't think she was pretty, did you?
My life, didn't his Lordship have an eye for you! Where'd
you get that frock? – really, you are a dark horse.'

When Terry came on the Monday he didn't look the
side I was on, and that suited me fine, if it would just
stay like that. All the same I felt pretty unsettled all that
week – until the following Monday when I was transferred to the reorganized cash office in the main works.
Then the sight of all the money I would be handling
soothed me like a tranquilliser.

There was a lot of extra work to do that week. I was
technically 'under' Susan Clabon, but in fact I'd had a
rise in salary and was on equal terms with her. The

same week a holiday list was posted up in the main office. Susan Clabon at once put down for the fortnight beginning Saturday 10 September, so I wrote my name in for the following fortnight. She would be due back on the 26th. I began to work on these dates.

On the Thursday I was alone in the office when Mark Rutland came in. He went to the safe and put some books in, and as he passed on his way out he dropped a ticket on my desk. I stared at it.

He said: 'Just in case you're really interested.'

It was a ticket for the National Rose Society's show. I looked up at him in real surprise, nothing pretended.

'Oh, thank you. You shouldn't have bothered, Mr Rutland.'

'No bother.'

'Well, thank you.'

At the door he said: 'First day's the best. But then you can hardly get there, can you. They're still pretty good on Saturday afternoon.'

He'd hardly spoken to me except in the way of business since I came. And after all, nothing could be more innocent than being given a ticket for a flower show.

After he'd gone out I took up a compact and powdered my nose. I exchanged a look with myself in the mirror. I was imagining things.

The only rose I had ever had was the dusty rambler that bloomed every year in the back yard at Plymouth; but it always got smothered with greenfly and fizzled out.

It used to make me wonder about that song, 'Roses of Picardy' and why anyone should bother to go nasal and wet-eyed about a plant as feeble as the rose I knew. I've never had any room for things that gave in without a struggle.

Not that 'Roses of Picardy' didn't mean something special to me. One day I'd been watching some men clearing a bombed site in Union Street when they found an old portable gramophone buried in the rubble. They turned it over and laughed, and one of them said: 'Yur, ducky, you 'ave it.' I went scuttling home with it and found it still worked, but the only unbroken record in the bottom shelf was 'Roses of Picardy' sung by some Irish tenor with adenoids or something. For three years after that I couldn't afford to buy any others, so I just played that and played it until it was worn out.

I used to come home from school at half past four. Mother and Lucy would be out at work still, and Mother used to leave a paper with the things she wanted, and I'd go shopping. Then I'd get the tea ready, which was usually ham and chips, or kippers, with bread and butter, in time for when they got home about half past six. Always I'd play 'Roses of Picardy' over and over because it was the only tune I had.

Sundays were sombre because they were all church; but Saturdays, with Mother and Lucy at work, I was free most of the day. Of course it was my job to clean the rooms, but I'd fly through this and be ready to join the others by about ten. We'd go mooching around Plymouth and watch the bulldozers and the builders at work; then when they stopped we'd wriggle under a gate and scavenge around on the site seeing what we could pick up. Sometimes we'd lift off the bricks that hadn't set and bury the spades and fill the cement mixer with stones. Later we'd walk round the stores, or go into one of the pin-table arcades or find some boys and stand at a corner giggling, or we'd climb up by the railway and throw stones at the trains.

One Saturday, in the February that I was fourteen, I'd been out all day with a pimply girl called June Tredawl, whose mother was doing three months; there'd been these two other girls with us but we'd split up, and all afternoon June and I had been hanging around looking for trouble.

It was a cold day, I remember, with a frosty look, and when we went on the Hoe the sea was grey as a skating rink. We wandered about for a time, kicking our cheap shoes together to keep our feet warm, and talking about all the things we'd like to do if we had money. When we came to the car park we looked over the low wall at the cars. There was every proprietary brand there, from little Austins made before we were born to smart MGs and Rileys.

June said: 'I'll dare you to go in and let down the tyres.'

'Go'n do it yourself.'

'I'll give you half a dollar to see you do it.'

'Shut up.'

'I'll give you these stockings as well. I'll dare you. Are you scared to try?'

'Be a dope,' I said. 'What's the *good* of it? It doesn't help *us*, so I'm not doing it. See?'

We snarled at each other and walked on. Round the corner there was no one in sight, so we got on the wall and looked over the car park.

June said: 'Well there, look at that there shoulder bag in the back of that car. I'll dare you to pinch that, and that's something we *both* want!'

This leather shoulder bag was lying on the back seat.

I said: 'Go on, the flaming car's locked, and I'm not going to break it open, even for you, you pimply tramp.'

We walked home mauling each other, but when she left me it was still only five and still quite light and I reckoned if I walked back to the car park again it would be going dusk by the time I got there. I didn't like being dared, and I thought, if I get the bag I'll show it to her tomorrow.

I walked back and loitered past the car park, and the car hadn't gone. I walked past twice because I wanted to see where the attendant was. He was at the other end and busy. The third time I climbed over the wall. When I was arguing with June I'd seen that one of the triangular front windows for ventilating didn't look as if it was quite closed, and sure enough when I sidled up and touched it with a finger it moved on its swivel. If you've a small hand it's easy then to put your fingers in and flick open the catch of the door. Then you stop to squint round the car park at all the silent cars. Then you open the door and lean over to the back seat and grab the shoulder bag.

I hid the thing under my coat and slithered back over the wall. Then I began to run.

It was the first thing I'd stolen since four years ago

when Mam had beaten the fear of God into me, and I was in a panic for a time. It wasn't till I got near home that I really began to feel good. Then I showed the first bit of sense. I remembered that when I was caught before it was because the girl I'd done it with had turned yellow and gave us both away. If June saw the bag I was never really safe any more. I went into a dark alley and looked what was in the bag. There was two pounds eleven and sevenpence and a book of stamps and a cheque book and a handkerchief and a compact.

I took out the money and the stamps and left the rest in and I walked as far as the harbour near the Barbican and dropped the shoulder bag in the sea.

So I went to the Rose Show on that Saturday afternoon. I didn't care whether I saw the flowers or not, but I thought he might ask if I'd been, and it's not easy to pretend if you haven't an idea what a thing looks like.

When I got there I really did get rather a lift out of seeing those masses of banked roses, and I realized my miserable rambler wasn't much of a specimen to judge by.

There were a lot of people about – people of the type I'd only really seen since I came to London. Although I'd like to have put a bomb under them, you had to admit they carried their money well. I stood by and listened to one woman ordering six dozen Peace and four dozen Dusky Maiden and three dozen Opera, and I tried to think what the size of her rose garden was, because she only wanted these as 'replacements'. I heard two men talking of a lunch they had had in New York yesterday. Someone was complaining that her villa in Antibes grew better roses than her house in Surrey and she wanted to know why. It was a far cry from this to the local Labour Exchange with its scruffy staff and its dead-duck unemployables. I wondered if these people knew that they lived on the same planet.

Well, maybe someday I should have my villa at Antibes, wherever that was.

'Ah, so you came, Mrs Taylor. I hope you're enjoying it.'

Mark Rutland. You never knew your luck, did you.

'Yes. I'm awfully glad I did come. I've never *seen* such flowers!'

'They get slightly better every year. I sometimes wonder how successful a thing has to get before it becomes vulgar. Have you seen the new Gold Medal Rose?'

We walked across the hall together. I thought, well, is he really another one? I didn't want to end up having a fight with this partner too.

He was better dressed today – usually at the works he wore an old suit – but his hair looked as if it had been combed with his fingers, and he hadn't a trace of colour in his face. Yet he wasn't bad looking.

I didn't want either him or his cousin, I only wanted to be able to rob them in peace.

Just as I was trying to think up an excuse for leaving him he said: 'I have to be back in Berkhamsted for six o'clock, but I think there's just time for a cup of tea. Would you like to join me?'

I was caught not thinking and said: 'Where?'

He smiled. 'Just round the corner. There's a teashop that makes rather good toasted muffins.'

In the teashop, which was quite a discreet sort of place, with pink curtains and alcoves – not a bit like the A.B.C. or Lyons – he began to ask me about the firm and whether I liked my job and whether I thought the reorganization of the cash department was going to be OK. I thought, well, it's a change, and he's not interested in me after all, thank God.

He said: 'We're a family firm, as no doubt you've heard too often; but the trouble with these firms is that they get into a rut. When sons inherit and don't come up the hard way it's very much a toss-up whether they have a talent for the job. My father wasn't temperamentally suited for business. Flowers were his hobby and his life. Nor do I think that some of the present . . .' He stopped, and a quick smile went across his face. 'But that's another story.'

'You've only been in the firm quite a short time?'

'Yes, until my father died I was in the Navy. I had a brother, six years older, who was going in the business, but he was killed in the war.'

'I'm told you've made big changes in the firm.'

'Who told you that? But never mind; it's true. Some of the departments hadn't been touched since about 1920. I ran the firm into a handsome loss last year. Considering the state of business generally I think that was rather ingenious.'

'I enjoyed the dance last month,' I said. 'Do you always go?'

'No, it was my first time. The first year I joined, my wife had just been taken ill. Last year she'd just died.'

So Terry Holbrook was being bitchy.

'You must find this a big change from the Navy, Mr Rutland.'

'I find it's equally possible to be at sea in either.'

Personally I doubted that, though I didn't say so. He looked very much like someone who knew what he wanted and generally got it.

'Why do they dislike each other?' Dawn said. 'Well what else could you expect, really? Family jealousy, and him coming into the firm like that, when they were all set to go along at the old jog-trot, drawing their fat salaries. Sam Ward practically ran it. Mark and Terry are *opposites*, if you see what I mean. And opposites in a family are worst of all. Their women were opposites too.'

'Did you know them both?'

'Well not exactly know them. Mrs Terry was an actress – still is, of course – she played fast and loose with some TV producer, so Terry divorced her. Blonde, she is; tall and wuh-huh. Sort of 38–25–38. *Handsome* of course, but going places. I don't think our Terry ever quite caught up.'

'And Mrs Rutland?'

'Mrs Mark Rutland? I always thought she was a bit queer. Brainy type. Not pretty. *Attractive*, but made nothing of herself. Used to dig up old stones – arche –

what do you call it. They say she was writing a book when she died.'

I combed my hair and turned it under at the ends with my fingers. 'Does Mark ever do like Terry?'

'What d'you mean, do like him?'

'Take the staff out – make passes at them.'

Dawn laughed. 'Not Mark. Not as far as I know. Why, has there been a pull on your line?'

I noticed as the weeks went by that nobody checked the weekly takings on the retail side against the size of the cheque drawn for the wages each Thursday. Of course, it all had to balance up in the books; but if the wages to be paid were £1,200, and the weekly retail takings were £300 no one except the cashier had the responsibility of taking 3 from 12. If she took 3 from 12 and made the answer 11, so that the cheque to be drawn was £1,100, no one would know until at least the following Monday.

Late in June Mark Rutland sprained his ankle playing squash, so nothing was seen of him at the works for two weeks. Terry Holbrook had hardly spoken to me since the night of the dance, but he'd looked at me quite a bit when he thought I wasn't noticing. He made me more uncomfortable than any man I remember.

One day I had to go in to him, and he was standing by the window thumbing over a copy of the *Tatler*. After I'd done what I came to do he said: 'And how is my *donna intacta*?'

I said: 'I'm sorry I don't know what that means.'

'Can't you guess, my dear?'

'I can guess.'

'Well, I'm sure you're on the right track.'

'I didn't have that sort of education.'

'No,' he said, 'that's exactly what I suspected.'

He'd turned my meaning round. 'I can't stop you thinking what you like. I'm sorry it bothers you.' I turned to go.

He put his hand on me. I don't know why but he always managed to find the place where your sleeve ended and your arm began. 'Must we fight?'

'No . . . I don't want to.'

'I mean to say, dear, most women don't consider it an *insult* to be thought madly attractive. Why do you?'

'I don't.'

He looked at me sidelong but rather seriously, as if he'd been considering it.

'I'm a persistent fellow. Water weareth away stone.'

'Not in one lifetime.'

Looking back, I suppose that sort of answer wasn't smart, but I felt I had to say something because he was seeing too much, seeing too deeply into what I was, and I wanted to cover up.

He let me go then. He said: 'Life's awfully short, Mary, and seven-eighths of it is spent in work and sleep. You should try to enjoy the other twelve per cent. Give out, let your hair down, *spread* yourself, dear. Give some man a run. It's all right while it lasts, but it doesn't last long, nothing lasts. One should try to make hay, even at Rutland's . . . Do I bore you? That's a great

66

mistake. I can't believe you were born to be an accountant. It's contrary to nature.'

That same week the holiday season was beginning, and in a small firm like Rutland's people had to double for each other at times. Mr Christopher Holbrook's secretary was one of the first to go and Mr Ward told me to do her work in the mornings. The first morning, I went into his office before he came, opened his post and put it out on his desk ready for him to read. About half an hour after he came he rang the bell and I went in with a pencil and pad.

'Oh, Mrs Taylor, did you open these letters?'

'Yes, Mr Holbrook.'

'Did you not notice that two of them were marked "Personal"?'

'I believe I did see it on one envelope.'

He looked through me. There was no electric fire on this morning. 'It was on two envelopes.' I saw he had fished them out of the waste paper basket. 'It's not customary in this firm, Mrs Taylor, for a secretary to open such letters – nor is it in any firm I know.'

'I'm very sorry. I hardly thought anything of it.'

'Well, remember it in future, will you?'

'Yes, sir.'

I went out, duly torn apart. I tried to recollect what the letters had said. The first, if I remembered rightly, was from a firm of stockbrokers in the city. It said they had purchased on Mr Christopher Holbrook's behalf the two hundred and fifty shares held by Mrs E. E. Thomas in John Rutland & Co. Ltd. They said they had been successful in obtaining them for only three shillings above the latest market quotation. And they remained his faithfully.

The second was from a firm called Jackson & Johnson Solicitors & Commissioners for Oaths, and it was a personal letter from one of the partners telling Mr Holbrook that they had been making further inquiries following Mr Terence Holbrook's visit of last Monday and indications were that the Glastonbury Investment Trust was interested. 'However,' the letter went on, 'it is perfectly clear that with so few of your shares in public hands, you cannot be coerced into taking any steps that would be out of accord with the wishes of your present board. Let me know what your feelings are, either as a board or, if you differ from the rest, as an individual. In the latter event I am sure that a private meeting with Mr Malcolm Leicester can be arranged.'

One letter seemed to tie in with the other. If he hadn't made a fuss about me opening them I should have forgotten them.

The whole of June was hot, but the third week was hottest of all. On this Thursday afternoon Mr Ward sent for me and said: 'Can you drive a car, Mrs Taylor?'

'No.' I could, but I had no licence in that name.

'A pity that isn't among your many virtues. I hoped you could have helped us.'

'What is it?'

He unhitched his spectacles and looked at them as if he didn't like them. 'It's this printing job for the Livery Company. It's promised for Wednesday next and I'm not certain as to the layout. In the ordinary way I should change it as I thought fit, but it is one that Mr Rutland has taken on personally, and of course it involves the dinner they're giving to the Queen Mother, so we have to have it right. I've been speaking to Mr Rutland about it.'

'Do you mean he wants to see it?'

'Yes. And of course, as you may have observed, he's still laid up.'

'I could take a taxi,' I said.

He looked at me down his long thin sarcastic nose, and you could see him working out what it would cost. 'Yes, I suppose you could. He's at his house at Little Gaddesden. If Thornton was not away I'd send him . . .'

I thought it would be cooler out, but it wasn't. The day had been clouding up and the atmosphere was as heavy as one of Lucy Nye's yeast cakes. The clouds were over London and looked as if someone had exploded the H-bomb. It took the taxi the best part of forty-five minutes, and the house was on the edge of a golf course, not big but smart-looking with tall chimneys and long windows and lots of grass all round to give it prestige.

A middle-aged woman in a striped apron let me in. He was in a room with open french windows that looked over one of the lawns towards some pine trees and the golf course. One of his legs was up on the sofa and he was watching a race on TV.

He smiled and said: 'How are you? Sorry to bring you over like this. Do sit down.'

I smiled back and gave him the programme. 'I expect you know what Mr Ward wanted to know. Is your ankle better, Mr Rutland?'

'It's doing fine. Now let's see.' His thick wad of black hair was as untidy as ever, but in an open-neck shirt and old flannel trousers he looked less pale than in a city suit. It was funny that he looked less delicate when he ought to have looked more.

While he turned over the programme I looked at the TV.

'Yes, Ward was right. I don't like this a bit.' He took a pen up off the table. 'Hot, isn't it. Did you come by taxi?'

'By hire car. Yes. He's calling back in fifteen minutes.'

'Switch that thing off if it annoys you.'

'No . . . it's nearly over. It's Kempton Park, isn't it.'

He began to write on the margin of the programme. 'Are you interested in racing?'

'I love it.'

He looked up as if he'd caught something different in my voice. 'D'you often go?'

'Not often. When I can.'

'Going to race meetings seems the sort of thing one does in company or not at all. But perhaps you do have company?'

'Not now,' I said, remembering in time that I was a widow.

70

'Your husband was fond of it?'

'Yes.'

He went on tinkering with the programme. There was a rumble of thunder. It began as nothing but came nearer, bumping downstairs like a garden roller. I got up and switched off the TV just before the race finished.

He looked up when I didn't sit down again. 'This will probably take me another five minutes. If you like roses go out in the garden. They've been very early this year, but there's a bed of Speke's Yellow round the corner.'

'I think it's going to rain.'

He nodded. 'Perhaps you're right.'

The room really was dark now. The sky outside was a ghastly coppery yellow and the leaves of a tree by the window glistened like old spoons. There was a flicker of lightning that made me jump about nine inches, and I did a graceful retreat towards the back of the room.

Old Lucy Nye. You couldn't get away from her, you really couldn't. 'Cover the mirrors, dear,' she'd say. 'If you see the lightning in 'em you'll see the Devil *peering* out at you. 'Tis true. 'Tis God's way of showing you Hell. Cover them knives; let the lightning get in 'em and it'll get in you next time you pick 'em up. I seen folk struck by lightning, split like a tree. I seen a man with his clothes cut in ribs, his face black and purple, his poor burned hands twisted up like he was boxing. He was still alive when I got there even though 'is eyes and face had gone . . .' You couldn't beat her at that sort of X-certificate stuff.

71

It was nearly too dark to see at the back of the room, all shadows – and the furniture was pretty depressing anyhow. There were shelves with old cups and figures and vases on them, some of the vases chipped and broken, and some were so smothered in old dry mud or clay that you wanted to get at them with a scrubbing brush. Just in front of the shelves was a grand piano as big as two coffins, and on the piano was a photograph of a young woman standing at the entrance to what might have been a bit of Stonehenge. Dawn had been quite right; she wasn't pretty; her face was too long; but she'd got nice hair and her eyes were big and bright.

A flash of lightning: the thunder that followed was near and nasty and noisy. 'We're all corrupt,' Lucy'd say, holding me on her knee as if I was going to slip down a nick somewhere. 'We're corrupt an' the worm'll eat us. But better be eaten than *burned*. See that one, ah, ah, nearly got us! Come just inside the window, it did, I seen the tongue flickering. Just didn't reach us. The Devil's out tonight all right, lookin' for 'is own. Keep your 'ead covered, dear, don't *look* at it, guard your eyes!' You couldn't beat Lucy, she really was laughable. I laughed.

He looked up, but I turned the laugh into a cough. 'That's about it,' he said, looking again at the programme. 'Anyway it's decently balanced now. Look, can I explain it to you in case Ward doesn't follow?'

I went back to his sofa half a step at a time and he began to explain. But while he was doing it there was a flash that cut right across us, and I gave a yelp and dropped the sheet I was holding.

'Sorry,' he said, 'did it startle you?'

I began to say something, but it got nowhere in a rattle of thunder that stamped down on the house. The whole room shook and shivered like with an earth tremor. Then there was an awful silence.

I could see he was waiting for me to go back to him by the window but I didn't. So he said: 'Put the lights on if you like. The switch is by the door.'

I went over and fumbled around, but I couldn't find it and my fingers were trembling. There was not a sound outside, no rumbles, no rain.

'It's like waiting for the next bomb to drop, isn't it,' he said. 'Would you like tea? It's nearly time.'

'No, thanks. Shall I help you away from the window?'

'No, I can get about with a stick.' There was a wait. 'I think it's moving away.'

'Sorry; I always get in a panic over a thunderstorm,' I said.

'That's rather surprising.'

'Why?'

'Well, when you ask me, I don't know. Except that perhaps you don't give the impression of being a person who would get in a panic easily over anything.'

'Ho . . . you don't know!'

'Quite true. We don't know each other really at all. Look, it's beginning to rain.'

I edged diagonally nearer the window. Two spots the

size of shillings had fallen on the step and were spreading as they dried.

He put down the proof programme and eased himself out of his chair. Then with a stick he got up.

'You interested in Greek pottery?'

'I don't know anything about it.'

'I noticed you looking at it. They were my wife's things. She collected them, mainly before we were married.'

'Oh.' Another rattle of thunder.

'What about my taxi?' I said.

'Oh, I doubt if he'll be back yet.'

'I don't want to go in this, anyway.'

'Don't worry, it'll soon be over.'

I suppose he saw I was in a state, so he started talking about the Greek things to take my mind off it. I heard him say something about Crete and Delos and so many hundred BC, and he put a little pot in my hands and told me it was a stirrup cup, but all the time I was waiting for the next explosion.

It came. The room lit up – two mirrors, the tiles of the fireplace, the glass over the photographs, all flickered and winked, then there was darkness. Then there was a sound as if the sky was made of cheap tin and was cracking under the weight. Then the sky split open and the weight fell on the house.

Death and disease and disaster. Thunderstorms and judgment and corruption. The worm dieth not.

'And did she – bring it back – with her?' I asked.

'Yes. I don't know if it does anything to you, but to me, to hold in my hand as my personal property a piece of pottery that has been turned by someone living five hundred years before Christ . . .'

Another flash was followed right on top by a great tearing roar of thunder, all round our ears.

'That was a bit close,' he said, looking at me. I wondered if he could see the cold sweat on my forehead. Anyway he hobbled across and switched on the lights. 'Sit down, Mrs Taylor, if it worries you that much. I'll get you something to drink.'

'No, thanks.' I was irritable as well as scared.

'The chances of being struck by lightning are awfully small.'

'I *know* that. I know all the answers.'

'And it doesn't help?'

'No.'

He said: 'In a sense I suppose you and I are in much the same boat.'

'I don't follow.'

'Well, you have lost your husband recently, haven't you?'

'Oh . . . oh yes. I see how you mean.'

He put the cup back and shifted a couple of other things on the shelves. 'How did it happen – with you?'

'Well, it was – it was very sudden, Mr Rutland, Jim – was on a motor bike. I just couldn't *realize* at first, if you know what I mean.'

'Yes, I do.'

'Then when I did begin to realize I felt I had to get away. I couldn't have stayed. It's much worse, isn't it, like you, to have stayed.'

He eased his foot. 'I'm not sure. In some ways it's a

challenge. In others it's a comfort, to be among the things that she knew . . .' He stopped. 'One hears a lot about the way one *should* take these things but when it comes to the point it's a new page, absolutely new. What you write on it is anybody's guess. The only thing certain is that it never runs to rule.'

The lull came to an end with a flash and an explosion like a bomb hitting the damned house. The lights went out and there was a crackle and a crash outside. I don't know who moved first but we somehow collided. I was in such a panic that I didn't know it was him until some seconds later. Then he seemed to be holding me while I trembled. I was trying to get my breath.

In the silence there were voices somewhere. It was the woman in the apron.

Then it began to rain. The noise grew until it was a noise like the drums at a firing squad.

I was standing on my own now and he had moved to the door. The woman came in. 'Are you all right, sir? It's that maple tree: all down the side; and the lights has fused! Lucky you wasn't by the window: I was afraid for you! All right, miss? There's a car outside. I wonder: oo, look, yes, see it's broken the glass in the dining-room window!'

Mark hobbled back towards the window, but I wouldn't go. By the time I got half-way I could see the lawn already under water and bobbling like with fish, and rose petals had drifted off the trees. A branch of a tree had been split and had fallen across the step.

'It's real dangerous today,' said the woman. 'Worst I

ever remember.' She pulled the french windows shut and bolted them. There was water already on the carpet.

'There's some brandy in the dining-room, Mrs Leonard. I think Mrs Taylor would like a drink.'

I sat down in a chair well back in the room, clutching my hands together to keep them still. He seemed cheerful, more cheerful than he had before, as if the whole foul thing was rather fun.

'The chances of being struck by lightning are very small,' he said. 'In future I'll keep my big mouth shut.'

'That taxi-dr-driver. He'll be get-getting drenched.'

'Not if he stays where he is.'

'I really can't go yet, not till this is over.'

'I don't expect you to.'

'Mr Ward will be fuming. He wanted the proof back by four.'

'Let him wait. It won't do him any harm to wait.'

There was another clatter of thunder as Mrs Leonard brought in the bottle and the glasses, but after that last crack ordinary thunder seemed nothing. He poured me something. 'Swallow this down. And you too, Mrs Leonard.'

I swallowed some and coughed. It was as strong as paraffin. But I gulped at it and you could feel it like fire, burning as it went down. Mrs Leonard went out to see if there was any damage upstairs. I began to let go of my hands.

'Well,' I said, 'I wonder who won the three-thirty.'

'Who was leading when you switched off?'

'North Wind. But Gulley Jimson was the favourite.'

After about ten minutes the lights came on again, but by now you hardly wanted them. The rain had begun to ease. Water still dripped from the gutter and gurgled in the pipes. Mrs Leonard put her head in to say there was no damage upstairs. He rang Mr Ward to say what had happened.

I got up to go. I was still quivering like a drunk round the knees, but he couldn't tell that. He gave me the proofs and hobbled with me to the door. He was friendly and easy. You'd hardly have known him. When we'd had tea after the rose show he'd been picking his way, not sure of himself or something. Now it was different. But there still didn't seem much risk of him heading the way of his cousin.

When I got in the taxi I began to feel a bit cheap and ashamed of myself, which was something rather new for me. I thought at first I was developing a disease. It took a time to work out what was wrong; and then at last I pinned it to that conversation we had had about me losing my husband and him losing his wife.

CHAPTER FIVE

WITH SUSAN CLABON taking her holidays from 10 September until the 26th the best date to set my sights on was Thursday the 22nd.

The staff was paid from eleven o'clock onwards on a Friday morning. Making out the pay packets was quite a major operation. In calculating a journeyman's wages – that is, a printer – you had all sorts of additions and subtractions to make. First you put down his basic wage – say £11 a week – then to that you added overtime, which might be £4 in a week. Then there was merit money which was a sort of bonus bribe to keep everyone happy, which might be £3. Then in some cases there was an agreed extra if the work was specially awkward. When all that was added up you began with deductions. First there was Lost Time – if anyone was late or absent – then each man had his PAYE number, which of course was usually the same over a period. Then there was National Health, and finally there was Voluntary Contributions which were not listed separately but which might be two or three small items for the annual dinner and the yearly summer outing, etc.

Susan Clabon and I operated together, one working

79

the machine and the other putting the money in the pay envelope along with the slip showing how the wages were made up. Usually I did the second part, and then Susan would check the money before sealing the envelope and putting it in a flat tray against the number of the particular printer or binder. These were usually finished on Thursday evening before we left and locked in the safe until the following day; but sometimes we had to run the work over into Friday morning.

Luckily in August Susan was away with tonsilitis, and I told Mr Ward I could do the job all on my own and did. The one thing that would wreck everything would be an 'assistant' while she was on holiday; and I thought now with luck I wouldn't get one.

In some ways I would be glad to go when the time came, even though it was by far the best and most interesting job I'd ever had.

All the time I was there, more or less, Dawn had been plaguing me to go out with her one night and I'd stalled, not wanting any more complications. She lived in Barnet and I'd been to tea with her and her mother one Sunday, but this didn't satisfy her. So now, feeling it was near the end, I said all right, and we joined up with two young men she knew and went along to a road-house called the Double Six near Aylesbury.

It was only after meeting and speaking to people like Mark Rutland – and even Terry Holbrook and Alistair MacDonald – that you realized what awful drags most young men were. The one I had to deal with was a big clammy pink-faced type with close-set blue eyes and the skin peeling off his nose. He talked all the time about his TR3 and golf and a holiday he'd had in Spain. He never stopped talking and seemed to think it was part of his charm. Also he chain smoked, which isn't particularly lovely for a non-smoker like me. I suppose I pretty well shared his cigarettes.

The road-house was the phoniest place with awful black beams and lampshades made out of old wills and tankards with glass bottoms; but I could see Dawn was enjoying it, so I didn't really mind being there; and we'd had a couple of dances and were sitting talking while more records were put on, when a short man with a red bow-tie came across to me and said:

'Pardon me, now, but aren't you Peggy Nicholson?'

Well, I didn't need to act, you see, because I wasn't Peggy Nicholson, and was certain I never had been, so that my blankness was quite true and I'd shown it before the knife went in.

I looked round first to make sure that he was talking to me, and then I said: 'I'm afraid you've made a mistake. My name is Mary Taylor. Mrs Taylor.'

He stared and pressed his spectacles on his nose.

'You're – not . . . Oh, I'm awfully sorry, but I thought a man called Don Weaver introduced us in Newcastle two years ago – I was certain you were . . .'

'I'm not,' I said and smiled. 'I'm sorry I've never been to Newcastle.'

'Not even with coals,' said Dawn's partner, and laughed.

The man looked very sheepish. 'Then I beg your pardon. It must be just a resemblance. I'm awfully sorry.'

'Not at all,' I smiled. 'I'm sorry I can't oblige.'

'*That* was a darn silly thing to say,' muttered the young man I was with as the other man turned away. 'You don't want to oblige a cheapjack like that barging in and pretending he knows you, just to get on speaking terms.'

Obviously the man, whose name I honestly couldn't remember, didn't know anything about Peggy Nicholson being wanted by the police. Not that they could prove anything anyway. But it just showed. I saw him looking at me once or twice when I passed him dancing. And I saw Dawn looking at me too.

Later in the evening in the Ladies she said: 'You are a dark horse, you know.'

'Why, what have I done now?'

'Nothing, only I thought you looked a bit peculiar when that man came up. Honest, you didn't really know him?'

'I've never seen him before in my life.'

She shook her head. 'Of course I believe you. All the same I think you've got a past, dear.'

'So has everybody who's more than one day old.'

'Too true.' She said no more then while she traced out a new cupid's bow. She didn't draw it very well; she always did it like one of those men marking out a white line over the old one on the dangerous corner. But as we were going to leave I thought perhaps I could learn something about myself if I tackled her, so I said:

'What d'you mean, you think I've got a past?'

'Well,' she narrowed her eyes and then laughed. 'Don't be mad with me, dear, I don't want to pry, but you don't ever *talk* about yourself, do you. Not like I do. Not like you expect a girl to do. It's only *that*. Anyway I was only joking.'

'All right,' I said, 'joke.'

She put her arms round my shoulders. 'Now don't be cross. But honest, you've been with Rutland's more than six months, yet I don't feel I *know* you. I don't feel I can get *at* you. I like you, of course, but I don't know what you're thinking at this very moment. You're like somebody behind a glass wall. There, now you can be as mad as you like!'

I laughed. 'Look out; one of these days somebody might throw a stone!'

On 7 September Mark Rutland came into my office while Susan Clabon was out, and his hair was as if he'd been running his hand through it both ways for a change. He said abruptly: 'I don't know if you're doing anything on Saturday but I'm going to Newmarket to the races. Would you like to come along?'

I had to think round that one pretty quickly. And a nice girl doesn't ask questions.

'Thank you very much, Mr Rutland. I'd love to.'

'Good.' His face had a flush on it for once. 'I'll pick you up here at twelve-thirty. Any clothes will do.'

'Thank you very much.' And that was that. Not another word.

In the last two months, since my visit to his house, we'd eyed each other every day at the firm but we'd hardly said more than the usual things. Of course I could tell there was interest by the way he was nice to me; and every now and then when we were alone in an office he wasn't so much the business man; I noticed this specially when Terry wasn't about, especially when Terry was away for three weeks in August.

But this was the first sign of heading for anything more. It was just cruel luck. I know I've the sort of face and figure that people call fashionable nowadays, but it could easily have happened I could have worked for ten firms with young directors and they would hardly have noticed me. It never rains but it pours, as Mother would have said, coining a phrase.

I'd have done better to have said no. Terry and Mark really were madly jealous of each other and ever willing to fight over anything; I'd be a new excuse; and if Terry knew I was going out with Mark after turning down an invitation from him he'd look on it as the deadliest insult.

However, I felt it was no good caring about that; in three weeks I should be away from it all. The other reason which I just couldn't resist was that, because Rutland's worked Saturday mornings, I had hardly seen a race meeting for three months. Mark had made the one suggestion I couldn't bring myself to sabotage.

Saturday was wet in the morning but it cleared by ten and it looked as if the going would be just right. I had brought things to change at the office, and after I'd changed I hung about for a few minutes to let most of the staff go. I particularly wanted Dawn to go off, and I saw her away before I went down to the car park where Mark was waiting. But of course Mr Ward happened to be there getting into his car, and he raised a sarcastic eyebrow. Mark didn't seem to care, and he handed me a package with some sandwiches in.

'This is your lunch, I'm afraid. If we don't stop on the way we may just make the first race.'

We made the first race, and we watched it from the enclosure. I hadn't been in there before. I'd only been twice to Newmarket before, and once I'd watched it from the Silver Ring, and once from the opposite side of the course, where you didn't have to pay.

I found I knew more about the runners than he did. For the three o'clock I told him Telepathy, a grey filly that I'd seen being trained as a one-year-old. I knew she'd come in second twice in the last month over longer distances, and each time she'd been passed near the post. The going wasn't heavy today so over this distance she would surely win.

'All right, I'll put a fiver on her,' Mark said good-humouredly. 'Shall I put something on for you?'

'Me? No, thank you. I don't bet.'

'Why ever not?'

'I'm afraid of losing the money,' I said straight out, and he stared at me and then we both laughed.

I said: 'I just don't have any cash I want to risk.'

'Well, I won't press you if you really feel like that.'

By the time he came back the horses were lining up in the distance, and I couldn't have used his binoculars more eagerly if I'd had a hundred pounds at stake. Telepathy won by a head. Mark laughed and went to collect his winnings. He brought back six pounds for me.

'I put a pound on for you for luck. She was second favourite anyhow.'

'Well, I can't take it, Mark. It was your money you put on. If you'd lost you'd have paid.'

It was the first time I'd used his Christian name. He pressed the notes on me, so I took them.

I had no fancy for the three-thirty. He backed his and lost.

'Tell me something,' he said. 'I'm not a great gambler myself but if I didn't have a few pounds on each race it would spoil the fun. If you don't bet, why are you so fond of race meetings?'

'I like the horses.'

'Just the horses?'

'Yes. I love to see them. I think there's nothing more beautiful.'

He crumpled up his tote tickets and dropped them in a basket. 'Do you ride?'

'A bit.'

'Not as much as you would like?'

'Well, I haven't the time. And it costs money.'

We began to look over the runners for the four o'clock. As it happened the favourite was called Glastonbury Thorn.

'By the way,' I said. 'What is the Glastonbury Investment Trust?'

'What?' He looked at me sharply. 'Why do you ask?'

'I can't remember where I saw their name recently.'

'You could see it anywhere. They're a big investment trust with plenty of money behind them. They recently bought two publishing firms. Vaughans and Bartlett & Leak.'

'Oh,' I said, 'well I shouldn't back him, then. How about Lemon Curd? He won last week at Kempton Park.'

Mark stared at his card. 'The small printer could be their target next – like Rutland's. Of course they could swallow us tomorrow and not feel it, but fortunately they can't because eighty per cent of our shares are still in the family.'

He backed Lemon Curd, but it was a photo finish and Lemon Curd was placed second.

We were standing by the rails at this time, and quite near to us, but of course in the Silver Ring, were seven or eight semi-Teddy boys of about eighteen.

They were dressed like usual and they were rowing with two fat men of about forty who might have been bookmakers or something. These two fat men were really scared, but it all died down when two policemen showed up. There were a lot of cat-calls and colourful language.

'Unhealthy little rats,' Mark said.

'What else d'you expect from sewers?'

He looked at me, surprised, not quite sure how to take it. 'D'you like Teddy boys?'

'No ... but they're not true Teds, for one thing. They're just ordinary rough types following a fashion.'

He rubbed his hand through his hair and looked at his race card.

I said: 'It's just a fashion, that's all, the things they

wear, just as it's the fashion for you to wear a jacket – with – with slanting pockets or for me to cut six inches off my skirt.'

'But we don't gang together and become offensive nuisances in the street and the pub.'

'No,' I said, 'and if you did you ought to be ashamed of yourself because you've been brought up in a decent home to know better. You should see some of *their* homes.'

'Have you?'

'Yes,' I said, and stopped there. I was going too far.

His eyes followed the eight boys. 'It may be something rotten in the state of Denmark that breeds them, I agree. But they don't all turn out like that . . . that sort, they've no brains and their physique is terrible. They couldn't stand up to any decent man so they gang together and become bullies. Whether it's all their fault or not, I still don't like them.'

'I don't like bullies,' I said.

When I didn't go on he said: 'And you think they're not?'

'Oh, the real Teds, yes. These are just fringe Teds. Pretty dumb characters, maybe, and not lovable. But nothing terribly *wrong* with them. Most are just – restless. You don't understand. They've nearly all got jobs that bring them in good money, but they're caught on a sort of treadmill and they'll not earn much more over the next forty years. They've brains enough to know that. You try it out and see if it wouldn't make you restless. Maybe if they were all in the Navy they'd be better. But you can't expect them to see that.'

'Oh, the Navy,' he said; 'I'm not holding that up as a solution.'

'Then what is the solution?'

He looked at me and suddenly smiled. 'To put my shirt on Ballet Girl for the four-thirty.'

After the races we had dinner together in Cambridge. On the way he said: 'You know, I know absolutely nothing about you, Mary. Every now and then you seem just about to catch fire. And then suddenly you withdraw yourself again.'

'There's nothing to know,' I said. I think that was the moment when I realized I had really stayed on this job too long. He was the third character who had said I was a mystery, who had got interested enough to want to know more. It was nearly always the flaw in my schemes. In seven weeks you could up and away without anybody wanting to get to know. Seven months was too long.

'Well,' he said, 'I know you're twenty-three, that you were married at twenty and are now a widow. Your father and mother are in Australia and you went to school in Norwich. That's about all, isn't it? Apart from that, I know you've a head for business and figures. Since you came to us you've never put a foot wrong. You're terrified of thunderstorms, and you go to race meetings but don't back horses. You know how to dress well – as now – but you don't in office hours apparently care. You have generally good manners but now and then you don't seem to understand simple bits of etiquette that most people take for granted.'

'Such as?' I said quickly.

'Never mind. You say you went to a High School, and your accent's right, but sometimes you seem to let it out that your childhood has been very tough. You're never lacking in initiative so far as your work is concerned, but you seem to be in your play. I've never heard of you saying a catty thing about anyone, but you're awfully tough about something inside and ready to fight the world. What's the secret, Mary? Tell me.'

I said: 'What are those simple bits of etiquette?'

Over dinner I thought it looked as if it might be getting serious. He didn't paw like his cousin, but the light was on. Oh, Lord, I thought, and to keep his mind off it I asked him about himself.

His mother was still living, and had a flat in Hans Place.

'Why did you leave the Navy?'

'You might say, why did I *go* in the Navy. When I was thirteen my brother, who was to have come into the business, had already been killed, but by then my father had made up his mind that I was going to be saved the unpleasantness of working in a family firm, so I was sent off to Dartmouth. And from there, of course, it was straight on.'

'The unpleasantness?' I said gently.

'Yes. My father and Christopher Holbrook never hit it off. Christopher's one ambition has always been to squeeze out the other members of the family in favour of his own son, and when Tim was killed it looked as if he was going to succeed. Then when my father died I wrecked everything by leaving the Navy and coming in in his place.'

'Did you mind leaving the Navy?'

'No, I wanted to get out. In my opinion it's a dead end now – sadly enough. In peace it has a sort of skeleton usefulness, but in war, which after all is what it is designed for, it will become about as serviceable as mounted cavalry. I couldn't see it as a proposition at all, so I was glad to go.'

'So you came to fight at Rutland's?'

'I'm not all that combative. I haven't looked for trouble. But I think the worst is over now.'

For a moment I thought of two letters marked PERSONAL lying on Christopher Holbrook's desk.

'I've wondered sometimes,' he said, 'if my cousin Terry Holbrook has ever made things difficult for you.'

'Difficult? How?'

'I thought that might have been clear. I'm glad if it isn't.'

'Oh . . . well. There hasn't been anything serious.'

'Sometimes I wonder . . .'

'Wonder what?'

'As you know, Terry's wife let him down. I sometimes wonder if he gets all that much fun out of his present philandering or whether half the time he isn't trying to prove something to himself.'

I said: 'Perhaps your father was right, and it was a

mistake to come back. You should have become an archaeologist.'

It was always a surprise when his smile came. It softened up all the rather off-key determination in his face. 'You're dead right, I should. But I've done quite a bit of digging up of old bones at Rutland's.'

He drove me home about eleven-thirty. The street where I had my rooms was a cul-de-sac and there was no one about, only five or six parked cars and a street lamp and a stray cat sitting near by licking its back foot.

'Thank you awfully,' I said, trying to talk even more the way his sort of girls talked. 'It's been a gorgeous day. I have enjoyed it all.'

'We must do it again,' he said. 'Let's see, next Saturday, I don't think there's anything near enough.'

'I can't next Saturday,' I said too quickly.

'Another engagement?'

'Well, sort of.'

'There's something the Saturday after at Newbury. What about it?'

'Thank you. That would be lovely.' By Saturday the 24th I should be out of his reach.

I put my hand on the door of the car to open it.

'Mary.'

'Yes?'

He put a hand on my shoulder and drew me to him and kissed me. There was nothing particularly passionate about it, but you certainly couldn't say he was inefficient. His hand moved over my head.

'You've such lovely hair.'

'D'you think so?'

'It's so strong and yet so soft . . . are you cold?'

'No.'

'I thought you shivered.'

'No!'

'It's been good today – for you?'

'Yes, Mark, it has.'

'So far as I'm concerned,' he said, 'to say it's been good is quite an understatement.'

'I must go. Thank you again. Thank you, Mark. I'll see you on Monday. Good night.'

That night I woke up in the middle of the night dreaming I was crying, but it wasn't feeling sentimental about Mark Rutland. It was a dream I sometimes had, although often I didn't get it for twelve or eighteen months. In fact it wasn't so much a dream as a sort of dream memory.

I sat up in bed and looked at my watch and cursed; it was only half past three.

Lovely hair he'd said I'd got. Maybe that was what had started it off, him saying that. I wondered if he would have thought the same ten years ago.

It didn't really start with the hair; it started when Shirley Jameson said something insulting in the playground about my mother. I can't even remember what it was she said but I know at thirteen years old it seemed frightful and I flew at her with waving fists and there was a fight there on the paved yard. In the end I was dragged off and there was a row and we were both kept

in, and then we had to go and say sorry to each other
in front of the headmistress.

At this time I was sleeping with old Lucy, and old
Lucy wasn't clean, especially her hair, and I got lice in
mine. Mother used to comb my hair out over a newspaper with a small-tooth comb and you could hear the
little tat-tat as the lice fell on the paper. Then she would
empty the newspaper into the fire and the lice would
slide off and *crick-crack* as they went in. After that she
would rub in ointment, but I don't think she ever told
me that it might be helpful to use soap and water.
Anyway, one day soon after that first row, I was coming
home from school when Shirley Jameson and two other
girls she was friendly with caught me up, and Shirley
Jameson said she'd seen something crawling in my hair
that afternoon in school. If it had only been her I should
have told her to go jump in the sea, but with the other
two there I couldn't do that, so I just told her she was a
bloody liar. Then she said if she was a liar I could prove
it by letting her look through my hair then. We were in
an entry, and there didn't seem any way out, so I had
to let her. All the time she was doing it I was grinding
my teeth and praying to God she wouldn't find anything. At first I thought I was going to be lucky, and
then suddenly she squealed with delight and came away
with a thing between her thumb and forefinger.

I lost my head then because I screamed at her that
she'd never found it in my hair at all and that she had
taken it out of her own hair and had it in her fingers all
the time. I was going to lay into her but the other two
girls grabbed my arms and twisted them behind me and

Shirley said, take that back or I'll slap your face. So I said I wouldn't take it back, because it was God's truth, so she gave me a good swinging slap that I think surprised her as much as it surprised me because she stopped and stared at me. Then she said, will you take it back now, so I said no, and then a queer look came into her eyes as she suddenly realized she was going to enjoy this.

So she gave me a slap on the other side of my face that made my head ring, and one of the other girls said, go on Shirley, go on and make her cry. So Shirley went on, first one side and then the other. But of course I wasn't nice to hold, and eventually I kicked myself free and butted her in the stomach and knocked her against the wall and ran up the alley. And they came baying after me. I ran like mad all the way and they never let up till I got to my street.

When I got there I didn't dare go in because I knew I'd get half-murdered coming in like that. My nose was bleeding and I'd lost my school bag and they'd pulled all the buttons off my blouse and torn the strap of my vest.

In the dream I was always crying at this point, and I always woke myself up, because if I didn't it would begin all over again. But when I really woke I never was crying, my eyes were always hard and dry. I've never cried, except for effect, since I was twelve.

In fact – though I never dreamt this part – things went on quite differently that day from what I expected. After I'd sat on the back step for a bit I went in with a story that I had been coming round the corner of Prayer

Street and had gone to cross the road and had been knocked down by a bicycle. But when I got in my Uncle Stephen was there, he'd come in on his ship that day and they were making him supper. I told my story, and Mother and Lucy swallowed it hook, line, etc., especially as they were busy all the while with their guest and hadn't much time for me.

But I noticed while I told it *his* eyes were on me in a rather queer way, and that made me uncomfortable because I always admired him and thought him the person I should have wanted to be like if I had been a man. He was a good bit younger than Mother and tall and good looking but he had gone grey early, because at the time of this visit he would only have been forty, and he was certainly grey then.

I remember, besides looking at me in that rather sceptical way, he also looked me up and down with a certain amount of surprise because by now I was just on my fourteenth birthday and I was growing up. I remember holding my torn blouse up at my neck when he looked at me because although I knew Uncle Stephen could have nothing but decent thoughts about me, yet I knew he was seeing me as other men would see me and was thinking I was nearly a woman.

After supper he said he would walk with me to the place where I had been knocked down and perhaps we should find the lost school bag, so I could hardly say no. So we went, and on the way he talked about South America, where he had just come from, and I asked him about the horses there. Then I found the corner where I was knocked down and we cast about for the school bag and I casually went down the entry and found it lying under the shadow of the brick wall, so we were able to take it home. But half-way home he said, 'What really happened, Marnie?'

I was so angry at being disbelieved, and by him of all people, that I went into the whole story again, describing the bicycle and the boy on it and the woman who picked me up and what she was wearing and what I said and what they said; because by now I almost believed it myself.

So in the end he said: 'All right, my dear, I only wondered.' But I could tell from the tone of his voice he still didn't believe me and that made me madder still, because I cared what he thought.

We went the rest of the way home, with me in a sulky silence, until at the door he said: 'Have you thought about what you want to do when you leave school? What would you like to do?'

So I said: 'I'd like to do something with animals, chiefly with horses.'

'A lot of girls do. If you couldn't do that?'

'I don't know.'

'What are you good at at school?'

'Not much, really.'

'Isn't that over-modest? Your mother says you've a head for figures.'

'I can add up.'

'Only that? Well, Marnie, in another year we'll see. I'd like to be able to help in some way, to send you perhaps to a secretarial college, to give you a chance of getting out in the world. There's more to life than this, Marnie. I'd like to get you away.'

On Thursday the 15th I did all the pay packets myself. They offered me Jennifer Smith from the progress department but I said I wouldn't have her, so they didn't press. At two o'clock on the Thursday I made out a cheque for £1,150 payable to Cash and took it to Mr Holbrook to sign. I then gave it to Howard, the caretaker, who went across to the bank with it, accompanied by Stetson, the foreman. They came back with the money in two blue bags and left it with me. To the £1,150 I added £250 takings from the retail side and began to make out the pay packets. I was left undisturbed and I worked, never stopping. By five o'clock I'd done more than three-quarters of the job, and when Mr Ward came in to lock the money and the pay packets away he asked sarcastically if I was trying to do Miss Clabon out of a job.

So another week went past. I got a postcard from Susan, whom I'd softened up quite a lot by this time. 'Glorious weather. Went Shanklin yesterday. Have just bathed. See you soon. S. C.' Like Hell she would.

During the previous weeks I had loitered through the works several times and fingered some of the papers that were stacked in the storeroom and about the works. On the Tuesday I went up to one of the young men, called Oswald, who was on a cutting machine and said to him: 'D'you think you could do me a terrific favour?

I'm organizing a Church social on Saturday afternoon and we're going to play games. I want a lot of small pieces of paper for them to write on. Do you think you could possibly cut me some?'

'Of course. Just let me know the size. What sort of paper do you want?'

'Well any plain paper – no lines – so long as it isn't too thick. And I want the pieces about postcard size or a little longer, about an inch longer. I wonder, could I go and choose from those stacks over there?'

'Sure. Go right ahead.'

So I went and chose my paper and he cut it up into the required size just like I asked.

Thursday the 22nd was a windy day, and the dust and leaves blew along the street outside the works. Autumn was coming early, and I felt sorry for types who were going to take their holidays by the sea, skulking behind walls and walking up draughty dismal piers. But it would be all right for riding. It would be just right for riding. In my handbag today I brought 1,200 slips of paper ready cut to size and rubber-banded in packages of fifty. Oswald had done them for me.

Mark made things easier by leaving straight after lunch. One of the girls told me he was going to a sale at Sotheby's. I wondered if there was going to be another Greek stirrup cup in Little Gaddesden.

The amount taken on the retail side during the week was about £350, but Mr Holbrook wasn't to know this. I made out the cheque for £1,190 and he didn't query it. Afterwards I wished I'd risked more. I took the cheque to Howard, and he and Stetson got the money.

They were back by two-thirty and I began work at once with Adcock, J. A., No. 5, whose basic wage as a journeyman printer was £10. 15s. 3d.

When everything had been added and deducted the total amount to go into his pay packet was £18 2s. 6d. I took up the first envelope and opened my bag and took out eighteen slips of paper from the first rubber-banded package and put the slips in the pay envelope. The eighteen pounds went into the other pocket of my bag. I had tried the slips against a similar number of one-pound notes in envelopes at home, and it just wasn't possible after shuffling them to tell which was which.

I went at it flat-out today. As I've said, the next office had only the telephone switchboard and some filing cabinets in it, and the one girl, Miss Harry, at the switchboard. The frosted-glass partition between us didn't quite reach to the ceiling, but there wasn't any real communication; we could hear the low buzz of the calls and she could hear our Anson machine and probably the chink of money. The door beyond her office had to open and about six steps be taken before anyone opened my door, so I had several seconds if necessary to shut my bag and look innocent. In fact, except for the little alteration at the end of each calculation, I was working as usual.

I was only interrupted three times all afternoon.

When Mr Ward came in at five I only had £260 left.

'Hm,' he said, rubbing his mole. 'Better even than last week. We'll give Miss Clabon notice.'

I smiled. 'It wouldn't work. She's really very good. Let me just finish this one, will you?'

He stood picking at his finger-nail while I finished off Stevens, F., journeyman apprentice, £8 4s. and put the money in an envelope and sealed it. Then I arched my aching back while he picked up the tray with its neatly stacked and named and numbered envelopes and carried it to the safe. While he was putting this in I got together the rest of the silver and notes and clipped the notes with rubber bands and put them in the cash-box. I carried the cash-box and the ledgers to the safe and held the door while he put them in. He locked the door and put the key in his pocket and took out a packet of cigarettes. He looked as if he was going to help himself, but he thought better of it and offered me one.

The generous impulse must have nearly killed him. I smiled and shook my head.

He said: 'No vices?'

'Well, not that one.'

'Quite *the* paragon, eh?'

'No.' I smiled again. 'Do you dislike me, Mr Ward?' I felt like challenging him tonight.

He was frightfully occupied shaking out a match and looking at the watch-spring of black smoke that came from it. 'It's not my business to like or dislike employees of this firm, Mrs Taylor. My business is to see that they do their work.'

'But you must have your own opinions.'

'Oh, yes.' He squinted down at his cigarette. 'But those opinions *are* my own, aren't they.'

This obviously wasn't his day for confessions. 'I'm glad you have nothing against me.'

'What could I have? You're so efficient. Everyone agrees.'

I picked up my bag, which suddenly seemed to me to look fatter than it should have done. I looked at my watch, Five-twenty. They weren't working overtime today, and most of the printers would be on their way out. It'd be murder if one came to the hatch now and asked for his wages tonight. It had happened once in April.

I went to the door. 'You'll be here tomorrow, Mr Ward?'

'No, I'm going up to a meeting of paper wholesalers. Why?'

'Mr Rutland will be back?'

'Oh, yes, he'll be here; and both Mr Holbrooks.'

I went out of the office and walked slowly, pretending to fumble with my shoe, until I heard Mr Ward lock the door. Linda Harry was putting on her jersey and she followed me out. We went along together to the cloakroom, where there were still two or three girls powdering their noses. I stayed there talking to them until I saw Sam Ward leave the building.

As I was just going to go out Linda Harry asked me if I had a light. I darned nearly opened my bag to see. But I said, no, I was sorry I hadn't.

We were about the last. You wouldn't believe how quickly the place emptied. I said good night to Howard and went down towards the High Street tube.

When I got home I locked the door of the flat and took the money out and counted it. I had over £1,270. In fact £1,272 10s. It was my best haul.

CHAPTER SIX

SO FROM then on it was the same old routine.

A gin and french first. It always tasted specially nice. Then I combed my hair out quite loose until it fell nearly to my shoulders. While I was finishing my drink I went over the train times.

Then I took everything off, throwing it in a heap on the floor, and went naked into the bathroom. I never would if I could help it take a flat without a private bathroom because as I've said soaking in warm water seemed to wash something away; not guilt because I never felt guilty, but the sort of old contacts with things and people. You skinned them off and left them in the water. When you stepped out you were being born again. Or *reborn* again as Marnie Elmer. I was a real person again, Marnie Elmer, not someone I'd made up and dressed up for half a year. Mary Taylor, the pathetic widow, had gone and left her old clothes on the floor.

She really had been a bit of a fool, Mary Taylor, getting so involved. Mollie Jeffrey had had much more sense. When that man Ronnie Oliver had rung up Marion Holland just after she'd helped herself to a large sum of money from the office of Crombie & Strutt, right under the nose of Mr Pringle, the manager – when Ronnie Oliver had rung her up when she was in her bath just before she left Birmingham for ever, I'd said never again. Don't be a fool, getting entangled. So Mollie Jeffrey had taken that advice to heart. But Mary Taylor had forgotten it. Mary Taylor had let herself be pawed about in private flats and she'd been taken to the races by a director. This was the worst and most incautious ever.

I packed all my old things in my case and dressed again in new clothes, all not to be noticed and not dear. Then began my usual round of the flat. Everything, magazines, newspapers, hand tissues from the waste paper basket, they were all gathered up, and this time it was easy to burn them because the flat had an open grate. I picked up my suitcase and packed the money in a corner of it, then I slung my coat over my arm and went to the door of the flat, stopped for a last look.

It was funny. There was nothing. Mary Taylor was as real as nothing. She left behind her a bank account containing seven pounds in Lloyds Bank, Swiss Cottage, and a few ashes in the grate. In a way, I thought, I was a bit like that man Haigh, was it, who dissolved his victims in an acid bath. I was dissolving Mary Taylor. She was going, going, gone.

I left and took the tube to Paddington, changing at Baker Street. At Paddington I caught the eight-thirty-five for Wolverhampton and got a meal on the train. At Wolverhampton I took a late bus for Walsall and I spent the night there. The next morning I was up early doing some more shopping, and then I went to a hairdressing salon and had a new hair-do.

But sitting there in the chair I began to think to myself that Mary Taylor had lived too long. I should have killed her sooner. It wasn't as easy as usual to get out of her skin.

By now – it was twenty past eleven – they'd know the worst. Who would be the first to find out? Probably, when she didn't turn up, someone else would take over the rest of the pay envelopes – but there really seemed no reason why anyone should find out until the first of her envelopes was opened.

In a way it was rather sad that Mary Taylor wouldn't ever see Mark Rutland again. Whatever else, you had to admit he was different. I mean, if you like to be heavy, he had class. And then there was Terry too – and Dawn. They'd all somehow got themselves into three-dimensional figures, not just cut-outs any more; and they stuck in your memory.

I left Walsall in the afternoon and went by bus and train to Nottingham. It took me eight hours to do fifty miles, but doing it I covered four times that distance. I did this sort of looping the loop every time after leaving a job. You just couldn't be too careful. I also lost my old suitcase, deposited at a left-luggage office to rot for ever, and went on with my new one. I stayed at Nottingham at the Talbot as Miss Maureen Thurston. On Saturday night I stayed at Swindon.

On the Sunday morning I left Swindon and made for the Old Crown, Cirencester.

It was like going back to old friends now, it really was; it was like a second home, and in some ways more homey than the first, because when I went back to Torquay it was sort of going back to being a kid again. The old Crown was a new life I was making for myself, and this wasn't a sham either, it was real.

I stopped only long enough for a couple of sandwiches in the bar and to change, and then I jumped on a bus that passed Garrod's Farm. I had dropped a postcard saying I was coming so they were expecting me, and you'd have thought Forio was too.

He knew it was me before I even got into the yard. He whinnied and stamped his foot and made noises that I've never heard another horse make.

When I went to him and rubbed my face against his muzzle he kept putting his soft mouth over the knuckles of my hand to find the piece of apple that I had for him. Always when I was away a long time I was scared he'd have forgotten me; but I never broke my rule not to visit on a job.

When he was saddled and we clattered out of the yard John Garrod followed me saying to take it easy because he hadn't been able to give Forio enough exercise, but I was too crazy to care, and as soon as we got going Forio nearly ran away with me; if it hadn't been for the heavy going and a slope he would have.

But of course it didn't matter. Nothing mattered; it was a lovely day and the heavy showers didn't count, and I was full of something though it couldn't be food as I'd only had the two sandwiches since breakfast. This was all I wanted, to hell with people; they cloyed and stuck and twisted you up inside and everything went wrong; this was simple, clean, easy, no complications; a woman and a horse. No more. Nothing to be fought out or explained. You just rode together. That's the way I wanted it always.

It rained heavily twice while I was out. The first time I sheltered in a copse, but the second time I galloped through it, Forio at full stretch, the rain pelting into my face. When we stopped, both with no breath, at the edge of the common, we were dripping all over and the last of the shower was leaving us, and the sun threw a rainbow over the woods towards Swindon.

I turned for home, and thought about Forio and the way I'd bought him.

It was after the second job I'd done, the one at Newcastle, and I'd seen Mother all right and still had money in my pocket and had gone to the races at Cheltenham. Not that I was going to bet, but there I was, enjoying myself all by myself.

One of the races was a selling plate, and after it was over I heard a man on the rails next to me say: 'Let's see how much the winner makes,' and walked off, so I followed him and the winning horse was being led into the ring with a few bored-looking people leaning against the rails, and a man suddenly started putting the horse up for auction.

Well, it never occurred to me to be interested until I saw that the horse had hurt its leg in the last few yards of the race and was limping badly and I thought, I suppose no one will bid for him now. And he was a *lovely* horse, with plenty of bone, and *big*, a bit big for me, but it was a good fault. He was almost black, with a lighter patch on his nose and his chest. Something wasn't quite right about his ears but that might not matter. Of course I knew nothing *really* about horses, except riding a few hacks and what I'd read in books, but he seemed such a wonderful bargain, and you know how it is, before you know where you are you've started bidding. And suddenly I had nodded once too often and the auctioneer said: 'Going for the last time – *Sold* to the lady in the corner, for two hundred and forty-five guineas.'

After that it was a sick panic to make all the arrangements, to leave a deposit with the owner and swear I'd be back with the rest of the money in the morning. Two weeks later I found myself the owner of a horse, boarded at Garrod's Farm at an *awful* cost per week, no job, and less than forty pounds left.

So I had to get work quickly, and I'd been lucky to get a promising job almost right off with Crombie & Strutt, the Turf Accountants. But it had been a bad grind for some months, living myself and paying for Forio out of eight pounds a week.

Not that I'd ever regretted it, not for a second. From the first ride he was wonderful; he'd got a great heart, always good tempered, and such an *eye*. His mouth was the softest thing; you couldn't feel his teeth. And I learned to jump with him and he was such a fine jumper. And when we galloped he'd a lovely long swinging stride. I hadn't had him six months when a man wanted him as a hunter and offered me five hundred pounds for him.

The sun had set before I got back to the stables and I stayed a long time with Forio, rubbing him down and brushing and combing his mane and tail. He loved this sort of thing and almost talked while I did it.

Being Sunday there were people about, and a crowd of half a dozen schoolgirls were in the yard chattering in fluting voices that weren't at all like the voices I used to hear in Plymouth. A dog barked in the farmhouse.

I was hungry now, fairly ravenous. I went through into the farmhouse and looked at the bus timetable. The next one passed the house at seven-thirty. That would get into Cirencester at seven-fifty-three. Time for a bath and a change before dinner. Then an early bed.

Mr Garrod came out as I passed. 'Oh, by the way, Miss Elmer, there was a gentleman asking for you about an hour ago.'

'For me?' My heart's all right; it keeps steady most times, but it gave a bit of a lurch now. 'What did he want?'

'He didn't say. He asked if you was here and I said you was out riding. I don't know if he'll be back.'

'Thanks, Mr Garrod.'

I soon calmed down. I suppose I might have asked what he was like, but I thought, I expect it's that stable-boy from Mr Hinchley again, wanting to see if I've changed my mind about selling Forio. Well, I haven't. Nor ever will.

But when I stepped out of the farm I just took the precaution of looking about carefully. It was now half dark and there was no one about. I walked down the muddy path and along the short lane to the main road. The bus was due in five minutes.

In the main road there were the sidelights of a car parked about twenty yards away. Just to be on the safe side I turned and walked the opposite way, and as I did so I bumped into a man who had stepped out from the hedge.

'Miss Elmer?'

It was Mark Rutland.

I don't know what they felt like when they dropped the first atomic bomb, but a sort of Hiroshima happened to me then. He took my arm to stop me from falling.

'Where are you staying? I'll drive you home.'

CHAPTER SEVEN

WE GOT to the car. Somehow I sat myself in the passenger's seat. He slammed the door on me, and it was like the clang of a prison cell. My heart was using something thicker than blood and it was clogging up my brain like dying. I thought it's not happening, you're making this up to scare yourself; this man doesn't know Marnie Elmer, he only knows Mary Taylor. Let him stay there. Let him bloody stay there.

He stuck the key in the ignition and switched on and started the engine.

'Which way?'

God help me, it was the same car as the one Mary Taylor had been to the races in. There was the same scratch on the dashboard and the same indirect yellow lighting. Supplied by Berkeley Garages Ltd., Hendon.

'Which way?'

I wet my lips and tried to speak but there wasn't any sound.

'Cirencester?' he said.

I nodded.

He started the car and we went off just ahead of the bus which was stopping to put someone down and which should have picked me up to take me back to the Old Crown. You know, that was the point where the two lines crossed. That was the point where I wasn't separate any longer from the girl I'd left yesterday. It was like dreaming a knife-stab and finding it was real.

We drove on, saying nothing.

As we got to the outskirts of the town he said:

'Where do you live?'

'The – Old Crown.'

'Under what name?'

'. . . Elmer.'

'Is that your real name?'

I tried to say something but my tongue stuck. He said: 'It'll save time if you tell me the truth.'

I looked at his face in the light of a street lamp. He was wearing an old mack and his hair was damped down as if it had been wet. I wondered how long he'd stood there waiting.

'Is Elmer your real name?'

'Yes.'

'Where do you come from?'

'Cardiff.'

'Where is the money you stole?'

'Some of it is here – in Cirencester.'

'The rest?'

'It's safe enough.'

'Not lost on the races yet, then?'

'I don't bet.'

'Ha!'

'It's true!'

He didn't speak then until we came into the square by the church. 'Which is your hotel?'

'On the corner over there.'

He drove across and stopped at the door. 'I'll come in with you while you get your things.'

'Where are we going?'

'You'll see.'

He got out and opened the door of the car for me. I slid out. God, my knees were weak.

Mark went to the desk. 'I'm sorry, Miss Elmer is my secretary and she has to cut her holiday short because of illness. Could you make out her bill, please? She'll be leaving right away.'

'Certainly, sir. Well, she's only just arrived so there's really nothing to pay.'

'I'll come upstairs with you, Miss Elmer,' he said as I started to move.

The receptionist raised her eyebrows, but nobody tried to stop him. I hated him for coming into my room because this was the one place where I'd been really myself. This was at the centre of my *own* life, not anybody else's. I didn't see why he had to force his way in here.

He'd gone across to the window and was staring at the thirty-foot drop.

'Where's the money?'

'In there.'

He picked up the attaché case, opened it to look inside, snapped it shut. 'I'll take this and wait in the corridor. I'll give you ten minutes.'

I could have done it in five but I took fifteen. I was like someone coming round after being thrown on their head. I had to take my time.

I was in the completest hole ever. I had always thought, if I'm caught as Mary Taylor or Mollie Jeffrey, that's not me. Even if I go to prison for it, that's not me. With luck I could keep them from ever knowing who I really was. I might have been able to write a note to Mother saying I was going abroad or something, keep up a sham until I came out. But there was no sham here. By some foul swivel-eyed piece of bad luck Mark Rutland had found me out as Marnie Elmer. And while, so far as I knew, there had been no link between Mary Taylor and Marnie Elmer, there certainly was a dead straight line linking Marnie with Plymouth and Torquay.

If he checked everything I told him, then I just had to tell him the truth – or part of it. It all depended on whether he was taking me to the police. You'd think it the obvious thing.

He was waiting for me, smoking, at the head of the stairs. The dismal light made his face look darker and more delicate. But I knew it wasn't now. I knew it was as tough as rock and for almost the first time in my life I was afraid of someone.

'Got everything?' he said, and led the way out to the waiting car.

'Where are you going to take me?'

He put my case in the boot. 'Get in.'

I looked round once, thinking of even running for it

because if there's one thing I know it's how to run, but there was a policeman on the other side of the square.

We drove off. He didn't speak while we left the town. I saw a signpost on the road marked *Fairford. Oxford.*

'Now,' he said. 'Just tell me why you did this.'

'Did what?'

'Took the money.'

'What are you going to do? Where are we going?'

'If you don't mind I'll ask the questions.'

I kept my mouth shut for a long time. I had drawn away from him as far as I could. He glanced at me and then leaned across and locked the catch on the door. I wondered if there was any hope of softening him up.

I said: 'Mr Rutland, I'm – terribly sorry.'

'Let's skip the emotional content. Just tell me why you did it.'

'How did you find me?'

'I'm asking the questions.'

I put my hands up to my face, not needing to act the misery I really felt. 'If you turn me over to the police I'll tell them *nothing*; I'll not say a *word*; they can send me to prison and you'll not get the rest of your money back; I don't care!'

'Oh, yes, you do.'

'But if you promise you won't, I'll tell you everything you want to know.'

'Good God, girl, you're not in a position to strike bargains! I could turn you over to the nearest police station and drive away and have nothing more to do with it! And will quick enough if you try those tactics.'

'They're not *tactics*, Mark . . .'

I looked at him to see how he took the Christian name. His hands were fairly tight on the steering wheel. 'All right, I'll begin. Where do you want me to begin?'

'What's your real name?'

'Margaret Elmer.'

'Where do you come from?'

'Plymouth.'

'Oh-ho, so you were lying again.'

'I can't help it—'

'No, it seems not.'

'I don't mean *that* . . .'

'Well, go on.'

'I – I was born in Devonport but lived most of my life in Plymouth itself. I went to the North Road Secondary Modern School for girls, from seven to nearly fifteen. Is – is that what you want to know?'

'Are your mother and father in Australia?'

'No. My father was killed in the war. In the Navy, Mark.'

'And your mother?'

'She died soon after . . . I was brought up by an old friend of mother's called Lucy Nye.'

'And when you left school?'

'My uncle – my mother's brother – he's at sea too, an engineer – he paid for me to go on to another school, St Andrew's Technical College, where I learned shorthand and typing and bookkeeping and accountancy.'

I looked at him again. He had dipped his lights, and the light from another car reflected off the road on to his thin angry face.

'I suppose this really is true, is it?'

'You can check it if you want.'

'Don't worry, I will. I was only reminding you to keep your imagination under control.'

I was wild at that. 'Have you never done anything wrong, never broken any law? It's different for you, of course, with always as much money as you needed—'

'Get on with your story.'

I struggled for a minute trying to swallow my breathing. 'When I left I got a job in Plymouth. But I was hardly settled before Lucy Nye was taken ill so I gave it up to – to nurse her. I nursed her for eighteen months, until she died. When she died I found she'd left me the house we were living in and – and two hundred pounds in cash. I spent some of the cash on – on elocution lessons and some more on accountancy, and then I got a job with Deloitte, Plender & Griffiths in Bristol. While I was there I first saw horses – horses as I know them now, not old broken-down things pulling vans but long-legged thoroughbreds, jumpers and – and—'

'All right, I've got that. You saw horses.'

'And I fell in love with them. Does that mean anything to you? . . . After a bit the house in Devonport sold for a thousand pounds. It was all mine. I reckoned I could live for two years or more, live like a lady, on what I'd got and what I'd saved, buy a horse, ride it. I bought Forio and—'

'Forio?'

'My horse at the Garrods. So I gave up my job and lived like that. I lived like a lady as cheap as I could, but all day free. I wonder if freedom like that means

117

anything to you. I used to ride nearly every day – then sometimes I'd get a temporary job round Christmas time to get a bit of extra money. But I just spent my capital most of the time. Then last year, about November, it was all gone . . . So I came to London and looked for work. I got a job at Kendalls but looked out for something better.'

'And you found Rutland's.'

'Yes . . .'

'That was quite a bit better, wasn't it, with a clear profit apart from wages of some twelve hundred pounds.'

I burst into tears. 'I'm s-sorry, Mark, it was a sudden temptation. I hated to do it but it was a sudden thought of being able to afford perhaps two more years like those I had had before I came t-to London. I shouldn't ever have taken a cashier's job, I-I suppose. It was handling so much money at – at one time. Oh, Mark, I'm so very sorry . . .'

The tears were turned on, of course. But if it had been possible for me to cry naturally I really could have cried – for disappointment, and for being found out, and because I was so scared of what was going to happen.

We were through Faringdon by now and on the main Swindon–Oxford road. I dabbed at my eyes with a handkerchief that was too small. But he didn't offer me his.

After a time he said: 'And Mr Taylor? Where does he come in?'

'Mr Taylor?'

'Is he a little more of your imagination or does he exist?'

'Oh, no. There . . . was nobody. She had never – I've never been married.'

'You've been somebody's mistress?'

'*No* . . . Good Heavens no! Why should you think I had?'

'I don't think anything. I'm asking. Why did you call yourself Mrs Taylor?'

I paused to blow my nose. Why the hell did I call myself Mrs Taylor? But I hadn't really. I had just made Mary Taylor a married woman three years ago when I thought her up.

'Mr Taylor was an old friend of my father's. He's been dead for years but the name came to my mind.'

'Why did it have to come to your mind at all? Why did you open an account in Cardiff in that name three years ago?'

I had been expecting that one. 'Mrs Nye has – has a nephew. He's abroad most of the time but he's not much good. I was afraid of – if he knew Lucy Nye had left me all that money he'd want a share.'

'Are you sure he isn't working with you in this?'

'Nobody's working with me! You speak as if it was all cut and dried, planned weeks ago, in cold blood!'

'And wasn't it?'

'No!'

'It was all so impulsive and child-like that you changed your name to Taylor when you came to London nine months ago? That is if you haven't been Mrs Taylor for three years.'

119

'I didn't change it for that. I changed it because I thought it would be like a *fresh start*! I didn't want Mrs Nye's nephew looking me up while I was in London! I – I thought I'd stick to the new name, make it something better than the old!'

'Well, you're not really trying to tell me that this theft just happened on the spur of the moment are you? Susan Clabon away on her holidays; a cheque made out deliberately for two hundred and twenty pounds more than we needed to draw; a supply of our own paper cut correctly to size and brought into the office that morning. What do you call cold blood?'

'No, but it was only the last few days that I really thought of it! Then when the chance came I just hadn't the strength of will to resist. I hadn't Mark, really. I know I'm weak. I should never have done it but . . . You see, it was the week before, when Susan was away, that I realized it would be possible, but even then I never seriously thought . . . It wasn't really till Wednesday. And then I couldn't rest, couldn't sleep because of it.'

Another shower came and he put on the screen-wipers. Through the Japanese fans they made on the screen you could see the suburbs of Oxford squeezing up round the car.

'Have you stolen before?'

I hesitated. 'Twice in Plymouth when I was ten – and got beaten for it.'

'Not that sort of thing,' he said impatiently. 'Since then.'

I thought it was risky to be too pure. 'Yes . . . once in Bristol.'

'When?'

'About three years ago. I was in a shop and . . .'

'How much did you take?'

'Oh, only a scarf. It wasn't worth much.'

'How much?'

'About two pounds . . .'

'And since then?'

'Not since then.'

In Oxford the rain had cleared the streets, and only buses and cars splashed through them. Out in the country again we drove past a signpost I couldn't read.

'Where are you taking me?'

He said: 'What proof have you of what you've told me?

'Proof? Nothing on me.'

'What can you get?'

'How do you mean?'

'Is there someone from Plymouth who knows you?'

'Well, I . . .'

'Well, is there?'

'. . . Yes, I suppose so; but if you aren't going to hand me over to the police I'd rather—'

'I didn't say I wasn't.'

'I can find my birth certificate – a – a bookkeeping and accountancy certificate – a character from the North Road School . . . I haven't kept much.'

'Where are those?'

'I could get them.'

'Where are they?'

'Well, various places . . . I expect I could get a letter from the South Western Electricity Board saying I worked for them. That was my first job. And Deloitte, Plender & Griffiths would say the same – though I was only with them six months . . . I think I've still got the receipt for Forio when I bought him . . . It's – it's hard to think of things. What do you want me to prove?'

'Prove? I want you to prove that you—' He stopped. He sounded choked – with irritation or something. 'Never mind.'

'That I'm not just a common sneak-thief?'

'If you like.'

'But I *am* . . . What else can you call me after this?'

'Never mind. I'm not sitting as a judge on you; I'm only trying to understand.'

I sighed shakily. 'I think perhaps that's impossible. When I'd done it, stolen that money, I could hardly believe it or understand it myself.'

'I didn't notice you rushing back.'

'No . . . And I shouldn't have done.'

'Well, that's honest anyway.'

'For one thing I should have been too afraid.'

We didn't say anything more for a while.

'It isn't always so easy to know the truth about yourself,' I said. 'Or is it with you? You've lived a different, easier life.'

He said nothing.

I said: 'Maybe you don't have two thoughts at the same time. I often have two thoughts – one belongs to the person I'm trying to be now, the other belongs to the kid from Devonport. And she's still a back-street urchin. I mean, you don't *suddenly* grow out of knowing what it's like to be hungry and knocked around and treated like dirt. You don't honestly. I mean, you may think you have, but then when you find yourself holding a thousand pounds in pound notes, well, you suddenly discover you want to bolt down the next dark alley. It's all mixed up with that. I can't explain to you, Mark.'

'In fact,' he said, 'that's the most convincing answer you've given me tonight.'

We had passed through Thame and seemed to be making for Aylesbury. I knew in the last minute or two I'd gained a bit – I wasn't any longer lying flat with him kneeling on my chest – I'd made the first move for wriggling out from under him. But it was chancy work – I had to move fast, but not too fast.

'The reasons for what I did – they were more mixed up even than that, even than you think.'

'How?'

'I can't tell you.'

'You'd better.'

'Oh . . . there were other things besides the need for money behind it. There was the need to get away.'

'To get away?'

'From you.'

'Thanks.'

I hesitated then, wondering if he was really taking it.

'Well, don't you *see* . . . Or don't you? We were getting – friendly.'

'Was that any reason why you should run away?'

'*Yes*. Or I thought so. Maybe I began to take it a bit

123

too seriously. I expect it was fine for you but it began not to be fun for me, and I thought it was time I opted out.'

'Go on.'

'Well, don't you see?'

'I'd like to hear.'

'Look, Mark, I can't help it, I felt that way. And I thought, what crazy chance is there of anything worth while coming of it?'

'So?'

'I thought, he's pretty well out of the top drawer. I'm not out of any drawer at all. I'm just something sucked up in the vacuum cleaner. Well, so well, what was going to happen? Nothing that I could see that wasn't going to be a nasty mess for me.'

'So you thought? . . .'

'So I thought I'll get out, and get out in a way that will finish it good and proper: so I did. The back-street urchin made a pretty fine haul, didn't she? Only she never thought – I never thought you'd find me again – so quickly – like magic . . . I don't want to start again – hand me over to the police and have done!'

He took his hand off the wheel and I thought he was going to touch me. But he didn't.

After a minute he said: 'Don't worry, you're not in jail yet.'

As we got to Aylesbury there was more traffic again because it was closing time.

He said: 'I suppose I've got to start calling you Margaret instead of Mary.'

'I've always been called Marnie.'

'Marnie . . . Marnie . . . Marnie; all right.'

'Where are you taking me? Won't you tell me that?'

'Home.'

'Where?'

'To my home. You'll have to spend the night there now. It's too late to do anything else with you.'

'I – what will your housekeeper say?'

'What should she say?'

I wondered now if I *had* been going too fast. 'She won't think it odd?'

'Are you worried about your reputation?'

'What's going to happen in the morning?'

'You're going back to John Rutland and Co.'

I sat up. 'What? Oh, don't joke about it.'

'I'm not joking.'

'But how can I?'

'You're going back as if nothing had happened – for a few weeks anyhow. If you want to give in your notice then you can do; but I'm having no unnecessary scandal.'

I put my fingers on his arm. 'Don't you understand, Mark? You must have been there yesterday. Everyone will know. Even if you don't turn me over to the police Mr Ward or one of the others will!'

He said: 'When you didn't turn up on Friday we tried to get in touch with your flat but there was no reply. So I decided, as Miss Clabon was away and as Dawn Witherbie was busy on the retail side, I'd finish the wage packets myself. I did about half a dozen before I noticed that there wouldn't be enough money to finish off the wages. Then I checked up how much you had drawn out on Thursday and how much there should

125

have been in cash from the retail side. So it didn't take me long to open one of the envelopes you had done and find what was inside.'

'Well, then, you see—'

'Oh, yes, I saw. I saw perfectly well.'

I sat and watched him.

He switched on the screen-wipers again.

'I thought all round it. I checked up one or two of the pay slips and they were perfectly correct. Odd you should have gone to that trouble when it wasn't going to matter.'

'I—'

'The careful worker coming out, I suppose. All that was missing was the money. So I went across to the bank and drew out another thousand pounds in notes. Then I came back and started reopening your envelopes and typing new ones.'

I stared hard at him in the dark to see if he was just trying to be plain funny.

'Of course if Ward had been there I couldn't very well have put it over; but there was no one else to interfere. When it came to eleven o'clock I called Miss Smith over and got her to distribute those I'd done. Those I hadn't done had to wait. I sent word round that Miss Clabon was away and Mrs Taylor had been taken ill. I finished the last by half past twelve. Apparently I only made two mistakes in my haste, and those I had to put right yesterday.'

We were nearly in Berkhamsted. My mind was working like a jet now, but it kept flying around one solid fact that just didn't fit with the rest at all.

'Why did you *do* it?'

'Ward always said you were too good to be true.'

'He was right.'

'Yes. And I was wrong. I'd hate to hear Ward say "I told you so!"'

I waited. He was being funny. He seemed to have finished.

'It can't be just that.'

'Near enough.'

'You wouldn't go to that trouble just for that. You wouldn't, Mark. No one would.'

'Don't you think it's a good enough explanation?'

'No, I don't.'

'Well, I suppose I had my own ideas.'

'What were they?'

'Never mind.'

When he got to his house Mrs Leonard had gone home. There was a note and some cold supper in the dining-room. He got some more cutlery out of a cupboard and we had tongue and salad and a bottle of beer. I was nearly out for food, and I tried not to eat like a wolf in front of him. I was still on a knife-edge, I knew. I still had one foot in jail. But it was on its way out. I could see that. Because he was still sweet on me. That was really what it added up to. It was a miracle of luck. But it was still a knife-edge.

And it was different here from being in the car. Then we'd been in semi-darkness, side by side, nothing but voices. Here we sat opposite each other, over a table, like the dinner in Cambridge. I was seen as well as heard, so I'd got to look just right all the time as well as sound it. I'd snatched a look at myself in the mirror in the hall and been able to powder the tears off my face, to comb my hair. But it wouldn't do to look too tidy, too composed. I was surprised how flushed my face was. But it didn't look bad.

He was white like a sheet, looked very tired. And his dark eyes kept staring into me as if they would skewer into my soul.

He said: 'How much money is there in that case?'

'Six hundred pounds.'

'The rest?'

'In a bank in Swindon, and a post office account in Sheffield. And the Lost Property Office at Nottingham.'

'You were spreading your risk.'

'I couldn't pay too much into one place.'

'You thought of everything, didn't you.'

I fumbled with a piece of bread. 'Apparently not; you found me.'

'I found you.'

'How?'

Perhaps that wasn't too clever. I saw his face tighten again.

'I'll keep that under my hat for the time being. Just to make sure you won't run away again.'

'Mark, I *can't* go back tomorrow as if nothing had happened! Really I can't. Somebody must have suspected something.'

'They can't suspect much if there's no money missing.'

'Where was Terry? Did you tell him?'

'I told nobody. Anyway he was interviewing clients all morning.'

'. . . How will I get the rest of the money – from Swindon and Sheffield, I mean – and it would take me all day tomorrow.'

'Come back first. When you go to these places I'm coming with you. In the meantime I can pay six hundred into the firm's account out of my personal account to make up the balance. That will keep the books all right if Ward or one of the Holbrooks should ask during the week. But the chances are very much that they won't anyway.'

A good deal of the bite had gone out of his voice. He'd sounded so angry at me at the beginning but now he was cooling off. In a way we might have been working together for something. If I didn't make another bloomer like that 'How?' you never knew your luck. This wasn't a threat any more, it was negotiation. But what was it a negotiation *about*? Even when you're sweet on someone you're not all Christian forgiveness. What did he want? Well, he wanted me; that was it, wasn't it? My skin crawled.

He was watching me now and I had to be careful.

'You're a strange creature. The strangest I've ever met.'

I lowered my eyes. 'Suppose I am?'

'According to what you've told me, if it's true, you don't have much contact with other people. You say you ride a horse – good exercise, but what about the rest of the twenty-four hours? You say you've spent over two years this way. Didn't you have friends?'

'I didn't have boyfriends. I got to know a few people. There was always something to do. I wasn't lonely.'

'But living that way is only half living. You're too withdrawn.'

'I enjoyed it.'

'Perhaps it all helps you to make up these exciting stories, does it? I'm thinking of what you told me about your husband. You were so upset after the motor accident that if you'd stayed on in Cardiff you'd have become a nerve case. But it was easier for you than for me because you'd been able to move and take a job.'

'Don't remind me please. I was – very ashamed of that.'

'You were? That's something anyhow. And about your mother and father in Sydney, and how they found it too hot in the summer months. And your father watching the Davis Cup matches. It was quite an effort on your part, wasn't it?'

'I'm *sorry*. I'm desperately sorry.'

'I wonder how much of what you've told me tonight is out of the same book.'

I raised my head again.

'I'm not lying *now*! They're two different *things*! I was a fool, but it didn't occur to me that I should get to know anyone well in my job. I've told you, I like to be solitary! When I found I was getting to know people I found I had to go on adding to my – to what I'd said at first. It's like a snowball. It piles up and up.'

'It's a common consequence, Marnie. But why send your parents to Australia in the first place, when they were both dead? How did that help?'

130

It was the first time he had used my name. 'It *didn't* help. I somehow wanted to make up a life quite different from my own.'

'There's such a thing as a pathological liar. Are you one?'

'I don't know. Anyway you're going to check everything I've told you tonight, so you can see for yourself.'

He was still looking at me sort of funny, half-way between a doctor and a lover. 'I can't check everything. I can't check what to me is the most important thing you've said tonight.'

'What's that?'

'That one of the reasons you committed this theft was because you wanted to get away from me, because you were afraid of getting entangled and getting hurt.'

'It's true!'

'I wish I could be certain.'

'Mark, it's true! D'you think I have no feelings at all?'

'I'm certain you have some but I want to be sure what they are.'

It was getting a strain, sitting there looking at him all the time, and I knew I was running into a packet of trouble of another kind. But there was no way out.

He said: 'I wonder, if you're such a smart girl, that it never occurred to you to play this the other way round.'

'What way?'

'I don't know whether to be pleased or insulted that you didn't.'

'Didn't what? I don't know what you mean.'

Thank God he pulled abruptly away from the table,

his chair creaking, moved across the room with a queer energy. His collar had got untidy as he talked.

'Next time you stand opposite a glass look at yourself. Have you never had men interested in you?'

'Yes. Oh yes. But I—'

'Did it never occur to you that I had lost my wife less than two years ago and, in some ways at least, was a fairly eligible person to become friendly with?'

'People in the office made remarks.'

'Did they? Well, putting aside for the moment the fact that you may not have thought much of me as a – as a proposition, didn't you ever think that if you hooked me you hooked quite a bit more than twelve hundred pounds?'

'It depends what you mean by hooked.'

'Married.'

The clock in the hall was striking midnight. It took a long time to strike. Well, it wasn't like that clock in Mother's kitchen but it seemed to strike into my spine just the same.

'That wasn't possible,' I said in a panic, in a suddenly stifling smothering panic.

'Why not?'

'We come from different worlds.'

'You've got rather old-fashioned notions, melodramatic notions about class, haven't you?'

'Maybe I have. Maybe I'm a fool. Anyway it seems less dishonest to me to take money the way I did than to trade myself for money like that!'

'You dislike me?'

'No, of course not. That's not it at all!'

'Then what is it?'

'If I—'

'You said you wanted to get away from me because you were afraid of getting hurt. That sounds as if you were not exactly indifferent. Then in what way would you have been trading yourself for money by marrying me?'

I was cornered – like a rat in a coal bunker. It was a completely new experience for me, because I've never been at a loss for an excuse or an explanation or a way out. For the second time that night he seemed to be cleverer than I was, and did I hate it.

To give myself a breather I put my hands up to my face. You've only got to think long enough about anything to find a way out. After a minute he came over and put his hand on my shoulder; it was the first time he'd touched me all evening.

'Tell me, Marnie.'

I said in a desolate voice: 'How can I tell you what I don't know? I thought it wasn't possible. Anyway it's too late now.'

Even while I took that line I was afraid of what he was going to say, and my God he said it.

'Doesn't that rather remain to be seen?'

'How?'

'You tell me.'

I knew I had to look at him. I knew that this might be about the last moment to bale out. Yet there wasn't really any place to go. If I told him no, it was as clear as gin what would come next – the police. It was a ghastly moment. His hand tightened slightly on my shoulder. I looked up, hoping my eyes didn't show what I was thinking.

'Mark, I'm a *thief*. Don't deceive yourself. There's no getting away from it. Just – forgive me if you can and let me go.'

'Is that what you want?'

'I'm sure it's for the best.'

'For whose best? Yours? Mine?'

'Yes. Yes, I think so.'

'I differ from that. D'you know, I happen to love you. I suppose you've guessed it, have you?'

'No.'

'No? Well, that's really the nigger in the woodpile. I love you, Marnie.'

'Mark. You're . . . you're *crazy*.'

'It's a symptom of the complaint.'

I said desperately: 'Look . . . be *sensible* . . . I've robbed you and lied to you. That's no – no basis to build a sparrow's nest on, let alone a marriage . . . Do you trust me?'

He half laughed. 'No. Not yet.'

'You see. How can anything begin like that? Love's got to be built on trust.'

'Nonsense. Love grows where it grows. What it builds on is anybody's guess.'

I didn't answer. He had me in the corner and I wasn't even like that rat – I couldn't bite him.

He said: 'After following you half-way across England do you think I'm going to let you go?'

CHAPTER EIGHT

So the impossible happened and I went back to work on the Monday as if nothing was different. Nobody said a thing except that one or two asked me if I was better, and Sam Ward looked down his nose a bit more than usual. Susan Clabon was full of the Isle of Wight, and that helped to pass the day. I found in the waste basket all my pieces of paper that Mark had snatched out of the pay envelopes and thrown away.

On the Thursday he drove me to Swindon and the other places where I had left the money, and I drew it out. On the Saturday he asked me to marry him.

It had been coming at me of course ever since Sunday night like a railway train, and me on a level-crossing. But I was tied there and there was no way of dodging it.

There was just no way.

He wouldn't say how he'd traced me, so I didn't know what mistake I had made. All I knew was that if he looked too hard the way led from Cirencester, clang, right back to Mother like one of those old-fashioned cash systems they used to have in shops. I had to go on lying to him about my mother being dead because if he once knew she was alive it was all up. If Mother knew I was a thief and had been keeping her on stolen money she'd froth at the mouth. In fact I knew it would kill her: she'd never be able to swallow the disgrace. If he ever met her the whole story of Mr Pemberton and his millions came crashing down, and then in no time they'd both discover I had been taking money for three years. Then as well as Mother having a stroke or something I would go to prison quick. Even marrying him was better than that.

So I had to stop him probing too hard, and the only way I knew was to let him think I loved him. Many of the things I'd told him were true – except that I'd left gaps – so I went painstakingly about getting him the proof he wanted. If I could get him proofs of what was true – birth certificate and the rest – he might not dig into what was not true. In fact he took a lot on trust. Perhaps he thought he ought to if he loved me, even though he'd said he would not.

He seemed pretty crazy about me. So I didn't say no to him, though by turns I fumed and shivered at the thought of it. But I kept thinking, there's months yet – something'll turn up. If I shut my eyes and think and wait, something'll turn up.

He said not to tell at the firm for the time being, and that suited me. But he wouldn't let me take my holidays, so I went on working right through October. He said he wanted to keep me under his eye. The way he said it was like an officer putting an Able Seaman on probation. He ought to have stayed in the Navy, I thought, that suited him, and I wished to Heaven he had.

Yet sometimes in fairness you had to admit he did his best to be nice. There weren't many men who would have done what he did, have found out about a woman what he had found out, and then said marry me. The most the average man would have suggested was a flat in London somewhere to visit when he wanted, and me installed there terrified to shift in case he set the police on me. I wondered why he hadn't suggested it. Terry would have, first go. He was a fool not to have tried that first anyhow and fallen back on marriage if he found there was nothing doing.

But every now and then, just when you thought he was being rather stupid about something, he'd say something that suddenly showed he was still a jump ahead of you, and that was what I liked least of all. I could have managed a man who was really *dumb*. But Mark I could never be sure of. I hated that. It was a nasty trick not telling me how he had found out. I wondered what he was going to spring on me next.

In October he said he wanted me to meet his mother, so I said all right, because what else was there to say; and he picked me up and we drove into London on a Sunday afternoon. While we were driving through Regent's Park he told me he thought we should be married in November.

I got heartburn at that. 'Oh, Mark, that's crazy! We're not officially engaged yet!'

'There's no such thing,' he said in his quiet down-right way. 'My mother knows. Who else is there?'

'I – have to get some clothes.'

'All right, get them. Give in your notice next week,

leave at the end of the month, that will give you two weeks to get ready.'

'Are you really satisfied?' I said. 'Satisfied that you really want to marry a thief and a liar?'

'I'm satisfied I love you. Anyway, who hasn't been a thief and a liar to some extent at some time of their lives? It's only a question of degree.'

'Yes, but . . . be reasonable. We've only known each other a month or two. It's too soon.'

'We've known each other seven months. Do you mean you're not sure yourself yet?'

'Oh, it isn't that,' I said, uneasily.

'Well I've been in love with you pretty well since the day you came about the interview, so I don't see there's any need to wait.'

'Not since the *interview*.'

'Yes. Sam Ward and I had already agreed to engage the girl we'd just interviewed, when you came in. He was going to tell you that but I stopped him. He didn't want to change his mind, but I persuaded him.'

'As you – persuade most people.'

'I also persuaded him to send you that day with the programme when there was the thunderstorm. I suppose you guessed that.'

'No, why should I?'

'Well, we don't usually employ cashiers as messenger boys even when we're short staffed.'

I swallowed my spittle. 'So I suppose that meeting in the rose show wasn't accidental then?'

'No.'

'It must have been a double shock that morning, when you found I'd gone.'

'It was.'

'What did you do – I mean when you had finished the pay packets?'

He wrinkled his forehead at me teasingly. 'I set about finding you.'

'Did you know where to look?'

'No.'

'Then? . . .'

'I'll tell you on our honeymoon.'

I'd thought of Mrs Rutland as tall and dignified and grey-haired – like one of those illustrations in the fairytale women's magazines – but she was a short stout twinkling woman with spectacles and beautiful small hands and feet. I didn't think she'd ever been particularly good looking but you could see that she had had a slight figure that had thickened as she got older. Her colouring was the same as Mark's, olive skin, dark brown eyes, thick dark hair.

I don't know what she felt like but I know what I felt like at the meeting: like a caged cat pretending to be a blushing timid canary. I wonder what she would have thought as I shook her hand and smiled at her if she had known that I was no more in love with her son than I was with a jailer.

I must say, though, that we both got through it fairly well; she was neither patronizing nor too anxious to please, and in a way I liked her better than Mark. Or perhaps it was just because battle and strife didn't come into it. She talked to me as if she'd known me half her life, and I answered and smiled and looked at her and looked round the flat, which was simply beautiful. You didn't have to know about furniture to admire the colour of the mahogany and the curve of the chair backs and the tapering legs and the oval table and the Regency sofas.

We stayed to tea and talked about her family and she carefully didn't ask about mine – so I suppose Mark had primed her a bit – and it was pleasant enough in its way. I think if I had come into these surroundings differently I should have enjoyed them; they were what I should have got for myself if I had ever had the money. It was right in the centre of London but very quiet, and the rooms were high and the windows tall and looked over a small square where the leaves were just falling, and we drank out of cups that showed the shadow of your fingers through them, and Mark watched us while pretending not to. After tea he wandered round the room while we talked, and once I glanced up at his face as he bent to light his mother a cigarette and I thought, my God, he's happy. And just for a moment then I nearly got up and ran.

But in this life it's Number One that counts most, and after all it was his own fault for pinning me here, and if he got hurt, well, so should I, but not as much as by going to prison; so I stuck it out.

And anyway there was still three weeks.

I thought of Forio, eating his gentle beautiful proud

head off at Garrod's and waiting for the touch of my hands. Whenever I was in a spot I thought of him.

When we left I went out to the car first and sat in it while Mark had a word with his mother. Presently he came down and we drove away.

I said: 'She's not as terrifying as I expected.'

'She's not terrifying at all. I was watching you both and I think you'll get on together.'

'I think we shall, Mark.' I meant that I thought we should have if we had met any other way.

'What does she do with her time?'

'When my father died she sold up his house in the country because she said she wanted the minimum of personal possessions. She does a lot of welfare work and sits on various committees.'

'I thought she had *lots* of personal possessions. Far more than my mother ever had.'

'Oh, in a small space, yes. My father was a great collector and she kept the best.'

'Don't you think you're cheating her taking me like that and passing me off as a – as a normal person?'

'Aren't you a normal person?'

'No.'

'Marnie, you're awfully anxious to keep on beating yourself. Give your conscience a rest.'

'I think you should tell her about me before we marry.'

'Well, that's my problem, isn't it.'

I wondered if I should go to see Mrs Rutland in private and confess what I was, in the hope that she would stop the marriage. But it was too risky. She might have a social conscience.

'What are you thinking?' he asked.

'I'm thinking what it must be like for her, welcoming another girl as a daughter-in-law so soon.'

'It's the crowning tragedy for every widow that she can't be her son's wife.'

I looked at him, and I knew suddenly again that he'd gone deeper than I could go. In some way what he said seemed to strike at me specially.

I said: 'You've never told me anything about Estelle.'

'. . . What is there you want to know?'

'She must have been very different from me.'

'She was.'

'Did you love her?'

'Yes.'

'If you loved her, don't you still love her? If so, then why me? How can you change?'

'I haven't changed.'

'Can you love two women at the same time?'

'Yes. Differently. However hard you try you can't love a memory in the same way you love a living person. I tried . . .' He stopped.

'Yes?'

'You were the first person I'd looked at in that way for eighteen months. I knew that, living the way I had been living, one can get dangerously myopic—'

'What does that mean?'

'In this case ready to fall for the first pretty face . . .' His fingers moved on the wheel. 'I sometimes think one's feelings and motives are like a succession of Chinese boxes, one within the other, and Lord knows which is the innermost. Anyway, they are with me. So I tried to be dispassionate about you.'

'And did it work?'

'No, I'm afraid it didn't. I soon couldn't get away from the fact that you were the woman I wanted – and no other.'

He said this in such a quiet voice that for a moment I felt touched and pleased. Perhaps this idea about the Chinese boxes was a good one for me to think of, because God knows a third of the time I was a bit flattered because he was so gone on me and a third of the time I hated him deeply, and a third of the time I was sorry for him, and all I could be sure of was that if I married him it would be the biggest mess alive for both of us and that I couldn't stand the thought of it.

By now he was feeling much more sure of me, and when I said I had to go to Plymouth to see the lawyer who had settled up Lucy Nye's estate he said all right. I'd mocked up a gorgeously detailed story to tell him, proving why I must go, but it wasn't needed and I was slightly disappointed at the waste. I got the feeling that now I'd given him some proofs, he was making a point of not asking for more. You know, a sort of love-and-trust gesture.

All the same I did not go straight to Torquay. I went first to Plymouth, then back to Newton Abbot, then to Kingswear. By the time I walked up Cuthbert Avenue I was sure I wasn't being followed.

It was the first time I'd been home since they moved, and Lucy Nye, my dead auntie, was waiting on the doorstep for me so that I shouldn't mistake the house.

In the last two weeks I'd had this awful worry over what to tell Mother. I mean, I could say nothing to her at all – or I could give her a sort of Revised Version, I mean the Gospel of Mark according to Marnie – if that isn't a bad joke. Or of course I could tell her everything – but that was out from the start.

I didn't think I wanted to go through the rest of my life tied to the secretarial strings of Mr Pemberton. In any case he was getting to be a nuisance. If I broke it to her now that I was getting married to somebody I had just met, a Mr Rutland, a wealthy printer, though not so wealthy as Mr Pemberton, she might not take it too hard.

Or she might. You never knew with Mother. And that way there was the frightful danger that she might demand to meet Mark. That could never be, because if once they got together, however careful Mark might be not to mention me stealing from his firm, Mam was dead *certain* to tell him what a good daughter I was and all the money I'd given her in the last three years, and that would start him asking questions again, and in no time he would have found out about Manchester and Birmingham and Newcastle etc.

I wondered if I could take the risk of telling her and still be *certain* of keeping them apart.

When I got in Mother was dozing in the front sitting-room and I thought she looked younger asleep. When she woke she seemed to take a minute or so to remember where she was.

Then she said: 'Why, Marnie, I told Lucy to look for you; we didn't wait tea but there's a tasty bit of ham cooking, I always believe in bay leaves, it adds just that to it; Lucy shut the door, this house is colder than the other, more outside walls.'

One thing about Mother: even if she hadn't seen you for six months she took up the conversation as if you had just dropped in from across the way. First I had to be shown the house. It was miles better than the other, with a sitting-room in the back, and a sun porch and a kitchen, and three cream-painted bedrooms with new fawn curtains and a toilet separate from the bathroom, and an attic with a view of Torbay between the chimney-pots.

It really was nice, only all the time I couldn't help but see how different it was from Mrs Rutland's flat with its lamps and its pictures and its arched recesses and its damned good taste. The two places weren't really in the same world. Neither were the two women. My mother had been the better looking of the two, but it was like comparing Forio with a horse that has been used to pull a dust cart all its life. It wasn't fair. It just wasn't fair. But there was nothing more I could do about it than I had done or than I was doing.

Mam said: 'How do you like this black marocain? Got it in the summer sales, model, reduced to four guineas, just my fit, isn't it. You're thinner, Marnie; been going easy on potatoes? I like that way you done your hair; more classy than last time.'

'I'm all right,' I said. 'I'm fine.'

We talked for quite a while, and then suddenly

without being asked she answered nearly all my questions.

'Your cousin Doreen was here last week – first time for two years – I said to her she might not have an aunt; what with her own mother being dead and her father in Hong Kong, you'd think she might have some thought for me. But no. She's a Sister or something now; gets a better screw, but d'you know what she came down to tell me; she's getting married. And to a doctor of all people. I had to pretend, of course, say yes, yes, fancy, but at the end I couldn't help but put in my spoke; I said, Marnie never thinks of marriage – or of men; I said Marnie's a model daughter to me, and I said she makes more in a month than most people make in a year. And d'you know what she said? She said, well, I hope it's honest. I could have slapped her. I said, in one of my sudden tempers, don't go raking up that filth that happened thirteen years ago; I said Marnie's as honest as the day. I said God took much from me but he gave me one jewel and that's my daughter!'

'Jewel,' I said. 'Woolworth's best.'

'No, Marnie; the very best there is. A real jewel if ever there was one.' She dabbed one corner of her right eye with a bit of lace. I'd never known Mother cry anywhere else but just out of the corner of her right eye.

'How's your rheumatism?' I said to change the subject.

'Well, not but what it couldn't be better. Mrs Beardmore in No. 12 recommended sour milk. Dear Heavens, I said, if it's that or knobs I'd rather have my knobs.

This weather doesn't suit it, of course, and what with the chimney smoking. How's Mr Pemberton?'

'All right. Mother . . .'

Mother's eyes had been looking absent-minded but they sharpened up like pencil-points at something in my voice.

'What is it?'

'You said I never thought of getting married. Well, maybe I don't. But what would you say if I changed my mind ever?'

We were at the top of the stairs from the attic. Down below Lucy Nye was clattering about trying to hurry on the supper. Mother buttoned her cardigan.

'Have you got to?'

'Got to what?'

'Get married.'

'No, of course not! What ever makes you say that?'

'Tell me if you have. Now tell me.'

'Look,' I said. '*No!*'

'Women often go like you, go thinner when it begins. I did. It's what I've often been afraid of with you. You're too lovely looking. A lot of men must have wanted after you.'

'Well, they've got nothing for their trouble,' I said, angry with her now. 'I was only asking you a straight question and I thought I might get a straight answer. Women do get married sometimes, you know. Surprising, but there it is. Even you did. Remember?'

She looked shocked. 'Marnie! We'll not go into that.'

'Why not?' I said. 'You talk as if getting married was

a disgrace! If you felt like that I wonder how you ever came to have me!'

She didn't speak while we got down the stairs. But at the bottom I saw her hand was trembling on her stick.

'I went into it not knowing,' she said. 'It was my duty to submit.'

There was a ghastly silence as we went down the next flight. The sizzling noise of chips came from the kitchen. Mother led the way into the sitting-room.

'That new telly is giving trouble,' she said in a queer voice, and I could see she was trembling all over. 'Keeps snowing. When I twiddle the knob the picture goes round like Ernie stirring the Premium Bonds. There was a wedding on it last night in one of those plays. It's all a sham. I said to Lucy, all that giggling and screaming and laughing; marriage isn't like that, marriage is what happens under the sheets, pawing and grunting, you don't giggle then. Marnie, you won't let me down?'

'Let you *down*?' I said, really angry, but holding her drumstick arm. 'What're you talking about? Who's talking about letting you down?'

'You were. You were. Even in a joke it don't do. I bank on you, Marnie, you're all I've got. You're all I've ever had.'

'All right, all right, don't get so *excited*. I was only asking a simple question. Can't I ask a question without you going off the deep end?'

'If you ask the questions it shows you've been thinking of it.'

'Get away, don't be silly!' I patted her face. 'You live alone here with Lucy and fancy too much.' I went across and switched on the TV and waited for it to warm up. 'Sit down here till supper's ready. And if I ever think of getting married I'll pick a millionaire and then he'll be able to keep us both!'

Mother lowered herself into her favourite chair. She looked better now. As the picture came on she said: 'Don't joke about it, Marnie. I'd rather have you as you are. I can't picture my little girl – that way.'

On the train back to London next day I worried about it. It would have been an awful lot easier if I could have just faced them both out with the truth, like it or leave it. I suppose I might even have looked better to Mark as the only support of a widowed mother, stealing for her.

And in a way all my life I *had* stolen for her, though it was too easy just to leave it at that. I'd taken money for myself too. It was all mixed up.

On the train I thought of my Uncle Stephen paying for my lessons in elocution and accountancy, and about my first few jobs – where I'd been honest enough – after all it's hardly worth being anything else behind the counter of an electricity shop, our home didn't even get any free bulbs. And then the job in Bristol – two pounds a week more and prospects – but I'd hardly settled there before Mother got this varicose ulcer, and the first I heard was a dirty bit of paper from Lucy saying she was in hospital and probably had to have an op. I hung on then waiting for news, but after a week I couldn't wait any longer and got two days off to visit her.

She was in the South Western General, and a flu epidemic was on, and she was in a ward as long as a railway platform and she was just by the door and had just caught flu herself and she looked like death. I'd only the one day really to see her, and I wanted to know what was wrong and nobody had any time for me *at all*. Mother said they'd done nothing for her in nearly three weeks and that she was getting worse and that she was in a perishing draught and the door beside her bed slammed a hundred and twenty times a day, beginning at five o'clock in the morning, and she thought for all the nurses cared she could very well die there before they did anything for her.

Well, I had words with a sour-faced sister and then a short interview with the matron who acted as if she'd just come from the presence of God; so then I really lost my temper and demanded to see the surgeon and there was a row because he was busy on some other case, but in the end I got to see him.

I told him just what I thought of his hospital and the way they were treating my mother, and he listened with a sort of tired patience that really got me raging. Looking back now, of course, I can see just what I must have looked like to him. I hadn't learned how to dress at all, and my new accent was too new to stick with me when I was mad. I remember I was wearing a print frock that was a bit too short and nylons that were cheaper because they only just reached above the knee and unsuitable white shoes, and my hair had been permed and I was carrying a big plastic hand-bag. I expect he thought I came from a snack bar or an amusement arcade or something – if I wasn't actually a tart.

Anyway when I stopped for breath he said: 'I quite
see that you are feeling anxious, Miss – er – Elton, but I
can promise you your mother is in no danger of dying
just yet. Perhaps you don't realize that a varicose ulcer
is caused by overwork, too much standing and by
general neglect. The skin gets into poor condition, it
breaks down and an ulcer forms. We can't operate on
the vein until we've cleaned the ulcer up. The time your
mother has been in hospital, when you wrongly suppose
we have been neglecting her, has been necessary to give
her rest and to help the ulcer to heal by seeing she gets
proper food.'

I said: 'Is it much rest when she can't sleep for the
slamming of the door behind her? And she says the
food is terrible.'

At least that took the look of strained patience off
his face.

'Young lady,' he said, 'I don't know if you are aware
that an influenza epidemic is raging in this city. We
can't find beds for all the urgent cases of one sort and
another that exist, and most of the staff of this hospital
is run off its feet. In an ideal community your mother
would have a private ward, but it doesn't run to that;
nor will it in my lifetime or yours. So we do the best we
can with the present material and in the present circumstances. I'll try to get your mother moved from the
door. I shall hope to operate on her next week. The
sooner you have her home the happier we shall be. But
– she's in a shop, isn't she? – I'd warn you that in future
she'll have to take sedentary work of some sort. She'll
just have to keep off her feet or she'll be back here in

three months with the same trouble or worse. And although she's in no danger of dying she's certainly in danger of becoming permanently crippled. Now I'll have to ask you to excuse me.'

I went back to Mother, feeling I'd done what I could but still boiling.

'Don't worry,' I said to Mother. 'They're going to move you soon from this door. I seen to that . . . I have seen to that. They've got to keep you here for a bit to get your leg healed, but it'll be all right, I promise you.'

I sat on her bed thinking over what the surgeon had said at the end. Just then the nurse came along.

'You'll have to go now,' she said. 'This isn't a proper visiting day, you know. You've only been allowed in as a special favour.'

'Thanks,' I said, and added 'for nothing' under my breath. 'Don't worry,' I said to Mother. 'We'll soon have you out of here. Did I tell you, I've got the promise of a marvellous job?'

'You have? Where?'

'Swansea. I don't know the details yet. I only heard of it last week but I think I'll get it. If I do . . .'

'Is it respectable?'

'Of course it is. What do you take me for? But as a secretary. I may get paid quite a lot. Anyway it may mean you won't have to go to work right away when you come home.'

When I got back to Bristol I gave in my notice at Deloitte, Plender & Griffiths and went to live in Swansea. I took a job in a store in the name of Maud Green. Three months later I slid out with three hundred and ninety pounds. That was my first haul and I was pretty nervous about it then.

At the time I was dead sure I was doing it all on account of Mother. Now it seems to me I was doing it mainly to satisfy myself.

CHAPTER NINE

'WELL, REALLY, I always said you were a deep one,' Dawn said, picking at a tiny mole on her cheek. 'Well, really, and how long has it been going on? Don't tell me. I really believe it was love at first sight, wasn't it? I thought one time it was Terry: you remember after the dinner; and I am sure he was interested in you; but of course you've done better. Mark – Mr Rutland I'd better start calling him to you, I suppose – oh, very well, dear, thank you, just between ourselves – Mark is a different kettle of fish. More *serious*, if you know what I mean. With Terry you put it on the slate and it washes off again. Where are you going to live, Little Gaddesden? We shall miss you, you know . . . Tell me, do these things grow? I'm sure it's bigger than it was last year. Of course some men call them beauty spots . . . Are we all coming to the wedding? Oh, very private. Well I know how you must *feel*. And I expect with you both having been married before. You *are* lucky, you know, two men before you're twenty-four; some girls have to slog it enough getting one.'

*

Sam Ward said: 'Well, Mrs Taylor, so we have to – hm – congratulate you, I suppose. Such efficiency – business efficiency – should make you a very successful house-wife, shouldn't it. Naturally I hope you'll be very happy. But then I'm sure you will be. Would you get me the costing report on the Kromecote? We want to see what the danger is of killing the gloss.'

'My dear,' Terry said, brushing a hand over his suede waistcoat. 'My dear, you *have* done it this time.'

'What have I done?'

'Well, my dear, Mark of all people. Not really your *style*, I should have thought.'

'What is my style?'

'A rather tortuous type. A man with a few wrinkles in his soul. Mark's too downright.'

'Have you told him?'

'He knows what I think, I'm sure. It would be unfair of me to dot the i's and cross the t's.'

He was breathing through his nose, the way he did at poker sometimes. And he was at his most cissyish – which was queer, because sometimes he wasn't that way at all. I thought he doesn't really care all that much for me, but he cares that Mark is getting what *he* hasn't had.

'Apart from that,' he said, 'you're a *mystery*, Mary, and mystery women are always a challenge. Dawn was talking about you to me the other evening.'

'What was she saying?'

'Never mind, my dear; nothing to your detriment in

my eyes, I assure you. You've got a past, I'd guess, but what sort I just wouldn't know. Not the *understood* sort, I'm sure.'

'Honestly, Terry,' I said, 'this talking in riddles doesn't amuse me at all. I doubt if it amuses anyone. If you think something, why not say it?'

'No, no, dear. I wouldn't want to offend you. In fact I hope we shall be bosom friends. On behalf of the Holbrooks I have pleasure in welcoming you into the family.'

'On behalf of the Rutlands, thank you.'

'Is it to be a *lavish* wedding?'

'No. Very quiet.'

Very quiet. So quiet as to be almost secret. Just his mother and two witnesses. But it was happening and there was no escape. It had crept up on me like a cat on a mouse; while it was ten days away it hadn't quite mattered so much; then it was seven, then four, then tomorrow. I should have gone off the night before, risked everything and run. But I didn't. I stayed and went to the register office and a red-haired square-jawed man in a shiny blue suit said some words to us and we said some words back and something was written on a piece of paper and we signed our names. My true name, that was what gave me the horrors. I wouldn't have minded so much if it had been happening to Mary Taylor or Mollie Jeffrey. My sham life didn't include Marnie Elmer.

And now for the first time I really had changed my name. I was called Margaret Rutland, and Mark kissed me on the mouth in front of his mother and the red-haired registrar and the two witnesses, and I flushed because, although maybe he saw it as a promise, I saw it as a threat.

Afterwards we went back to his mother's and had champagne cocktails which I didn't like, but we hadn't long to spend because we were catching the three o'clock plane for Majorca. While we were standing about talking and trying to be natural I thought of Forio, just to keep myself sane.

Before we left his mother took me on one side and said: 'Marnie, I won't say, Make him happy, but I will say, Be happy yourself. I think you're capable of much more than you think.'

I looked at her and half smiled.

She said: 'It will be twenty-eight years ago next month since he was born to me. I felt then I had everything – and I had! A husband, a son of eight, a mother and father still alive – and a baby son. I felt as if I were the centre of the universe. Since then they've all gone – except Mark. I expect it will seem a long stretch of time to you, but it doesn't look very long to me, looking back. Life slips so easily through your fingers.'

I didn't know what to say, so I said nothing.

'Life slips so easily through your fingers. So make the most of it while you can. Grasp it and savour it, my dear. Now, good-bye . . .'

We stayed at a hotel in Cas Catala about four miles out of Palma. Over the evening meal I asked Mark how he had traced me.

'Must we talk of that tonight?'

'You promised.'

'Well sometime on our honeymoon, I said. Are you itching to know?'

'Not *itching*. But curious. I – thought I had been clever.'

'So you had.' He rubbed his cheek. He was quite good-looking tonight because as usual holiday clothes suited him. Except that the shape of his cheek-bones wasn't right you could have taken him for a Spaniard. 'There was nothing ever more premeditated than that theft, was there?'

'I told you how it was. But I want to know how you found me.'

He looked me over. That was truly what he did. 'Can you imagine how I felt that Friday morning? I was in love with you, and I suddenly found I'd been made a complete fool of. I was so upset I could hardly think – and very, very angry. I could have strangled you.'

'You looked as if you could when you found me.'

'I might have done earlier but you were out of reach. The one important thing in my life from that moment was to catch you. I decided to cover up the theft and at the same time follow you and find you, wherever you'd gone and however long it took.'

'You weren't sure, then?'

'I hadn't an idea where you were. But all the time I was working, putting the money in the envelopes, I was really thinking about finding you. That's what surprises me, that I only made two mistakes with the pay envelopes; it shows one's mind can work in separate compartments—'

'Yes. Go on.'

He half grinned. 'I think perhaps I'll keep the secret for a day or two more. Why can't you sit and enjoy the view?'

'*No*. I want to know, Mark! I'll enjoy the view afterwards.'

'But it might spoil it for you. It was largely luck the way I found you.'

He poured out the last of the wine and sipped at his glass. 'Odd how much better this Rioja tastes here than in England.'

'It was largely luck?'

'Well, I thought to myself, what did she show herself *really* interested in? Not me, certainly. But wasn't she genuinely interested in horses? Was that a sham too, all that enthusiasm and knowledge? It couldn't be. So I thought of horse racing.'

'Yes, I see.'

'I thought, what will she do with the money? Go to race meetings, probably, and bet. What race meetings are on next week and the week after and the week after? If I follow them every Saturday I'm bound to catch her out eventually even if it takes a year.'

'But it only took a day.'

'Two.' He offered me a cigarette. I shook my head.

He said: 'I went carefully over everything we'd said to each other at all our meetings – piece by piece. And when you feel about a girl the way I felt about you it isn't difficult to remember because – well because you think a lot about it in any case and that fixes it in your mind. And presently I came across something you had said at Newmarket. You advised me to back a grey filly called Telepathy and you said you'd seen her training as a one-year-old.'

'Oh!' I said. 'Oh!'

'Yes . . . Anyway, it was the only trail I had. I looked up Telepathy in *Ruff's Guide* and saw she belonged to a Major Marston of Newbury, but that she had been bred by a Mr Arthur Fitzgibbon at Melton Magna, near Cirencester. On the Sunday morning I phoned Marston and got details from him and then went down to Melton Magna. Unfortunately Fitzgibbon had left, and it took me most of the morning tracing him to Bath. Even then he couldn't help me; he knew no one who answered to your description. So I went back to Melton Magna, and just got in the Oak Leaf before closing time at two. Saunders, the innkeeper, didn't know anyone of your description either, so then I asked him if – apart from the ex-Fitzgibbon place, which was private – there were any riding stables around where it was possible to hire a horse. He gave me the names of three. Garrod's was the third I tried.'

'Oh,' I said again, dismally.

'I almost gave it up just before getting to Garrod's. The sun was setting and I was very tired and feeling very played out.'

I looked at him. 'It was just as if you had come out of the ground.'

'Like your conscience.'

'Like the devil.'

He laughed. I stared out at the view now, thinking over my mistake. We were on a closed veranda looking over a small cove. A quarter moon was going down, and the small boats anchored in the bay cut the moon's track like into a glimmering jigsaw. I suppose it was beautiful. But I thought only of my mistake. How I could have done it. If I hadn't been such a fool none of this need have happened and I should have been free and happy.

I looked down at the gold band on my finger. I had been feeling sick and frightened but now I felt sick and angry.

'You might not have found me,' I said. 'You might never have found me again. What would have happened to your money then?'

'I should have had to make it good out of my own pocket and written it down to experience.'

'You have so much money?'

'No. But I thought you were worth the risk.'

'I'm not.'

'I think you are.'

'I'm not. I know I'm not. You should just have taken your money back and then let me go.'

'Darling, what's the matter?' he said later that night. 'Are you afraid?'

'Yes. I can't stand it, Mark. I'll die.'

'It seems improbable. Tell me what's the matter. Do you hate me?'

'I hate the thought of *this*. I screw up. I feel – *sick*.'

He put his hand on my bare leg just above the knee, and I moved quickly to cover it. He said: 'Why do you shrink from me like that?'

'I don't shrink from you. It's just the contact.'

'Isn't that the same thing?'

'Not quite.'

'Marnie, do you love me?'

'I don't love this.'

'Aren't you fighting against something in yourself?'

'Not in myself.'

'Yes. The physical act of love is a normal outcome of the emotional state of being in love. Surely.'

'Maybe. For some people.'

'Of course without emotion there is only sex. But without sex there is only sentimentality. Between a man and a woman the two elements of love become one. Don't they?'

I stared up at the curved stone ceiling which was quite low in the alcove over the bed. 'To me it's so degrading.'

'Why?'

'I don't know.'

'Give me one reason why you think that.'

'It's . . . animal.'

He made a first little movement of annoyance. 'We *are* animal – in part. We can't take our feet out of the mud. If we try we fall slap on our faces. It's only by accepting our humanity that we can make the most of it.'

'But—'

'We can degrade anything, of course – that's the price we pay for our brains and our ingenuity – but if we do, it's our own silly fault. We can just as easily exalt it. Whoever made us gave us the whole pack.'

In the café on the quay outside someone was playing a guitar. It sounded twenty miles away from me just then. I was trying not to tremble because I knew if I started he would know at once, and I'd really have hated to give myself so much away. It wasn't exactly a trembling of fear but of sheer nerves. All those nice nerves that kept so steady when I was stealing money had gone back on me just now. And my mixed feelings for him weren't mixed any longer; I didn't like anything he stood for, male body, male superiority, male aggressiveness disguised as politeness. I hated him for having humiliated me, for having come into the room when I had practically no clothes on and put his hands up and down my body so that I was sick and hot and ashamed of myself and him.

Of course it was what was expected. I knew that. You don't live the way I'd lived without knowing it all. But it doesn't mean you have to want it all. Right through the evening I'd been trying to set myself to see it sensibly, like not happening to me, like it might have been if Mollie Jeffrey had got sent to prison, something you could keep at a distance. But you can't always do what you set yourself to do.

He said gently: 'I'd give a lot to know how your mind works.'

'My mind? Why?'

'It turns too many corners. It never goes the straight

way to anything. It ties itself up in little knots and sees things inside out.'

'Why d'you say that?'

'These quaint ideas you have about sex. If they were nothing else they'd be desperately old-fashioned.'

'I can't help it.'

'You're a very pretty girl – made for love. It's like a bud saying it won't open, or a butterfly that won't come out of its chrysalis.'

I looked at him. I'd thought when it came to this, when there wasn't any escape, I'd be able to pretend that I liked it. But I knew now I couldn't, not for all the tea in China. But I daren't risk yet being outspoken about it – not any more than I had been. I wasn't sure enough of him.

I sighed and said: 'I'm really most awfully sorry, Mark. Perhaps I've got it all wrong tonight. But I promise you, it isn't just something wrong with my reasoning. It's something I feel afraid of and have got to – to overcome. Give me time.'

He was really too easy to cheat. 'That's a very different matter. Perhaps you're tired and overexcited. Perhaps too much has happened in one day.'

He was even giving me excuses. I said: 'The plane upset me a bit. Don't forget it was my first flight. And don't forget either that this is my first wedding. It would have been better for you if I really had been a widow.'

'Well, we'll carry that over for consideration tomorrow.'

*

The next day the weather was bright but showery. We hired a car to take us across the island to see the stalactite caves and a pearl factory. I bought some earrings and two or three brooches. In the evening we went to a night club and watched Spanish dancers. When we'd seen the best I was taken ill with pains in my stomach and we had to get back to the hotel by taxi. That took care of that night, but I didn't think it was going to be a good excuse for long. The day after we spent in Palma. We bought a decanter and wine glasses in the glass works, and a handbag for me and a wallet and some shoes for him. I quite enjoyed it, just as I'd found it all right being with him at the races. That part was all right – though I should have been just as content on my own. When night came I was all tensed up for another argument and with a new set of excuses, but to my surprise he was quite matter-of-fact and didn't try to touch me. We had twin beds, and except for the embarrassment of sharing the room I'd nothing to complain about. The same the next night *and* the next. I mean, it was surprising.

During the day I could tell he was watching me sometimes, and now and then I caught a look on his face as if I was a puzzle that wouldn't come out. But all round he was considerate enough, except that we did so much in so short a time.

Now I'm as strong as a horse, but even I felt tired with all we did. He might be thin and pale, but I realized he was about as delicate as a four-minute miler. Perhaps he was trying to tire me out.

On the fifth day we flew to Ibiza and took a car to

watch a Saint's Day fiesta in one of the tiny villages. It was queer and strange, with the sun reflecting off the blank white wall of the church, and the mass of black-clothed peasants seething in the square like a lot of beetles that have just hatched out. The only colour was the procession of sacred images bobbing through the crowd, and the young girls who wore bright fiesta costumes with lace and silk and coloured underskirts.

I saw one of them who was specially pretty standing next to Mark. She had long plaited black hair with a great satin bow and she was chattering to a crowd of these older women who were all in black, and wrinkled and weather-beaten as if they'd spent forty years in the sun and the rain. He caught my look and smiled, and I think he saw what I was thinking because when we moved off he said:

'Youth doesn't last long here, does it? A year or so, and then she'll marry a farmhand and it'll be all childbearing and work in the fields.'

'It's so unfair,' I said. 'She's trapped – no escape.'

'Oh, yes, I agree. Though if you weep for her you weep for all the world. We're all trapped the instant we're born – and we stay so until we die.'

I felt he was blunting the point; by making it general he was taking the edge off what I felt for that girl; but I could not find the right words to say so.

Afterwards we sat in a café and drank cognac at fourpence a glass and watched the Spaniards crushing to the bar trying to get served. Quite a lot of the young men were already pretty well on and we could hardly hear ourselves speak for all the noise. Three young men at the door of the café were trying to get three girls to talk to them. The girls were giggling behind their hands and acting like the young men weren't there.

I said: 'Men only want one thing from a woman really, don't they? Something that's over in five minutes, and then they can pass on. It doesn't seem to me it matters what woman it is as long as it's a woman.'

Mark drank his brandy. I knew as soon as I saw his face that I'd said the wrong thing, and afterwards I wondered why I'd said it, knowing it would really sting him.

'We're all caught up in systems bigger than ourselves, Marnie. This isn't a very good one: most of the girls here will be elderly drudges by the time they're thirty. But it doesn't follow that their standards are lower than ours. In fact what you've just said comes from a lower view of life than theirs, not a higher. Most of them would despise you for it.'

'Like you do?' I said gently.

He took a slow breath. 'Darling, you're a big girl now. If someone gave you a new system of bookkeeping to learn, you'd learn it. Quicker than I could. Well then, try to keep an open mind, be ready to learn about other things.'

'Such as this, I suppose.'

'Such as trying not to have set ideas – other people's ideas – about love.'

There was an awful wild cackle of laughter from the men at the bar. It reminded me of Keyham. If that was love I thought . . .

Mark said: 'Everybody's experience is something new – absolutely new to themselves – unique. Right?'

'I suppose so.'

'Well, have you ever been to a Spanish fiesta before?'

'No.'

'Would anybody telling you about it be the same thing?'

'No.'

'Then don't let yourself be told about sex. It's a nasty trivial little indulgence only if you make it that.'

'It isn't what I've been told, it's what I feel!'

'You can't feel about what you haven't known.'

I moved my glass into one of the damp rings on the table that other glasses had left.

He said: 'If you study some of the Eastern religions you'll find that the act of love is closely linked with the act of worship. Not necessarily in the way of orgies, but because they think that on the rare occasions when there is great love between a man and a woman, it copies on a lower level the love of man for God and the ultimate union of man with God.' He stopped. 'All right, that's high-flying stuff you may think. But it's better to keep that in mind than dragging it all down to the level of the lavatory and the gutter and the brothel. You pays your money and you takes your choice.'

There was a sort of scuffle at the bar, and three men began to sing through their noses. Others began to stamp and clap their hands.

Mark said: 'Darling, if you have memories of some sort, can't you try to forget them?'

'I haven't any memories – of that sort.'

He put his hand over mine. 'Then I wish you'd help me to make some.'

That night we spent at a hotel at San Antonio. He ordered champagne before our dinner and some sort of red wine with it, and then we had three big liqueurs afterwards. This with the brandy I'd swallowed at the fiesta should have knocked me silly, but I just haven't that sort of head. At the end of the dinner I caught sight of myself in a mirror, and although the holiday had browned my skin the drink had only had a sort of paling effect around my mouth and nose.

I was wearing a crimson taffeta frock, off the shoulders with three-quarter-length sleeves. It looked all right. I suppose I looked all right too, which was crazy on my part because this was the time if ever to look a frump.

After dinner we went for a walk, but there wasn't much to see and we came back fairly soon, and when we got into the bedroom I knew this was it. And it was too late to develop an illness. Even he would have seen through it tonight.

He came across and tried to kiss me. 'Darling, d'you remember that you made promises when you married me?' He was very gentle and half teasing.

'Oh, yes.'

'And are you willing to honour them?'

'Sometime maybe.'

'I think it should be now.'

'No.'

'I think it should be now,' he said again.

I could feel the panic growing up in me. 'You knew what you were marrying.'

'What?'

'A liar and a thief.'

'Even in this?'

'Yes, even in this.'

'In what particular way have you lied to me this time?'

I looked past him at the room, at the amphora in the corner, at the beaten copper plate on the wall, at my coat carefully hung and his coat thrown anyhow over a chair.

'I don't love you,' I said.

He pulled a bit away from me and tried to look in my eyes. But he could only see my face, and that was empty, I should think. 'Marnie, look at me. D'you know what you're saying? Do you know what love means?'

'You've tried very hard to tell me.'

'Perhaps it's time I stopped talking.'

'It won't make any difference.'

He didn't let me go. 'Why did you marry me?'

The amphora thing had come out of the sea, they said, and was centuries old. Mark had been very interested.

'Because I knew if I didn't marry you you'd turn me over to the police.'

'You – really believed that?'

'Well, it was true, wasn't it?'

'Honestly, Marnie, dealing with you I'm in quick-sands. Where does your reasoning lead you? How could

170

I have turned you over to the police? Once I'd covered up for you it was only my word against yours.'

I couldn't explain anything more, so I shrugged.

He kissed me. He took me by surprise and he made no mistake about it this time.

'Don't you hate me?' I said, when I could get a breath.

'No.'

I tried to tug away from him, getting in a worse panic every minute. 'You're not listening to what I'm saying! Don't you understand plain English! I haven't any feelings for you at all. It was all a lie, right from the beginning, first because I wanted to steal the money and then afterwards when you caught me, I had to say *something*, I had to pretend, so that you wouldn't hand me over to the police. But all the time I was playing up to you, *nothing* else, *nothing*! I don't love you. I didn't want to marry you but you left me no way out! Now let me go!'

Perhaps after all the drink was in me. I know I sounded pretty shrill even to myself. Anyway I hope it was that. I hadn't intended to blurt it out then, and when I did I'd wanted to make it sound decenter than that. He still looked at me, and now I was looking at him. The pupils of his eyes were big and the whites were slightly bloodshot. He said: 'I've been thinking something of the sort for the last two or three days. But even that doesn't answer all the questions.'

'What questions?'

'Never mind. When I married you I didn't do so with my eyes shut. Love isn't always blind.'

'Let me alone.'

'Nor is it always patient. Nor is it always gentle.' I suppose the drink wasn't lying quite silent in him either.

I tried to swallow the panic. I'd never felt really scared since I was thirteen; I'd never been really scared of anyone, not even the police, never in my life. But I knew now I'd not gone the right away about this at all. I couldn't tell whether he believed me, but even if he did it had worked the contrary way. Now when it was too late I said: 'Mark, we're both talking rubbish. We really are. We've both had too much to drink. I'm feeling a bit muzzy in the head. Let's talk about this in the morning.'

'All right,' he said quietly, and then as quietly as doom began to undo the buttons at the back of my frock.

After a minute I wrenched away and got clear of him and went towards the window; but the window was high up, miles above the rocks, and there was no other way out of the room. As I came round the corner he caught my arm.

'Marnie!'

'Let me *alone*!' I snarled. 'Don't you know what I mean when I say, *no*? Leave me go!'

He grabbed my other arm, and my frock slipped down. I felt an awful feeling of something that seemed to be half embarrassment and half disgust. I was fairly shivering with rage. One minute I felt I'd let him get on with his lovemaking and be like a cold statue dead to every feeling except hate, and just see what he made of that. But the next I was ready to fight him, to claw his face and spit like a she-cat that's got a tom prowling round her that she doesn't want.

He took me to the bed and slipped the rest of my clothes off. When I just hadn't anything on at all he turned off the light above us, and there was only the small pilot light shining in from the bathroom. Perhaps that prevented him from seeing the tears starting from my eyes. In the half dark he tried to show me what love was, but I was stiff with repulsion and horror, and when at last he took me there seemed to come from my lips a cry of defeat that was nothing to do with physical pain.

Hours later light was coming in from the window, and I got my eyes open to see him sitting in a chair beside the bed. He must have been watching me because he saw right off I was awake.

'Are you all right?'

I made a sort of movement with my head.

'That can't have been very pleasant for you,' he said. 'I'm sorry.'

I looked up at the pattern that the grey light was making on the ceiling.

He said: 'Nor was it for me. No man ever really wants it that way, however much he may imagine he does.'

I moistened my lips.

He said: 'You don't realize perhaps what you said before this began – how much it goaded me. You threw all my love back in my face. It didn't mean a damn to you, did it? Not a bloody damn. At least that's what you said.'

He waited then but I didn't speak, didn't deny it.

He said, 'Are you surprised I didn't like it? I still don't like it. I'm still trying to swallow it. If it's true it's a real poison pill.'

I wet my lips again and there was a very long silence, perhaps ten minutes.

'Cigarette?' he said at last.

I shook my head.

'A drink?'

'No.'

He moved to pull the quilt over me, but I wouldn't have it.

'It's six o'clock,' he said presently. 'Try to go to sleep again.'

I went on staring up at the ceiling. For a bit my mind was all blank, as if everything that had happened before that night had been rubbed out. I hardly saw Mark, except the arm of his pyjamas on the edge of the bed. I was watching the play of light on the ceiling, which must have been caused by some reflection from the water outside. But I watched it as if it had some sort of extra meaning for me.

It must have been an hour before I dozed off again, and when I woke the next time it was full daylight and Mark had fallen asleep in the chair beside the bed.

I shifted my head and looked at him. He looked very young with his head forward on his chest, and still as slight as ever. I looked at his wrist and forearm and there was nothing there to show the strength there was in it. I thought over his brutality to me last night. There was something – well, feline about him, because his strength, like a cat's strength, didn't show. I thought again of what had happened, at first not caring much, like someone still under dope; and then all of a sudden I was awake, and in a second my mind was full up with every second of recollection as if suddenly an empty cage was full of flapping vultures.

Horror and rage came up in my throat, like something I'd swallowed, and chiefly it was rage. Before this I'd more or less felt for Mark the sort of dumb hostility you feel for someone who's generally outsmarted you, a feeling of frustration and irritation. But nothing above that: in some ways, given a chance, I could have liked him. But now it was quite different, all that much more. It was like being infected with something that made your blood run hotter. It was like being stabbed and seeing your blood run.

It was a hazy mix-up of hatred and blood. If I could have done it at that minute I would have killed him.

We flew back to Palma and the following day went out as far as Camp de Mar. It was the warmest day of the holiday, though by now a blight had settled on us like Alaska in December. The sea in the sandy cove looked like fluid green bottles, and he said should we bathe? I said I didn't care, so he said well, then, let's; but when I was ready I stood for a long time on the edge hugging my elbows and afraid to take the plunge. In the end he took my hand, and I went in.

The water was lovely after all, not really cold, and after a while we climbed on to this bathing pier and lay in the sun. I lay with my head over the edge and looked down at the water and at all the sea urchins growing like mussels on the supports of the pier. I didn't want him to break in on my mood by talking, and in fact he didn't try to, but sat hugging one knee with his eyes narrowed against the sun.

Well, presently I slipped off the pier to swim back to the sand. It was so lovely that, although I'm just an ordinary swimmer and not strong in the water, I didn't head back at once but swam parallel with the shore towards the rocks at the side of the bay.

After I'd been going for a few minutes I lay on my back and floated and saw that Mark was still sitting where I'd left him. The slanting sun made his body dark like a spade's, and I thought squatting there he might have been a pearl diver or something in the South Seas. And I thought how two nights ago his body had done what it wanted with mine.

Lying in the water like this a sort of tiredness came over me. I felt as if I didn't have the energy to hate him any longer; I just knew there wasn't any point in me living at all. I never had added up to much, perhaps, but at least for a while I'd been some help to Mother and old Lucy. I'd counted for something the way any protest counts for something. But now my life had run bang into this blind alley of marriage, and there was nothing more to it. I was trapped for good, pinned down like a moth on a paper. If I ended now I would simply help to tidy up a thoroughly nasty mess.

But I knew I wouldn't have the guts just to let myself go bobble, bobble under the water. As soon as you start breathing sea you start fighting to live. It doesn't make sense but there it is. So the important thing was to get so far out that I couldn't get back if I wanted to. I turned over and began to swim easily as anything towards the mouth of the bay.

As soon as I'd decided I knew I'd decided right. It just drew a simple neat little line under everything. Mark would be a widower for a second time at twenty-eight – good going that – and could look out for a female of his own type who could make something of his slushy ideas about sex. Mother could manage, would *have* to manage somehow. It would all be sad – and satisfactory.

I don't really know how long it was before I saw he was swimming after me. First I noticed he wasn't any longer on the pier. Then I saw something on the water, a whiteness of broken water a long long way behind me. Well, he'd be too late with his help this time.

I swam on a bit quicker, fixing on a special point at the edge of the bay. I certainly couldn't reach it. I was getting very tired.

When the first wave slopped in my mouth it was a nasty shock. Sea water tastes nasty and when you swallow it it makes you want to fetch up. It wasn't going to be a bed of roses, this end, but it would soon be over. I just dreaded the first breath. All that gasping and retching. It would soon be over, though.

And then I heard him shouting at me not far away.

Right off all the fear went. I just stopped swimming and sank.

Yet even though I tried not to, I found I was holding my breath the way I'd done jumping off the pier by the Hoe when I was a kid. I tried to force myself to let go of life, but I came up again like a cork choking and coughing. As I came up he got me.

'You fool!' he said. 'You'll drown yourself!' He was clutching my arm.

I shook him off. 'Let me *go*!'

I tried to dive, but it's hard to go down when you're already in the water, and as I thrashed away he caught me by the leg and then round the waist. We struggled for a few seconds and then I almost got free again. At that he gave me such a slap on the side of the face that he made me taste blood. I screamed and scratched his arm with my nails; then he closed his fist and hit me on the jaw. I remember my teeth clicking together with a sound like lift gates shutting; and that was all.

When I came out of it I was lying on my back in the water. He'd got my head between his hands and was lying on his back too, swimming with his legs, towards the shore. I tried to get my head free, but he held me tighter as soon as I tried, and that way we came back to the sand.

We lay there together, absolutely dead-beat both of us, but luckily there were no other bathers today, and the only people in sight, two Spanish women shovelling seaweed into baskets at the other end, had seen nothing and looked as if they couldn't care less if they had.

As soon as he got some breath back he began to go for me. He used most of the words you hear around a dockyard and a few more besides. It looked as if nothing I'd done before had got under his skin like this. I suppose it was the final insult.

I stood it for a bit and then one of the words he used made me giggle hysterically.

He stopped and said: 'What is it?'

'There isn't a female of that.'

I giggled again and then turned my head away and was sick.

After I was better he said: 'I didn't know there was a female like you, but I'm learning.'

'It makes a change, doesn't it? I don't suppose Estelle was ever like this.'

'No, you blasted bloody little fool. She wanted so much to live and couldn't.'

'Whereas I want to die and can't.'

'Than that,' he said, 'there are few uglier remarks a woman of twenty-three can make.'

We lay quiet, getting our strength back. Then he said:

'If we stay here any longer we'll both begin to shiver. Come on, I'll help you back to the hotel.'

'Thanks, I can manage,' I said, and got to my feet. So we walked back a few paces apart, with him a step or two behind me, like a warder whose prisoner has nearly got away.

CHAPTER TEN

THE GARDENER at Little Gaddesden was called Richards. He came three days a week, Mondays, Wednesdays and Fridays. He was a quiet little man with an ailing wife and three pale-looking children under teenage. He'd a funny sort of enthusiasm about the garden that I couldn't quite understand, because it wasn't his. He seemed to like me and he always called me 'madam' as if I was royalty or something. 'We've got some *lovely* tulips over here, madam; they'll be showing in another week or two, I shouldn't wonder.' 'I'm going to tidy up these paths this morning, madam; then they'll be nice and clear until the spring.' He obviously got a sort of joy out of it. I shouldn't have thought there was much joy in his life, with his wife bent up with bronchitis and him often going home wet and soaking and having to look after the children. Sometimes the eldest, a girl called Ailsa, would call in on her way home from school. She didn't remind me of myself at eleven. I think I must have been fairly hard bitten by the time I was eleven; anyway I'd knocked about plenty. Ailsa was soft and gentle like her Dad. The chances were in this world that sooner or later she'd get trampled underfoot. Richards said she'd asked for a Bible for Christmas, an illustrated one, and Mr Mark was getting him one through the trade at cost price. I thought why doesn't Mark *give* him half a dozen, but when I said something about it Mark said: 'That would never do; he'd hate charity.' I suppose I didn't understand.

The garden at Little Gaddesden was about one acre. At the end away from the golf course was an old shed and an old garage and a small paddock. Leading to this was a path bordered by a thing I thought was a yew hedge, but Richards politely corrected me. 'It's Lonicera, madam. I grow it in my own garden, you can train it just the same way. I've got a *beautiful* bush shaped like a church. I hope sometime, madam, you'll come and see it.'

I went and saw it. I met Mrs Richards and the two youngest. I didn't know what to do about the charity side of it, but I risked buying some sweets and I baked some buns and took those along. It didn't seem to offend them.

The trouble with Richards, I soon saw, was that he was too conscientious. What's the good of a conscience if it makes you stay out in the rain when you can potter around and pretend to do things in the greenhouse. Mrs Leonard and I began to work out schemes for him to do jobs in the house on the bad days.

I was somehow managing to live with Mark. When we got home he'd given me a separate bedroom, and although the rooms had connecting doors, he hardly ever came in and never without knocking. He never *touched* me. I suppose I'd frozen him up, at least for the time being. We were quite polite to each other, the way we had been during the last ghastly days of the honeymoon. When he came home at night he told me things that happened at the firm. Once or twice we went into London to the theatre, but he didn't suggest a race meeting and I didn't ask. I could never be quite sure what he was thinking.

Luckily I got on well with Mrs Leonard. I told her right at the start that I had never run a house before and could only cook the simplest things, and she seemed quite pleased to carry on as she had before Mark married me. Of course I could talk her language, and I knew how she looked at things. Perhaps I should have pretended, but I didn't, and soon she was calling me dear, instead of Mrs Rutland.

The house was peculiar to live in because I kept coming on things belonging to Estelle. A pair of slippers in a cupboard, two old blouses, a pair of nylons still in their cellophane – they were too short for me – books, a notebook, an engagement diary. And of course the photographs in the drawing-room and in Mark's bedroom. I could see how a second wife could be made jealous. Not that I was. I only wished she could come back and claim her man. I mean I never for a second felt *married* to Mark. Perhaps married isn't a thing anyone feels, it's something that grows on you. Well, it didn't grow on me.

One thing I found in the garage was an oldish twoseater car. It had belonged to her – she'd used it going to her excavations, and the boot looked like it – but

Mark said I could drive it if I wanted, so I did go off one or two afternoons exploring round about, though I hadn't anywhere special to go.

After a few weeks, when he still kept his distance, I began to let go, to relax, to feel easier in the house. There was no way of leaving him yet, except the way I'd tried at Camp de Mar – and I knew I'd never try that again – so for the present it was a case of making the best of it.

One night after supper I'd opened up a bit about myself and he said suddenly:

'Marnie, why don't you do this more often?'

'Do what?'

'Talk about yourself. It might help.'

'Help what?'

'It might help you to get free of – of things that at present get in your way. It even might help us to understand each other better.'

'I don't see how.'

'Well, at its lowest it interests me. It's important to talk. Otherwise one gets ingrown. Any psychiatrist would tell you that. So would a Catholic priest.'

'I'm not a talker.'

'I know. That's what I'm saying. Tell me about losing your brother, for instance.'

'What about it?' I said sharply.

'Well, you did lose one, didn't you? Wasn't it through neglect?'

I told him. He said: 'If it went as far as a court case the doctor was lucky to get away with it. I suppose it was wartime. Is that why you hate doctors?'

'I don't think it happened because it was wartime. I think it happened because we were poor.'

'Well, that shouldn't apply now, should it?'

'Oh, but it could. You don't realize; you've never been poor, Mark. When my—' I stopped.

He was watching me. 'When your what?'

'When my aunt had a varicose ulcer,' I said carefully. 'You know, the one who brought me up. She was in hospital and I went to see her; I had that job with the accountants in Bristol and I came back to see her and she wasn't being well looked after at all. I made a fuss and it helped a bit, but I could see she was being treated badly because they knew she was poor and couldn't stand up for herself.'

'From what I've seen of the Health Service I shouldn't have thought that was often so. It may be pretty rough and ready, especially if you're not too seriously ill, I grant that, but I shouldn't have thought it made much difference, once you were in, whether you were rich or poor. Of course, if you can stand up for yourself, that's a help. But the important thing in hospital these days is to have a rare and interesting disease. If you have, then you're treated like royalty. If you haven't, then you take your chance.'

'What's the use of asking me to tell you these things if, when I tell you, you don't believe them?'

'It isn't that I don't believe them. But I try to see it through your eyes and then I wonder if I should see it the same through my own . . .'

'Well, of course not. I—'

'But never mind. Go on.'

'You think I've a chip on my shoulder about poverty and being poor. Well, perhaps I have. But no one's entitled to criticize me who hasn't tried it.'

'You've a chip of some sort on your shoulder, Marnie, as big as an Admiral's epaulette, but I doubt if it's just poverty that's caused it. I can't tell you what it is. I wish I knew. Maybe a psychiatrist could tell. But you wouldn't let him try, would you.'

'Try what?'

'To find out if there was something wrong.'

'No.'

'Would you be afraid?'

'What of?'

'Of going to see one.'

'A psychiatrist? Why should I be afraid? It would only be a waste of time.'

'Perhaps yes. Perhaps no.'

'Do you go to a doctor when there's nothing wrong with you?'

'Do you think he would find nothing wrong with you?'

'Oh, they always make up something to earn their money.'

He was quiet for a bit. Then he got up and went over to one of the bookcases and began to leaf through a book. But he wasn't looking at it.

'Marnie, tell me something . . . Perhaps you don't know but . . . since we were married you've shown pretty clearly that you hate the physical side of love. What I want to know is, do you hate love as such or do you merely hate me?'

I picked up one of the Christmas cards on the table and read the name inside. It didn't mean a thing.

He said: 'Try to tell me exactly the truth if you can. Could you imagine finding pleasure in love with another man?'

'No.'

'Then I think a psychiatrist might help.'

'Thanks. I'm all right as I am.'

'Are you?'

'*Yes*. Everyone isn't made alike! Some people love music. Others hate it. It would be a poor world if we all wanted the same thing.'

'Ah, but—'

'The only mistake you made, Mark, was forcing me to marry you. The mistake I made was being caught.'

It was the nearest we had ever come to the horrible things we'd said to each other on our honeymoon. He seemed to swallow it now and push on.

'That's all right as far as it goes. But it doesn't go far enough.'

'Because you think I should be like Estelle?'

'Because sex is a fundamental instinct that you can't compare to love of music. If it isn't there in some form something is wrong.'

'I'm not the only woman who's ever disliked it.'

'God, no. Some people put the number as high as thirty per cent of the female population. But there are degrees and yours is an extreme degree. And you haven't the face or figure of a frigid woman—'

'Is there such a thing?'

'I think so.'

'Well, I'm sorry. I'm sorry if you've been deceived.'

The next morning, Sunday, was wet, so he spent it mostly rearranging his wife's Greek pottery. But over lunch he said:

'I've been thinking about what we said last night. There's a man I know called Charles Roman. I wish you'd meet him.'

'Who is he?'

'A psychiatrist. But a very practical one. The sort of person one can talk to.'

'Oh, no.'

'I thought I might get him over to dinner one evening. He's about fifty, and very wise, and very simple. No frills.'

'Ask him to dinner one evening when I'm out.'

Mark ate for a few minutes in silence.

'Perhaps we could do a deal.'

'A deal?'

'Yes. You oblige me and I oblige you . . . Supposing I promised to have Forio brought here. It wouldn't cost much to turn the old garage at the end into a stable, and the paddock beyond is empty. Then he could be here permanently, and you could ride him whenever you wanted.'

I crumbled bread in my two hands, waiting for the catch. 'Yes? What do I do in return?'

'You agree to go to Roman for one hour, say, twice a week to see if he can help you.'

'I don't want help,' I said, but my thoughts were jumping like fleas. I'd expected Mark was going to make the one condition I couldn't consider. But this . . . Well, it had to be thought of.

'You want Forio?' he said.

'Well, of course.'

'It might make you happier?'

'Yes, of course it would.'

'Well, there's the proposition. Think it over.'

I said: 'I'd – think much better of you if you let me have him without conditions, Mark.'

'I expect so. But I'm afraid they have to come into it.'

At lunch I said to him: 'You mean I could keep Forio for good? You mean I could ride him any time I liked? You would pay for his keep?'

'Of course.'

'And how long would I have to see this man?'

'It would depend on what he said. Perhaps he wouldn't feel he could help you at all. But if he did try, it's only fair to say it might be a long treatment. These things are usually very slow.'

'What would he do?'

'Chiefly encourage you to talk.'

'I'm not a talker. I've told you.'

'I know. That would be his problem.'

I didn't say any more then, but all through Monday my mind was working hard. If I couldn't escape from Mark altogether – yet, I might escape in a way by having a horse to ride. And just to have Forio here, with me, would be like having a friend to turn to.

I thought highly of the idea. The more I thought of it the more I liked it. But to get it I took a risk; Mark would see to that. People like this man Roman had a way of inching into your thoughts so that in the end you gave something away. I couldn't afford to give anything away.

But only two hours a week. Couldn't I hold my own with any doctor for two hours a week? The fact that I hated them all would make it that much easier. It would be a battle of wits, a question of keeping on the alert. Was it worth the risk to have Forio?

I said nothing until the Tuesday morning, and then I said: 'Mark, I've been thinking over what you suggested.'

'Oh?' It was too casual, trying to hide the look in his eyes.

'Yes. I – haven't decided yet. But if you like to ask this Dr Roman to dinner I'll look him over and see if I think I can bear him. But, mind, I haven't agreed to anything.'

'No doubt he'll want to see what you look like too. He's pretty choosy.'

'What would you tell him about me?'

'I hadn't thought of it. Principally, I think, that you would like treatment. The rest is up to him.'

'I mean,' I said, 'I mean, if you're going to begin by telling him about me stealing the money, then it's off right away.'

'My dear, it's up to you, what you tell him. I shan't. Anyway – as you should know – that's not what worries me.'

'So you say.'

I could tell Mark was pleased, and it didn't give me any satisfaction to please him. But I'd agreed now. Did he really think something helpful to him would really come out of it? Did he really think a few talks with a psychiatrist would turn me into a sweet and loving wife? How hopeful, I wondered, could one really get?

Although living with Mark might mean I'd no special need to worry about money for myself, it did not mean all my money troubles were over. For the last three years I'd never given Mother less than four hundred pounds in any one year; and it was usually more. She and Lucy lived the way they did only because of what I gave them. I'd taken on the responsibility when I bullied Mother into giving up that awful shop job in Plymouth and got her the first home in Torquay. She'd been miles better in every way since she'd given up work. So there it was. If I'd been able to pull off this Rutland job I should have been easy for eighteen months or more. As it was I only had dribs and drabs of money scattered about the country. Two hundred and ninety-one pounds ten shillings.

On the Thursday Terry called. I happened just then to be sitting at the desk working all this out on a piece of paper, so I stuffed the paper away and asked Mrs Leonard to show him in.

He was wearing a tweed hacking jacket with a yellow silk scarf and pale brown cavalry twill trousers. It was funny how, after not seeing him for a time, it was his dandyism again that hit you first. He didn't look particularly sharp, like he really was; and he didn't look sly; and he looked sure of himself, which he wasn't. Not nearly as sure of himself as Mark, I thought, who *looked* so modest.

We talked for a minute or two, and he made a few silly remarks, but I knew he hadn't come just to be silly. After a time he got up and walked round the room, stopping to finger one of the Greek vases.

'What does it feel like, being married to Mark?'

'All right.'

'Compare favourably with your first? You know it *shouldn't* work.'

'What shouldn't?'

'Your marriage to Mark, my dear. I've said so before. You're far too *submarine*. We can't all be dashing naval craft like him, churning up a hell of a froth on the surface. Anyway, where does it get you?'

'Do you expect me to answer that?'

'No, I will. It gets you one of the fashionable stress diseases before you're fifty – and a *lot* of money which you've no time to spend.'

'I shouldn't have thought Mark was like that.'

'Ah, that's newly-wed loyalty. Wait till you've been yawning your head off here for a couple of years. Life's a gilded *cage*, my dear, for girls like you. What do women really want in life? I'll tell you. Lots of new clothes, lots of leisure, lots of admiration, lots of sex. But you can't trade the first two for the last two – as you'll find. Woman's no more monogamous by instinct than man.'

'Well, thank you for telling me.'

He smiled in a crooked way. 'Anyway, I'm sorry you won't come to my party next Saturday.'

'What party?'

'Didn't Mark tell you? I invited you both after dinner for drinks and maybe a little gamey. All friendly like, but he said he couldn't make it.'

I tucked my legs under me on the sofa, and then, seeing Terry's look, pulled my skirt down.

'I expect he was speaking for himself,' I said.

'Mean to say you'd come without him?'

'No, I didn't say that.'

'Pity. You did so well last time.'

'So well?'

'At poker. The MacDonalds are coming and three or four others. You're a natural, you know. A natural player. Alistair was saying so *only* last week.'

Neither of us said anything for a minute. Terry was staring at a piece of broken pottery. 'Can't think what people see in this sort of thing,' he said presently. 'You can get as good on Hampstead Heath any Sunday.'

Last time, me a beginner, I'd won twenty-two pounds.

'I don't get it,' he said again. 'The whole thing's bogus. If anyone was ever chi-chi it was Estelle, the way she used to go around excavating bronze-age barrows. What conceivable use is that to a girl?'

'Tell me about Estelle,' I said.

'I'm telling you. She slouched about in slacks, and only put on lipstick at sundown. I should think even

192

Mark was absolutely distraught with her. What's the good of being bronze-age in bed.'

'You men have only got one idea, haven't you?'

'Well, it's rather a good one, isn't it?'

Of course twenty-two pounds was nothing much. It wouldn't really solve anything.

'Isn't it?'

'Isn't what?' I said.

'Never mind, darling, don't *listen* to what I'm saying. Just tell me if you're coming to my party on Saturday.'

But I hated gambling. It made my heart thump.

'I don't know. I'll see. I'll see how things go.'

'Well, it's nine o'clock for drinks if you can.'

He left soon after. I went to the door with him. He said: 'If you love me, don't tell Mark I've called. I'm on firm's business, and I don't think he'd *approve* of my spending time with you. He doesn't approve of me at all, you know.'

As I watched him go I thought, I don't approve of you either; somewhere you've got a streak. But it isn't my streak; you're wrong there.

It seemed to me that he felt for sex what I felt for money. At least it was never lonely in his company.

That evening Mark said: 'I telephoned Roman and he's coming to dinner on Friday.'

'Oh . . . So soon? What did he say?'

'Not very much. At first he didn't want to meet you socially.'

'Why not?'

'He seemed to think it better to see a patient as a patient without other meetings.'

'What did you say about me?'

'The least possible. But I said I thought you'd come more willingly if you had met here first.'

Now that the thing was on top of me, right on my head, the idea of it got me worried. I think he must have cottoned on to this because he said: 'I've also telephoned the local builder to come in tomorrow morning and you can tell him what alterations you want to the old garage. You should have Forio here by this time next week.'

Forio. I don't think I even liked Mark talking about him that way. Because Forio was a *personal* possession, a personal companion and friend. I wanted him here but I wanted him still to myself.

I said: 'Is he coming alone? This man, I mean, to dinner.'

'I thought we'd get Mother over. She hasn't been since we came back, and it will make it more of a social evening.'

'Very social for me, feeling like a maggot under a microscope.'

'He isn't that sort of man.'

'I wish I hadn't promised even to see him.'

'Well, if you hate the sight of him we can always try someone else.'

I looked at him, thinking, Should I try to persuade him out of it, say, You don't want me brooding all day over my *symptoms*, people like Roman always do more harm than good. But I knew this was a bargain he'd hold me to.

'Mark, I want to go out myself on Saturday night. I'm going out with Dawn Witherbie. We were friends before I married you. I can't suddenly drop her.'

'There's no reason why you should. Where are you thinking of going?'

'We haven't decided. Probably only to her house. It's after dinner. But I may be late.'

'I turned down an invitation for Saturday. From Terry. He asked us over to his flat.'

'Why? Didn't you want to go?'

'. . . There aren't a lot of people who get under my skin, but Terry's one of them. Don't you feel it – or does he appeal to you? Honestly I can't bear the sight of him, and I have far too much sight of him in and out of the office every day – anyway too much to want to prolong it into the evening.'

He went across to pour himself a drink. 'It might be a good idea to ask Rex and his mother for Friday as well, if you can bear it. We need their moral support in the firm, so it would be politic as well as polite.'

'In the firm?'

'Yes. The Newton-Smiths have a big minority holding, but with their help I have enough of a hand usually to do what I want. Only about eighteen per cent of the capital is owned by the public, and usually the public never turns up at meetings or uses its votes. The rest, about thirty-five per cent, is in the hands of the Holbrooks.'

'Well, then, you're safe enough,' I said.

'It's not cast-iron. There's been a good deal of traffic in the public shares recently and the price has rocketed. I know the Newton-Smiths have had an offer from a merchant bank for part of their holding, and they're tempted to cash in. I'm trying to persuade them not to. A merchant bank sounds innocent enough, but they may be acting as nominees for some other firm or person.'

'Do the Holbrooks know about this?'

'Well, of course; they're part of the board and part of the family, even though I sometimes wish they weren't.'

All Friday I was in a flap. I suppose I wasn't geared right for social life after the way I'd grown up. I got more butterflies in my tummy over a meal for a few elderly people than over taking seven hundred and forty-six pounds from the Roxy Cinema, Manchester.

One you could do in secret, nobody knowing a thing till it wasn't your business any longer. But this. I mean, did you go to the door when they came or wait till they took their coats off; what did you talk about, the weather wouldn't last for ever; who offered drinks and when; and when you got to the table did I have to start eating first or did I wait for Mrs Rutland?

In the end I got through it somehow. Mrs Leonard as usual did most of the work. At the last minute the zip of my frock stuck when someone was already ringing the doorbell, and I *wouldn't* ask Mark for help, so I had to wriggle out of the frock again and half zip it up and then wriggle back. And then the soup was salt and the drawing-room fire smoked.

It wouldn't have been so bad if you had just been having Mark's family for the evening. But Roman on top of it was too much. I'd got to be hostess for the first time to three high-grade relatives and at the same time keep a wary eye on him.

In fact when it came down to rock, Dr Roman wasn't so frightening. I expected somebody like Dracula, so it was a kind of a relief when this tired-looking baldish man came in in a brown suit that needed cleaning and long pants that showed when his trouser-leg worked up. He talked about his two children who were at a co-ed school, and about his holiday abroad and about the diet he was on, not as if these were a front for his secret microscopes but as if they were what chiefly interested him. We talked a half-dozen times during the evening, but he didn't seem the least bit curious about me. You got the feeling he was just out for a good dinner and nothing more, and he certainly ate it.

If I'd wanted a sympathetic, all-understanding, father-confessor figure I should have thought, well I can write off Roman. But as a person to go to only to fix my end of the bargain with Mark, he looked just the right answer.

I couldn't help liking Mrs Rutland in spite of her disadvantage of being Mark's mother. She was just that much helpful to me without ever being patronizing, and though you'd never mistake her for anything but a lady, she wasn't stiff-backed and *awful* like many old women of her class. They really are awful, so many of them: about nine feet tall and big-busted and thin-ankled, and they never mix with any but their own kind, and they talk about their shopping at Fortnums and Harrods, and they're always frightfully poor, which means they can't afford caviare, and they have voices like the high notes of a Welsh tenor. Old Mrs Newton-Smith was a bit like that, and it was an ordeal when I had to take the two women upstairs and help them to powder their noses. God, I was glad I had had those elocution lessons, even though perhaps that made me the most counterfeit of the three.

When we got downstairs again things were helped because Mark told them about my horse, and it turned out Rex was mad about horses, and right off he wanted to know all about Forio. Of course it sounded wonderful me having bought him in a sale and keeping him on a farm in Gloucestershire; it put me right alongside them among the landed gentry. Anyway, it turned out that Rex hunted regularly with the Thorn – heaven knew what size horse he would need to get him over the gates – but, as that was only about eighteen miles from Little Gaddesden, he said would Mark and I go over one day for a Meet. I said yes out of politeness, but thought I could probably slink out of it later as I'd never hunted and didn't like the notion.

When it was all over and the last of them had gone Mark said: 'That was pretty good, Marnie.'

'Good?' I said, looking for sarcasm or something.

'Yes, I thought it could hardly have gone off better. Didn't you?'

'I was nervous as a nit.'

'You didn't show it.'

'We must have this chimney swept,' I said, jabbing at the remnants of the fire.

'You know,' he said, 'dinner parties were one of the things Estelle could never manage. I'm so very glad you can.'

I straightened up, and for a minute thought he was going to touch me. So I edged round out of his reach and asked: 'Did Dr Roman say anything?'

As usual he was too sharp not to notice the move, and his face cooled off. 'He made an appointment for Tuesday at two.'

'Just that?'

'Not much more. You'll go?'

'I haven't decided.'

'He suggested you might go first for five or six weeks as a preliminary period. By then he should know whether he can help you.'

I straightened the photo of Estelle on the grand piano. I might not want her husband, but it was nice to know she hadn't been perfection in everything.

'And the shares?' I said. 'Did you persuade Rex and his mother not to sell?'

'I've persuaded them to hold on for the time being. I think if they really make up their minds about it I may have to buy them myself. But I'd have to borrow heavily from the bank to take the lot at the present inflated price.'

'You say the shares have been going up. Why, if you made a loss last year?'

'We made a loss the year before. There's quite a big

profit in the new accounts that have recently come out. But all our premises and stock are much under-valued, that's really the answer. People are buying the few shares there are on the market as a long-term speculation.'

I thought, maybe not so long term, thinking of those letters I had read.

When I got to Terry's about nine on the Saturday night the same round-the-clock top-of-the-pops were playing, but I didn't know any of the people there except the Macdonalds. Gail said vaguely, 'Why darling, *such* a long time,' and patted her urchin cut. Alistair raised his eyebrows across a lot of bottles and sandwiches and nattering people. Terry introduced the others. There were six of them, and they were an odd lot. One was a Jewish film director with a disillusioned expression as if he'd gone right through the alphabet and there wasn't anything more; two were hard-bitten women in their forties, with thin silly lines for eyebrows and the sort of faces that look ancient because they're trying to look young. The other three were all men and they'd all got plenty of money. You could see that right off.

As soon as we got playing, which we did about ten, I saw this was a different game from the last. Last time it had been ordinary middle-class folk having fun and a gamble. This time it was serious. And there weren't any beginners, except me.

And the maximum raise was one pound. I had brought five pounds with me, but I saw from the stuff the others were handling that this wasn't going to count for much if I lost. So I began very cautiously, dropping out every time when I didn't have much and not bluffing at all. I watched the others and tried to learn from them. And I tried to work out the odds, the way I'd done before. But it was all nerve jarring, and if the cards hadn't come slightly my way I should have lost. I was mad when I got out on a limb playing against the film director, and knew in my bones that I had a better hand than he had but didn't dare to call his bluff.

By one o'clock I was two pounds to the good, and by three I'd made nearly nine. Then I had two nasty jolts, and in the second, when I was sure the film director was bluffing again, I found he wasn't and went down eleven pounds on one hand. I played safe as hell after that, and when we stopped at four I was only thirty shillings out of pocket. But I felt sick to the stomach, and even thirty shillings seemed a fortune.

I'd forgotten completely about the time and about Mark, and when I looked at my watch I jumped and said I must go at once.

Terry gave me one of his smooth lop-sided glances. 'The old man likely to cut up rough? Well, I hope it's been worth it.'

'Yes, I've enjoyed it ever so. Thank you, Terry.'

'Come again. I have a party once a week. No needy person ever turned away.'

I thought, no, but sometimes they'll be needy when they leave.

I drove home in Estelle's car, trying to tell myself I didn't mind being a loser.

CHAPTER ELEVEN

'Do sit down, Mrs Rutland,' said Dr Roman. 'Over here, if you don't mind. Can I take your coat? That's better. Not a very pleasant day. Did you come by car?'

He lived in one of those tall narrow houses looking on Regent's Park. Everybody raves about them and it just beats me why.

'I want you to look on this first meeting not so much in the light of a consultation as of a friendly chat. Indeed, as I expect you know, much of our time together will be very informal.'

Roman was different now you met him on his beat. I suppose he had a 'manner' that he lifted off a nail and wriggled into before the patient came. From the plate outside it seemed he shared the house with another doctor, a consulting surgeon. A manservant had let me in, and I wondered how much all this was costing Mark.

'What has my husband told you?'

'Very little, Mrs Rutland. Except that you agreed together that you should consult me.'

'I'm only coming because he wants me to.'

'Well, yes, I gathered that the idea was his. But I assume that you're not unwilling to see me?'

We'd been for Forio over the weekend. 'No . . .'

'Of course it's necessary to make that clear at the beginning. I can do very little to help you without your willing co-operation.

I tucked my blouse in at the waistband.

'I shall sit here just behind you,' he said. 'I don't make notes, so nothing you say will be recorded. What I would like you to do today, if you will, is just give me the general factual background of your life, i.e. where you were born and that sort of thing. That will give me a chance of getting the broad picture.'

I thought he was sure to want to be put in the picture sometime or other. Nobody ever talks any other way nowadays. I was sitting on the usual black leather couch. But it was fairly wide and there were two green cushions on it to give it the glamour treatment.

'What, now?' I said.

'When you're ready. No hurry.'

Naturally no hurry, I thought, at X guineas a visit.

I thought of Forio. We had driven down to Garrod's Farm on Sunday morning, almost before my eyes were open. (Mark must have guessed I was late back but he didn't mention it.) It had been a lovely drive because the sun was shining, and for miles and miles at every church we passed the bells were ringing. Sort of royal procession.

'I'm twenty-three,' I said. 'I was born in Devonport. My father was a draughtsman in the dockyard. When war broke out he joined the Navy and he was drowned at sea. The same year my mother was killed in the Plymouth blitz and I was brought up by a sort of aunt called Lucy Nye. I went to the North Road Secondary Modern School for Girls. Then my Uncle Stephen paid for me to go to St Andrew's Technical College, where I learned shorthand and typing and bookkeeping and accountancy.'

I didn't much like the idea of him being behind me. I was telling him exactly the same mixture of truth and make-up that I'd given Mark, but I couldn't see how he was taking it all. When I stopped he didn't speak, so I waited. I waited while a clock somewhere chimed the quarter hour and I thought, well, that's fifteen minutes of the first visit gone already.

That cheered me up, so I went on with the rest of the stuff, about going to work and Lucy Nye dying and leaving me a house, and me getting a job in Bristol. Then I said I'd used all my money and taken work in London. Then I moved to Rutlands and met Mark and we got married. It all sounded so straightforward that I believed it myself.

When it was over he said: 'That's excellent. That's exactly what I wanted – a brief biographical sketch. Now, what I would like you to do for the next few minutes is to tell me about some of the personalities involved in your life.'

'How do you mean?'

'Well, starting with your mother and father. Do you remember much about them? What they looked like, for instance.'

'My father was a tall man, with greyish hair and a quiet voice. He had very strong hands with the nails cut short and keen grey eyes that seemed to know what you were thinking before you said it. He was the one who first called me Marnie, and it has stuck ever since.'

'And your mother?'

It was pretty well only as I stopped speaking that I realized I hadn't described my father at all, but Mother's brother, Stephen.

There was a long pause. 'I don't remember my mother so well.'

'Anything at all?'

'A bit. She was smallish, with high cheek-bones, rather strict. She worked very hard, *always*; when we were poor she did without things to give to me. Everything was for me. I always had to be *respectable*. That was the *most* important thing. She took me to chapel, three times every Sunday.'

After a wait. 'Anything more?'

'No.'

'You've already told me far more about your mother than your father.'

Another wait. He said: 'I don't quite understand one thing. Why were you poor?'

'Why not? We hadn't any money. That's the way you are poor.'

'But your father was in work?'

'As far as I remember. I was too young to remember much.'

'You'd get a pension, of course, as the orphan of a sailor killed in the war?'

'I don't remember. I expect Lucy Nye drew it for me.'

'After your father died, how long was it before your mother was killed?'

'About nine months.'

'And then this aunt, this Mrs Nye, took you in?'

'Miss Nye. Yes.'

'Can you tell me about her?'

I told him about her.

It really wasn't bad, talking like this. Three-quarters of the time you could tell the truth, and the other quarter was already fixed in your mind and you could play around with it as you pleased.

If he asked you a question you didn't want to answer, you simply said you didn't remember.

If I stopped he didn't hurry me on, and once or twice I was able to go off into pleasant little day-dreams about Sunday. When we got to Garrod's, a loosebox Mark had ordered was already waiting. I'd gone running through the yard and out into the field to find Forio, and he had come galloping across at the first sound of my voice. Mark had really done his best to be nice all the time, and I could see the Garrods liked him. He seemed to know a bit about horses and he didn't hurry me to start back. In the end we left about three, driving slowly behind the horsebox; and just before dark we got home and let Forio loose in the paddock, and I rode him round bareback half a dozen times just for the sheer pleasure and just to let him know we were going to be together again.

'Were you not an only child, then?'

I dragged myself back and heard a clock striking. It

was all over for this afternoon anyway, and I could forget it till Friday.

'I had a brother but he died at birth.'

'How old were you then?'

'I'm not sure.'

'You don't remember anything about it?'

'No.'

'Do you remember anything about when your father died? Do you remember the news being brought?'

I had to think about that. My father hadn't really been killed until I was turned six. That is, I knew he was killed after we'd been blitzed out of Keyham and gone to live at Sangerford, because he died in June 1943, and my brother was born in the September, but for the life of me I couldn't remember coming home from school and being told, or seeing Mother get a telegram and collapse, or even hearing of it second hand from Lucy Nye.

'No,' I said, still thinking.

'It's not unnatural. Your memory is remarkably good. It's most exceptional in that you have hardly had to hesitate over a date or anything.'

'No?' I said. So I was being too pat.

'And do you remember anything of your mother's death?'

'I remember being told. But I wasn't there. I'd been evacuated to this bungalow in Sangerford, near Liskeard where my aunt Lucy lived. Mother was – was going to join us but she left it too late . . .'

'Well,' he said, rising. 'I think that's a very good

preliminary talk. On Friday perhaps we shall be able to go into a little more detail.'

He helped me on with my coat and saw me out. It was still raining, but I walked to the tube instead of spending money on a taxi.

I played poker again on the following Saturday. It was much the same crowd. I won six pounds. I was coming along fast. Except for the film director and Alistair MacDonald, they weren't all that good. They weren't mathematical about it. They went by 'hunches' and by watching how many cards their neighbours drew. They'd never get any *better*. All the same I didn't really enjoy playing. It was too nerve-racking.

The Friday visit to Dr Roman had run on the same track as the first. I did the talking, he asked the questions. They were the sort of questions I'd have asked anybody for nothing, not expecting to be *paid*. It was such a bogus business; we could have worked it all out over a cup of coffee in an espresso bar for eightpence each. This man put his name on a brass plate and people paid him *pounds* just to sit on his couch and talk. It made you think. Maybe I had been an honest citizen, just taking money out of tills.

When it was over for the day he had offered me a cigarette and said: 'You've done well so far, Mrs Rutland. It always heartens me to be trying to help someone of your calibre.'

'My – er—'

'Well, for a patient to benefit from psychiatric treatment at all, he or she must be intelligent. It's simply a waste of time working on dullards.'

'Thanks.'

'Please don't think me patronizing. But I do feel you have a quick and clear brain. It stimulates an analyst, to work with you.'

I gave him a quick and clear smile. 'Next Tuesday?'

'Next Tuesday. Mind you . . .' He had stopped and scratched his chin, which hadn't been shaved too closely that morning. 'The intelligence in our work can be both a springboard and stumbling block. There is a point at which you will have to decide which yours is to be . . .'

'I'll think of that,' I said, but I hadn't thought of it or had time to think of it until I happened to remember it at this poker party. Now I did remember it I got a slightly uneasy feeling as if there was more in the saying than met the ear. There'd been something in the way he'd said it. It wouldn't do to underrate Roman and imagine you were doing awfully well with him if you weren't doing awfully well at all. It was never clever to be too sure. I'd learned that early in life.

After Christmas things were better between Mark and me, even though it didn't last. I think he'd probably had a word from Roman that I was playing fair; so he was hoping I might be cured of whatever he thought I needed to be cured of. And also he was very quick to notice when I was brighter.

I felt better than I'd done since when he caught me in Gloucestershire. I could ride every day, and if that wasn't being free it was a fair copy.

Also Mark still kept his distance. I suppose if I'd been as bright as some people thought, I should have guessed how much this was costing him. But the longer he left me alone the less I thought of it.

Money for Mother still nagged. At Christmas I'd sent her twenty pounds and explained I was frightfully sorry I couldn't get home; but thought, in the New Year I'll look for a part-time job afternoons, say, in some shop or something. It would be easy to get there in my car and Mark need know nothing about it. I could work under another name; but it seemed doubtful if I could do anything worth while. Of course you could lay a false scent, but it wouldn't really *ever* be satisfactory or safe to be anything but honest so long as I had to come home every evening as Mrs Rutland.

I thought around the idea of a begging letter in the Personal Column of *The Times* and even went so far as writing out an advertisement. 'Will a few kind and generous people help Reverend Father, working in great poverty in East End, to purchase a small second-hand car for use about his parish? All gifts personally acknowledged. Write Box etc.'

You could easily fix an address for *The Times* to post the letters on to, where you could pick them up, and you could easily get notepaper printed 'St Saviour's Vicarage' for your letters of thanks. But I thought somebody in *The Times* office would see the forwarding address wasn't a clerical one and might start asking questions. It would need more going into before I did anything.

On Twelfth Night we had Mrs Rutland coming for dinner. I'd had a busy morning. I'm no cook, not really; but cakes I do well and I'd been baking a big birthday cake for Ailsa Richards. Mrs Leonard had been helping me to ice it. It's pathetic, I know, but sometimes you get more fun out of doing things for other people than doing them for yourself, and even missing a ride didn't matter compared with taking the cake down to the Richards's cottage and seeing their pleasure.

I felt fine. When I got back Mark was just in from a round of golf. He kept wanting me to try, as the eighth tee was practically at the bottom of our garden, but I kept putting it off and saying I'd be awful. We laughed about this. We didn't often laugh together, it was quite a change. Mark had a funny side that I'd hardly had a chance of seeing. Just for a few minutes it was as if that horrible night at San Antonio had never happened.

Somehow at the end of lunch talk of the firm came up, and I thought, I'm not playing fair with him, not telling him about those two letters I'd read; it's up to me to tell him and then he can think what he likes. So I told him.

He heard it all through without saying anything. Then he gave an uneasy shrug as if his coat was uncomfortable, and looked at me. 'The Glastonbury Investment Trust. That's Malcolm Leicester. I wonder what Chris is *playing* at. Is he trying to get control of the firm entirely out of my hands? Or is he trying to sell? If he's selling on the one hand, why buy on the other?'

'That's all I know. Terry's never mentioned it to me.'

'D'you mean before we were married?'

'Yes, of course.' I covered up.

'In any event they should have brought the whole thing, whatever it is, to the attention of the board. It'll have to come out now.'

'Don't say how you got to know.'

He wrinkled his forehead. 'No . . . On second thoughts it hadn't better come out – yet. But I'll make inquiries . . . I'm enormously grateful to you for telling me.'

'Not at all,' I said, copying his politeness, and that made it sound more off-track than ever.

He lifted his head and half smiled. 'D'you feel married to me, Marnie?'

'No.'

'Nor I to you. Perhaps it will grow . . . Have you ever been to a concert?'

'What sort?'

'Orchestral music. Festival Hall stuff.'

'No.'

'We'll go next week. Like to?'

I said: 'I suppose it's the sort of thing you hear on the radio.'

'Very much. But it sounds different not coming out of a box.'

'All right . . . You're very patient, aren't you, Mark?'

'Have you only just realized that?'

'Patient,' I said, 'but you keep on. There's no let-up.'

'I'm playing for high stakes.'

'You want a nice cosy wife, who'll be here every evening to warm your slippers and – all the rest. I could pick six for you.'

'Thanks, I do my own picking.'

'Yes,' I said, and got up. 'But it doesn't always work out. What are you taking me to hear?'

I suppose that talk was about the high spot. After that we went down.

CHAPTER TWELVE

IT WAS that next week that Roman began different tactics.

As soon as I sat down he said: 'Now, Mrs Rutland, I think we've been making enough progress these last two weeks to pass on to the next stage. It's very simple really, and really very much the same. But I shall stop asking you to tell me about your life and instead I just want you to talk. In the course of the hour I shall put one or two questions to you or perhaps even just one or two words – and I shall ask you to talk about whatever ideas come into your head as a result of that question or that word. I don't want you to reason anything out, I just want you to say the first thing that comes to you, even if it's nonsense – more than ever perhaps if it is nonsense. Do you understand?'

'Yes, I think so.'

We sat in silence for a minute or two and then he said: 'Are you happy coming here?'

'Oh, yes . . . Yes, quite.'

'Do you come by tube?'

'Yes, usually.'

'Rain. What does rain suggest?'

'It's always raining when I come here. Every time so far. My umbrella leaks a pool in your hatstand. The buses make noises with their tyres like kettles boiling. Hiss, hiss.' I thought that was quite clever really on the spur of the moment.

'Water,' he said.

'Isn't that the same thing? Not quite, I suppose.' I looked down at my ankle. That woman *had* caught my stocking in the tube with her crazy stick. Some women ought to be locked up, not looking where they were standing, and all the time telling this friend about Charles's gallstones.

I thought I'd give Roman a run for his money. 'Water? It rains a lot in Plymouth where I was born. And there's water all round there. Why do they call it Plymouth Sound? The sound of kettles boiling. I love tea, don't you? It's the cosiest drink. They were always drinking tea at home. Come in, dear, and have a cup, it's not five minutes since we made it. Sugar? No, I gave it up during the war. Wasn't rationing awful?'

He waited a bit but I didn't go on.

'Baths.'

'Baths?'

'Yes.'

I didn't speak for a long time but leaned back and shut my eyes. I thought, this isn't bad. He just waits as long as I wait, and the hour ticks by.

'Baths,' I said. 'Do you take baths, Dr Roman?'

He didn't answer. I said: 'Sometimes when I'm in the mood I have two and three a day. Not often, but sometimes. Mark says, What do I waste my time for,

215

but I say, Well isn't it better to take too many than not enough? People who don't wash smell. You wouldn't want me to smell, would you?'

He said: 'What do you associate with baths? What are the first things that come into your mind?'

'Soap, plugs, water, rain-water, Boers, Baptists, blood, tears, toil . . .' I stopped, because my tongue really was getting ahead of me. What was I talking about?

'Baptists,' he said.

'Blood of the Lamb,' I said. 'Made pure for me. And his tears shall wash away thy sins and make thee over again.' I stopped and giggled slightly. 'My mother used to take me to chapel three times every Sunday, and I suppose it's coming out now.'

'Did you learn that so young?'

'And Lucy Nye too,' I said in a hurry. 'Lucy was just as bad after Mother died.'

The hour went on like this. Most of the time he seemed to keep on dodging around the same dreary subject of water. I don't know what was biting him, but after a bit I didn't enjoy it so much and thought, let him go and run after himself. Why should I work so hard? He was getting paid, not me.

So we stuck there for a long time, until he mentioned thunderstorms, and I thought, oh, well, this'll colour his life, so I told him all about Lucy Nye and how she'd made me afraid of them. And even then I had this funny instinct that he wasn't believing a word of it.

Anyway, when it was all over I came away with a

feeling that for a non-talker I'd talked a lot too much . . .

So on the Friday I went all set to say nothing at all.

But it wasn't so easy because almost the first thing he said was: 'Tell me about your husband. Do you love him?'

I said: 'But of course,' in one of those light brittle voices, because keeping quiet here might tell more than talking.

'What does the word love mean to you?'

I didn't answer. About five minutes later I said: 'Oh – affection, kissing . . . warmth, friendly arms . . . a kitchen with a fire burning, come in out of the rain, m'dear . . . God so loved the World that he gave His only Begotten Son . . . Forio knowing my step. Mother cat carrying her kitten away. Uncle Stephen walking down the street to meet me. That do?'

'And sex?'

I yawned. '. . . Masculine and feminine. Adjectives end in euse, instead of eux. Male and female . . . Adam and Eve. And Pinch-me. Dirty boys. I'll slap your bloody face if you come near me again . . .' I stopped.

There was another long wait. OK. I thought, I can wait.

It must have been another five minutes. 'Does sex suggest anything else?' he asked.

'Only dirty psychiatrists wanting to know,' I said.

'What does marriage suggest to you?'

'Oh, what's the good of all this?' I said, getting hot. 'I'm *bored*. See? *Bored*.'

It was so quiet I could hear my wrist-watch ticking away.

'What does marriage suggest to you?'

'Wedding bells. Champagne. Old boots. Smelly old boots. Something borrowed, something blue. Brides-maids. Confetti.'

'Isn't that the wedding you're thinking of, not marriage?'

'You told me to say what came into my head!' I was suddenly angry. 'Well, I've flaming well said it! What else d'you expect! If that isn't enough I – I . . .'

'Don't upset yourself. If it upsets you we can pass on to something else.'

So it went on. On the following Tuesday we had a real set-to. Then I clammed up and said practically nil for a complete half-hour. I pretended to go to sleep but he didn't believe it. Then I started counting to myself. I counted up to one thousand seven hundred.

'What does the word woman suggest to you?'

'Woman? Well . . . just woman.'

I relaxed and dreamed about jumping a hurdle.

'Woman,' he said much later. 'Doesn't it suggest anything?'

'Yes . . . Venus de Milo. Bitch. Cow. I once saw a dog run over in the street. I was the first one to get to it because it was still yelping and it bit through the arm of my winter coat and there was blood on the pavement, and the boy driving the baker's van said it wasn't his fault and I shouted at him yes it was, yes it was, you should take more bloody care, and the poor little perisher died in my arms and it was awful it suddenly going limp, just limp, like a heavy old rag; I didn't know what to do so I left it there behind the dustbins meaning to go back for it, but when I got home I got in a screaming row for getting my arm and coat bitten . . . Queer; I'd forgotten all about that. Queer how you dig things up.'

He didn't say anything. Each time I came he said less.

'You want to know about sex,' I said. 'All this beating about the bush really comes down to that, don't it? It's the only thing any of your trade are interested in. Well, all I can tell you is *I'm not*. Mark wanted me to come to see you because I won't sleep with him! That's what he told you, isn't it? Well, it's the truth! But I don't aim to be put in a glass case or stared at through a microscope – a sort of – of freak at a side-show – simply because I have my own likes and dislikes and choose to stick to them! See? Everything I've said you've tried to twist round to one meaning, haven't you? I know your sort. Most men have pretty dirty minds, but psycho-analysts are in a class by themselves! God, I wouldn't like to be your wife! Have you a wife?'

After a while he said: 'Go on, say exactly what you think. But try to relax while you're saying it. Don't tense up. Remember you won't shock me.'

Oh, won't I, I thought. I could if I really got going. All those filthy rhymes that Louise taught me. Your kind don't know the half.

He said: 'Tell me one thing, Mrs Rutland. Apart from this question of – not wanting your husband, are you happy generally speaking, in other ways?'

I kept my mouth shut this time.

'What I mean,' he said, 'is, do you feel you're experiencing and enjoying life to the full?'

'Why shouldn't I be?'

'Well, I'd be surprised if you do.'

'That's your opinion, isn't it?'

'I suspect that for a good deal of the time you live in a sort of glass case, not knowing real enthusiasm or genuine emotion; or feeling them perhaps at second hand, feeling them sometimes because you think you ought to, not because you really do.'

'Thanks, I'm sure.'

'Try not to be offended. I want to help. Don't you sometimes slightly pride yourself on being withdrawn from life? Don't you sometimes feel rather superior about people whose feelings get the better of them? – or ashamed when you give way to them yourself?'

I shrugged and looked at my watch.

'And isn't that pity or feeling of superiority an attempt to rationalize a deeper sensation, an overreaction if you like against a feeling of envy?'

'D'you like hysterical people? I don't.'

'I wasn't talking of hysteria but of genuine natural emotion, which is essential in a balanced liberated human being.'

I pulled up my shoulder strap, which hadn't slipped after all.

He said: 'But even hysteria is much easier to set right

than your condition. You've grown a protective skin to defend yourself against feelings. Unless you try to come out of it the skin will harden until the real *you* inside shrivels and dies.'

'And d'you think all this talking is going to help?'

'It will, I promise you; but only on certain conditions. That's why I'm breaking my general rule and trying to interpret your problems far too soon. So far, Mrs Rutland, except for one or two rare outbursts like today, you have been watching your step all the time. Whenever anything has seemed to come to your lips that represented the true Free Association I'm seeking you have bitten it off sharp. Well, that's not uncommon at the beginning, especially in a woman of perception like yourself – but I have to differentiate between involuntary suppression and deliberate suppression. An analyst can only help a patient who tries to help herself.'

'What d'you expect me to do?' I said sulkily.

'I want you to stop being frightened of what you're going to say.'

It was that night we went to the concert at the Festival Hall. I went in the wrong mood to sit still for two hours while a lot of sad-looking men and women played prim classical music. The only thing that could have done me any good at all was perhaps jazz, which did at least set your blood moving, your arms and feet twinkling.

I yawned all through the first part of the concert – or at least half the time I struggled not to. The lights and the noise and the dressed-up audience made me sleepy and yet at the same time restless. The second half I thought I was never going to get through, except for the last piece. By then I'd soaked in some of the right mood, or perhaps it was the music. It was something by Brahms. I think it was his fourth symphony. But it might have been any of them.

Anyway, Mark saying it was different from when it was canned, I could see there was this difference. The horns and things showed you what 'brassy' meant, and the strings had a sort of reedy sound, like wind blowing through grass, like wheat stalks shivering, like the crying of trees. In the end it got me; it was like it had slid under my skin and was playing on exposed nerves. I forgot all the sad-looking people and Mark next to me and the gangway on the other side and the lights and the antique faces in the orchestra, and I felt as if I was alone on a peak of a mountain and what I'd done with my life so far was pretty much of a dream and only these few seconds were real.

But you couldn't stay up there, it was too cold or the light was too bright or something, and suddenly the music had stopped and people were getting up and moving out. I wiped the sweat off my forehead and nodded to Mark and we followed the others down to the January wind and the waiting cars.

Afterwards we went to a night club. It was his idea not mine, but by then the want to jive had left me because something else had been there and taken its place. But the something else had gone and left an emptiness, and nothing much mattered any more. We got home about one. I don't know if he thought the evening a success, but for me it had been too up and down; somehow except for just those few minutes I'd never been in step – and even those minutes I hadn't so much been walking as flying.

When we got home I said I was tired and went quickly to bed and put the light out. I watched his light for a time, afraid because of something about him that evening.

Thought up two or three different excuses, including of course the most obvious one. I'd never used it even on the honeymoon because I was shy of speaking about it to a man. But I thought I might keep it as a sort of last resort tonight.

I heard him moving about for a long time. It must have been three before he put his light out. But he didn't come in.

I'd missed two Saturdays at poker, but the next one I went again, and this time I gambled heavily. It was quite unlike me. I was losing my judgment. But I won twenty pounds. That's the way it is sometimes; you get the luck when you don't deserve it. That week I'd sent Mother a hundred pounds in two Money Orders, so I was within scraping distance of rock bottom.

On the Sunday morning Mark said: 'These Saturday nights with Dawn Witherbie get later and later. What do you do, go dancing?'

'No, we went to the pictures and then I went home with her, and her mother wasn't well, so I stayed on until the doctor came . . . How did you know I was late?'

'I thought I heard the car about two, so I waited and then went and looked in your bedroom and it obviously wasn't.'

'No, it must have been later than that.'

'It was nearly four. I didn't get to sleep again until after I *had* heard the car.'

I rubbed a small stain on my riding breeches.

He said: 'Anyway you seem to come up bright and fresh every Sunday . . . How are you going on with Roman?'

'Doesn't he tell you?'

'No, he hasn't said anything yet.'

'I'd like to give it up. It's upsetting me.'

'I'm sorry.'

'I've done weeks and weeks now. It's far beyond what I promised. I don't *want* to go on. I come away feeling tired and depressed.'

'Shall I ring him next week, and ask him what he thinks?'

'Oh, I know what *he'll* say. It's only the beginning for him. He's making a good thing out of it.'

'He's far too honest to go on only for that reason.'

I could see Mark wasn't giving way, so I turned and went out into the garden.

For once Forio wouldn't come to me. It was so out of character I could hardly believe it. He'd let me get nearly to touching distance and then he'd toss his head and trot off. It had been wet practically all week, so I suppose he hadn't had enough exercise. After four or five times I gave up and walked back to the house. A piece of apple would fetch him.

As I got in I heard Mrs Leonard call out: 'I don't know where they are, Mr Rutland, not this week. I was out, and Mrs Rutland must have put them away.'

'What is it?' I said.

'My new shirts,' Mark said.

'Oh, I put them in your wardrobe. Wait a minute.' I ran upstairs and into his room. He was standing there in front of the mirror with a handkerchief in his hand. He was wearing a pair of old grey flannel trousers but he hadn't anything on above that.

He said: 'Sorry, I thought you'd gone.'

'I had but I came back. I took the shirts out of the box and put them with your others.' I went to the wardrobe. 'Here they are.'

'Thanks. I thought I'd just try one.'

I lifted the top one out and pulled the various clips and things out. On the table were his keys and his pocketbook and a diary and some loose change. He always put them there each night when he undressed. 'I never knew before people ever did buy six shirts at a time.'

He laughed. 'It's not a sign of extravagance. They wear longer.'

When you saw him without his clothes you could see he wasn't delicate, or even thin. His skin was pale and smooth, but the muscles lay under it; there when need be.

I said: 'Forio's being tiresome. I came in for some bait.'

He took the handkerchief away from his face. 'As you're here, d'you think you could get this eyelash out of my eye? I think I shoved it in with the towel.'

I went to him and he bent his head. I honestly believe this was the nearest we'd been to each other since we came home. And taking an eyelash out is very much of a close-up project. Your own eyes stare into the other eyes at nearer than love-making range. You see the pinkness under the lid and the tiny blood vessels; but even that doesn't matter so much as the pupil, because that seems to stand for about the closest you can ever expect to get to the personality. It was harder still for me this time because I had to put my other hand somewhere when now and then it wasn't wanted, so I had to put it on his warm shoulder, and of course my body was touching his.

I saw the eyelash and edged it towards the corner. Then with me standing there like this against him it was just as if my own body hadn't any clothes on either. I got the feeling just like it was really happening.

Just about in time I got the eyelash out and shifted away, feeling sick and short of breath.

'There you are. No charge at all.'

He took the handkerchief from me. 'Oh, heaven, that there were but a mote in yours.'

'What?'

'Nothing. Only a quotation.'

I went to the door.

'Marnie.'

'Yes?'

He smiled at me. 'Thanks.'

I went out and ran downstairs and went into the kitchen for a minute or two to try and get the thing out of my system. When I went to fetch Forio I realized I'd come out without his bit of apple. But it didn't matter because this time he came to me like a lamb.

I rode till lunch-time and was late back for lunch, but I felt frightful all day. I felt so depressed I could have howled. I was becoming a melancholic. That'd be something fresh for Roman to unscramble.

I was depressed all week, and had dreams enough to keep all the psychiatrists in London on time and a half.

On the Wednesday I went down to see Mother. I found I could do it well enough in a day, so I made the excuse I had to settle up something with the Garrods.

Mother was looking much better. She was mixing in nicer company here, she said, and the house quite suited her. For once she jarred; I suppose because I was still feeling depressed. I thought, here she is having a good time on my money and not really caring where it comes from. Then I remembered how she'd been four years ago and what a difference the money had made.

She went into a sulk when I said I couldn't even stay one night, but she only asked casually about Mr Pemberton and seemed to take it for granted things were going on as usual. Just after tea, while Lucy was washing up, I said: 'Mam, when did Dad die?'

'Die? He was killed, drowned. Nineteen-forty-three. Why?'

'I was only wondering. I was thinking of it the other

day. I don't remember it. I mean I don't remember who told me or what they said to break the news.'

'Why should you indeed? You were only six at the time. Why should you remember anything about it?'

'Well, I remember other things. After all six isn't all that young. I remember Uncle Stephen coming when I was five and bringing me a pair of fur-lined gloves. I remember the girl next door—'

'All right, you remember one thing and forget another. That's the way of it. If you want the truth, I didn't tell you for months after. I thought it'd upset you, like. I thought, Marnie mustn't know. So in the end it just didn't make an impression on you at all.'

I edged around on my seat. 'What part of nineteen-forty-three was it? We were at Sangerford then, weren't we? Did he visit us in Sangerford? I mean earlier. I mean one Christmas. I seem to remember he did. Didn't he bring me a present of a box of chocolates? And some sugared almonds. I remember the sugared almonds . . .'

She said: 'Wait,' and got up with her stick and limped to this old stool we've had since the year one and lifted the top and took out her black bag. 'I'll show you,' she said, and began to fumble among some papers. 'I keep it here. I keep everything here.' She passed me a yellow news-clipping.

It was from the *Western Morning News*, 14th June, 1943, under 'Deaths on Active Service': 'Frank William Elmer, H.M.S. *Cranbrook*, on June 10th: Aged 41, late of 12, Mulberry Street, Keyham. Beloved husband of Edith and father of Margaret.'

I gave it back. 'I don't remember seeing it before. Thanks.'

Mother dabbed her nose. 'It was Whit Monday that came out. It was a lovely day. People was on holiday, even in the wartime. I cut it out to keep. That's all I had left.'

'It's years since I saw a photo of him,' I said. 'There used to be one in Plymouth on the mantelpiece. You know.'

'There's one here. Same one but not framed.'

I looked at that face. I'd come from that face. A stranger he was, because I only knew the photograph. Somehow I'd come from him. He wasn't a bit like what I'd told Roman. His hair was fair and thick and cut short, his face was round, his eyes blue or light grey, small, and I should think twinkling. The oddest thing was he looked *young*. Mother had got older and he'd stayed young.

'How old was he here?'

'About thirty.'

'Can I have this or is it the only one?'

'You can have it if you take care of it.'

Old Lucy came in with some dishes then, so I put the photo in my bag before she saw. But later when she went out again I said: 'Mam, what was the name of the doctor – you know, the one that let you down with the baby?'

'Why?' she said. 'What's it all about? Gascoigne was his name – may God have mercy upon him, for I can't.'

'Was I all right?' I said. 'I mean when I was born. No trouble then?'

'Of course not! But that was before the war. You – why, you never gave me a minute's worry. Not till you were ten, that was. And that was all because of the common company you had to mix with. What's the matter with you today, Marnie? All these *questions*.'

'I don't know. I sometimes think I'm a bit queer.'

'*Queer*. Well, be thankful you're not like other girls. Trollops and flying after men. Painting their toe-nails. You're worth three of any ordinary girl, Marnie, and don't let anyone tell you different. You're so clever – and so good.'

'Were you a bit out of the ordinary when you were young?'

'I was always one to want to get on – a wee bit proud perhaps – kept myself to myself. Your father used to say I was too good for him. But I was never as clever as you, dear.'

'I'm not sure it's wise to be too clever,' I said. 'Sometimes you overreach yourself.'

That Sunday at breakfast Mark said: 'Are you never going to tire of your poker parties?'

I swallowed something that wasn't food and said:

'My what?'

'The poker parties you go to at Terry's.'

'Have you been having me – followed?'

'Not really. No.'

'Then how did you . . .'

'A few weeks ago I asked Dawn Witherbie how her mother was and she told me she hadn't been ill. After that it wasn't hard to find out the rest.'

I broke a piece of toast. 'Why shouldn't I go if I want to?'

'Is that the point? Surely the main question is, why lie to me in the first place?'

'Because I thought you'd disapprove.'

'So I do. But only because it's Terry. Otherwise I try to let you live your own life.'

I was feeling scared. Supposing he'd had me followed to Torquay!

'Well, it's Terry. Why shouldn't I go out with Terry if I want to?'

'Two reasons. Perhaps they're both personal and you won't think they affect you. I think Terry is one of the misfits of this life. I spend one-third of the time feeling sorry for him and two-thirds hating his guts. I feel he's utterly misplaced and out of his true element as a printer. But there's no job on earth that I can think of that would *be* his true element. Can you? He's – to me – a jumble of ambitions and frustrations that don't quite add up to a real person. He wants to be a first-rate business man, but he never will be. He wants to be a great lover, and is always trying to be, but I don't think he is. He teeters around on the edge of things, dressing beautifully, picking up the latest fads and phrases, running his little poker parties and his jam sessions. You see, Marnie, if he was a really tough bad character, perhaps I could make something of that, but he isn't even big enough to be really bad. And what's worse, along with his failures – perhaps as a result of them – there's a sort of slyness that gets under my skin. He has the sort of ingenuity that turns sour everything that it touches.'

'Perhaps it's because he's a misfit that I – get along with him.'

'Don't underrate yourself. Look at this business of the Glastonbury Investment Trust – and it's you I've to thank for putting me on to it. I haven't tackled him yet, but it seems to me perfectly typical of the man. I don't resent his enmity but I resent his back-door way of showing it.'

'What are you going to do?'

'I don't know. That's reason number two for your not going to these parties. Just at the moment I don't think you, as my wife, can possibly, decently, have a foot in both camps. It would be less impossible if the blood-letting were above ground. But it isn't yet.'

I began to put one or two of the things together on the table.

He said: 'I hate unpleasantness. And the feeling that all this is going on underneath all the time poisons every day as soon as I get to the works. I told Rex about the Glastonbury Trust, and he has some weird idea of having the Holbrooks and ourselves over to dinner one night to see if they'll make the friendly move and come out in the open. I've told him he's crazy, but he says it's a pity if an old family firm is going to have to come to a split for lack of an effort on his part.'

'When does he want us to go?'

'I don't know. I think the week after next. Anyway

you see how it is. You see how impossible it is for you to be out until all hours with Terry, don't you?'

I piled the dirty plates on the dinner wagon. If something was put to me rationally I nearly always saw the point. But I was feeling mulish. I expect I looked mulish, because after watching me he said:

'Ours is about the oddest sort of life anyone could live, isn't it. That's if it can be called a life at all.'

'I didn't suggest it.'

'No, but to some extent you acquiesced.'

'You know the reason for that.'

He came over and stood beside me. His eyes were very dark. 'I've done what I can to leave you alone, Marnie. It hasn't been much fun, I can tell you. Sometimes it gets me down. That's another form of unpleasantness, to feel that you're being treated as a jailer by your own wife. That, and all the other pressures involved . . . It puts me off balance at my job, it comes between me and my sleep. I'm irritable and short-tempered with things. Sometimes I feel I could kill you. But I don't. I leave you alone. Except for Roman, you do whatever you want. You go your own way. I hope for better things. I keep on hoping. It's the only thing that makes the present set-up tolerable at all. But if you start playing fast and loose with Terry I shall have to think again.'

'I don't play fast and loose with him! I can't bear him to touch me!'

'I know he wouldn't be Terry if he didn't try.'

'I really believe you're jealous of him.'

He took me by the shoulders and tried to bring me

round to face him. I wouldn't move. He pulled me round.

'You're hurting me, Mark.'

He didn't let go. 'So I'm jealous, Marnie. I'm jealous of the men you speak to, of the people you go out with, of the hours you spend here alone while I'm at the works. I even have to be jealous of my miserable back-door sham-smart wise-cracking cousin. More than ever jealous of him because he seems to be the only man you favour. The whole damned feeling is something I've never felt before and never need to have felt, because with any sort of proper relationship between us it wouldn't have arisen.'

'You're hurting me.'

He let me go, shrugged. 'I don't want to start getting melodramatic . . . I've made my own present – and yours too. And for the time being at any rate we've got to live in it. I'm trying to let you go your own way and at your own pace. That's fine – we've agreed to it, and if it's wearing on me that's my funeral. But the bargain doesn't include your going out and staying out with Terry. I'm sorry if you thought it did, but it doesn't. It just doesn't, Marnie.'

I pulled my arm away and left him there at the door.

CHAPTER THIRTEEN

MY MIND sometimes went to Mark's keys which he took out of his pocket in his bedroom each night, but so long as I stayed with him there wasn't a thing I could do about them.

At this time I had my chief pleasure out of being friendly with the Richards and their neighbours. In the cottage next to them were two old men. One was blind and the other half blind and they used to go for walks arm in arm – one eye did for two of them, they said – it was startling how happy they seemed; but their cottage was in a mess, and I couldn't bear to see it like that, so one day I went down with Mrs Leonard and we had a gorgeous spring-clean. I also found some old curtains which were sixty times better than the cast-off nappies or whatever they'd had over the windows till then. The two old men were puzzled but grateful. Then I found *they* liked my cakes too.

That week Dr Roman said: 'We're almost at the beginning of our third month, Mrs Rutland. We made quite substantial progress in January, but at the moment we seem to have struck another bad patch. I have been wondering whether you would submit to hypnosis.'

'D'you mean— Who by?'

'By me. But I have to tell you at once that unless you willingly allow it, the attempt is useless. Nobody can be hypnotized against their will.'

'Well,' I said. 'Why d'you think we're not going on all right as we are?'

'I think we might get over the present difficulty. We've made no progress now for five meetings.'

It sounded safe enough. 'When, do you mean?'

'Now, if you like.'

'All right. Do I close my eyes?'

'No. In a moment I'll ask you to watch this silver ring that I shall hold up. But first I'll lower the shades a little.'

Twenty minutes later he said in a dry voice: 'Yes, I suppose I might have expected it.'

'Expected what?'

'Well, you may be giving the appearance of submitting but in fact you're resisting with all your might.'

'I'm not! I've done everything you told me to do!'

I liked it better when I'd got him face to face like this. He was polishing his glasses, and he looked tired. Without his glasses you could see the bags under his eyes.

'You *always* do everything I tell you, Mrs Rutland, but always with great inner resistance. Had you been a less interesting personality I should have given you up weeks ago.'

'I'm sorry.'

'Are you?'

He said that as if he was going to make something out of it.

'If you're sorry, may I put another suggestion? I can produce the effect of hypnosis artificially with a simple injection. You will have heard of pentothal. It has no unpleasant after-effects and will, I think, do a certain amount to help us both.'

I looked down at my nails. 'I think I ought to ask Mark first.'

He sighed, 'Very well, Mrs Rutland. Tell me on Friday.'

On Friday I said: 'I'm awfully sorry but Mark doesn't fancy the idea of me being drugged. He's funny that way, but he has a prejudice against any form of injection.'

'I see.'

'But let me carry on, will you, just as we are for a week or two yet? I've had some extraordinary dreams since I saw you last . . .'

'I think you yourself would never agree to pentothal, would you? Isn't that really the truth?'

I said: 'Mark won't let me anyway.'

'And you won't let yourself.'

'Well . . . why *should* I? It isn't fair to – to get people like that. It's like bullying them – it's like getting them down in the street and holding them there. I won't give my – myself – away to anybody on earth. It's like giving away your soul.'

*

237

WINSTON GRAHAM

Later he said: 'Tell me this, what more do you want in life, beyond what you already have?'

'Why?'

'Well, tell me. What's your ambition for the future? You're twenty-three. Most women of your age want marriage. You have it but cannot accept it.'

'I don't mind being with a man so long as he leaves me alone.'

'Do you want children?'

'No!'

'Why not? It's a natural instinct, isn't it?'

'Not for everyone.'

'Why don't you want them?'

'I don't think it's any sort of a world to bring them into.'

'That could be why you don't *have* them. It would not be why you don't want them.'

'I don't see the difference.'

'You're trying to find a rational explanation for something you feel emotionally.'

'Maybe.'

'Do you love your own mother?'

'Yes . . . I did,' I added just in time. 'I love her memory.'

'Don't you think it right and reasonable that some-one should come into the world who feels for you what you feel for her?'

'Could be.' God, I felt queer just then; he might have *given* me his drug; I was sweating all down my back and in the roots of my hair; might have been in a Turkish bath.

'If a child could be got by an injection, without

238

having any intercourse with a man at all, would you object then?'

'What the flaming hell does it matter what I would object to!' I shouted. 'I don't *want* children or anything to do with 'em! See? Now d'you understand?'

'I understand you're angry with me because I'm asking you questions you don't want to answer.'

'All right, you are! Well, you said you never pressed a patient, so now you can change the subject!'

It must have been ten minutes with neither of us saying a word. Trouble is, though, you can't hide your breathing. I watched the brooch on my frock going up and down. Reminded me somehow of old Lucy. Not that she had much to go up and down, but she always snorted when she was mad. If I—

'Does the thought of childbirth frighten you?'

'What?'

'Does the idea of giving birth to a child frighten you?'

'I've *told* you! I'm not *interested*!'

'Will you give me your free association of thought with the word childbirth.'

'Twilight sleep. I wish my analyst would take an overdose. I wonder why *he* was ever born. I wonder why I was. Better if all the doctors in the world were killed off. Maybe better if all the world was. Not long now perhaps. Strontium 90. Deformed babies then. Monsters. That blasted clock's striking eleven. If you—' I stopped.

'What clock?'

'The one in mother's kitchen. I hate its guts. Like a bloody little coffin. It's got a glass front. The top half is the face and the bottom half has love-birds painted on it. It was Grannie's . . .'

'Tell me more about it.'

'About what?'

'The clock.'

'Kettle on stove. Boiling water. Nearly out of coal. Lucy Nye. Cold weather. We need more blankets. Maybe newspapers will do.' I gave a sort of strangled cry that I turned into a cough.

'Were you very cold?' he asked after a wait.

'Cold? Who said anything about cold?'

'You said you needed more blankets.'

'I didn't. I was warm as warm . . . Always till that tapping at the window.' The sweat down my back had suddenly gone different and I shivered; I really *was* cold then. For a minute I thought I wasn't going to be able to stop shivering.

I said: 'Why does Daddy tap at the window? Why doesn't he come the ordinary way? Why do I have to be turned out?' And I began to cry; believe it or not I began to cry like a kid. It really was like a kid in a funny way; not like me making grown-up noises. I darned near frightened myself. So I tried to stop. But all I did was choke and cough and start again.

I cried on, and in a mixed muzzy sort of way I was back as a kid being lifted out of a warm bed and put in a cold one; and just before that there'd been tapping; sometimes it was like with a nail and sometimes it was like with a knuckle, but it always meant the same thing. And it was always mixed up with that clock striking away. And I was standing with my back against the wall, the other side of the bed the light was on and the door was shut but they'd been groaning in there, and I knew in a minute the door would open and those who'd been torturing in there would come and do it to me. And God help me, just at that minute the door did begin to open, and I stood in my art-silk nightie pressed against the wall watching it. And the door came wide open, and who should be there but Mam.

But it didn't mean the end of anything; it didn't mean the end of the horror but just the beginning, because there she was coming in, and it wasn't Mam at all but somebody just like her, somebody who looked like her but older and torn about, in a nightdress with her hair trailing like a witch; and she looked at me as if she knew me, and she was carrying something that she was going to give me, something that I couldn't *bear* to have . . .

Roman got hold of me as I was half-way across the room. 'Mrs Rutland, please. Do sit down.'

'There's a clock striking now!' I said. 'That's the end of my hour!'

'Yes, but please don't hurry. I have a few minutes in hand.'

'I've got to go! I'm sorry but Mark's meeting me at the station.'

'Then stop a moment and rest. Would you like to wash your face?'

'No, we're going out this evening. I've got to meet him now.'

'Wait five minutes.'

'*No!* I've got to go.'

I shook myself free of him, but he followed me out into the hall. There I calmed down and sat down for a minute and rubbed my face with my hankie and powdered most of the stains away; so when at last I got out in the air I looked just as normal as any other woman. It was the first time I'd cried properly since I was twelve.

Of course I wasn't going out, and I was home ahead of Mark by best part of an hour. I went out to Forio who was grazing in a corner of the field by the golf course. We'd had to have the fence raised there because once he'd got out and we'd only just rounded him up before he invaded the seventh green. It was nearly dark but not cold and I went over and gave him a bit of apple, and he took it without ever letting me feel he had teeth at all. He was restless tonight and kept putting back his ears and stamping his feet and snorting. I'd ridden him yesterday, but it was a week since I'd given him a real work-out. I wondered sometimes about hunting. Two or three of our neighbours round here hunted, and I knew the excitement would be lovely and the jumping and the galloping.

One day last week Mark had hired a hack and ridden with me. We'd been out half the day and had stopped for lunch at a little public house, and for a while it was as if all the rows and the coldness between us had taken time off. I don't mean that I felt loving towards him but just more natural. You could forget for a bit and act as if he was a casual friend.

I led Forio back to the stable, and switched on the

light and lifted up his left forefoot. Yesterday he'd picked up a stone which in a dozen paces had wedged in tight enough to be a job to get out. He'd limped on the way home and I wondered if there would be any swelling today, but there wasn't. I began to brush his long mane, which had grown more than it should have, but I liked it that way. It was as fine and silky as a woman's hair. Horses don't purr but they make noises that mean the same.

While I was doing it I kept thinking about that little bungalow we'd lived in at Sangerford near Liskeard. I suddenly remembered toddling out to the dustbin in the back yard with some old cabbage leaves Mother had told me to throw away. The smell of the cabbage leaves was as distinct as if they were still in my hands. I remembered the lavatory pan was cracked and the cheap tiles had been so badly laid that you could turn your ankle on them. And the table in the kitchen would never stand firm because the floorboards sloped. Jerry-building. Mother often said so.

After a while I tired of grooming Forio and went into the house and the telephone was ringing. It was Terry.

CHAPTER FOURTEEN

So there was this dinner party at the Newton-Smiths the following week. The night it was fixed for, Mark came home early and we had our usual drink together – that was about the easiest thing in our married life – but I could see tonight he was thoughtful about something and wondered if it was because he didn't want to go. He never had wanted to go because he thought if there was a deal being planned by the Holbrooks behind his back, a social evening wouldn't affect them one way or the other, and it was naïve of Rex to think they could do more over dinner with women present than round the boardroom table.

But over his second drink Mark said: 'Roman rang me today. He says you haven't been near him since a week last Tuesday.'

'No . . . that's right.'

'Any special reason?'

'I don't think I'm getting anywhere at all.'

'Roman seemed worried about you, asked if you were all right.'

'Why shouldn't I be?'

'He said you were upset when you left him last.'

'Upset? No . . . I was sick of being third-degreed all the time.'

I accepted a drink from him. He said: 'I hope you don't mean this is the end.'

'I – think it has to be.'

He sipped his drink. When I looked at him now, I saw how much this business had meant to him, what a lot he'd banked on it.

'Terribly sorry, Mark. I've *tried*.'

'Roman is certain you have a deep-seated psychoneurosis which only long and patient treatment will cure. But he thinks he could do a lot for you if you went back to him.'

'It's making me so unhappy, Mark. You don't want me to be unhappy, do you?'

'He doesn't at all want to give you up. He asks me to *ask* you to go back. But . . . he stresses that if you return to him you must do so of your own free will.'

'Oh.'

'So I suppose I mustn't bribe or blackmail you into anything. I can only ask you – as he asks you – not to throw everything away now.'

I didn't feel I could say anything useful, so I didn't reply.

He said: 'All this is a terrible disappointment to me, Marnie. It's like groping along in hope of finding some way out and suddenly coming up against a brick wall. If you don't go back to him there isn't any hope any more.'

We went up to change and went out for the evening in very much this mood. We didn't speak to each other all the way there. I looked at his face sometimes and thought, he's a sticker, he's a fighter, but he's got to give in now.

The Newton-Smiths lived in a big house in the country, and when we got there we were surprised to find that there were going to be twelve to dinner. I thought, well, this is a funny idea, having us here for an evening with the Holbrooks apparently to talk about the firm, and then they invite outsiders. But perhaps that was true to intention; that was what they'd said, just a social evening. They were a well-meaning couple but not awfully bright. Terry was there before us looking just shaved and yellow-haired, but a bit furtive and hot as if something hadn't turned out the way he expected it. The MacDonalds were there too and a Mr and Mrs Malcolm Leicester were introduced to me, and I couldn't make out where I'd heard the name before. But all that was suddenly swallowed up because through the open drawing-room door I saw another couple arriving, and he was somebody I *did* know, a man called Arthur Strutt.

He was a partner in a firm of Turf Accountants called Crombie & Strutt who had a branch office in Birmingham. It was at the branch office in Birmingham that a Miss Marion Holland had once been employed as a confidential clerk.

Well, there it was, suddenly staring me in the face like the muzzle of a gun. At first it didn't really knock me out at all because as usual I had the feeling that the gun was pointing at Marion Holland, not me. We were different people.

But it was going to be quite embarrassing if it turned out we both had the same face.

Mr Strutt had travelled up from London once a month while Marion Holland worked there. That meant he'd seen a lot of her. He usually spent a whole day in the office going through things with the branch manager, Mr Pringle. Twice he spent more than an hour at a time with Marion Holland.

When I could get my tongue away from the roof of my mouth I clutched Mark's arm. He'd been talking to Mrs Holbrook and he looked surprised.

I said: 'Could I – have a word with you. I've just remembered something.' When he'd excused himself I went on, 'I've just remembered I've left the oven on.'

'What oven? At home?'

'Yes.' I laughed weakly. 'I put it on about five and quite forgot it. I think I'd better go back and—'

'Oh, it'll be all right, surely.'

'No, it won't, Mark. I put something in the oven and wrapped it in grease-proof paper. I was cooking a cake, experimenting. If it gets too hot it might catch fire. It might set the house on fire.'

'If you're that worried, ring Mrs Leonard and ask her to come up from the village. It'll only take her ten minutes.'

'She can't get in.'

'Yes, she can. You know she always has a spare key.'

'She told me yesterday she'd lost it. I – really, Mark, I think I'd better go.'

'My dear, you *can't*. It would take you an hour and a half to get back here. It's impossible. Why if—'

'Mark, I have to get *out*.'

'Why—'

'At once. In five minutes it'll be too late. I'll explain later. Please, please trust me.'

Terry came up. 'Hello, my dear, you're looking quite ravishing. But pale, I think. Pale. Is Mark treating you badly?'

'No. Very well,' I said, and took two steps and then saw it was too late. Mr and Mrs Strutt had come into the room.

Rex was making the introductions. I saw Arthur Strutt smiling at Gail MacDonald, and I thought, perhaps I have changed myself enough. You can never tell. Colour of my hair's different, of course, and the style quite; I was wearing my hair behind my ears in those days. And it was two years. Maybe he never really looked at me. He was a fat little man, and his wife was thin and faded, and—

He saw me and his face changed.

Rex said: 'And this is my cousin and his wife, Mr and Mrs Mark Rutland.'

We said the usual things. I didn't look at him much but I could see Strutt blinking behind his library spectacles the way he did when he was excited.

After what seemed about an hour he cleared his throat and said: 'I think we have met before, haven't we?'

I stared at him in surprise and then smiled. 'I don't think so. At least I don't remember. Where was it?'

'In Birmingham. With Mr Pringle?'

I shook my head. 'I'm awfully sorry. I haven't often been up there. How long ago?'

'Two years. Rather less.'

His wife was looking at him suspiciously.

'No,' I said, 'I lived in Cardiff two years ago. I'm sorry.'

'*I'm* sorry,' he said, but he moved on. He had to be introduced to this Malcolm Leicester and his wife.

I took a gulp of the drink the maid had just given me. It was strong gin but I needed it. My hand was shaking so much I had to put the glass down before anyone noticed me.

Then someone was holding my arm. 'Bear up,' Mark said under his breath. 'He's gone. Can I help now?'

I think if anything could have warmed me to him it was that. It did me more good than the gin to know he was like that about it. I smiled at him and shook my head.

But Strutt wasn't satisfied yet. I saw him talking to his wife, but he didn't come over again because Mrs Leicester started talking to him, and by the time she'd got through it was time to go in to dinner.

It was one of those good dinners, with plenty of the right food cooked the right way. You could see how the Newton-Smiths kept their strength up. Mark might think it was all a waste of time, but I saw now that the Newton-Smiths weren't so simple after all, because of Malcolm Leicester. Somehow by inviting him as well as Mark and as well as the Holbrooks, Rex was calling the Holbrooks' bluff. It was a new sort of game of poker, and afterwards I wasn't so sure I'd have liked to play poker with fat Rex.

I had Terry on one side and a man whose name I forget on the other. Although it was all so good, everything I ate sat like an iron lump on my stomach.

Half-way through dinner I heard them talking about Rutland's at the other end of the table. Leicester leaned across and said something to Mark and Mark said something back that made them all laugh; but I could see Mark had taken the point all the same.

I looked across sidelong and saw Mr Strutt watching me. I lowered my eyes just as quick as he looked away. His wife was on the other side of Terry, and she wasn't exactly being showered with attention by Terry.

Terry said: 'D'you mean it's true – you can never come again to one of my little parties, my dear, my dear?'

'I didn't say so.'

'We're having a special one next Saturday. No holds barred. Think you can make it?'

'Terry, is that Malcolm Leicester of the Glastonbury Investment Trust?'

An uneasy smile went across his face. 'Yes. How d'you know? Did Mark tell you?'

'No. I do it with tea-leaves.'

'Or with reading letters? I remember my father saying once that you read personal letters when you were in the firm.'

It was the only bit of talk I recollect over that dinner, and I waited for the meal to finish. Afterwards all the women went upstairs. I knew I was in for more trouble yet, but I wasn't expecting Mrs Strutt to start it. She came over to me when the others were all chattering and said:

'I understand you knew my husband some years ago?'

'No,' I said. 'I'm sorry but he's confusing me with someone else.'

She looked at me in the mirror while I made up my lips. I mean, it wasn't easy to concentrate. She was a drawn sort of woman, not too old, but she'd lost her looks.

'Arthur never forgets a face.'

'I don't suppose he's forgotten it, Mrs – er – Stott. I think he's just mistaken it. Anyway, does it matter?'

She looked over her shoulder at the others. 'I knew he was infatuated with a woman all through 1958,' she said in a low voice.

'I'm sorry.'

'I could never find out her name. He used to go off on these *business* trips . . . Did you *leave* him or something?'

I screwed the lipstick back in its thing and put it in my bag. 'Honestly, Mrs Stott—'

'Strutt, as you well know. He tells me some story now about you being in the Birmingham office; but I know he would *never* have blurted it out if you hadn't taken him by surprise. He's always so *careful* . . .'

There was a whole burst of giggles from the other women.

'I sometimes look in his suitcases, his pockets . . . Only once in 1953, I really caught him. And even then . . .'

Well, I looked at her again in the mirror, and her eyes were brimming up with angry tears. And I suddenly felt awfully sorry for her, so I said: 'Look, Mrs Strutt, honestly, your husband's never been in love with me. Really, dear. He's making a mistake and so are you. We've never even *met* before. Won't you believe me?'

Mrs Newton-Smith had come up to the table. 'Are you girls ready to go down?'

'Yes,' said Mrs Strutt, and she turned away, but I didn't know which one of us she was answering.

I knew of course he was going to have another stab at me. In a maddening sort of way his poor suspicious wife made it all the more necessary for him to prove himself right. Apart from that, he wasn't the type of man who'd easily part with money. I expect Mr Pringle had got it hot at the time for not making more sure of my references.

I kept near Mark all the time. It looks silly when you come to think of it, but I felt he was a protection. I felt he was on my side. I'd never felt him on my side before.

We stayed on and on talking and drinking and chatting. Then Rex came over to me and started talking about hunting. But I've really no idea what he said. Ten-thirty came and eleven. At half past eleven the MacDonalds got up to go, and then there was a general stirring around. Like a dog off the lead Arthur Strutt came over to me, with his wife just behind.

He blinked and said: 'I'm sorry to keep on about this, Mrs Rutland, but you were Miss Marion Holland before you married, weren't you.'

It wasn't a question at all. It was just him stating what he knew to be true.

'No,' I said, not politely. 'I wasn't.'

Strutt blinked up at Mark, then glanced at his wife. 'The Marion Holland I mean was employed by my firm as a confidential clerk between September 1958 and February 1959. In Birmingham that was, under my manager there, George Pringle.'

I sighed. After all, I'd every reason to be getting impatient by now. 'Is it necessary to say it again? My maiden name was Elmer. But in 1958 and 1959 I was living with my then husband in Cardiff. He died late in 1959. His name was Jim Taylor. I've only been to Birmingham twice and that was five years ago.'

He stared at me, as if any minute he was going to call me a liar. Then Mark suddenly said: 'I can confirm that, Mr Strutt, if it will give you any satisfaction. Though I don't know what all the excitement's about. I knew my wife before we were married.' I was staggered by him coming in like this.

'When?' said Strutt. 'In 1958?'

'Yes. I met her first in Cardiff in June 1958. I've known her ever since. I don't know what's worrying you about the resemblance, but I can assure you it can only be a resemblance.'

That really upset him. You could see the conviction,
the absolute certainty, dying away, and in its place for
the first time, real doubt. 'Well I'm jiggered . . . I've
never seen such a resemblance, honestly. I admit,
Marion Holland was a blonde, but you know how
women change their hair . . .'

Someone behind us laughed. It was Terry.

Mr Strutt looked at me. 'I beg your pardon, Mrs
Rutland. I'd – you see, I'd a special reason for wanting
to meet Miss Holland again. She – well, there it is, I
think I've made rather a fool of myself. You haven't a
twin sister, I suppose?'

'No sisters at all,' I said, smiling now that he was
backing down.

The suspicion crept around in his eyes, like quick-
silver in a saucer. 'You even smile like her . . . Well, I
promise you I'll never disbelieve one of those *Prisoner
of Zenda* stories again.'

They left soon afterwards, and we were not long
behind them.

Terry came down the steps with us, and instead of
going over to his own car walked with us to ours. He
talked away about this and that; but one thing I was
certain, he wasn't thinking what he was talking about.
He kept darting little glances first at me and then at
Mark.

He said: 'I didn't know Leicester was a friend of
Rex's before, did you, Mark?'

'No.'

'I never met him before,' Terry said, 'but he seems a
nice chap. Powerful in his own way, too. By the by, I

didn't know either that you two knew each other as early as 1958. You weren't ragging, were you?'

Mark said: "Fraid not. You remember I was in Wales in June 1958 on that dispute with Verekers. I met Marnie then.'

'While Estelle was alive?'

Mark hesitated. 'I didn't know Marnie well. We wrote once or twice.'

Terry laughed. 'Deceitful, wasn't it, my dears. All this business of her coming and asking for a job. Why so roundabout, eh?'

Mark hesitated again. 'People talk, Terry. Even you. I didn't want some silly scandal to get around.'

'Ha, ha. Well, you see how your misdeeds find you out.'

He slammed my door and we drove off.

We drove off in one of those silences. I waited for Mark, but he said nothing at all. And his face had really nothing you could read on it.

It was freezing in the car and I leaned down to switch on the heater. It began to whirr but the engine was so cold that only cold air came in to begin with. The air swirled round my ankles and I shivered. I pulled the collar of my coat up. There was another car on ahead that had come from the house but I couldn't remember who had left before us. There were one or two icy patches under the trees and once the car in front skidded. But it kept ahead of us almost half-way home. The moon was rising and sometimes it looked like a headlight coming the other way. A slight warmth began to come through the heater.

I said: 'Mark, I want to thank you for what you've done tonight. You've been a real friend tonight, sticking up for me the way you did – I shall never forget it.'

'No?'

'No. I – it was wonderful and reassuring to feel that you wouldn't let me down. I really am most awfully grateful.'

He said: 'Well, d'you think in that case it's time to start being most awfully truthful?'

'About – tonight?'

He said patiently: 'What else?'

'Are you angry with me?'

He glanced at me. 'Angry isn't quite the word. Rocking on my heels, you might say – and anxious.'

'It was marvellous the way you backed me up.'

'So you've said. But let's not make too much of that. Just put it down to the fact that I still don't like the idea of your going to prison.'

I sighed. 'Well, thank Heaven for that.'

'I honestly think, Marnie, that it's time you stopped thanking Heaven, or me, or anyone else, and faced up to the facts of life.'

'Which are?'

'That you're going to have to tell me about all the other money you've stolen in the past.'

'What d'you mean? Who said it was anything to do with money?'

'I asked Strutt.'

'You *what*!'

'I asked him. I was entitled to know why he was so worked up at the thought of meeting Marion Holland. Eleven hundred pounds is enough to work any man up.'

'But he'll think—'

'He's suspicious anyway; but no more so than he was before. I think we've pretty well choked him off, at the expense of making Terry believe I was trailing round after you while I was married to Estelle. Oddly, it's just the sort of explanation Terry would most easily swallow.'

'Well, I'm sorry about that—'

'You needn't be.'

The other car had gone. We went miles in silence. He said: 'I must know, here and now, I've just got to know what the real score is. Helping you at all may be unprofitable, but helping you blindfold is a fool's game.'

'I suppose it looks as if I've cheated you. But you see, I never wanted you to know—'

'I can believe that.'

'Let me finish. I never wanted you to know because I felt you had faith in me, and if I told you any more, that would destroy it. You may think I care nothing about you but . . .' My voice broke.

'Whatever else happens tonight,' he said gently, 'for Pete's sake let's not get the issues blurred with crocodile tears.'

We turned in at our drive and he drove into the garage.

'D'you remember,' I said, 'when you caught me before, when you brought me back here and we were having supper, I said I was a thief and a liar. I told you so plainly then. I said forgive me and let me go. And I said it later too. You wouldn't let me go.'

'So what's followed is really my fault?'

'I didn't say that—'

'But I have to bear a share of the responsibility? Is that it? Well, quite right too.'

He cut the engine and we sat a minute in the dark. I wriggled my handkerchief out and blew my nose. In the garden you could hear the wind sighing through the bare branches of the trees.

'Quite right too,' he said. 'I *wanted* to believe what you told me before we were married. I checked some of it and took the rest on trust. After all, I was in love with you, and trust must begin somewhere. To tell the truth, I was afraid even then of going too deep, just in case there *was* something wrong with your story. I thought, what's over is over. We love each other. Surely we can begin from here. If you deluded me, I was a willing victim. So in a sense you're absolutely right.'

'Mark—'

'But it was pretty bad reasoning all the same. What's over isn't over. I've got to go into your past life, Marnie.'

'I'll tell you everything I can—'

'You mean you'll tell me everything you can't avoid. I'm afraid that won't do this time. We've really got to go a bit deeper.'

I opened the door of the car and moved my legs to get out.

He said: '*Marnie*.'

'All right.'

'No, it's got to be more than all right this time. I'm no longer the man you married. With your willing aid I've become cynical and disillusioned. So, though I still want to help you, I swear to God that if I find you out in any lies tonight I'll go to Mr Arthur Strutt and tell him of the mistake I made. After that nothing can save you from the police. So bear it in mind, will you?'

We didn't go to bed that night until five. Except that he was so polite about it he'd have made a good man for the Inquisition. His face got whiter and whiter as the night went on. He looked like the Devil. Sometimes I cried, sometimes I screamed at him; but he just went on.

In the end I told him all about the Birmingham affair, all about the one in Manchester, all about Newcastle. In the end I was so exhausted I couldn't stand. And I hated him more than ever. All the good he'd done by sticking up for me at the Newton-Smiths was lost.

Even then I didn't tell him about Mother, and I didn't tell him about Swansea. He thought he'd squeezed me dry but he hadn't quite. I clung on.

But three was bad enough. I'd never have thought anyone could have made me tell so much. I've heard about prisoners being questioned in the war, how once they *started* talking they went on.

At five o'clock he made a cup of tea and we drank it together. We'd been in the kitchen all the time because it was warmest at that time of night. The windows were steamed as if it was with all the hot air.

After we'd been sipping for a time he said: 'I still don't know why you did it, why you began.'

'If you ask me anything more now I shall faint.'

'Not with that warm tea inside you, you won't . . . But anyway I think we may be getting to the end of our tether tonight. You're sure you've not forgotten anything?'

I just shook my head.

He helped himself to more sugar. 'The thing now is what we're going to do about it.'

I shrugged.

He said: 'Well, my love, it's just not possible to leave it as it is.'

'Why not?' He didn't answer. I said: 'Why did you lie for me if you didn't want to leave it as it is?'

'I lied for you to save you temporarily, and to gain time. But it can't be a permanent thing. You can't live a normal life when you're wanted by the police of three separate cities.'

'*I'm* not wanted—'

'Not as Marnie Elmer, not as Mrs Rutland. But you're at the mercy of every wind that blows. Next time I might not be there. Next time you might not be so lucky.'

I shivered as if I'd caught cold. 'Let me go to bed, please.'

'There may be some way out of this, but if so I don't know it. You just can't live all your life as a wanted criminal.'

'Let's think of it in the morning.'

He put down his cup and looked at me. 'I wonder if

that's one way you live, by saying when anything difficult turns up – let's think of it in the morning. Or else you've cohabited with this idea so long that the danger doesn't look so big. Well, it looks big to me. Not to mention the fact that I don't think one ought to live with that sort of thing permanently in one's personality.'

I watched him walk across the kitchen and back. His tie was round the side and his hair was sticking up. 'Every time we went into a room together – think of it – meeting new people, keyed up for the chance accident; then denials, hasty lies, all the rest . . . until one day it doesn't work and you're caught . . .'

'There's nothing else for it,' I said.

'And apart from you – though you're the chief problem – I carry not only the moral but the legal load, as accessory after the fact. I don't want to go to jail, Marnie.'

'Just let me go,' I said. 'There's nothing else for it.'

'To jail, you mean?'

'No, just let me leave you. I'll quietly disappear. People will soon forget.'

'I doubt it. Anyway, that really solves nothing.' He came back. 'Perhaps that was good advice of yours after all. We'll see it clearer in the morning.'

CHAPTER FIFTEEN

IT WASN'T clearer in the morning, nor the day after that, nor the day after. We stopped talking about it, but I could see he hadn't stopped thinking about it. But each day when he said nothing and did nothing I felt that much safer.

Well, what was there to do, honestly? He either gave me up to the police or he didn't give me up. I didn't believe he would ever really get to the point of betraying me – and every day he left it he was more implicated himself. Anyway, he was still in love with me, or whatever it was he did feel – that hadn't changed – and the way he'd stuck up for me at the Newton-Smiths had been an eye-opener.

But I knew that for the next few weeks, while it hung in the balance, I depended an awful lot on his goodwill, and I was sorry I'd thrown so much of it away. I had to get on the right side of him again, or at any rate not give him cause for complaint. Of course if I'd been able to make up to him like other women it would have been easy.

Then one day, about a week later, he mentioned that Roman had rung him, and had I really decided to drop all that for good? I saw at once that if I could do it, this was the way to please him, so I said I'd try going for another few weeks. I didn't *want* to start again, I said, because it always made me so miserable, but I'd do it because he wished me to.

So he agreed, and I went back to Roman, and I felt that Mark had accepted this as the only way out.

About this time one of the two old blind men – the less blind one, the one called Riley – took ill and was in bed for two weeks with his heart. This was the bad time of the year for Mrs Richards's bronchitis too, and she couldn't help much, so I went down every morning after Mark had left and did for the blind men. I'd sometimes spend three hours a day down there, what with one family and the other. It was queer, the way those two men worked together. Even with Mr Riley in bed he would *talk* to Mr Davis, telling him where things were, so that Mr Davis had a sort of eye after all. They were closer than twins.

Mr Davis had a wonderful Welsh voice, and listening to him answering Mr Riley's instructions was like listening to someone singing responses in church. 'Over a little more to your left, David,' Mr Riley would say, and 'Over a little more to my left, John,' Mr Davis would answer. 'Mind that stool by your left ankle, David.' 'The stool has been minded, John.' By the end of the third week Mr Riley was up again and they were able to start their walks. I was afraid some motorist would run them down.

What with one thing and another I hardly had time to wonder whether there'd been any other outcome of that awful dinner party, whether Mark was any more on terms with the Holbrooks, or whether the Glastonbury Trust was persuading Rex to sell any of his shares; but I did notice Mark looking very preoccupied, and he was back later than usual. I could always tell if he was thinking something about me or when he was thinking about other things. In a way I was glad he had something else to worry about; he'd have less time for me on his conscience.

Then the second weekend he said he had to be away. He was spending Saturday night and part of Sunday with his mother at the house of some man whose name I can't remember; he said he was a second cousin or something, and did I mind if I didn't go because they had to beat out some family matter?

I said no, of course I didn't mind. And of course I went to Terry's.

Perhaps I asked for it, going like that, but I was getting pretty short of money.

When I got there I found only five of them besides myself, and it was a no-holds-barred evening, as Terry called it, meaning that the limit was off the raise. I did all right for a time and then I began to lose. It was easy to lose big money tonight, and I twice borrowed from Terry. Then I got in an awful hand with Alistair MacDonald, when everyone else dropped out early, and I had a full house. I thought from his discards he had threes and we bet against each other until he 'saw' me, and when he put his hand down he had four sevens.

I lost forty-seven pounds that night. This is the last time, I thought. Never again, this has finished me. When we broke off the Jewish film director came across and said:

'D'you know, Mary, you're the best woman poker player I have ever met.'

'Are you being funny?' I said.

'No. There's only one thing wrong.'

'What's that?'

'It isn't card sense you lack. It's a sense of knowing when your luck is in. When I'm playing, I know. It is almost like being aware of a gentle breeze. If it blows for me I know that with reasonable cards I shall make money, with good cards I may make quite a lot of money. If it blows against me I have to cut my coat accordingly. I know that if I pick up a good hand, someone else, against the run of the distribution, will probably have a better.'

'Well, anyway,' said Terry, coming up, 'she ought to be lucky in love.'

'I'll pay you next week, Terry,' I said. 'Or I'll send you a cheque.'

'Take it out of the housekeeping. That's if Mark gives you any.'

'He's generous enough that way.'

'Interesting evening at Rex's, wasn't it?' Terry said, when the film director had gone to pick up his winnings.

'Yes?' I said cautiously.

'Well, yes, I thought so anyway. All that business of a man out of your past. What did Mark really think?'

'Darling,' I said, 'he wasn't out of *my* past. I thought that was clear at the time.'

'Well, yes and no, my dear. It was clear that you'd

had a man in your past. The point that didn't emerge was, had it been Strutt or Mark? They both seemed to be claiming the privilege.'

'Really, Terry, how silly you are—'

'And Strutt's wife looking daggers. I've never seen such a *diverting* situation. And where did your first husband come in? I honestly think you should tell me all about it.'

'There's nothing to tell. I met Mark. We were just friends. When the job at Rutland's came vacant he knew I was a widow and wrote to tell me.'

'Night, Tommy! Night, John!' Terry called, but when I was going to move for my coat he put those fingers of his on my arm. His eyes were that gum colour again. 'Why d'you come here, Marnie?' he said, quite roughly for him.

I looked down at his fingers but didn't answer.

'I know Mark wouldn't want you to come. Things are pretty taut between us just now. Shall I tell you why you come? It's because you're much more like me than like Mark. You breathe freely here. You're not restricted by trying to behave as you think he *wants* you to behave. There's no "naval discipline". You're not put on a charge for whispering when the admiral goes past. Why pretend to yourself? Snap out of it, my dear.'

The others had all gone, all except the MacDonalds who were still in the bedroom. I was surprised at the feeling in Terry's voice; there was no shrug-off about this.

He said: 'I know you're bogus, my dear. What sort

and how much I haven't troubled to find out, even if I could. Why *should* I? It doesn't *worry* me what you've been and what you've done. You could have poisoned your first husband for all I care. In fact, to me it would make you more interesting. Get that in your *head*.'

He pulled me towards him before I could stop him; but if I'd wanted to I could have stopped him kissing me. But I let him. Perhaps I saw it as advance interest on the money I'd had to borrow. But chiefly I wanted to know if I'd changed at all. An awful lot had happened to me in the last few months, and I wondered if it made any difference to the way I felt about him. Or about men generally.

It hadn't. I got away.

He was smiling now. 'Don't come here again if you don't want to; but don't stay away just because Mark tells you. Understand, there's no right or wrong so far as I'm concerned; there's only survival. You've survived. That's what I like about you.'

Since I went back to Roman, I had been trying to play fair with him. Because of me depending on Mark's goodwill to do nothing about Mr Strutt etc. I had to make some effort. I felt Roman would let Mark know if I did nothing to help. It was like being a schoolgirl who'd had one bad report and couldn't afford another until after her birthday.

So we had a sort of honeymoon two weeks, with me trying to be helpful and him not trying to probe too hard. I even went so far as to tell him I'd once stolen money and it worried me I couldn't pay it back, but he didn't seem very excited or impressed by that.

Somehow, though, as time went on, even though he didn't probe, I began to talk. More things began to leak out, not only in my talk but in my memory. I remembered odd bits of events that didn't seem to link together. I remembered looking out of the kitchen window at Sangerford at the rain splashing down the drainpipe; there was a break in the drainpipe and the water gurgled and splashed against the sill. The taste of brandy-snaps was in my mouth, so I suppose I must have been chewing them. And the heavy jangle of trucks was in my ears (we overlooked a railway siding but it wasn't used more than twice a day). There was a man in the kitchen talking to Mother and Mother was at her most frigid. The man was trying to persuade her to do something, to sign something that she didn't want to, and Mam kept saying: 'Part with her? Not if it's the last thing I do!' I could hear her voice so clearly, but I couldn't remember who or what she was being asked to part with.

And another time there was somebody fighting; I don't think I was actually in it, but I remembered the heavy clump of fists and the grunting of men's breath. And there was a woman of about forty I remembered very clearly now. She was probably a nurse from what I could recollect of her clothes, but I was *scared* of her. She'd got braided fair hair that had lost its colour, and a tight upper lip, and she always smelled of stale starch.

One day when things had been dragging rather, Dr

Roman said: 'Let's see, have you one parent alive or both?'

I stopped then. 'What d'you mean? You know they've been dead seventeen years, both of them.'

'I beg your pardon.'

'You're thinking of your next patient, not me.'

'No,' he said, 'I was thinking of you.'

'So you don't believe anything I've told you at all?'

'Yes, I believe a great deal . . .' He paused.

'Well, go on!'

'No, you go on, Mrs Rutland.'

'I've told you over and over! Dad died when I was six. I remember he used to carry me round in his arms. No one's ever carried me round since. Coh! I wish I was back at that age now, and none of this palaver. Then maybe *you* could carry me around instead of leaving me floundering on this couch like a landed seal!'

'You'd like that?'

'I might like it if I really was six and if I knew you better. I don't know a thing about *you*, while all the time you're prying into my life. You just sit there behind me like a – like a father who's no good. What good are you, to me or to anyone?'

'Why was your father no good?'

'I didn't say that! I said *you* were no good. You never advise me! You never tell me anything. You never suggest what I ought to do.'

'As a real father should?'

'Well, yes.'

'But yours did not?'

'Who said not? Now you're putting words in my

mouth! When he died I had a picture book with an elephant on and I didn't say anything but just put my head down on the book and let the tears run on to the elephant. It was a cheap book because there was a sun behind the elephant and my tears made the colour run until it looked as if I'd been crying blood.'

'Who told you, Margaret?'

'Lucy Nye. Mother wasn't there and Lucy told me. I'd been playing with the kitten next door – there was an old wash-tub in the garden and a broken pram – and she called me in and I didn't want to come and I sulked and at first she didn't tell me why she called me in and I sat and read the book.'

Tears were running down my face and I grabbed my bag and took out a handkerchief. This was the second time now I'd cried at these sessions – really, I mean, not for effect. I felt such a fool crying there because I'd remembered something I'd forgotten and because I felt again the twist of the grief inside me, remembering that day and how I knew I'd never have complete protection or shelter or love again.

Mark had invited this Mr Westerman to dinner. Mark said he was a very old friend of his father's, and I rather got the idea that he had something to do with the underground squabble that was going on around Rutland's. He was a lean man of about sixty with a sharp nose and grey hair slicked back. I suppose I ought to have guessed something by the way he buttoned his jacket.

After dinner Mark said: 'I've some business to talk over with Humphry, so I'm going to take him into the study for a time. You'll be all right on your own, Marnie?'

I said I would, and after powdering my nose I helped Mrs Leonard to clear up. As I passed the study I could hear the murmur of voices, Waterman's booming over the top of Mark's.

When I dried the dishes for Mrs Leonard she said: 'The first Mrs Rutland was awfully nice – a real sweetie – but she never did help like you do and it makes a difference, don't it, just that little bit extra. She was one on her own as you might say. Often you would talk to her and all the time she was thinking of something else, you could see. Mr Rutland used to laugh at her – really laugh. You don't often hear him like that now. They used to laugh together. You'd hear them sometimes in the mornings when I was getting the breakfast. It was lovely . . . But by midday every day she was deep in it. Books on the table in the study piled half-way to the ceiling. Then she'd be away three or four days – didn't care how she looked – he used to join her at the weekends. They used to dig up things called barrows, or some such. Funny what interests some folks have.'

I put away the wine glasses. Funny? I wondered what sort of companionship Mark had expected from me. I mean, we laughed sometimes, and of course there was the day-to-day business of living in the same house. But there hadn't been any *real* companionship, not the sort I suppose there might have been. Often he made some move and then froze off short.

Mrs Leonard said: 'Was the lamb *really* all right?'

'Yes. Lovely.'

'I said to Mr Rogers we don't want anything but the best tonight. It's important, because we've got a bigwig coming, and one that'll be on your trail fast enough if you sell us mutton dressed as lamb.' Mrs Leonard tittered at her own wit.

'D'you mean Mr Westerman?'

'Well yes. Chief Constable and all that. I mean to say.'

'Chief . . . Mr Westerman is the Chief Constable? Of – of Hertfordshire?'

'That's right. I think he retired last year, didn't he? I ain't sure, but I think he did. But once one of those always one of those, I say. Not but what I haven't always been law-abiding myself. And what with that great telly aerial you have to put up, you just have to pay your licence these days.'

She went on talking. I went on drying knives and forks. Mark and this Humphry Westerman were in the study.

I felt as if someone had clamped an iron band round the top of my head and was slowly tightening it. I went on drying the things until they were all finished. I looked at the clock and saw that they had been in the study now for fifteen minutes. I thought, I can go in and ask them if they want more coffee, but if I do they'll stop talking and wait for me to leave. And if I don't leave, if I won't take any of the hints, it will only delay whatever they're discussing until another time.

Because if Mark wants to betray me, nothing will stop him sooner or later.

Mrs Leonard said: 'I'd dearly love to have been there. Of course Mrs Bond, who used to work for the Heatons, swore that he used to come home drunk practically every night, and they . . .'

If I went out and stood in the passage I might hear part of the conversation. But Mrs Leonard would be certain to come out of the kitchen and catch me.

There would be enough lamb left for tomorrow's lunch. We could make a casserole. We were nearly out of coffee, that sort you had fresh ground. It was twenty minutes to ten. The study had french windows that looked out on the lawn.

I said: 'I'll just go and look at Forio. He was restless this afternoon.'

'Well, put your coat on, dear. It's damp outside.'

I could hear everything if I crouched down and put my ear against the glass.

Mark was talking. I don't think he'd been talking long – about this – but it was long enough. When it came to the point it was hard to believe. Even in spite of everything I'd thought I must be mistaken. It's hard to believe when you listen and hear your husband betraying you.

'. . . I had no idea, of course, when we were married. But all the same I'm absolutely convinced of one thing – that at the time she committed these thefts she was mentally distraught, temporarily unstable. And she no longer is that. You can see for yourself.'

'She certainly seems a very attractive young woman, but—'

'That was one reason why I asked you here, so that you could see her for yourself. Already there's been a big change since I married her; and I'm absolutely certain that as time goes on, if she hasn't to face criminal charges, she'll become absolutely normal – even more normal than she is tonight.'

'Has there been any—'

'Wait a minute before you say anything. Let me finish. My wife is probably wanted under three different names by the police. There are pretty certainly warrants out for her arrest. But the police have *no clue at all* which can connect the women they want with Marnie. So if she went in and made a full and frank confession to the police of all that she had done, it would be entirely voluntary. That's the first point. Unless she surrenders I'm convinced they haven't a *hope* of tracing her. The second point is that I'd be perfectly willing to repay out of my own pocket all the money that she stole, to the persons or firms from whom she stole it. The third point is that she is already receiving psychiatric treatment, as I told you. But if she were so ordered I know she'd willingly accept any sort of additional treatment that the police or the police doctor – who must have had cases like this before – would prescribe.'

There was a pause and I crouched down as someone's shadow fell across the window, but it was only one of them moving his position.

Mark said: 'The one thing I'm certain of at this stage is that any sort of public charge or trial would be disastrous. Naturally *I'd* hate it like hell, but that's not the important point. She's the one who has to be considered, and at the moment she's very delicately poised. If she goes on living the sort of life she's living now I'm certain she'll become – and remain – a perfectly normal, completely honest woman. But if she's charged and sent to prison you'll be creating a criminal.'

The blood was thumping in my ears as if there was an express train somewhere. I thought, Mark's stretching the case, for his own ends; he's told at least two lies so far.

Westerman said: 'No, thanks, just water please . . . I must say it is a pretty problem, Mark.'

'I'm sorry to let you in for it. I could, of course, have gone to a good criminal lawyer; that would have been the smart thing to do. But it happened I knew you and have known you pretty well all my life, and I thought this was an occasion to come straight to the fountain-head. Nobody can know better than you what the official attitude would be.'

'On that point at least we agree, Mark.'

'But on no other?'

'Oh, I'm not saying that. But I don't think I'm quite clear enough yet on all the facts. There's a lot more I should want to know about your wife before making any comment at all.'

'Such as?'

'You see . . . No, have one of mine this time; they're ordinary gaspers . . . You see – well you obviously want me to reflect the official attitude, don't you. Supposing you had come into my office last year, before I'd retired; suppose that; then there'd be certain questions I'd want to ask right away.'

'Well, ask them now.'

'In the fifteen years I was Chief Constable I often came up against problems in which the human element conflicted with the official attitude; and often there was no completely satisfactory solution. A police official is a very decent human being, but he inevitably becomes a little case-hardened to the hard luck story. You see, he knows, we all know, that there are generally speaking three main classes of thief. The first type, who are the great majority, are very silly and careless. Their thefts are unpremeditated and often quite motiveless. You find them in our prisons, unhappy men and women who have to be locked up in defence of the laws of property and common sense, people who can't keep their fingers to themselves, kleptomaniacs in varying degrees of addiction. Then there is the second class, the people who steal – or more often embezzle – only once or twice in their lives. They are the people who find themselves in a job where money comes through their hands or where the books can be cooked, and they perhaps experiment once or twice and get away with it, so they yield to the terrible temptation and disappear with the staff funds or with money they have manipulated at the bank. Their thefts are not as senseless or as unpremeditated as the first class, but often, indeed usually, they act on impulse, or at least with lack of real preparation and foresight.'

I waited, knowing now what was coming.

'The third group are the clever, the intelligent ones. They are genuinely immoral – that is, they recognize right at the outset just what sort of life they intend to lead, and they proceed to lead it. They usually work out one particular line as their own and they usually go on repeating it, in general design. That's how they get caught. But sometimes they are too clever for us and they go on and on. Now the first thing a police officer would ask himself is, into which category does the present history seem to fall?'

Mark said: 'Yes, I recognize all that. It's very natural and necessary to want to classify criminals. But I think if you try to fit Marnie into any hard and fast group you'd be making a tragic mistake.'

'That may be so. I'm prepared to accept it. But you spoke of psychiatric treatment. Now, I've seen psychiatry and analysis do fine things for the kleptomaniac, the sort of women who will go into a shop and steal twenty-three bottles of tomato sauce or twelve egg-whisks or something equally unprofitable. Such a woman is sick, she's mentally unstable. She may not be curable but it's certainly worth a try. Where does – where does Mrs Rutland come in such a picture? What, for instance, persuaded you she needed treatment before you heard of these thefts?'

It was raining again now, and a cold wind blew the drops in a fine mist over me.

Mark said: 'After our marriage she was awfully – I suppose distressed is the best word I can find for it. She seemed to feel an overbearing sense of guilt and horror.

Sometimes in her confusion she almost turned against me. All this must have been very much on her mind, because she repeatedly told me I should never have married her. I think her confession to me the other night is a direct consequence of her visits to the analyst.'

Well, I thought, he's clever. But this man isn't going to swallow any of it . . .

'How much do you know of her background, Mark? Is she quite open about it?'

'She's become more so. Both her parents were killed in the war and she was pretty well dragged up. If she—'

'Any convictions?'

'Not that I know of. And I've been into it pretty thoroughly with her.'

'Well, of course, that would be the first thing we should check. She doesn't know you're telling me tonight?'

'Not yet.'

The shadow passed the window again. Westerman was walking up and down. 'You see, what really troubles me about your story, and what I know will trouble my successor if you put it to him, is that all these embezzlements, all three of them, were undertaken with the utmost premeditation. This isn't a case of a girl cashier who can't resist the notes crackling in her fingers. In each of these cases she took the job under a false name. In other words she *took* the job with only one end in view.'

'I tell you, she was mentally disturbed at the time. If she—'

'About what? Had she some reason to be mentally disturbed?'

'That I don't know yet. The psychiatrist should be able to tell us in due course.'

'What's worrying me, Mark, is how far you have deceived yourself in this—'

'It's one of the risks I have to take.'

'But it's not one that others – especially the police – will readily take.'

'I know that, but I'm talking to you as an old friend tonight.'

'I agree, but as your friend I have to try to help you to see this straight.'

'And you think I'm not?'

'I can't answer that. I think there's a risk that you may not be doing so.'

Nobody spoke; it was as if they were stopping to cool off.

'Look, Humphry, tell me this. Suppose you were in my position and were convinced of the facts as I've told you them. What would you do?'

'There are only about two things you can do . . . Of course embezzlement is not the most serious of crimes. But it's a felony. You know, I wish she hadn't done it three times; that's really your biggest snag.'

'I know.'

'Well, as I say, there are really only two courses open to you. The simplest and straightest is to go with your wife to our headquarters in Hertford. Ask for Inspector Breward – he's a very reasonable and civilized man –

and get your wife to make a full and complete confession. At the same time make it clear that you intend
to return all the money. She will be charged in the
normal way and will come before a magistrate, who
may deal with her summarily or, if the prosecution ask
for it, will commit her for trial at the next quarter
sessions. In any event get a first-rate man to take your
case, and when she comes up he can go all out for the
many redeeming features. Free and voluntary confession
and surrender to the police, eagerness to return all the
stolen money, the prisoner's deep and heartfelt regret,
newly married woman, first offender, etc. It will sound
very well. If you get a decent judge – and most of them
are only too glad of an opportunity to show they're
human beings – your wife, having pleaded guilty to the
Indictment, will be bound over to keep the peace – and
at once released.'

'What would the chances be?'

'Oh ... better than fifty-fifty. But if by then you
could arrange for her to be with child, I should say at
least four to one against any sentence.'

I was cramped and stiff with cold.

Mark said: 'That makes the whole thing completely
public. And it puts her to all the mental stress of going
through the normal processes of the law. What's the
alternative? Is there one?'

'Well ... off the record, yes, though it's altogether
more complicated. Go with her and make private calls
upon each of the three firms who have lost money,
express your deep sorrow at the trouble she has caused
them and her earnest contrition etc., and while you are

saying this show them your cheque for the amount stolen, press it into their hands and ask them as a special favour to an anxious husband if they will withdraw the charge.'

'That sounds *less* complicated.'

'Perhaps. But it's more tricky. If you follow the first course you are at the most subject to the decision and the outlook of one man, the judge who will try her. I agree it's a risk, he might be a man who feels compelled to make an example of her; but I think it's the risk I personally would take. In the second course you are subject to the views of three lots of people – perhaps three boards of directors. If they are decent people they will take the money back and let the whole matter drop – though there's a snag attached to that – but if there is *one* vindictive one among the three, there is nothing to stop him saying "Thanks, I'll take the money back but I'll still proceed with the charge. We've been put to a great deal of trouble and expense, and it's necessary for the sake of other people, our customers, the rest of our staff, to make an example of this woman." There are plenty of self-righteous people in the world. And once that has happened, if she comes to trial then, she can never stand as well with us, or with the judge.'

'. . . and the other snag?'

'Warrants for the arrest of the thief will have been issued. It would be necessary for the firms concerned to communicate with the police and ask for the warrants to be withdrawn. It would then depend whether the police were in fact willing to withdraw them.'

'Would they not be?'

'Well, they too have been put to trouble and expense. They have their duty to do, their duty to the public as a whole, don't forget. They might at first refuse to get the warrants withdrawn by the Justices concerned . . . Though I suppose in the end, yes, after a period they would agree.'

I was wet through and shivering.

Mark said: 'Well, thank you, Humphry. I've got to mull this over for a bit; then I have to consult her. Whatever I do has obviously got to be with her willing co-operation.'

'. . . Perhaps this psychiatrist fellow might be able to advise you and her. There's only one thing, of course.'

'I think I know what you're going to say.'

'Well, I'm sure you do appreciate that by the act of telling me about your wife you have made me a party to the concealment. The fact that I no longer have an official position doesn't affect that. If I do nothing about what you have told me I'm guilty of misprision of felony – as indeed you will be too.'

'What do you suggest?'

'Obviously there's no immediate hurry, and I shall naturally treat this talk in the strictest confidence. But if you could give me the assurance that you will do something within a reasonable period of weeks . . .'

'I intend to,' Mark said.

I got in and Mrs Leonard exclaimed and said whatever had I been doing getting soaked to the skin like that, and my lovely frock; and I said Forio wasn't well and I thought I'd have the vet in the morning, but anyway don't say anything to Mr Rutland about me being wet, just apologize to them for me and say I have a headache and am going to bed.

I stumbled upstairs and stripped off my things and ran the bath and lay in it for a few minutes trying to take a hold of my nerves and push my brain around. But for once even lying in the water wouldn't do anything. I mean, I was really up against it this time. I got out of the bath and wrapped a towel around me and went into my bedroom. I caught sight of myself in the mirror, a draped half-naked figure with damp hair and eyes too big for her face. My face had shrunk. I dropped the towel and dusted my arms and back with talcum powder. My legs were still damp and I rubbed them. Voices downstairs. Mr Westerman was going.

I went across and fiddled with the portable radio. It came on to Radio Luxembourg and a sudden voice said I ought to turn to the Lord; but instead I turned to some Latin American music on the Light. But I didn't listen to it. Not properly. It was as if I'd overheard I'd got an incurable disease.

I tried to get into my nightdress, but my back must still have been damp because it stuck and I tore the shoulder strap. As I wrestled my way into it I saw my suitcase on top of the wardrobe.

I'd have to go. That was the answer. There wasn't any other now.

I stood on a stool and got the case down; it was nearly empty but there was a bathing cap and some sun-tan oil that I hadn't taken out since Majorca.

I heard a car start. So he was off. Suppose he didn't trust us and rang one of his inspectors tonight.

I went to sort out some things in the dressing-table and drop them in the case. Then I stopped. It wouldn't work. I couldn't leave tonight. More haste etc. I shut the case and clicked the catches and pushed it under the bed.

There was a knock on the door.

'Who is it?'

'Mark!'

'Just a minute.' I shut the drawers and pulled on my dressing-gown. 'Come in.'

He came in. 'Westerman's just gone. Are you all right?'

'Yes . . . I had a headache.'

'What's the matter?'

'Nothing's the matter.'

'You look so pale.'

'I feel pale.'

He stood hesitating. His eyes went round the room and he saw my frock.

'Is your frock wet?'

'I went out to see to Forio.'

'Without a mackintosh?'

'Yes.'

After a minute he said: 'You know what we were talking about?'

'Yes.' I sat on the bed. It creaked as if I was double weight.

He shut the door behind him. 'Did you listen?'

'What does it feel like to behave like Judas?'

'Is that the way you see it?'

'How d'you expect me to see it?'

He dragged over a bedroom chair and sat on it, quite close to me, quietly facing me. I pulled the dressing-gown across my knees.

'Marnie, it isn't a thing I could talk over with you any more. I had to make the choice myself, after weighing up the risks and the probabilities.'

'You did that, I'm sure. Sneaking to the highest policeman you could—'

'I'm not being moral or superior or righteous, I'm just trying to use my common sense. I wish you'd use yours.'

'Perhaps I could if it was your liberty that was at stake.'

'If it was my liberty that was at stake I'd do exactly the same. Don't you see, you can't just go on living in a dream world until something else happens? I'm by no means sure that Strutt is satisfied by what we've told him. What's to stop him making some further inquiries? It's no good appealing to the judge then, or offering to pay the money back. *We* have to make the first move. Otherwise you'll get three years as certainly as you are sitting here looking so hurt and so beautiful. You wouldn't have the luxury of three baths a day, and daily rides, and poker with Terry; and maybe that lovely fresh skin would react badly to three years indoors—'

'D'you think I don't know all that!' I shouted, getting up. 'Don't you see what you're doing – what you've flaming-well done! If I go to prison it'll be your bleeding fault and no one else's! You've ratted on me – like a dirty rat – like a dirty crawling rat – a dirty filthy crawling—'

He got me by the shoulders and shook me. He shook me till my teeth clicked.

'You're terrified, you fool. I know that! So would I be. But can't you use your head at all! This way, you stand a good chance of coming out of it with *no harm whatever*. If we act now, but *only* if we do, *only* if we spike their guns by following up what I've begun tonight, you may be absolutely free.'

I tried to wrench myself away. I haven't lived delicate and I know how to fight and I tried to get away. So while we ranted at each other we scrapped too.

So when he'd got my arms behind my back I gave up and just stood there and he said: 'D'you know I understand you better when you go back to being a street urchin . . .'

'You filthy—,' I said.

He kissed me. I could have spat at him but I didn't.

'Listen again,' he said. 'I agree with Westerman that open confession is the safest way. But I know you won't stand for that. And I don't want it either. The way to get you free without stigma is by approaching these people privately. *I'll* approach them to begin, not you. I'm certain— Are you listening?'

'Westerman'll go straight to his own kind tonight.'

'No, he won't. He won't act even in a month – I know that. But *we* must. Aren't you convinced?'

'Why should I be? It's just a dirty . . .'

'Won't you try to trust me?'

'No!'

In this fight we'd had, my dressing-gown had slipped off one shoulder, and my shoulder was bare because the strap of my nightdress had given way before.

He put his hand on my shoulder and then to my disgust suddenly brushed the nylon down and put his hand right over my breast. He put his hand right round it. It was just as if he held something that belonged to him.

'Let me go,' I said.

He let me go. I dragged my dressing-gown up to my throat. He looked at me with a sort of grief, as if the steeliness had gone out of him.

At the door he stopped and turned the handle a couple of times, looking down at it. 'Marnie, you said just now, would I have done the same if my liberty had been at stake? Well it is. Or if not my liberty, my happiness. I'm gambling with that just as much as I am with yours. You see, I can't disentangle myself from you – even though I've tried.'

I sat on the bed again. He said: 'It's my future as well. If you fail I fail. Try to remember that, can you?'

When I didn't answer he said: 'Try hard. I don't like fighting you. I still think of myself as on your side. I want to fight for you. In fact I will whether you want me to or not. We're in this together.'

I thought when he'd gone how crazy it all was that even while he betrayed me he still wanted me. *He* wanted me, Terry wanted me, the police wanted me, Mother wanted me, all in their several different ways. I'd nothing to give him back; not Terry, nor the police, nor maybe even Mother any longer. It was best to go.

CHAPTER SIXTEEN

ON MY way to see Roman on Tuesday I called at Cook's and asked them what was the easiest way to get from Torquay to the Continent? Well, the young man said, how did I want to go and where? I said, somewhere in France. Mid-France, maybe, or Paris. I wasn't particular. He thumbed through some booklets and said, well the easiest way was to come back to London, but if I *wanted* to start from Torquay then the best route was from Exeter airport to Jersey. I would have to spend a night in Jersey and then I could fly on the next day to various places in France and Spain.

'Nothing from Plymouth?'

'By sea? Well, possibly. There's the French Line.'

'What's that?'

'Atlantic liners call at Plymouth about twice weekly and pick up passengers for Le Havre. We can book you right through to Paris. You leave Plymouth midday, spend a night on board and get to Paris next day in time for lunch.'

'What days do they leave?'

'Well there's one next Tuesday and one on Saturday.'

'Is there ever one on a Friday?'

'Yes, the following Friday, the eighteenth. The *Flandre*. That's in ten days' time. Shall we book you that?'

'I don't know the language,' I said. 'I suppose I shall be able to get along.'

He smiled. 'Oh, yes, miss – madam. You can get along with English anywhere in Paris. But would you like our courier to meet you at the station?'

'No, thanks.'

Then there was the business of foreign money and a passport. He gave me the address of the chief passport office, and I went out of Cook's and straight into one of those quick places in Oxford Street where you can have your photo done in a few hours. I said I'd call back later. But the question that worried me a bit was, what Justice of the Peace, or solicitor or bank manager or doctor was going to testify that they had known me X years and that the details I was going to fill in about myself were correct?

I was ten minutes late at Dr Roman's, but when I got there I gave him good value. I was inspired that day. I free associated like a junkie. I tried to think of all the dirty stories that had ever been whispered to me in the gutters, the attic bedrooms and the waste plots of Plymouth. And I told him a lot of invented dreams full of gorgeous symbolism. I told him I'd dreamt I was the third largest salmon in the world and that I was swimming round in an enormous glass bowl, and that outside the bowl were a whole lot of men trying to reach in and catch me, but I kept slipping through their fingers. (And while I was telling this I thought, what does it matter about getting somebody to testify to the truth of my statements for my passport? I can testify myself. Who's to know my writing?)

I told him I dreamt I was walking down a street, well dressed but I knew I had no underwear on, and I must buy some in case I was knocked down by a car. I turned in at a shop, but when I got in I found all the shoppers were rats. I could feel them running backwards and forwards over my bare feet. (And while I told him that I thought, Mark's keys, the keys of the printing works and the safe, those he leaves on his dressing-table every night. There's two Yale keys and a big ordinary key and two small ones like those for suitcases and a brass key.)

I told him I dreamt I was in a condemned cell waiting to be hanged for something I hadn't done, and I think I'm going to get a reprieve; and there's a knock on the door and the wardress comes in and she says, 'I think I'd better finish this off now,' and she snatches up a long knife and comes at me, and I've nothing to defend myself with and I struggle with her and get hold of the blade of the knife in my hands and feel it cut deep into my hands and I feel the blade grating on the bones of my fingers. (And while I tell him this I think, I'm going hunting with Mark and Rex next week. I'll have to get the keys copied by then. The Thursday night I can leave and the day after that see Mother and then cross to France. That's the way it's got to be.)

When the session was nearly over Dr Roman said: 'Last week we were making real progress. What's the matter today?'

'Nothing. I feel rather happy.'

'I think you ought to distinguish between being happy and being what the Americans call trigger-happy. Has something happened to upset you?'

'Heavens, no, I'm going hunting for the first time next week and I'm rather excited about it, that's all. Do you know the Thorn Hunt? One of the most popular, they say. I'm riding my horse over there the day before, and Mark's being lent one by the MFH. Mark's cousin, Rex Newton-Smith, has invited us. It's really quite an occasion for me. Isn't that what well-bred people call it – an occasion?'

He got up and prowled across the room. His black suit was shiny at the elbows. 'When you oppose me so implacably, you're really only opposing your own cure. It delays your progress. But of course it is only another form of protest from that part of you that doesn't want to be cured.'

'What part's that?'

He looked at me. 'Such protests are not altogether discouraging because they show that the core of the resistance is becoming sensitive to pressure. Next time perhaps we shall be able to recover the lost ground.'

'At five guineas a visit I suppose there's no hurry.'

'None at all. But I have a long waiting list. You need only come just as long as you want to.'

I went to Petty France and saw one of the passport officers. He said if I got the form filled in and signed there should be no delay. I went to a big ironmongery shop in the city and asked to see some keys. They had a big choice. The Yales were easy, as any Yale looks much the same as any other. I bought two or three brass ones and two or three key-rings because I couldn't remember just what Mark's was like. I told them I wanted the keys for amateur theatricals.

That night I argued with Mark. I asked him please not to do anything about going to see those people and paying the money back, not for a week or two. I said it had taken me by surprise and I had to get it straight in my own mind. I said two weeks wouldn't make any difference – not all that difference. I said perhaps in two weeks I could make up my mind to come with him. If I went to these people *myself* and they saw how sorry I really was . . .

He wasn't easy to persuade but in the end he agreed to hold everything for the time being . . .

My biggest problem of all was Forio. I couldn't take him with me, that was what hurt most. He was my oldest friend, in a way my only friend. I mean we seemed to understand each other just like that. Our moods were the same. I could have ridden him anywhere almost without a bridle. When he put his head against mine it was the gesture of a friend who asked nothing but my friendship in return.

I couldn't even sell him to someone I would be sure would care for him, because I couldn't let anyone know I was going. The best I could do was write to the Garrods the day before I left enclosing money and asking them to have him back. If I *gave* him to them it might be the best thing, but I couldn't bear the thought of him being used as a hack.

I went into Mark's bedroom a couple of times that week when he was dressing and got a better look at the keys and the ring. On the Tuesday I skipped Roman altogether but went into the city again and bought some more keys. All I had to do was get keys and a ring that he would see on his dressing-table without noticing the difference. It wasn't hard. I collected my passport. The vicar of Berkhamsted was called Pearson. Nobody at the passport office queried his signature. I got my ticket from Cook's and picked up some French money. I was scared of the whole thing, of being in a foreign country with only a few hundred pounds, of not knowing the language, of coming to a bad end.

I wondered what Mother would say when I went down and told her she'd been living on stolen money for the last four years.

She was tougher than she looked. Anyway, I'd got to do it. It was better she should hear it from me first than from the police.

On the Monday Terry rang me from the office.

'Doing anything this afternoon?'

'Why?'

'I want to talk to you.'

'What's the matter?'

'Can we meet for tea? Neutral ground.'

'If you like . . . St Albans? There's a café, The Lyonesse.'

'Right. Let's meet at four.'

When I got there he was waiting for me. His eyes had that funny angry look they'd had when we talked about Mark. I'd been afraid he might want the money I owed him but he never mentioned it. When he'd ordered tea he said: 'How much d'you know about what's happening at Rutland's? Are you behind it?'

'Behind what?'

'Well, those *clever* visits of yours to my poker parties which are supposed to be against Mark's wishes. Was it all a *glorious* little sham so that you could spy on me on his behalf?'

'Spy on you? How could I?'

'Mean to say you don't know Mark has sold out of Rutland's?'

'Sold out? What are you *talking* about? He'd never do that!'

'Oh, yes, he has – or next door to it. He told us at the board meeting this morning. He and Rex have sold out to the Glastonbury Trust.'

I stared at him. 'But I thought that was what you wanted.'

He laughed. 'Well, it wasn't. You've played us quite *the* dirtiest trick, haven't you?'

Tea came. I poured him a cup. He said: 'You read some letters of father's once. He told me. I suppose you told Mark what was in them, my dear.'

'I still don't understand.'

'Always the Rutlands have had control of the firm, *effective* control, with Rex's co-operation. It isn't a good thing for any company. But when Tim Rutland was killed, the old man, Mark's father, more or less let the reins slip, and for *years*, for *years*, my father kept things going. I helped him. They still had ultimate control but they never exercised it. I grew up to feel that we were building something worth while, that *all* our efforts meant something. But then along came this superannuated naval lieutenant who immediately tried to take all control in his *own* hands and turned the business into a glorified retail shop and threw his weight about as if he was fighting *the* battle of Trafalgar. It was particularly intolerable for my father, who's had thirty years' experience of printing and knows more about it in his little finger than all the tribe of Rutlands put together.'

I was quite startled at the venom in his voice. 'But I thought it was you who got this Malcolm Leicester interested in the business in the first place?'

'So we did. We knew the Newton-Smiths would not sell to us but we thought they would sell to an outsider. We thought that the Glastonbury Trust would be an enormous asset as a big minority holder. With a nominee of theirs on the board, we could between us slightly overweigh the Rutland interest and preserve a proper balance of control.'

With what had happened this last week and what I'd been doing yesterday and today, this thing he was talking about hardly seemed to concern me. I mean it was remote, like a happening in the life of one of the Mollie Jeffreys. In my mind I'd already run away.

'And what's wrong with Mark selling out? – though I can't believe he's done it.'

'He's going to do it. The Glastonbury Trust, instead of being a big minority holder who could act in co-operation with us or not at all, becomes virtually *owner*, and I and my father will be reduced to ciphers.'

My tea was too sweet. I added some water.

'But isn't that just what you've been trying to do to Mark?'

Terry fiddled with his tie. 'So you are on his side, my dear. I just wanted to *know*.'

'I'm on nobody's side. It doesn't concern me. Why should it? It's Mark's money. He does what he wants with it . . . Anyway, why are you telling me all this?'

'What sort of influence have you got with him?'

I stared. 'Over this? None at all.'

'I'm not so sure. Look, Mary, it's this way. The Glastonbury Trust has made an offer of seventy-two shillings for all our shares. Mark told us this morning. A circular's being printed to send to our outside share-holders, recommending acceptance. It will go out next Monday. There's still time to draw *back*, my dear.'

My mind was wandering again; I wasn't really interested. Who was he talking about?

'You think I could stop him? You're crazy. Why should I want to?'

Terry leaned back and watched a girl leaving the shop. His eyes started on her legs and worked up.

'*Why* did you marry Mark?'

I shrugged.

'You're not his type. I've told you before. You're more my type. Up against it. Know what they called me at school? Turkey. Because I'd got a red neck. That sets you off on the wrong *foot*, doesn't it?'

'Maybe.'

'Somehow *you* got off on the wrong foot too. I don't

know how but it hasn't left you feeling too good about life. Not *sure* of yourself. I'm never sure of myself, even though I act that way. D'you know the first girl I ever *had*, all the time I was thinking, she's really bored and disgusted. It puts one off, the knowledge that one is – different in a *disgusting* way. It's like getting out of step early on in the march.'

'You're making a lot out of nothing.'

'That's what you think. Oddly enough, I get on well with Dad. I'm sorry for him and even sometimes admire him. He held the firm together when it would otherwise have gone to pieces. But the rest of mankind . . . you've got to despise 'em before they despise you.'

He went on talking for a bit, off and around the point. He hadn't much to say, but again I felt a sort of link that he was trying to make stronger. But it wasn't anything he actually said, because I hardly listened. If I *had* listened I should have thought him a fool for supposing I couldn't see the truth, which was that in some way Mark had turned the tables on him. How he'd done it I didn't quite understand and I didn't care. I didn't care for Terry's problems at all, nor for Mark's. The firm of Rutland & Co. meant less to me than last week's laundry bill.

Maybe I should have paid more attention to the fact that he was talking to me at all. Asking my help and sympathy really was grasping at a straw, and the proverb says drowning men etc. That didn't register. All I knew was that he was plugging at something that went deeper than what you might call logic. We were like two houses on opposite sides of the street connected by a land-line.

I didn't mention it to Mark that evening or the next day. Most of the time I was busy with my own thoughts. And part of Tuesday I was riding Forio over to the Newton-Smiths for the Wednesday meet. That was a horrible ride because I knew it was the last time I should ever be alone with him. Wednesday, riding in a crowd, wouldn't be the same.

I found when it came to the point there were other things I should miss. There was the Richards family and the blind men. Even in a short while I'd got friendlier with them than anyone I ever remembered before. And it wasn't unpleasant being your own mistress, having your own house, and a nice house at that.

. . . Mark was talkative at breakfast. We were driving over and the meet was to be at ten. Seeing Mark like this, I realized how quiet and moody he'd been these last weeks. And this was next to the last breakfast I should ever have with him. Tomorrow night I was going to go into his bedroom when he was undressing and while he wasn't looking change over the keys and . . .

I said: 'Is it true you've sold Rutland's, Mark?'

He looked up and smiled. 'More or less anyway. An offer has been made. We're recommending all share-holders to accept it.'

'But why? I thought you would never do that.'

'So did I a few months ago. And then I thought, how ever long I work there and whatever I do, we shall never be free from the friction that poisoned half my father's life. And I thought, what's in a name? Let it go.'

'But what will you do?'

'Probably go into partnership with someone else. There are one or two printers I'm interested in who do some of their own publishing. That's more attractive to me. I was going to tell you, but I waited till the whole thing was settled.'

'And what will the others do?'

'Rex? He's drawing out as I am. Anyway he has plenty of money. The Holbrooks? If they want to stay in I'm sure they can keep their seats on the board.'

'Do they feel badly about it?'

'This move? Yes. But I honestly don't see what they have to complain of; they first interested Malcolm Leicester. Of course Rex has been the organizer of this coup.'

'He's smarter than he looks.'

'Except for the first two meetings with Leicester I've tried to do everything openly. The choice is put fairly before the shareholders now.'

'Yes. Yes. I see.'

He got up. 'It's time we were off . . . It's been a big wrench, but now I've decided, it's like throwing off a hair shirt. It's pretty unpleasant, Marnie, to have this to contend with month after month. And I honestly think that the Holbrooks, once they've swallowed the first pill, will find it better too. Jealousy's a nasty thing: it's bad to suffer under and it's bad to feel oneself.'

I got up slowly. He said: 'Marnie, I hope you'll let me start approaching Strutt and the other two firms pretty soon. I want to go and see them on my own. I think I could bargain.'

'How?'

'Well, it's something Westerman couldn't suggest because it's illegal. But I could put it that I would return the money stolen from them *provided* they agreed not to prosecute.'

I shook my head. 'It isn't much to bargain with. They'll have been insured.'

'Probably. But not certainly. Everyone doesn't do everything he should. Anyway it's worth trying.'

The sun was breaking through thick misty clouds as we drove down. Just before we got there he said: 'How did you know about Rutland's?'

'Dawn told me.'

'She doesn't know. None of the staff has any inkling yet.'

I sat in silence.

He said: 'When you tell a silly lie like that I get depressed all over again.'

We were following a horse-box now which was evidently going to the same place as ourselves.

He said: 'If you'll only *trust* me there's no limit to what we can do, how far we can go together. If you don't trust me then we've no solid ground under our feet at all. We're still struggling in the same dreary morass where we began.'

He overtook a farmer on a big strong bay which looked as if it might not be very fast but would last for ever.

'Was it Terry who told you?'

'Yes.'

'So you still see him?'

'No. He telephoned and suggested it. We had tea at a café in St Albans.'

'Why did he want to see you?'

'He seemed to think I might be able to persuade you to back out of this deal.'

'And are you going to try?'

'No. I know it's no use.'

'But you might if you thought it would be? Whose side are you on, Marnie?'

I stared out of the window. Once again I didn't seem to care. It wasn't my concern. 'Isn't this where we turn left?'

'If you are on the other side, say so.'

'No,' I said. 'I'm on your side, Mark, in this.'

But I suppose I didn't have enough feeling in my voice, because he looked at me as if he knew it wasn't true.

The meet was in the grounds of a big house called Thornhill. It was a Victorian place, I should think, built of brown brick with a lot of ivy climbing up it and chimneys as tall as rows of pencils. At the side was this large conservatory with a glass roof the shape of the covers you see in cafés to keep the flies off the cakes.

There were quite a lot of people already about when we rode up with Rex Newton-Smith. There were ten cars and four horseboxes and two trailers and about a dozen people mounted or dismounted and a farmer or two, hands in corduroys. Before I agreed to come I'd asked Mark to find out if Arthur Strutt was a hunting man but it turned out he wasn't, so I was safe from that risk.

Mark was on a big brown horse that was pretty restive so I steered Forio away from him because Forio, although the sweetest-tempered thing, easily caught nerves. Then a man came along in a velvet cap and a scarlet coat, and Rex introduced him as one of the Masters. We all got down and talked for a bit, but I didn't listen much to what was being said because this was all new to me and, although I was still thinking more about tomorrow than today, I was glad in a way to experience it all once before I bolted. I'd seen horses and dogs streaming over the Gloucestershire countryside but somehow had never come full tilt into them and certainly had never been one of them before.

Just then the hounds came, bobbing and making strange noises and waving their tails all ways. Then suddenly there seemed to be more people everywhere, people talking, people tightening girths, people mounting, a huntsman talking to the dogs, three men in bowler hats and yellow breeches, horses pawing the soft turf, a girl in a blue habit – I'd like one like that – on a horse with white stockinged forefeet, an old man with a crab-apple face; Forio was excited now, he'd never been in so much company; I checked him as well as I could with one hand; just in time we moved off.

Everybody moved off talking, chattering to each other like a Sunday picnic, waiting their turn at the gates, then off down a rutted muddy lane. They were a queer-looking lot, a good many of them ugly, even the women, and hard in a way; I mean tough. I'd swear none of them had ever been short of anything important all their lives. 'Good crowd,' Rex said to me in his squeaky voice. 'More than usual for a Wednesday. It's the weather I suppose.' The sun was still trying to shine, weakly, like one of those poached eggs that come pale. Mark was just behind me but his horse was straining; it was one of those animals that always must lead, like some men; it's a question of temperament. Forio was still lively, kept trying to rear. 'Hullo, Mark,' somebody said. 'It's a long time.'

We got to the end of the lane, just by a coppice. Somebody in the front had stopped and everybody was jostling each other. 'They've found!' a man in front said, and it was like an electric current going through everyone. A man next to me was biting his bottom lip and trying to edge forward even though there was no room. Then there was a movement up front and people were turning off through a gate and up the hill beside the coppice.

Suddenly there was this horn. I'd heard it before in the distance, but it's different when you're part of it. The hounds must have gone up the hill because everyone was following, but it was hard to get a move on; it was like driving a car in Oxford Street; I thought I'd sooner have a good clean canter any day.

Mark caught up with me, still checking this big brown horse of his. 'All right?' he asked, but his eyes were still cloudy with what had been said in the car. I nodded.

Suddenly we were through and galloping up the field. It was only a couple of hundred yards or so before we came up with the leaders who had checked, or whatever it's called, but it did us good to go full out, the wind whipping at my face; and I got a bit of nasty satisfaction out of the fact that Forio left Mark's mount behind.

'I'm thinking the fox has swung left-handed into Cox Wood,' said a man in a bowler, looking me up and down as if he liked the look of me. 'If so we shall lose him. Scent's always poor in Cox Wood.'

For about half an hour we jogged about, up and down fields and lanes, squelching and splashing, and waiting our turn and getting in each other's way, and I thought, there are too damned many of us altogether, and I thought, well done fox, you've had the laugh of us, stay in your hole, don't be a fool and give those hounds a chance to show how smart they are.

But at twelve they found another fox and this time it seemed the crazy thing hadn't been so careful. The horn began to blow like mad, and I followed Mark over a fence, noticing that his horse took it easily, and suddenly the field seemed to spread out and we were racing along level open ground beside a railway embankment. In the distance you could see the hounds and the man called the whip, I think, and the huntsman and about three other riders; then there was the Master and two more, then about a hundred yards behind came Mark and me, but I was leaving him again, and a cluster of about ten others. The rest had been unlucky and had got in a tangle at a bridge.

We had to slow at another gate and then the

ploughed field that came next was too heavy for anything but a trot. I was sweating, and I was enjoying myself now. The difference from just riding was that someone else told you what you were going to do, and it was exciting, and just for the minute you didn't think about what was being chased.

We went downhill then full-pelt and almost caught the hounds, which were scrambling and wriggling through a wire fence. Some of the riders in front of me were making a detour to get through a gate, but I saw the MFH take the wire fence and come to no harm so I set Forio at it and we went over. He never as much as stumbled and I'd gained on the rest of the field. I heard a crash and rumble behind me but it wasn't Mark, it was the man in the bowler; Mark had got over all right and was only twenty yards behind.

I'd turned at the wrong moment because a low branch nearly had my hat off, and a bit of it scratched my ear and neck. There were only three ahead of me now, and I was out of breath with excitement. The hounds had checked but only for half a minute and they were swinging in a sort of wide arc, past a farmhouse with a small boy leaning over a gate, across a tarred road and down a narrow lane past three cyclists who shouted and waved, over a thick fence of blackthorn and through a wood where pigeons were fluttering and a dog barked. Then out in the open again.

My eyes were watering with the speed, and Forio was white-flecked and his flanks were heaving, and we came to another bigger fence and this time just cleared it. The three men were still ahead of me but I'd gained on them. And then I saw the hounds. And then I saw the fox.

The ground was rising again, and I saw the fox black against the green of the short grass, and I could see he was nearly done. I saw him turn his head and I saw him sink once and then go on running. There must have been getting on for four dozen hounds. All the time they'd been baying, that odd sound; but now it changed somehow. They could see the fox and they'd got him, so it was a sort of different cry, and their hackles were up and their tails seemed to stiffen. And I thought, he can't get away from them. Whichever way he goes, it's open country. He's run well but now he's tired and done up and there's nothing for him left but a horrible death. Perhaps he's got young at home but he'll never see them again. And I thought no one will help him. No one.

I gave Forio the whip, trying to hurry him forward, with some sort of dim mad idea that I could stop what was going to happen. But all that happened of course was that Forio put on an extra spurt so that I was nearer and could see it all better. The hounds were only a few yards behind the fox now, and he'd no more cunning or strength left in him and he turned snarling for his last stand; and it was fifty to one. Just one minute he was there, a single lonely animal against all the rest, and then suddenly he was swamped in a mass of hounds snarling and fighting and bloodily tearing his life out of him.

Somehow I'd come to a stop, or Forio had stopped for me. The huntsman had gone in with his whip, beating the hounds off the dying fox, so that he could save the brush. That was all he cared about. And then the other three horsemen came up with them and hid the scene so I couldn't see it any longer. And then others came up, Mark with them, and the afternoon was full of blowing panting horses and people talking and people laughing, and somebody waved the fox's brush in the air and there was a cheer, and everybody was saying what a good run it had been. And the afternoon was full of laughter and satisfaction and cruelty and death.

'My God, you made a fine run of it, ma'am,' a man said to me. 'If you ever want to sell that horse, ma'am, do let me know. You quite outdistanced me.'

I didn't answer. Mark said smiling: 'You rode beautifully.'

I turned away because my throat was choked and I really wanted to cry although I couldn't quite. Because all these people were happy because an animal had been chased over miles and miles and then cruelly torn to pieces with no chance of escape. I looked at them all, the way I'd looked at them just as we were starting; they were all well fed, well turned out, just the way I'd seen them before. But now I seemed to be able to see something more in their expressions. They were the sort of people who would have sat in an arena and seen men tortured or horses gored or any other show of cruelty without being personally touched at all. They hadn't any real feelings at all. All they wanted was their own pleasure.

Mark was talking to Rex who had just come up.

Rex's face was a lot redder than the sun, and he kept mopping the sweat off his forehead and neck.

Perhaps there was something wrong with me just then; I'd like to think so because it all got out of proportion. I think I was *feeling* more just then than I'd ever felt before in my life. Instead of being able to stand aside from things, as I always used to be able to, this was right in my stomach like a knife. It was happening terribly to me.

And now these people, not satisfied with one kill, were getting ready to move off again. Another fox was going to be hunted to its death. And I fancied that, if they knew the truth, that I'd preyed on them, just the way a fox'll prey on chickens, stealing a few pounds from their banks and their offices, they'd just as quickly turn and hunt me. That fat wrinkled little man with his brass-buttoned coat and white stock and peaked velvet cap, that man looking after the hounds with his whip and his horn, could just as easily set them on me. And once the chase began, once the hounds had started baying, I could gallop and gallop and twist and turn, but I could never get away from them until I too was spent and they came at me with their tearing mouths. But the human beings, so called, would stop that. They'd step in and take me carefully away and very soberly bring me before a judge, and someone would pretend to put my case, although really he'd have his tongue in his cheek all the time, and then someone else would speak for the police, and I would be called to answer questions; but it would all be according to the so-called rules of evidence and I would never be given a chance to explain as I could explain in private and given proper time; and then the judge would speak a few words summing up and he would say, 'Margaret Elmer, you stand convicted on three charges of embezzlement and fraudulent conversion, it is my duty to sentence you to three years imprisonment', and I would be led carefully and firmly away.

It was all part of society – what was allowed and what was not allowed. Prison was allowed but they didn't consult me. Hunting was allowed but they didn't consult the fox.

So they were all moving off again, and I couldn't look at the blood of the fox staining the short grass. But Forio more or less turned on his own and went with the rest. I don't know how long we jogged on, but instead of it getting better inside me it got worse. The thing was boiling up in me like water inside a pan with its lid tied on. The jostling and the neighing and the creak of leather, and the high brittle voices of the women, and the squashing noise of mud and the yelping of the hounds, it all made it worse. 'You ought to distinguish between being happy and being trigger-happy,' Roman said. 'At five guineas a visit,' said the jailer, 'I have a long waiting list.' 'All right, damn you, have it your own way,' said a man near me, wheeling his horse. Forio whinnied and nearly had me off. 'They've found again!' a girl squeaked. 'What super luck!' 'How much do you know of her background, Mark?' Westerman asked. 'Well, she was pretty well dragged up.' Was a fox dragged up? Was it any more dragged up or I any more dragged up than a hound; was its mother less loving? Was my mother less loving than Mark's? To Hell with their damned patronizing beastliness. All of them. Hard-mouthed, cruel hunters. What had I done half as bad as kill a fox?

We were off again. The whole damned herd of us, off at a yelling gallop, the horn twanging, people thrusting their heels in, mud flying, faces alight with the blood-lust. We came to a fence and Forio checked and then took it perfectly; I suppose I helped, I don't know. Across another field full pelt and over a ditch and landing among some broken branches: nearly down. The whole hunt had swung right, up rising ground towards a wood. I jerked Forio's head left. He didn't like it. I dug my heels in and we galloped off and away from the rest. I heard Mark's voice: 'Marnie! This way!'

I went on. Forio gathered speed, fairly thundering down the slope. I didn't think I could ever stop him; I didn't want to. We breasted a blackthorn hedge, fairly flying.

'Marnie!' There was the beat of hooves behind me; Mark was following.

I gave Forio his head. He'd been winded when he got to the fox but in half an hour he'd recovered, and he was strung up with all the excitement. He'd never gone so fast. But Mark wasn't far behind. He was coaxing or whipping some extra speed out of his brown horse.

We were still going downhill. There was a lane on ahead with an open gate this side with a line of willows behind. Somehow I slid or slithered through the gate, hooves striking sparks, there was no gate on the other side but the hedge was low; anyway I couldn't have stopped Forio there. We took it and over into the next field. Mark followed and had somehow gained. I heard him shout: '*Marnie!*' again.

I let Forio go across the next field. It was as if not just Mark but all the things he stood for were after me, as I'd fancied they could be.

The next hedge was higher than any so far; and in the sort of flickering way these things come to you I saw that the willows were alongside a river or stream. I couldn't see whether there was room to land in between, but I knew Forio was going to try and I knew I was going to let him. Mark shouted behind me again and then we took off.

Half over I knew we were for it. The other side was a good four feet lower on to stones and sand, with a twist bringing the river almost up to the wall. Forio saw his danger and seemed to try to check; he'd have landed square but the height did it; he came down on his forelegs and went right over; I went up, and while I was falling I saw Mark somersaulting after me.

I just missed the river, crumpled backwards into the low willow branches, came head down on the ground but gently, breaking and bending branches, and my hat took the worst. I just hadn't any breath. That was the only bad thing at first. You had to gasp and strain to stay alive. Then I heard something or someone screaming. I tried to claw myself round and sit up. Mark nowhere. Mark's horse in the river up to its hocks, shaking itself, unhurt. Forio was still down. The noise, that unbearable noise was coming from Forio.

He was trying to get up but he couldn't. He was wriggling and fighting to get up but he couldn't. I pulled myself up and fell down again, got up again, staggered towards him. Then I saw Mark. He was lying very still. I ran towards Forio. He was lying there and rolling his eyes like a mad horse and the foam was flecking out of his mouth; and as I got to him I saw one of his front legs. Something white was sticking out through the skin.

I went up to him and knelt beside him and tried to unfasten his bridle. His mouth bit at me in a sort of agony, and I thought of that dog that had been run over in Plymouth, that mongrel that had bitten right through my sleeve. I got his bridle off somehow; someone else was making a noise and it was me; I was crying out loud as if I was hurt; I looked back and saw Mark hadn't moved. His head was down, almost flat in the mud. I got to my feet again and stared, and it was like being pulled both ways by ropes, like that torture they'd had in the Middle Ages, being pulled apart; but it wasn't my *body* that had to suffer. If only Forio would stop that terrible whinnying scream; and he kept trying to get up. Mark was dead perhaps; and Forio was alive and needed me. If I could hold his head, comfort him somehow, hold him till help came; Mark didn't need me, Mark was dead; Oh Jesus help me; help me to comfort my old friend. I was on my knees and I was crawling towards Mark.

He wasn't dead. The mud was plastered all down one side of his face and in his mouth. I tore his scarf or stock or whatever it's called and began to wipe the mud away from his mouth. He could only just breathe; in fact he was suffocating because the mud had got up his nose too.

'Gawd, you're 'urt!' said a voice. 'I thought you'd took a almighty tumble!'

A man, a farmer or something. 'Get help!' I screamed.

'Let me see,' he said. He slithered down the wall, looked at Forio. 'Gawd what a mess, whatever made you come that way?'

'Stop him screaming!' I said. 'For Christ's sake stop him screaming. Go and get an ambulance! Telephone!'

Pointing to Mark: 'Is 'e all right? 'E looks pretty bad. Something broken?'

'I don't know; I can't *leave* him. Look after my *horse*! Go for help! Don't ask questions.'

He scratched his head and then went scrambling up to the hedge again. I began to drag Mark out of the mud. He was right out, and as pale as paper, and perhaps he was going to die after all; and I knew what was going to happen to Forio; I knew, and if I thought of it I should die too, and for some reason until they came it was important to stay alive.

I dragged Mark as far as the stones, and I was panting and groaning myself, and I didn't look round, but thank Christ Forio had gone a bit quieter. I unfastened Mark's collar and dragged my torn coat off and put it under his head; and then there was a noise I thought I'd never want to hear again, the thud of hooves. I left Mark there and stood up and hung on to

a branch of a tree and was sick, and then I looked at
Forio again, being quieter as if he knew he'd never walk
again; and Rex said over the wall: 'My God, what a
mess. Jack, go for a doctor!'

'Somebody's gone,' I said, and wanted to faint and
couldn't. Now that 'they' were here I did so badly,
badly want to faint over and lose myself, faint and be
just another body for them to look after; but I wasn't
helped that way. I stood there and saw it and watched
it all, to the bitter and terrible inevitable end. After all
it was my fault so perhaps it was right that I should.

CHAPTER SEVENTEEN

I WATCHED Forio being shot, and I went in the ambulance with Mark to the hospital and I was treated for bruises and shock and then sent home. It was easy really. Everybody said, poor girl, her horse bolted, she's terribly brave, I do hope Mark will be all right; darling, the best thing for you is to go straight to bed. You have someone at home? Don't worry about Mark, he's in the best possible hands, I'm sure he'll be better in the morning. The surgeon said: 'We really can't tell you yet, Mrs Rutland; it's severe concussion. His arm has been set, but he hasn't broken anything else. By tomorrow morning we shall be much better able to judge.'

So I went home. And nobody blamed me at all.

I went home, and bubbles of pain and grief and sheer hurt kept rising and bursting in my heart. And Mrs Leonard who'd been sent for from the village came up and fussed, and then Mrs Rutland rang up. Mrs Rutland behaved exactly the way all the mothers must have done in all the wars England has ever fought, when they hear their son has been wounded and want to comfort an anxious daughter-in-law, even though they are really much more anxious themselves. She did it just right, and you couldn't fault her. And you couldn't fault me either. After all, how could I possibly be to blame? My horse too, she said, as an afterthought. It really was an appalling piece of misfortune. And I thought of those men, how brutal and cruel they'd been to a fox and how gentle and kind they were over a horse.

That night I wondered where I could hang myself. But Mrs Leonard stayed with me all night and never gave me a chance.

Next morning the reaction set in. I was black and blue all down one side and could hardly move my shoulder or my hip. And I slept. I slept as if I'd been short of sleep for a year. The doctor came once but I'll swear he gave me nothing. Maybe it was the shock.

Sometimes I'd wake out of a black cloud of sleep, and there'd be pain waiting for me somewhere like a sort of illness just round the corner of my mind. But it wasn't the pains of my wrenched shoulder and bruised back; it went much, much deeper than that. It was like the part of your heart that beat, the part of your brain that reasoned, as if there was something wrong at the hinge. I'd wake sometimes and feel this awful hurt and look at the clock and see it was five past three, and then I'd sink off gratefully into a long deep sleep. Then after it I'd wake with a start and see it was only ten past three, and the hinge would still be creaking and I'd look down a long dark corridor of empty echoing horror to the end of my life.

I drank something every now and then when Mrs Leonard brought it, and just about dusk I looked up and saw Mrs Rutland was there and I said like asking the time: 'How's Mark?' And she said: 'He's holding his own.'

I ought to have asked more but I drifted off again and had an insane jumble of dreams about Mother and Forio and how Mother said he had to be shot because it wasn't respectable to keep a horse in Cuthbert Avenue. Then I was suddenly in court and seemed to be both judge and prisoner in one, defending and condemning myself. Dr Roman was there testifying that I was unfit to plead. Once or twice during the day I tried to get out of bed, but each time the pain in my body woke me up, and I lay back panting and staring.

Outside the window were two trees – just skeletons, no leaves; all through the bright afternoon they nodded and leered at me. Then I saw the river again where we fell, and the water was a snake crawling slimy over the sheets of the bed. It wasn't till the Friday about noon, pretty well forty-eight hours after the accident, that I woke up with my mind really clear, absolutely clear, just like a glass that's been emptied and polished, and knew there was an appointment I'd missed today. The *Flandre* had sailed without me.

From then on a few things began to move normally. I couldn't sleep then for the pain in my shoulder and back, and I couldn't even close my eyes because of Forio. The minute I closed my eyes I saw him again. Perhaps it isn't any good describing everything as it happened, the way my thoughts went; but some time later there was Mrs Rutland in the room again, and I said again: 'How's Mark?'

'About the same. He isn't conscious yet.'

'What do they say?'

'They say we can only wait.' She came into the room; her hair was untidy. 'And you?'

'Oh, yes. I'm better now.'

'Can you eat a little lunch?'

'No. No thanks. I'm better without.'

That evening Mark came round and Mrs Rutland got back from the hospital more hopeful. The doctors said he wasn't out of danger yet, but they thought it was going to be all right.

'The first thing he said was, where were you, Marnie, and it seemed to help him a lot when I told him you weren't badly hurt.'

The next day I got up while Mrs Rutland was out, and managed to dress and hobble round the house. My back and hip were like somebody'd painted thunder-clouds on them, but a lot of the pain was going. The pain in my body, that is. Mrs Leonard found me out in the stable and tried to get me back to bed, but I wasn't going. I stayed in the stable all morning, just sitting there, until Mrs Rutland came back, and then I limped in and had lunch with her. Mrs Rutland said she'd promised to drive me in to see Mark as soon as I was well. I said I'd go the following day. I couldn't very well say anything else. Before dinner that evening I had to go into his bedroom for something, and his keys were there in the corner of the top drawer of his dressing-table . . .

At dinner Mrs Rutland said: 'These flowers are from the gardener, Richards. He brought them for you and he seemed specially anxious to make it clear that they were out of his own garden.'

Two daffodils, some wallflowers, a few violets.

'And a blind man came yesterday with a bunch of grapes. He said they were with love. Do you know a blind man?'

'Yes.'

We ate nothing much for a long while. Any other time I'd have felt screwed up inside at the thought of having a meal alone with her, but now there wasn't room for any of that. What had happened sat square in my middle like a stone ju-ju; you just didn't see round.

After a time she said: 'This reminds me of a meal I once had with Estelle. D'you mind my talking of Estelle?'

'No . . .'

'Mark was away, in Wales on business for the firm. Mark's father had been dead about eighteen months. I'd just sold our house, the family house, and most of the furniture, and was moving to the flat in London. And suddenly I got this terrible conviction that I couldn't go on. I suddenly felt as if I'd wrenched up my last roots; and *that*, on top of George's death and my other son being lost in the war, was more than I could bear. I couldn't live in London, I couldn't go on living *anywhere*. All I wanted was some warm and comfortable place to die. I asked myself to dinner with Estelle because I had to have company at any price, and some sort of sympathy and understanding if I could get it.'

It was too dark in the room; I wished I'd switched

on the table lamps. That curtain ring needed fixing; Mrs Leonard never remembered. Mrs Rutland's fingers were small and pointed, not at all like Mark's; she moved them along the edge of the table.

'Did Estelle give it you?'

'I never asked for it in so many words. When I got here I realized there are some pits of the soul that have to be climbed out of by oneself or not at all. This was one of them. You can't ask for understanding at twenty-five of the awful loneliness that can strike you thirty years later.'

She went on talking, and I watched and listened, thinking perhaps Estelle never had that loneliness, yet she must have had when she knew she was going to die.

'It isn't a question of age,' I said.

'What?' She'd gone on to something else.

'It isn't just a question of age. Weren't you ever lonely as a child?'

She thought. 'Yes. But it's different then, isn't it? When you're young you have something to feed on, an inner iron ration that keeps your strength up. When you're older, when your life is past, that's used up, there's only the hollow place where the nourishment has been.'

I didn't think to ask her why tonight reminded her of that time. She changed the subject right away, as if afraid I'd think her morbid.

Presently I said: 'Does Mark ever talk about me?'

'You mean, do we discuss you? No, I don't think so.'

'Hasn't he ever said we don't get on well?'

'No . . . Don't you?'

'Not very.'

She turned her wine glass round but didn't look at me.

I said: 'It's chiefly my fault.'

'That sounds half-way to a reconciliation.'

'Oh, it isn't just a quarrel. I'm afraid it goes far deeper than that.'

Mrs Leonard came in. When she had gone Mrs Rutland said: 'I hope you'll be able to make this up with him, Marnie, whether you feel it is your fault or his. I think it would bring him down altogether if he had another failure.'

'Failure?'

'Well, yes, in a sense. Isn't death at twenty-six a failure? It's contrary to nature anyway. It's a failure of life and vitality, and I think Mark looked on it to some extent as a failure of love . . .'

Her eyes were on me, and I didn't like it now; it was just coming through; they'd a liquid look, but shallow, like holding back at the last.

'Perhaps it's natural for me to think him an unusual man, being his mother. But I try to keep my understanding this side of idolatry; and I do see that he's a man who all his life will be bent on taking risks – risks with the usual things perhaps, but most of all with people. He's tremendously self-willed but also tremendously vulnerable. Estelle's death hit him hard. To fall in love again so soon . . . It doesn't often happen.'

I said uncomfortably: 'Did Mark tell you he was – what he was doing about the printing works?'

She still turned her wine glass. 'About accepting the Glastonbury offer? Yes. I persuaded him to take it.'

'You did? Why? Didn't the name matter?'

'The name matters very little if you put it alongside the other things. Mark will never get on with the Holbrooks; he hasn't the flexibility of his father. It's much better for everybody that they should separate now.'

'The Holbrooks won't like it.'

'Not the way it's turned out, no. But only because of that. Mark didn't want to do it; he said he felt responsible for the staff. But that's what he's been negotiating about, writing in some safeguards. As far as we can tell, no one will suffer.'

No one will suffer. I thought, it's a sort of epitaph. No one will suffer except me, and Forio, and Mark, and my mother, and, at the next stage, his.

On the Tuesday Mrs Rutland drove me down to the hospital. I tell you, I didn't want to go. I'd nothing to say to Mark. Except the things that couldn't be said. Such as, I'm sorry. And, I'm going soon. Goodbye.

He was in a room to himself – private patient I suppose – with a long window, and the sun was falling on a corner of the bed. Thank God she let me go in alone. I was surprised his head wasn't even bandaged, but that frail look that had foxed me when I first met him, it was more so than ever, he looked a stone lighter.

I didn't know *what* sort of way I should be greeted, but he smiled and said: 'Hullo, Marnie.'

'Hullo, Mark.' I tried not to limp on the way to the chair by the bed, and then just as I was going to sit down I remembered the nurse still standing by the door so I bent and kissed him.

'How're you feeling?' He got it out first.

'Me? Oh, I'm all right. *Stiff*. But you?'

'A headache and this arm, that's all. I want to come home.'

'Will they let you?'

'Not for a few days. I'm awfully sorry about Forio . . .'

'I'm sorry about it all.'

'But I know how much he meant to you.'

'It's my own fault anyway.'

'Or mine. I shouldn't have chased you.'

There was a pause. 'Anyway,' he said, 'thanks for dragging me out of the mud.'

'Who told you?'

'I was just that much conscious. I remember you wiping the mud out of my eyes and ears.'

'I can hardly remember what I did myself.'

'I seem to remember it pretty well.'

That's all. We hadn't any more to say. The nurse hadn't shaved him well and his skin would be dark in another hour or so.

He said: 'Have you let Roman know about the accident?'

'No.'

'Ring him, will you? Otherwise he may think you're deliberately dropping off again.'

I said: 'What happens to a horse when it's shot, Mark? Do they – bury it, or what?'

'I don't know.'

'I couldn't bear to think of anything else, of it being sold . . .'

'I don't think there's much likelihood.'

There were some flowers and grapes by the bed, and some magazines and two or three books. I suppose I should have remembered to bring him something.

He said: 'It's early days yet, of course, but . . . there are other horses. We can go round in the spring, pick up a good one.'

'I don't think I'd want one.'

'We'll see.' He patted my hand.

I must say it was awfully queer. Sometimes since I married him he'd looked at me as if he hated me. Because I was friendly with Terry or because I drew away sometimes when he touched me he could fairly go white and angry. But after this, after I'd led him a wild chase over impossible country and landed him with something near a fractured skull, well, he didn't seem to hold that against me at all.

Mrs Rutland went home on the Wednesday. I went to see Mark each day, and they said he could come home on the following Monday.

On the Wednesday night just as I was going to bed Terry rang. He said he was sorry about the accident and he hoped Mark was going on all right and that he'd inquired a couple of times about me through the Newton-Smiths and it was all too bad, wasn't it?

I said yes, it was.

He talked for a minute or two and then said: 'I

suppose you know the take-over of Rutland's is going through?'

'I – haven't had time to think of it.'

'No, I suppose not. Or me.'

'Or you. I'm sorry.'

'Well, I suppose it's no good gnawing over an old *bone*. We've got to live as we've got to live. When's Mark coming home?'

'Monday, I think.'

'Come out with me Friday?'

'Oh, Terry, I couldn't.'

'Feel ill?'

'Just miserable.'

'All the more reason to get away for a bit.'

'No, thanks, I can't. I couldn't.' By Friday I should be gone away.

'Tell you what,' he said, 'I'll ring you again tomorrow when I get back from the works, see if you'll change your mind.'

'All right.' I wouldn't be here tomorrow evening either.

'That's my girl. By the way, did you hear the six o'clock news tonight?'

'No, why?'

'Warning of hurricane force gales in the south-east. Close your *windows* and hold tight. Is Mrs Leonard with you?'

'Yes, she's sleeping here till Mark gets home.'

'Good . . . Look, I'm relying on you Friday evening, dear. Heaven knows, with all this take-over on our plate I shall need bucking up myself; and only you can do it. Shall we call it a date?'

'Ring me tomorrow evening,' I said. 'I'll tell you definitely then.'

I saw Mark again on the Thursday morning, and he was sitting up in a chair although he still looked shaky. It was just an ordinary meeting, and I couldn't quite believe it was the last.

I said he seemed cheerful and he said: 'I've got a hunch this may be the beginning of a new start for us both.' When I looked up he went on: 'No special reason, no logical reason ... I feel I'm making a fresh start where my job's concerned, and it may be – once certain formalities are out of the way – that I can make a fresh start where my wife's concerned.'

'You'd still be willing to try?'

'I am, yes, if you are.'

I liked him better when he was like this – or perhaps it was just the old funny human thing of liking more what you're going to leave behind. Anyway just for a second or so there was this twinge of regret in me for all the life there might have been between us. It was like seeing something through a door, suddenly. It was like being in a foreign land and looking through a door at a life you don't know anything about and have never led. You look in and then you sigh and move along. Perhaps for a minute you almost wish you could be a part of it. But really it's a sort of sentimental cramp, because it can't ever be your life at all.

When I got home I tried to write him some sort of note, just a line saying goodbye. But although I started six times nothing worth putting down would come at all, so I burned the lot. Maybe silence was best. That way he'd think the worst, and the worst was right.

I told Mrs Leonard I was going to stay with friends who lived near the hospital and would travel back with Mark on Monday. That way I could carry my bag out to the car without any hole in corner business, and she watched me go.

Just before I left I went into the stable and looked round for the last time. It still smelled of Forio. I seemed to remember reading somewhere that men often killed the thing they loved. That had happened to me.

It wasn't Richards's day in the garden, so I couldn't say anything to him; but driving away I passed the two blind men out on one of their walks. Usually I stopped the car or at least blew my horn and they waved, but this time I sneaked past. I felt awful. I felt like a thief. I felt like a thief again.

It would take an hour from here to Barnet, half an hour to get into the works and open the safe and get out again, and about four or five hours to drive to Torquay. That would mean Mother's before midnight. They were always late to bed and late up, so with luck I'd be there before they locked up. I'd sleep there and tell Mam everything in the morning, God help me. By noon or earlier I'd be away. I was going to take my chance at Exeter Airport.

I drove to Barnet.

As I drove I began to feel more and more queer. Not queer in the body but queer in the feelings. It was as if the death of Forio, the way he'd died, the fact that I'd *killed* him, was soaking into me all over again. Two or three times during the drive I had to wipe my eyes with my gloves, and once I nearly hit a cyclist. I wished my eyes had got screen-wipers.

It was a nasty evening with a thin fog every time you got away from the streets into a bit of open country, even if it was only a couple of fields. I missed my way once, and it took me more than an hour to get to Barnet.

I didn't drive up to the works, but there was a narrow street running beside the retail shop so I parked there.

Now of course the mist was a help, and I wished it was thicker. The hardest part was going to be to get into the building without being seen, and I wasn't sure which of three keys was the one that fitted the outer door. If you fiddle about there's always the chance of the stray policeman; but there was no way but to risk it.

The front door of the works was on the corner, and there was a lamp on the opposite side. Whoever went in would be seen by anyone passing.

I went right across and up the two steps without looking either way. After all I was the wife of the managing director. The first key went in but wouldn't turn, and then it stuck and wouldn't pull out. I wriggled and fiddled while two cars went past. I got the key out and tried the second. It worked. I let myself in.

It was all dark inside, and the only light was from the fanlight over the door. At two paces was a second door, and when I had unlocked this I didn't shut it behind me because of the bit of extra light that would come through. The passage beyond was dark, but I knew every inch of it. You walked down, turned right, and then there were the stairs.

At the foot of the stairs was the door leading to the printing shop. Usually it was shut at night but tonight it was open. I stopped in the doorway looking into the works.

There were a few shafts of light coming in through windows here and there, falling on the big machines and the bales of paper; but what got me most was the silence. I'd never been in the works before when it was shut, and somehow the quietness was twice as much because you expected and remembered all the noise.

Then in the absolute dead silence I heard a rustling. I stood there not moving and listened to it. It came from over by the paper. I found I was clutching the keys so they hurt. I let my hand relax. I went up the stairs.

I'd brought a torch but still didn't use it, and groped my way along the corridor. I jarred against a bucket that one of the cleaners had left.

I got a nasty feeling any moment that instead of my hands groping along hard things like walls and filing cabinets and doors they'd come up against a warm arm or a body or a face. I suppose it was the dark giving me the jitters. That and me still being under the weather from shock. I thought if I stopped I'd hear breathing near to me.

I got to the office where the switchboard was and

pawed my way across it. This time a chair got in the way; but a bit of noise didn't matter, no one would hear noise, it was light that might show in the street outside.

The door of my old office, the cashier's office was locked, but I found the key to fit and went in. A Miss Pritchett was doing my job now. Mark said she was middle-aged and efficient but slow. I wondered how many of the pay packets she and Susan Clabon would have done.

There were two windows in here but no proper blinds so it meant still working partly in the dark.

I went to the safe and put in the key. It slid in easily and the lock turned as if it was in Vaseline. I tugged the door open and switched on my torch.

Anyway none of the routine had been changed. The envelopes were stacked in their tray, the rest of the money was in the drawer underneath. I took out this money and emptied it into my bag. I took the notes, of course, and all the silver but left the copper. Then I pulled out the tray and began to flip the pay envelopes together.

I thought, so it's nearly all the same as it would have been six months ago. I'm taking the same sort of money from the same safe. Mark interfering has only made half a year's difference. Except that Mark interfering meant I was now known under my own name and would be wanted under my own name and would have to get out of the country to be safe. And Mark interfering meant I was married, not single, and Forio was dead, and Mark was in hospital, and tomorrow or the next day was in for a shock when he found I was gone.

I shovelled some of the envelopes into my bag and then stopped again. Just at that second for some forsaken reason all my grief about Forio was coming up more and more and I began to shake. God knows why I shook but I did. I felt mad with myself because I felt so weak. I felt so weak I could hardly walk out of here with this money and drive off to Torquay. But it wasn't just muscle-weak, it was will-weak, that was what made me so mad.

I looked at the money and I looked at my bag and I dropped them both on the floor and sat down and tried to work it out. It's awful when you get so turned up that you don't know where you are.

D'you know, I thought to myself, this is the second or third time you've felt like this. It's Forio's death, that's mainly what's done it. But also there was one time before. It means something, but Lord knows what.

So I picked up the money and put it into the bag and scooped up the next lot of envelopes. And then I thought, something really has got into you because you can't take this money.

I must have sat there half an hour in the dark fighting with myself. At the end of that time I'd worked it out that I didn't in the least mind taking the money – I hadn't suddenly gone all that soft – but there are just some things you can't do. You can *leave* your husband – and the thought of leaving Mark was still a glorious one – but to rob him, to pinch his keys while he's in the hospital, to take maybe a thousand pounds and leave him to do all the explaining, well, believe it or not, it wasn't on.

Sometimes you can plan everything in your mind, and it looks perfect, and then when it happens it all happens differently and you're in a jam. That wasn't so now, and that was what made it all the more crazy. Everything had gone according to plan – except me and I had just gone all to Hell. Or maybe it was that I'd really made all my plans a week ago, and now, a week later, I'd been following them more or less blindfold and in betweens time something had changed. I sat there with all that money around me, in the safe, in my bag, on the floor, and wished I'd never been born, wished the sea had taken me at Camp de Mar. I tried to think of all the bad things I could about Mark and our marriage – I thought of quite a few – and once I got as far as shutting my bag. But I couldn't even cheat myself now.

I opened my bag and started putting the money back and every bundle hurt just as much as taking teeth out. I cursed and cursed. Even while I put it back I couldn't help but reckon it up. The notes were in bundles of fifty pounds and the pay packets, well, I could guess what they were worth within a pound or so each. I thought, every bundle I put back, that's taken from Mother (because I'd intended to try to persuade her to take this lot and sit on it; it would have kept her for three years). But even that didn't wash. Because like as not she'd have winced away in scalded horror from accepting a penny more of my money once she knew it was stolen.

So after all if I went to her empty-handed I don't

suppose it would make much difference. But it would make a difference to me.

All I had in the world now was about two hundred pounds. I had to keep that myself until I got some sort of a job in France, or wherever I ended up.

When all the money was back I began to swing the great safe door to, and then I had to stand there for several minutes again before I could work up the will to shut it. I was breathing so heavy I might have run a mile. I sounded to myself like an old woman I'd heard dying once. I felt so awful.

When it was done I turned the key and then groped my way out of the office. Somehow I got downstairs, and there I was looking through this open door again into the printing shop and listening for the sound of rustling among the paper like half an hour ago.

This time there was just silence.

I let myself out and drove away.

I was in Newton Abbot by eleven-thirty. The fog hadn't got any worse. I never stopped all the way. Luckily there was enough petrol.

The only thing I was sure of was that the nearer I got to Cuthbert Avenue the less I liked the idea of telling Mother. I could just see her look. I was the apple of her eye, all she had. But if I didn't tell her, the police soon would. If I told her at least I could try to explain.

Explain what? How I came to steal instead of being content to stay a wage slave in the same office all my life? How I came to know I was smarter than most people and could use my smartness? How I found out it was easy to lead a double life and go on multiplying lives so long as you took certain precautions? How I got married and never told her?

Well, I thought, all that's going to take a lot of explaining between now and tomorrow morning. Explain it to yourself before you start on her.

It was raining in Torquay. I parked the old car in a municipal car park and took a taxi up.

There were no lights in the front of the house when I paid off the taxi, but there was a glimmer in the hall coming through from the back. I carried my suitcase up the three steps and rang the bell. There was a long wait and then footsteps. Lucy opened the door. Her face was all red and lumpy.

She gave a little scream and flung her arms round my neck. 'Oh, Marnie! Oh, Marnie! 'Ere at last! We was looking for you everywhere! We didn't know where you could've got to. It wasn't right, leaving no address. They said to me, but she must have *some* address. Look in the telephone book, they said—'

'Here, what's this all about, Lucy? What's the matter? What's to do?'

'Oh,' she wailed, looking at me, and suddenly she spouted tears. Then behind her came Doreen, Uncle Stephen's daughter.

'Marnie,' Doreen said. 'Your Mam died yesterday.'

CHAPTER EIGHTEEN

THERE WAS a long stain down the kitchen wall. It looked like a map of the River Nile. I had to draw a map of the River Nile once and I remember it well. There was a nail in the wall just about the place for Cairo. 'It was that storm,' said Lucy. 'You remember. It blew a slate off and the rain came in. First week in Jan. We sent down to Marley's but they never came.' One of the padded arms of the rocking chair had been recovered; it didn't quite match the other, and somebody, it must have been Doreen, had hung a tea towel to dry on the fretwork pipe-rack. 'She was took ill on Monday night,' said Lucy. 'A stroke, the doctor said. Down her side. She never spoke again, Marnie. But you know how she was about you. I thought, well, I *got* to find her; but I looked through your letters. No address. I found Doreen, that's all. Doreen phoned Manchester and Birmingham, didn't you, Doreen.'

'Dad's coming tomorrow for the funeral,' said Doreen. 'He's in Liverpool, luckily. Why didn't you leave an address, Marnie? We tried half a dozen Pembertons, but none of them was your man.'

'Yesterday morning the doctor says she can't last

long,' said Lucy. 'So we went to the police. They says they can't help us to find you, why not put an SOS on the BBC? So we done that. But she passed away peaceful yesterday five o'clock in the afternoon. Breathing heavy she'd been ever since Tuesday night, like she couldn't catch 'er breath. I sat with 'er, and Doreen too.'

'Funeral's tomorrow at two,' said Doreen. 'I've got to go back right after because I've left my husband and he's rushed off his feet. It's the time of year, all this bronchitis. I hope I did right but somebody had to make the arrangements. There's a policy. With the United Insurance. It was only a few pence a week but it'll cover the cost. I didn't know whether you'd be here or not.'

'I thought you'd *'eard*,' said Lucy. 'You coming like that I thought you'd 'eard. She was right as ninepence till Monday dinner-time; then she said she'd got a 'eadache so she'd lie down. She got up for tea again and baked. She was always one for saffron cake. She said to me, "Lucy, I've a feeling Marnie'll be down this month." Next thing you know she was on the floor, just where Doreen's standing now. I tried to get 'er in the chair but she was a dead weight, so I ran for Mr Warner.'

Doreen said: 'Aunt Edie had a cousin Polly, didn't she? D'you know where she lives? I wired to the address in Tavistock, but they said she moved soon after the war. Ooh, I'm tired; I was up at six this morning.'

Mother's stick was in the corner, propped up against the dresser, and a pair of her going-out shoes; very narrow and pointed: she'd always had narrow feet and wore pointed shoes long before they were the fashion.

'Y'know, tis 'ard to credit,' said Lucy. 'I still think I shall 'ear 'er coming down the stairs. Would you like to see 'er now, Marnie? We done a nice job, the nurse and me. You'll think she's just asleep.'

But she didn't look asleep to me. She looked very faded and very, very small. She didn't look like my mother really at all. I went up to her, and the more I looked at her the more she looked like something that's been left behind. She looked just as much like my mother as the shoes downstairs and the stick looked like her, and the dressing-gown behind the door. Whatever I cared for was gone and this could all be dumped. Maybe it sounds callous but it wasn't, it was how I felt.

I slept with Doreen, or anyway, I shared the bed and lay awake looking at the curtains, the way they went darker and then lighter through the night as the moon set and then the dawn came. I got up at six and made tea, but I didn't wake them. I felt like someone in the boxing ring who's had first a jab on the solar plexus and then a right hook. I'd been to boxing once or twice at Plymouth, and I'd seen that happen to a man. He came out for the sixth round, out of his corner quite normal, but I was close and I could see by his eyes that he didn't really know what he was doing at all. He went on making the motions of fighting, but it was just a question of time before the third blow landed and stretched him out.

I got my third blow about a quarter to seven.

I'd been sitting with Mother for half an hour, but as I say not really thinking of anything or thinking she was there. I mean I'd been sitting by the bed not far away from her as the sun struck in through a slit in the curtains, and I thought how crazy it was I couldn't get her a cup of tea, and there was a fly buzzing somewhere, and I knew how mother hated flies. She used to squash them against the window panes with her fingers sometimes; I hated her doing that. And then I saw that old black imitation crocodile bag of hers that she'd carried everywhere. It was on top of the wardrobe. I could see the corner of it and I thought, I wonder if there's that other photo of Dad in it, because I think she might like to have it with her in the coffin.

I mean you can be punch drunk one minute and as weepy and sentimental and silly as anything the next; so I got the bag down and clipped open the long tarnished clasp. The first thing I found was a photo of me at eighteen, and I thought perhaps that could go as well; and then there were some old newspaper clippings. The first one I saw was out of the *Western Morning News* again, announcing a birth. Frank and Edith Elmer had had a daughter. That was me too.

There was a bottle of the charcoal pills she took for her rheumatism, and then, Heaven help me, my baptism card. Then there was the newspaper cutting about Dad's death, the one she'd shown me. A wedding card, her wedding card, made my throat close up, and clipped to it was an old dance programme that made me feel worse.

Then I picked out another cutting. It was dated November 1943 but it hadn't a newspaper heading. The top of the column said: 'Plymouth Woman Bound Over on Murder Charge'.

I thought this must be someone Mother knew, until I saw the words Mrs Edith Elmer. Then I took that column in so fast I still can't remember which order the words came in.

'At Bodmin Assizes today Mrs Edith Elizabeth Elmer, aged 41, of Kersey Bungalow, Sangerford, Liskeard, was charged with the murder of her new-born child . . . Opening for the Prosecution, Counsel said that Mrs Elmer, an evacuee divorced woman living alone with her five-year-old daughter . . . Her neighbour, Miss Nye, helped to deliver the child, but there seemed some doubt as to the exact sequence of events before the district nurse was summoned . . . Nurse Vannion would tell how she came to the house and found Mrs Elmer in a state of prostration. Mrs Elmer informed Nurse Vannion that she had had a miscarriage but the nurse's suspicions were aroused, and going into the next bedroom she found the body of a perfectly formed child wrapped in newspaper under the bed. The child was dead and evidence would be brought to prove that it died of strangulation . . .'

I dropped the cutting and it fluttered to the floor like one of those paper streamers. I bent down for it and dropped the bag. Bits and pieces fell out of the bag and rolled under the bed. A cotton reel, a two-shilling piece, a thimble, a box of matches. I went down on my knees scrabbling for them in the curtained half-light, but I couldn't hold anything, my fingers were shaking so much.

I got hold of the cutting and sat up on my heels, and there a few inches away from my face on the edge of the bed was a hand. It was a thin knobbly hand, and as I looked at it it slid an inch down the slope of the bed.

Somehow I managed to straighten up. I hadn't any feet or knees. I sat balanced on cold water. I looked at my mother's dead face. I looked and looked. I'd sat there for half an hour and never had a qualm. But now I was like in some sort of frozen terror. And then it seemed to me she sighed. Any minute now, I thought, that old face is going to move, those lids will flutter and show grey blobs of evil staring at me, as they'd stared at me that time in Dr Roman's when I'd been a child again with my back pressed cold against the wall.

I made a move to the door but it was backwards, I couldn't get my eyes off her. Another step and I was there, the knob in my thigh. I got round, my hands were too sweaty and weak to turn the knob. I had to use the other hand and the news cutting got screwed up. I got the door open and backed out. I backed into Lucy Nye.

'Look, dear,' Lucy Nye said, 'don't 'ee take it like that. Listen, you was never meant to *know*. All these years we kept it to ourselves. I used to say to Edie 'twould be better to tell the girl, you never can be sure someone else won't. But she wouldn't. Oh, no, she was a strong one, was Edie, an' stubborn as a mule. I never dreamed she'd kept that newspaper, dear. I wonder why she done that? Now it's all come out on account of 'er own foolishness.'

Lucy poured me tea like liquid boot polish. She kept looking at me with her one big eye and her one small one. They squinted at me like marbles that had fallen into wrinkles in the sand. They didn't tell me anything. Only the voice went on.

'Drink this, dear, it'll do you good. Doreen isn't stirring yet. I'll take 'er up a cup in a—'

'Does she know?'

'About your Mam? I don't think so. She's only same age as you. That's unless her Dad's told 'er.'

'He knows?'

'Yes, dear. 'E was on convoy work but 'e was in Devonport refitting at the time.'

'I don't get it. I don't get anything at all.'

'No, dear. Well if you know s'much I'd better tell you. Drink your tea.' Lucy scratched in the parting of her grey hair. I remembered when that hair was a faded fair, and I remembered she'd scratched just the same way then, with her three middle fingers. 'I knew your Mam when she was a girl, dear. A 'andsome girl she was too. Not so pretty as you but striking, like. I used to live across the street. She was always with boys, always a different one, but always kept 'erself nice like. She was brought up strict. 'Er Dad was *strict* with 'er, make no mistake. An' she kept the boys in their place. I used t' watch 'er. She'd always make 'em leave 'er on the corner of Wardle Street and walk down alone, case the old man was watching. My mother used to say, she'll pick and choose once too often, all that dressing up, all that money on 'er back. Your Mam worked in Marks & Spencers then.'

Old Lucy rubbed the back of her hand across the tip of her nose. 'Then I moved Liskeard way, and I only

saw 'er off'n on. I knew she'd married your Dad, and I
seen you once when you was a mite of two. But I never
seen much of 'er until the war. Then she was evacuated
to the bungalow next to me. Your Dad was in the Navy.
She come along with you, an' you was, I s'pose, three
and a half or four. Lovely little thing, you was. No
trouble at all. I used to push you out. We got more
friendly, like. She used to say she was lonely, your Mam
did. She missed 'er friends an' the shops an' one thing
and another. But she 'adn't changed, always dressed
well, kep' herself to herself; *you* know 'ow she was.
Well, I say she 'adn't changed . . .'

I turned the newspaper cutting over and over. There
was an advert for Mumford's Garage on the back, and
a paragraph saying 'Enemy Plane Shot Down'. The
paper was yellow and had been folded a lot. How often
had she read it? How often had she read it through?

'. . . It was just then she got friendly with soldiers,
dear. I don't like to 'ave to say it but she did. Your Dad
was at sea and she was lonely, I s'pose. There was a lot
of soldiers round about Liskeard just then. *You* know,
time on their 'ands. Mind you, you never *seen* her with
one, that was the rum thing, but everybody knew it just
the same. The soldiers knew it too. I s'pose they told
each other. 'Twas the strangest thing you ever seen;
there she was living in that tiny bungalow along with
you, *respectable*, you couldn't find no fault with 'er,
well dressed, always partic'lar 'ow she spoke and who
she spoke to; out walking in the afternoon, never in a
pub nor nothing, but everyone *knew*. If a soldier came

along after dark, all he'd got to do was tap on the window and—'

I said: 'I used to be sleeping with her, and the tap would come and she'd lift me out and put me in the spare bedroom. The bed was always cold. She'd lock me in . . . D'you mean *any* soldier?'

'That I don't rightly know, dear,' Lucy said carefully. 'She'd never say. I didn't dare ask 'er then, and afterwards she'd never say, never talk of it, word never crossed 'er lips. I reckon soldiers was always being moved here and there. Maybe she 'ad only a few favourites, but of course idle tongues wagged and made it more and more.'

'Did Dad get to know?'

'Not for a year or longer, dear. When 'e came 'ome word 'ad gone round and no soldier came near the place. But I think 'e 'ad 'is suspicions. Because one night in the winter of '42, January or February, 'twould be, he come back unexpected.'

'So it's true, what it says here, "evacuee divorced woman" . . .'

'Yes, dear, 'e took it bad and divorced 'er. That's how she didn't 'ave no pension. She *denied* it, y'know, said 'twas all a pack of lies, even though he came back unexpected and found what 'e did find. So then she was on her own, as you might say.'

'Except for me.'

'Yes, dear, and you was coming along beautiful. I never seen a handsomer little girl. Five you was then. I used to take you out every afternoon. Your Mam wasn't strong. She'd go out shopping in the morning. 'Member her walk before she got that bad leg? No, you wouldn't. Rum walk she always 'ad – not like a . . . well, not like a woman who did what she was doing – partic'lar, respectable, feet in a straight line, you know, one knee ever so nearly touching the other. Never too much powder or paint. 'Twas just the same after the divorce as before. Vicar's wife she might have been. But she kept on with 'er games. I was nearest to 'er, y'know.

'I used t'run little errands for 'er; we was close, our bungalows was semis. I could see everything, but she never let on even to me. Once I says something to 'er and she says, "Lucy, there's evil tongues and evil thoughts; it is for you to choose your company." I shut up after that. Another time I know she says, "These poor boys, away from their hearths an' homes, 'tis the least one can do to give them companionship, to offer them the quiet fireside of a Christian home."' Lucy shivered. 'An' then she got caught.'

The clock struck half past seven. The paint was coming off one of those damned pink and green love-birds, and there was a crack in the face.

'She got caught, but she didn't let on. It wasn't long before the neighbours began to talk. It was Mrs Waters that spoke to me first, behind 'er 'and. I said, *oh, no*, I *don't think so*, but as soon as she spoke I knew 'twas true. We none of us said nothing for months and then Mrs Waters tackled 'er. She said, "Oh, Mrs Elmer, 'ave I to congratulate you?" Your Mam says, "I don't know what you mean." Mrs Waters says, "You're expecting a certain event, aren't you, Mrs Elmer?" and your Mam says – "How dare you be so downright insulting!" and goes off with 'er 'ead in the air. Well, after that—'

'Listen,' I said. 'What's that?'

'What's what?' said Lucy.

'I thought I heard footsteps on the stairs.'

We sat there like mice at the tread of a cat; it was a sunny morning but this window faced west and the curtains were drawn, so it was half dark; Lucy's cup began to rattle so she put it down.

So I said: 'I'd better go and see.'

'Nay, leave it be, Marnie.'

I thought of my mother and wondered if she was still upstairs or if she was standing outside listening with that thin knobbled hand of hers on the kitchen door. I couldn't move. I couldn't go and see. There was cold sweat on my face.

I got to the door somehow and wrenched it open. There was nothing there.

But it was darker than ever out in the lobby, and maybe there were things I couldn't see.

I shut the door and stood with my back to it. 'She said she wasn't going to have a baby.'

'No . . . that's what she said. She wouldn't admit it to no one. Not a soul. I was always in an' out, though she was never afraid to tell me to be off when I wasn't welcome or when she 'ad "a friend" coming. The last month, of course 'twas clear and plain to everyone, but if I so much as dropped a 'int she choked me off. You know 'ow she could. There was never sight nor sign to the very end of anything made ready, no baby clothes, no linen, no knitting, no nothing. Then on the night it 'appened she come to me . . . Sit down, dear.'

'Let me stand.'

'The night it 'appened she come to me and says, "Lucy, I'm very unwell. I think there's something the matter with me. Come in a minute." When I went in, there was you sitting in front of the kitchen fire crying your eyes out, and she fair collapsing on the bed in 'er bedroom as she followed in after me . . .' Lucy's face twitched. 'Well, I done what I could but I seen what was wrong and I was for going for the doctor, but she says, "No. I won't allow it, Lucy. Get the child out of the way. We can manage. It will all be over very very soon." Well . . . well, there 'twas, I should've gone, no doubt, but 'twas almost too late anyhow. 'Ow long it'd been going on before she sent for me I haven't the least notion. So I put you in the next bedroom and locked you in, poor mite you was trembling and trembling, and I came back to your Mam, and in an hour a fine baby boy was born. Cor, I was in a terror, I reely was. But when 'twas over, my dear soul, I felt a changed woman! I says to her, "'Tis what you deserve, Edie, for being so obstinate and stubborn, but God be thanked, all has been for the best and you have a lovely little boy!" And she looks at me and says, "Lucy, don't tell anyone yet. Leave me now for an hour or two to rest." And I says "I'll do no such thing, the baby wants washing and binding. You've got nothing 'ere, so I'll nip in my place and fetch what I can lay me 'ands on." So I went . . .'

Lucy poured herself another cup of tea. She slopped a good bit in the saucer too, and sat there all hunched up licking her fingers. Then she tipped the tea out of the saucer into the cup, and the rattle of the crockery in her shaky hands was like a morse code.

'So I went and – and when I came back in twenty minutes the baby was gone. God 'elp me, Marnie, that's how 'twas! She was there in bed, in a muck sweat, and looking white as paper and she stared at me with all 'er eyes. I never seen the like, God 'elp me, I never. I says to 'er: "*Edie*, where's the baby? Edie!" And she answers me in two words. "What baby?" Just like that: "What baby?" as if I'd dreamed it all.'

The milkman was coming round with his bottles. He rattled down a couple outside and then his footsteps went thudding off.

Lucy said: 'Maybe she was crazy mad, Marnie. Maybe I was too. 'Twas like looking at someone you loved and seeing 'er for the first time. But you see, I was never so strong-minded as 'er and if there was no baby 'twas my word against 'ers. You was screaming to be let out, and she just lay there with 'er great eyes and said, "What baby?" as if I dreamed it all ... Gracious knows what I'd've done in the end. My life and soul, I b'lieve I'd've let it go, but soon after she started a 'aemorrhage and it went on and nothing would stop it, an' I knew then I couldn't just stand there and let 'er die – though she said I must; she said: "Let me die, Lucy; no matter, you can look after Marnie, let me die." But Marnie, 'twas too much for me and I fled from the bungalow and sent for the district nurse. And when she come she found the baby, just as it say in that there paper, under – under the bed in the next room . . .'

I went away from the door and went through the kitchen to the scullery and I vomited there, as if I'd taken poison, and I ran the water and tried to run it over my face and arms. Lucy came out.

'Marnie, dear, I'm sorry. 'Tis all past and done with and long since forgotten. 'Tis no fault of yours and she suffered for it and no one'd have been the wiser but for her silly foolishness keeping that paper, and there's no call to take on so. Lie down and let me see for your breakfast.'

I shook my head and got away from the sink and took up a towel. My hair was hanging in wet streaks like seaweed. I dried my face and hands and I stood by the flickering fire and my fingers touched something on the mantelpiece. It was Mother's gloves. I pulled my hand away like I'd touched something hot. I started shaking my head to try to clear it.

'Marnie, dear . . .'

'What got her off?'

'Well, 'twas the doctor really. Dr Gascoigne. And then—'

'She told me it was all his fault for not coming when he was sent for!'

'Yes, well, dear, that was only 'er way of seeing it later on. It done him no 'arm because 'e was dead. It just made it seem better to 'er to tell it to you that way. If I—'

'Why should he try to get her off?'

'Well, 'twasn't quite like that, but he said in the box she was suffering from something – something like purple—'

'Puerperal.'

'Yes, puerperal. Puerperal insanity, caused by worry and distress and what not. It was true more'n likely . . . Women do get that way sometimes after childbirth. They go off their 'eads temporary like. A few days or so and they're good as new. 'Tis a sort of fever that takes 'em.'

I finished wiping my hands. I put the towel on the table. I put my fingers through my wet hair, threading it back from my face and eyes. I said: 'I still don't know why she did it. You've told me nothing. And I don't know why she fed me those lies. Why all that story, all that lying story about the doctor not coming and . . . Why did *you* let her lie?'

Lucy's eye was watering. 'You was all we got, Marnie.'

'That doesn't answer anything.'

'Well, dear, you was all we got.'

I said: 'I mean, if she didn't want to tell me the truth couldn't she at least have just kept her mouth shut? Couldn't she? Why couldn't she?'

'I believe 'twas comforting to her to feel you was on her side . . .'

There were real footsteps on the stairs this time and Doreen came in. She said: 'I had nasty dreams. My, Marnie you look as white as a sheet!'

CHAPTER NINETEEN

THE FUNERAL was at two. Uncle Stephen came about half past twelve. We hadn't seen each other for four years. He didn't look as good-looking as I remembered him, but he still had the same smile and the same grey eyes that saw through you. I went through that funeral like a sleepwalker, I really did.

There were seven of us and six wreaths. Doreen had ordered one for me. In fact she'd fixed everything. The only thing she hadn't fixed was the narrow turn out of the stairs into the hall. They had to get the coffin down by sliding it through the kitchen door but then, it wouldn't turn, so they took it up two steps and tried the other way. But it still wouldn't go so they had to stand the coffin on its end like a mummy-case and get it round that way. I wondered if the tiny thin corpse inside had slipped down and was going to be buried in a heap for all eternity.

I thought I ought to be buried too. Or I thought I'll go on the streets to celebrate. But I wouldn't be as discreet as mother. What the hell. No soldiers tapping on my window. The door would be open wide.

Just before we left the house I was sick again, but

after that I was all right. I nearly burst out laughing in church, but it's just as well I didn't as I should never have been able to stop. And it wasn't at anything funny either. It was the church on the hill. I forget the name, but from the churchyard you could see over the roofs of the houses to Torbay. The sea was like a blue plate with bits chipped out of the edges. Over to the west I fancied I could see the roofs of the new Plymouth, the Guildhall and the shopping centre, where the buildings had grown up out of the rubble and dust that I remembered as a kid.

It was bright but perishing cold; the wind whistled through the trees from the north and made my coat feel like rice paper.

I thought, I wonder what Mark's doing. It was the first time I'd thought of him since I came last night. I thought, well, no one will be after me in all that much of a hurry now because I didn't steal anything yesterday. I shan't be missed till tomorrow probably or the next day. By then I can still be in France.

But was it any longer all that urgent to run to France? For the first time now with this death I was really, truly free.

Uncle Stephen's hair was blowing in the wind. He'd gone quite white, though he was a good bit younger than Mam, five or six years. He wasn't like Mother at all, except that maybe they'd both got a good shape to the bones of the face. Christ, I thought, I've been living – what have I been living? Why didn't *he* tell me?

I remembered now that girl at school, Shirley Jameson, what she'd said. That had begun the fight; I'd gone at her with waving fists. She'd said: 'Garn, putting on airs ! Your mother done a murder!'

Well, so Shirley was right after all. Come to think of it, that often does happen – that the thing somebody tells you when you're a kid that makes you the most indignant at the time – sooner or later you find it's true. It's one of the things you learn . . . And me afraid to tell Mother I'd pinched a few pounds to keep her comfortable! I did laugh then, but somehow it must have sounded like a cough because no one turned round.

'Ashes to ashes,' said the vicar, 'dust to dust. If God won't take her the devil must.'

No, he couldn't have said that, I must have misheard him, I was going crazy. But of course I *was* crazy. That was obviously what had been wrong with Edie Elmer. I was her daughter, I took after her. Except that instead of going with soldiers I ran away from them. I couldn't stand them touching me. Perhaps that was just the other side of the penny.

All her life had been a lie. How much of mine had been? Bloody near all of it. I'd started from scratch and built up a beautiful life of lies – three or four beautiful lives all as phoney and untrue as Mother's. I wasn't even content with one.

I felt I wanted to break the top of my head off. What a fool she'd made of me! What a fool I'd made of myself.

The others were moving away now but I didn't move. The shiny brown box with the brass plate and the brass handles had gone into the red earth, the sexton or whatever he was was leaning on his spade. I didn't feel any grief. In a few weeks I'd changed from feeling too little to feeling too much – like a skin rubbed raw – but now I'd passed out of that into numbness again. I just stood and stared at the hole in the ground. It was like a slit trench. The wind blew a cloud over the sun. There was an oak tree about my height standing beside the next grave; it was covered with brown withered leaves that rustled in the wind; the leaves should have fallen long ago. They were like lies that had long since forgotten what they were told for but lingered on and on. You told a child about Father Christmas until he was ten and then you told him the truth. But some people fixed their children up in such a paper chain of make believe and sham that they never got free.

Well, now I was free, free as I hadn't ever been before. Free of Mark and free of Mother and free of Forio. They were all gone and as good as dead. I ruled a line under them. Now I started afresh.

Uncle Stephen touched my elbow. 'Marnie . . .'

'Go to hell,' I said.

'The others have left. I've sent them on. Anyway Doreen has a train to catch. Lucy can fend for herself . . .'

'So can I.'

'Presently yes. You'll have to. But before we do any more I want a talk with you. Lucy tells me you know about your mother.'

'Go to hell,' I said.

'Marnie, dear, we have to talk. I've a taxi here. Let's drive somewhere.'

'I'll walk, thanks.'

'Come on.' He got hold of my arm.

Suddenly I hadn't any more fight left in me. I turned away from him and went down to the waiting taxi.

We drove down and had tea somewhere; it was one of the posh hotels, and I thought afterwards he took me into a public place because there I couldn't give way or blow off altogether – that's while I still had some feeling for appearances. He was taking a hell of a risk. I felt like kicking the table over. But it wasn't temper, I swear it wasn't that, it was just the most awful despairing deathly empty desolation, which was more than any human being could stand.

He said: 'Marnie, take a hold of yourself.'

'What bloody right have you got to say what I shall do?'

'Marnie, stop swearing and try to see this thing straight. I know it's been a terrible shock, losing your mother and then learning all this about her so suddenly just afterwards. But see it in its proper proportion. If you'll let me talk about her – perhaps it'll help.'

'If you'd talked about her ten years ago you might have some right to talk now.'

'What, told you this when you were thirteen? In any case I hadn't any right to: you were her child, not mine. But if I had, are you saying you would have understood what I'm going to tell you now?'

I stared across six white tablecloths at a bowl of flowers; narcissus, iris, tulips. I realized for the first time that his voice had a west-country burr.

'Edie was older than me,' he said, 'but I was always very fond of her and I think in a way I understood her.

354

It's all the rage now to blame one's failings on one's mother and father; but if you blame any of yours on her, then you ought to blame some of hers on *our* father. Your grandfather was a local preacher; you knew that, I suppose?'

'She said so.'

'He was a local preacher but he was a plasterer by trade, and in the twenties he was out of work for more than eight years. It turned him sour, narrowed him in a funny way. He got more religious but it was religion gone wrong. When your grandmother, my mother, died Dad went more and more into his shell, and Edie took the brunt. Did you ever think of your mother, Marnie, as a woman? I mean apart from her being your mother. She was what you might call a highly sexed woman.'

'So I should think!'

'Yes, but don't get it wrong. She was always attractive to men – she always had a boyfriend but she was too strictly brought up to kick over the traces with them. I was her kid brother; I know. She stuck with Dad till he died. She was thirty-three then. Thirty-three. Does that mean anything to you? Heaven knows what sort of struggle went on in her. She took the brunt with Dad; he was terrible at times; he'd got tremendous authority too, like an Old Testament prophet. She got to be a bit like him these last few years, only not half as bad. I used to duck out. As soon as I could I went to sea.'

He offered me tea but I shook my head. He said: 'Two months after he died she married your Dad. I think they were happy. As far as I could tell they were happy. I think for the first time she began to lead a normal life. I think she – well, let's be blunt, I think she discovered what she'd been missing. I think Frank found he'd wakened something in his wife he'd hardly expected. Not that it mattered so long as he was at home . . .'

This hotel had a veranda overlooking the sea. The only people sitting on it were three tottering old ladies. They were like mother sitting there, like flies in the last sun.

Uncle Stephen said: 'When you were evacuated to Sangerford, she was alone, far more alone than she'd ever been before she married. Life had wakened her up – and wakened her late. Now it told her to go to sleep again. That's not so easy. She began to see soldiers.'

'Yes, it was plural, wasn't it?'

'I'm not defending what she did. I'm only trying to explain it, to try to see why it happened. With another woman, differently brought up, differently made, it might never have happened. The end, the business of the child, that certainly wouldn't have happened.'

'Are you trying to tell me that the way she was brought up made her murder her own son?'

He stopped at that and began to light his pipe. 'Marnie, your mother was a strange woman, I'm not pretending anything else. She was capable, especially in later years, of enormous self-deception. The way she swallowed your story of this wealthy employer – Pemberton – who showered money on you—'

'You didn't believe it?'

He took the pipe out of his mouth to shake his head.

'I don't know how you came by your money and I'm not going to ask, but I don't believe in Pemberton. Neither would she if she hadn't wanted to and been capable of willing herself to. Well, somehow during that fantastic period in Sangerford she succeeded in living in a world of make-believe. I know why she slept with soldiers – because she wanted to and had a consuming desire for love – but I don't know how she got it past her conscience. Have you ever thought what it's like to lead a double life?'

I winced. 'Well?'

'Perhaps she thought – and I don't mean this as a dirty crack – perhaps she thought she was helping the war effort by giving the soldiers her love. Somehow she went on through each day as if the nights never happened. She was still Abel Treville's respectable, carefully dressed, good-mannered daughter. She was still Frank Elmer's faithful wife. She was still your devoted mother.'

I made some noise, but it wasn't words he could answer.

He looked at me with his grey eyes. 'When the new child started coming it must have blown her make-believe world to shreds. God knows what she thought or how she reasoned then. But somehow she got herself into a frame of mind in which she could deny the child's existence even to herself. Of course the doctor was right. At the end her mind was temporarily deranged and she did what she did . . .'

We sat there then for a very long time. The waiter came and Stephen paid the bill and we sat there. And the old ladies began to feel chilly in the veranda and moved out into the lounge. A page-boy came past with the evening papers from London. Nobody bought one.

I said: 'If I'd been the judge and they told me a woman like that was mad I should have said, why did she make no preparation for the baby? Was she mad for nine months before?'

We got up and started to walk back to Cuthbert Avenue. We walked, and the cold wind was still blowing through the town. By the harbour a few boats bobbed and lurched, and over beyond it the palm trees rustled like raffia skirts.

I said: 'Did you know I was married?'

'Married? No. I'm very glad to hear it. Who is he?'

'Glad,' I said, and laughed.

'Shouldn't I be? Aren't you happy? Where are you living?'

I said: 'It never had a chance. It was queer from the beginning. I was queer. I don't like men. I can't bear them touching me. It disgusts me and turns me cold. I got pushed into it – into getting married. I didn't want to. The man – Mark's his name – tries to love me but it's hopeless. He means well but he hasn't a clue what's wrong with me. I went to a doctor, a psychiatrist. He began to pry around. But he hadn't unearthed in three months a quarter of what I've dug up in a night by finding that newspaper cutting. I remember it all now. But it doesn't help.'

'It must help. Any psychiatrist would say so, Marnie. The business of remembering is half the battle.'

'It depends what you remember. I'm queer – out of

the ordinary, see – I've been different from other people ever since I was ten . . . I'm queer and I'll stay queer. These last months I've learned about psychiatry. This doctor – Roman – has told me—'

'My dear Marnie, I can imagine the sort of shock you got that night; that by itself is enough to explain anything that has happened to you since—'

'But it's too easy,' I said. 'You don't explain people as X and Y. It doesn't work out. Maybe I had a shock. Maybe I've had another shock now. But it isn't all. Ever heard of heredity? What goes on when people are born? You take after your parents. You've just told me that mother was getting like *her* father. Well, I'm like my mother. What was she, I ask you? She was one of two things. She was either a murderess or a lunatic. You don't need psycho doctors to tot up what's wrong with me. I take after my mother, that's all. I've had proof of it more than ever these last weeks.'

His pipe had gone out. He stopped to knock it against a stone post on the promenade. I waited impatiently. He put the pipe in his pocket.

'There's always two to a marriage, Marnie. Frank, your father, was as normal as I am. And I'm her brother; is there anything specially wrong with me? You don't have to take after her. But even if you did, you wouldn't necessarily act as she did. You still don't understand her.'

'I don't want to understand her! What's there to understand anyway? Let's change the subject.'

'No. You're forcing me to defend your mother, so I will. You see – you see, my dear, she was a very passionate woman and a very inhibited woman – and also rather an innocent woman. Oh, I know you think that's fanciful, but imagine what an experienced woman would have done in her case. First she'd have taken good care not to have a child. Then, if that had gone wrong, she would have quickly seen to it that she lost it. My dear, anyone can if they know the ropes. She didn't. Perhaps she tried a few old wives' brews, I don't know. But nothing more. She went to her full time under the pressure of ignorance, her fantastic conscience ground into her by her father, and her own desperate make-believe. Under these pressures she became temporarily insane. There's no reason on God's earth why she should have passed on to you a character that would act in the same way even given those circumstances. Quarrel with your peculiarities if you like, but don't think they have to be incurable!'

We walked on. I wanted to be rid of him then; I just wanted to be on my own, to walk away somewhere completely solitary and think.

I said: 'Have you ever heard her talk about sex, about love? All her life she's tried to poison me against it. Can you beat that? Can you beat it really?'

'People come to hate the things they suppress. The man who loathes cruelty is often the man who's suppressed the streak of cruelty in himself. When your mother recovered from her illness and found sex was no longer for her – as she did – wasn't it natural, with her upbringing, to look on sex as the cause of all the evil that had come to her and want to warn you about it?'

'Well, it was the cause of all the evil, wasn't it?'

'Only because it was at first wrongly denied and then later wrongly used.'

'You argue like Mark.'

'Your husband?'

'My husband.'

'Tell me about him.'

'He's no longer important.'

'Sometimes, Marnie, I feel very guilty, going off to sea the way I did, first letting Edie take the brunt of Dad and then letting you take the brunt of Edie. Somehow I've got to stay now and help you – try to help you – to see things right.'

We turned up Belgrave Road. I said: 'I know you helped years ago. I think in a way you've helped now. But there isn't any carry on from here – between us, I mean. Tomorrow or the next day you'll go back to Liverpool, and I shall go – wherever I decide to go. If we talked this over to the end of our lives there wouldn't be an easy answer, because an easy answer – or an answer of any sort – I mean, it probably doesn't exist. You've told me your side of the story. Lucy's told me hers. But the one who could really tell me everything, from the inside, can't any longer. All my life she fed me with lies and she's gone to the grave never saying a word. That's a fact. There's no getting round it, and I have to live with it – if I want to live at all. And the only way I can live with it is fighting it out myself alone. So will you leave me now? I'll come home later. I can't face that house yet. I expect I'll be back some time tonight.'

He put his hand on my arm, and we stopped. 'Marnie, will you promise to come back?'

'Yes. I promise.'

'I'd rather stay with you.'

'I'd rather be alone.'

CHAPTER TWENTY

WHEN HE had gone, I turned back down Belgrave Road and began to walk back along the promenade. The wind was behind me now and it kept whipping at my skirt and thumping me in the back as if I ought to hurry.

The sun had just set, and there was a smear like a blood-stain in the sky over to the west, and the sea kept tumbling against the wall and then sucking itself away again. Two nuns were coming along the promenade and the wind was making ugly wings of their habits. They struggled past me, not looking up, their heads bent against the wind.

Well, I suppose I could go and be a nun. That would be one solution, getting rid of my sickness on God. If I took the veil I was at least out of harm's way. Or I could go to the opposite end of the seesaw and try some top-pressure whoring. I wondered if there were any professional whores in Torquay. I wondered how you went about it.

Or were the stones the best way out? Over these railings, and the sea would soon take away all the remains. That was easiest. In order to live, there had to be a reason for living, even if that reason was only staying alive. I hadn't any. The can was empty.

Funny, I thought, I'm free. Free for the first time in my life. I've told myself this twice before today, and it should have given me a thrill. Well, it hasn't.

What was the difference? Mother was dead, and she'd left a poisonous smear behind like a snail that's gone underground. But my sickness lay deep, deep, deeper than that.

I stood by the rails and got hold of them hard and then I went one by one over the things that had made life pleasant enough during those long months working in Birmingham and in Manchester and in Barnet. I counted them and not one of them helped me. I'd a mainspring gone. My life had been turned inside out like some gigantic awful conjuring trick, and I was like an animal turned physically, disgustingly inside out, walking the wrong way, looking cross-eyed, split down the middle of my soul.

I got moving again. I went past the Pavilion and then turned away from the sea towards the town. It was quieter and less blustery here, and there were quite a lot of people about. But it wasn't like Plymouth.

I walked up the main street. I turned into the pub on the corner and ordered a brandy. Although it wasn't long after opening time the place was nearly full. The man next to me had a mouth like the back of a lorry that falls down to let the gravel out. He was talking about the football match he'd been to last week. 'We was playing twelve men,' he kept saying. 'Twelve men.

The ref. ought to've been strung up. Little runt. Twelve men we was playing. If it's the same tomorrow I'll do for him.'

The man next to him started eyeing me. He was a little type in a check cap, and his eyes were all over. You could see what he was thinking; I didn't need to be Edie's daughter for that.

It was getting as smoky as an opium den in here already. The bar was wet and the barmaid, a fat black-haired girl, wiped it over with a cloth. I only had to smile at check-cap, just the one smile. He'd do the rest. I thought, what are you scared of? Coming to have a child and murdering it and living with that all the rest of your life? Wanting sex and telling your-self you hate it and it's dirty? Is that what you'll come to?

Well, what was stealing but lies? Why did I blame mother more than myself?

I turned away from check-cap and took my drink to a table. There was this one woman sitting at it. She was about forty and she was floppy, with big eyes and big lips and big comfortable breasts. She was wearing the sort of dress and coat I'd have worn five years ago before I began to learn. She said: 'Hullo, dear. Hot, ain't it?' One of those brown ale voices.

As I sat down, there was a mirror advertising Teacher's Highland Cream that reflected us. I saw her, and sitting down next to her was this girl in the short brown coat and the curling hair, and the fringe, with the yellow blouse with the stiff-pointed collars. She didn't look much different from usual. She didn't look like that crazy animal pulled inside out.

'Feeling queer, dear?' said the woman. 'All this smoke . . .'

Four new people pushed their way past. A fat man with check trousers and slits in his jacket bumped the table and nearly upset it.

'Clumsy clot,' said the woman. There were three empty glasses by her and a fourth half full of Guinness.

I thought, but it isn't only the lies that matter, is it? It isn't just mother sleeping with soldiers, it isn't even her strangling her kid. It isn't just all those things. It's everything that's happened to me on top of it. You get a bad foundation and then you build crookedly on that . . .

'Try a Guinness, dear,' said the woman. 'Them short nips are no good. What is it, brandy?'

Yes, I said to myself, but not to her. It was the first brandy I'd drunk since that evening in that other pub in Ibiza, when all the crowds had been revelling and I'd argued with Mark. And suddenly I found there were tears squeezing out of my eyes. God knows what they meant, but they came.

'What's the matter, dear? Quarrelled with your boy-friend?'

That girl in the mirror was fumbling about, and then she got a handkerchief out and dabbed at her face, but it took a time to stop. I thought, Teacher's Highland Cream? Rat poison for you.

'I had a boy-friend once,' said the woman. 'Here,

MARNIE

swallow that down and let me buy you a Guinness. It's
settling, is Guinness. Here, you, two Guinness. See?'

She said this to a barman in a white coat that was
spotty and unbuttoned. She leaned her breasts on the
tabletop. 'He was a sailor, this boy, this partic'lar
boy . . .'

I thought, Mark didn't know what he was taking on.
Neither did Roman. Some hopes they'd got, either of
them, of making a normal woman of me. Oh, Mark, I
thought, I did make a mess of it for you, didn't I . . .

'. . . I said, Bert, you've got a kind heart, and kind
hearts are more than what's-its; but it ain't enough.
You got to be loyal. I thought afterwards 'twas a funny
word to use. Of course I meant faithful . . .'

Loyal, I thought. Well who'd been loyal to who in
all this? There wasn't any loyalty except maybe Mark's
for me. It wasn't a thing human beings dealt in much.
Keep that for the 'lesser' animals, horses and dogs.

I drank some of the Guinness this woman had
bought. Had I even spoken to her yet? I couldn't
remember. Supposing I told her everything? What
would she say? All her experience was with the normal
things gone awry. Mine was with the abnormal ones.
Supposing I began: 'I'm a thief and my mother's a
whore . . .'

After a minute I looked in this mirror again and I
saw to my surprise that the girl was talking. And the
blowsy woman had stopped. I mean, she'd stopped
talking and she'd got her big comfortable mouth open
listening. And she looked startled and uncomfortable,

like somebody who's picked up a blind worm and found it's a rattle-snake.

I think I told her everything. I'm not sure. I told her enough to make her wonder if she's been getting acquainted with an escapee from the local mental home. Which I suppose was near enough to be true to make no matter.

While I talked I looked in the mirror and thought there goes Marnie Elmer, the old Marnie Elmer. She wasn't a bad-looking girl, and although she was hard-boiled, she didn't really want to do anyone any *harm*. She was just a certain dead loss from the day she was born. Better if her mother had done for her as well.

Well, she was done for now anyhow – this was the end of her, in this pub. When she'd finished telling this woman all her sad, sad troubles she'd walk right out and disappear for ever. Was there anyone going to be born in her place? Was there anything worth saving? Not Mollie Jeffrey, not any of those people. It had to be somebody utterly fresh.

Perhaps I was a fool to take it the way I did. While I talked I unburdened some of the horror and the shock. At least I was free. It was the fourth time I'd told myself that. I kept saying it, expecting a reaction, because all the time I was married to Mark I'd so desperately wanted to be free.

I could go out of here and say, maybe I am a bit mad like my mother, but what about it? I'd got by so far, and no one could call me a fool. I could live off my wits . . . Muriel Whitstone . . . that was a nice name . . .

I said: 'So that's about all. You wanted to know what

was wrong with me. Well, now you know. Thanks for the Guinness. Can I buy you one?'

She fairly gaped at me. I said: 'I'm not batty – or not very. It's all true, what I've told you. Funny what happens to some people, isn't it?'

I ordered a Guinness for her and a brandy for me. Some more people had come in and that man with the mouth started his same old story: 'We was playing twelve men. I tell you. That blasted ref.'

The woman said: 'You're having me on, dear.'

'God's truth, I'm not.'

I suddenly needed the brandy. I realized for the first time why some people take to drink. It's to drown the pain in their guts that being alive has put there.

The waiter came and I paid him and I splashed a bit of soda in and had gulped the glassful down while the woman was wiping a moustache of froth off her upper lip after her first swallow.

She said: 'But why did you leave your hubby, dear? Didn't you hit it off?'

'Well,' I said, 'it was more than that.' But I looked at her big easy breasts and broad gentle face and thought, it's no good, I can't explain *that* to her – or I could explain it but no amount of talking would ever clue her up. Because for her sex was like a comfy chair, a warm fire, a glass of Guinness. It didn't mean more and it didn't mean less. How could she ever understand what it had been like to be screwed up, horrified, disgusted; how would she have a notion if I explained that the repulsion, the dislike had been something more than I could deal with? Had been? Still was? I didn't know.

I said: 'I'd better be going.'

'Well, dear, you sure give me a fright. You look so young and innocent. Reely . . . But I shouldn't worry if I was you. Life's all right if you don't weaken. You can't help what your Mam did, can you? I mean, it's not sense. How do I know what my mother did when she was twenty? She was a dear old soul when she was seventy, but that's different. Dear life, I'd not want to tell my kids everything!'

As I left the pub check-cap was there. 'Like a lift, miss? Which way you going?'

'Not your way,' I said.

'Oh, come on, be a sport. I got a nice little Sprite round the corner. I'll give you a run round in it first.'

'I bet you would,' I said, stepping off the pavement.

He stepped off beside me. 'It's over there. See? The red one. New last year. Ever been in one? It's an education.'

'Being in yours would be,' I said, and shook his arm off and walked away. He followed for a few steps and then gave up.

I walked right up to the top of the street to where there was a church at the top. It was quite dark now. Muriel Whitstone, I thought, blowing out a breath with brandy on it, Muriel Whitstone is being born. I'll go and spend the night in Cuthbert Avenue and tomorrow I'll pick up my few things and push off. I'll go first to Southampton, and then I'll take a bus for Bournemouth. There I'll have my hair done a different way and my eyebrows plucked and maybe some other things done, and on Tuesday I'll leave for Leeds. It's all exciting really, just the way it used to be, building up a new history, making a new person. And this time the money I get I'll spend entirely on myself. To hell with the world.

At the iron gate by the church there was a kid crying.

I said: 'What's up with you?'

He said: 'I lost me Mum.' He was about eight.

'Where d'you live?'

'Davidge Street. Number ten. Over there.'

I thought, crazy, leaving a kid of his age to wander about after dark. 'Is it far?'

He shook his spiky head. 'Dad's there.'

It was nearly on my way. 'I'll take you if you like.'

'Don't wanna go.'

'Why not? Your Mum might be home before you.'

That started him crying again and then coughing. He'd got a lousy cough, like a shovelful of wet coal. I got hold of his hand, and began to walk with him. Under the light of the lamp he looked thin and hot. Dressed all right but thin and hot.

I thought, maybe if I was a nun I could care for sick children; maybe that would make up for the one that was put under my bed . . . This kid's hand was in mine, as trusting as if I was his maiden aunt.

'How did you come to lose your mother this evening?'

'Didn't,' he said.

'Didn't what?'

'Didn't lose Mum tonight.'

'What d'you mean?'

'Lost 'er Wednesday.'

We went on a bit. We came to Davidge Street and went down it. I hadn't got a toffee for him or anything. I thought suddenly, I don't care a *damn* for Muriel Whitstone. I don't *care* if she never comes to life at all! I'm not interested in her and her lousy secretarial jobs and her thieving. I don't know what's going to happen to Muriel Whitstone, but Marnie Elmer has *had* it. She can't invent other people any more. And she can't go on living herself.

'What d'you mean?' I said. 'Your Mum went away on Wednesday? When's she coming back?'

'She ain't never coming back,' this kid said. 'They told me she'd gone visiting but I knew better. I seen her. They carried her out in a box. She's dead.'

He began to cry again, and I put my hands round his head and held him to me. I thought that's right, be a mother for a change. Bite on somebody else's grief instead of your own. Stop being so heart-broken for yourself and take a look round. Because maybe everybody's griefs aren't that much different after all.

I thought, there's only one loneliness, and that's the loneliness of all the world.

CHAPTER TWENTY-ONE

I DON'T know what time I got back to Cuthbert Avenue. I suppose it couldn't have been all that long. I saw the boy in and saw his father and then walked home. It may have been seven or half past.

The kid's father was a thin weedy type with sandy hair.

'We come here from Stoke because of them saying the weather was better. Not so hard for Shirley. I changed me job. Three pound a week less. But so soon as she come here she started spitting blood. They wanted her to go to hospital, but no. "Never again," she says. "I'll die in me own home," she says. Bobby slipped out when I'd me back turned. He knew. Tried to keep it from 'em but they all knew.'

If he'd asked me I'd have stayed. There were three other children and he looked very down. But he didn't ask and I couldn't offer. Afterwards I wished I had. It might have given me something to do instead of just thinking.

If I could have something to do that took up sixteen hours of every day.

When I got to Cuthbert Avenue there was a car

stopped outside No. 9, and I thought I'd seen it before, and I suddenly had a funny feeling that it might be Mark.

Of course it wasn't Mark; he didn't know where I was, and anyway he didn't get out of hospital till Monday. But seeing the lights of the car reminded me of that time coming out of Garrod's Farm where he'd traced me and been waiting for me, and I thought, well, he wouldn't be as unwelcome now as he was then. I mean, in a way, I could have told him everything the way I'd told it to that woman in the pub, and perhaps in his case he might have partly understood. He'd always made a great effort to understand. You could hate him and yet have to admit that he did his best to understand.

Perhaps I didn't hate him any more. I was too tired and beaten up to hate anyone, least of all him.

And as I walked up the avenue I knew I would have been glad to talk to him. That was quite a shock but I had to admit it. Compare what the rest of my life had been, and the time I spent married to him had been comfort and sanity and decency and order. Oh, there'd been the big stumbling block, and perhaps it was still there and perhaps it would always be there, but the rest was all right.

And you *could* talk to him.

There was one personality I hadn't thought about when I was writing off all the Mollie Jeffreys and the Muriel Whitstones. That one was Margaret Rutland. What about her?

But anyway it was all too late. She'd gone out of the gun with the rest.

I was thirsty again and I stopped at the door wondering if there'd be any drink in the house. Not likely. Mother would see to that. Had she secretly wanted to be a drunkard too?

I hadn't a key and knocked on the door. Old Lucy opened it, just like last night, except that her face wasn't so swollen. She said: 'Oh, Marnie, we was hoping you'd come. There's a gent to see you.'

I went in and into the front room. Uncle Stephen was sitting there talking to Terry.

CHAPTER TWENTY-TWO

THE ROOM was badly lit. This bowl thing hanging from the ceiling was supposed to spread the light, but in fact it threw most of it up so that your face was in a sort of half shadow. Terry's face was in half shadow.

He said: 'Oh, good, my dear. I've only just come. I went to Cranbook Avenue first. I wasn't sure.'

He was wearing a yellow tie with a green sports jacket and a maroon waistcoat. I said: 'How did you know where I was at all?'

'I heard the SOS message. I never thought it was you until I rang you a second time today and there was no reply. Then it suddenly occurred to me, my dear. I thought, that was her mother.'

They were drinking beer. I suppose Uncle Stephen had got it from somewhere. I sat down in a chair. 'What have you come for?'

'I thought I might be able to help. I didn't know how you were fixed.' He was smiling sympathetically. There was still something not quite clear about it but I was too beaten up to bother. It was like a dream – going on with one I'd begun somewhere else on my own.

Uncle Stephen said: 'Mr Holbrook was telling me your husband had been seriously injured in a riding accident. I'd no idea. You should have told us, Marnie.'

I was still looking at Terry. 'He's not worse?'

'No.'

Lucy came in. 'I got supper ready, dear. 'Twill do us all good. Mr 'Oldbrook? I laid four places.'

'Thanks, I'd like to,' said Terry. 'Though I mustn't be late starting back.'

We had the meal in the dining-room which had all new furniture I'd bought for this house, so it didn't remind me so much as the other rooms. I wished I could remember why I hated that clock in the kitchen. I never could. But while I sat there pecking at some cold ham and pickles I remembered the rough feel of khaki on the back of my legs when I was lifted up and put on a man's knee. And I remembered a terrible thing like a battle, like a war, bursting suddenly over my head. It was Dad and another man who were fighting . . .

'Eat your 'am, dear,' said Old Lucy. 'If I'd known we was 'aving company I'd have baked.'

Nobody was talking much at the table. I suppose nobody knew how much anybody else was supposed to know, and they were afraid of saying the wrong thing. Terry and Uncle Stephen began to talk about under-water fishing.

'Marnie.' It was Terry.

'Yes?'

'Why don't you drive back with me?'

'Where?'

'Why don't you let me run you home?'

I dug my fork in a piece of ham but didn't lift it off the plate.

'Why don't you?' said Uncle Stephen.

'Why don't I what?'

'Let Mr Holbrook drive you home. It's been a hard day for you, and if your husband's not well you should be with him, otherwise he might worry. Lucy and I can tidy things up here. Can't we, Lucy?'

''S I reckon,' said Lucy, and looked at me with her big eye.

'I couldn't,' I said, 'go home.'

'You could come down again in a few days. Really, it's much the best way.'

'Mark's still in hospital,' I said. 'I can't help him that way.'

But even while I was speaking there was a sudden flush of feeling inside me that said, why don't you. Even though I knew it was mad I listened to it. You see, more than anybody else I suddenly found I wanted to talk to Mark. More than anyone else he'd forced me to talk when I didn't want to, so he really knew more about part of my life than anyone. I wanted to go back to him and fill up the gaps. I wanted to go and tell him and say, this is the sort of female I am, this is what happened to me, this is the rotten stock I came from: can you wonder I didn't fit in with your fancy notions of a wife?

You see, there was no one else I *could* talk to like that. No one at all, not even Roman. I felt if I could see Mark and talk to him and *explain* a bit, it would help me – and also it would help him to understand. I'd say to him, d'you realize who you've been living with, d'you realize who you wanted to be the mother of your children? And if I said that to him I think he would have some sort of a view of it that would make me better able to live with myself.

That was all. I just wanted to explain. It wasn't a great ambition.

I didn't want to go back to him permanently – I just wanted to talk.

Uncle Stephen said: 'If you'll leave tonight I'll promise to see personally to everything here. I can stay several days . . .' He rubbed his nose and looked at Terry and then said carefully: 'You see, Marnie, this isn't your life down here any more.'

Lucy was breathing on her cup of tea to cool it; the steam went across the table nearly to where Terry was cutting the bread on his plate into squares.

I said to Terry: 'Why have you come?'

Everybody looked at me. Terry said: 'My dear, I thought I might be able to lend a helping hand.'

'D'you mean that?'

'Why not? You don't think I came to this Queen of Watering places for *pleasure*, do you? I thought, Marnie's in difficulties and Mark's ill, so perhaps I can help.' His mud-coloured eyes flickered up at the other two and he grinned. 'Oh, I admit I feel no personal love for Mark. Would you, my dear? But I don't believe in carrying my grudges around on my back.'

'You'd – drive me home?'

'Of course. Or if you don't want I'll leave you here. It's all the *same* to me. I'm only offering to be neighbourly.'

I was still too tired to think quite straight. I got a feeling that I had missed something, but for once my brain didn't tick. It was still half-way through that dream.

He said: 'Or maybe you'd like me to do something else to help. What do you think, Mr Treville? Is there anything I can do here?'

'Take Marnie home. That's really the only thing. I'd be very grateful if you would and I'm sure she will be too.'

Wishing is like water caught in a dam. You let a little trickle of it escape and you don't think it's much, but in no time the trickle has worn a channel and the edges fall in and the water's doubled and then you get a flood carrying everything away. That's the way it was with me then. Obviously I'd be crazy to even think of seeing Mark again; but I wasn't answering to reason any more. I *wanted* to see him. I'd got to *tell* him.

All the same I didn't let on right away. I just let myself drift along to the end of supper, and then after supper I went up into Mother's bedroom and stood there for a few minutes, and I looked at the clothes in the wardrobe and the old blue dressing-gown with the silk buttons behind the door, and the high-heeled shoes – three pairs, very small, all black; and suddenly instead of being evil she became just pathetic. All she'd done, except perhaps one thing, was pathetic, and her lies and her build up and her crazy pride . . . I thought of her for one last time as the person I'd loved most in all the world, and the person since early this morning that I'd hated most – and the twelve hours since this morning seemed as long as all the rest of life. And now

I didn't seem to have any feeling for her any longer except pity.

And I thought, perhaps if you pity her enough you won't have any left for yourself.

The room was empty and cold, and there was the faint stale stink of hyacinths and corruption.

And I went downstairs and told Terry I would go back with him.

It was a cold night but the wind had dropped and I kissed Uncle Stephen and old Lucy and told them I'd come again in a few days, not perhaps ever really intending to.

I didn't imagine, I carefully didn't think it out yet beyond a certain point. I didn't face up to all that going back might mean.

We drove fast through the night. We went through Newton Abbot and skirted Exeter and took the A30 and the A303 through Honiton and Ilminster and Ilchester towards Wincanton. I thought, life's like being in an insane asylum. Everybody goes about with their own delusions hugging them close for no one else to see. So you plough through the wards among all the milling figures towards what looks like one sane man. That's what I was doing now.

Terry said: 'Queer, you know, I rang up on Wednesday, asking you to come for a drive round with me on Friday evening – and here we are, my dear, having that drive. You never know your luck, do you. You never know which way the dice is going to roll.'

381

That clicked something into place. 'But how did you know my name was Elmer?'

'My dear, I'd always felt your first marriage was a fake, you *know* that. I didn't care a cuss, but it irks me to have a feeling that way and not to *know*. So I went to the register office and looked up the entry of your marriage to Mark, and found that he'd married a Margaret Elmer, spinster, of the parish of St James's, Plymouth.'

'I see.'

'Care to tell me about it?'

'Not now, I wouldn't, Terry.'

'Did Mark know all along?'

'Fairly early on.'

Terry whistled a little flat tune. 'He's a queer character, Mark. He's like a weathercock; you never know which way he's going to blow.'

'It isn't the weathercock that blows, it's the wind.'

'Defending him for a change? It's so much more stimulating when a wife has a healthy antagonism for her husband. Why did you ever marry him, my dear?'

Why did I marry him? I might know that, but did I really know why I was going back to him? Did you go back to a man simply to explain? And after I'd explained, how was I going to leave again?

Terry said: 'Pardon me for sounding melodramatic, but did he have a "hold" on you or something? After all, it was plain as a wall that he was mad about you – and pretty soon it was nearly as plain that, behind that lovely give-away-nothing expression, you hated the sight of him. I mean, it was enough to make any fair-minded cousin curious.'

'Yes, I suppose it was, Terry.' If I hated the sight of Mark, why did I want the sight of him now? Had I changed? Had something happened? Had a lot of neat little gadgets inside me all suddenly gone into reverse just because I knew a bit more about them? No, it wasn't that, it couldn't be that. Even in a madhouse life didn't make that much sense.

Anyway, if anything had happened to me, I mean had happened to me to make any sort of difference in the way I thought or felt about Mark, it wasn't just this or that, it wasn't just the discovery about Mother or such-like, it was an add-up of everything that had been going on for weeks. It was Roman and Forio and living at that house and mixing with those people and finding out about Mother and being with Mark all in one, all tied up in one great unravellable mess, like a ball of string a cat's been playing with.

'You haven't answered,' said Terry.

'Answered what?'

'Are you in love with him?'

'Who?'

'Well, Mark, dear, who else?'

'I don't know . . .' My God, didn't I? Of course I wasn't, but it didn't do to tell Terry everything.

'And does he still love you?'

'I think so.' Does he? What have you done to keep it alive since you were married? Lived like a sulky prisoner, refused him love, thwarted his intentions

383

whenever you could, played his psychiatrist up, tried to drown yourself and then to break your neck and his as well. Why should he love you? Now you've got stomach cramp. What the hell's that for?

We went through Andover and turned off on the Newbury road. There was more traffic here and Terry had to pick his way.

Terry said: 'It's rather important to me to know if he still loves you.'

'Why?'

'Well, unless he does, there's not much point in my taking you back, is there?'

'. . . You're very kind.'

'We all have to do our deed for the day.'

What had Mark said once? 'I want to fight for you. We're in this together.' The stomach cramp didn't go away. Of course I knew what I was going back to. If I found Mark as I'd left him, still anxious to do something about our marriage, even with all this knowledge in front of him, and if I decided to stop and try too, then it meant facing one of the two choices about the stolen money. Even if he could, I knew he'd never settle for any other way, and I knew if I stayed with him I'd have to agree to let him go ahead with the attempt to buy people off, probably.

But was there any sense in even thinking of staying with him, seeing I knew now what I did about myself? Would he want me to? It was pretty lunatic ever to have let myself be talked into coming back at all.

I must have made some move because Terry said: 'Getting stiff?'

'No.'

'Why don't you go to sleep?'

If I went back now nobody would know I'd been away – that was odd. Except Terry nobody *need* know.

'Terry . . .'

'Yes?'

But that was the old way again. Lies and more lies clogging up the pores. I couldn't ever get straight with Mark or with myself on that platform.

'Yes?' Terry said.

'Nothing . . .'

We had to stop at a garage near High Wycombe for petrol. I thought of Estelle's little car I had left behind in Torquay, and wondered what would happen to it. In spite of myself I was feeling sleepy, and soon after we started again I must have dozed off for a bit. I woke up with the lights dazzling across the windscreen from an oncoming car, but I still felt drowsy and in one of those moods when you haven't got quite all your hard-boiled skin tightly buttoned on. I mean I suddenly thought, what if you do love Mark? You crazy cretinous ape, what if you think you love him now; is it any surer than the hate you felt at Ibiza? And I suddenly realized that I couldn't *reason* any longer, that my brain wasn't going to direct me what to feel any more; I was suddenly emotional and female and hopeless, and if Mark was there at that second I should have gone blubbering into his arms wanting love and comfort and protection. Hell, how feeble-minded can you get. I was glad he wasn't there; but who was to know that I shouldn't act like that when we did meet?

Anyway tonight I should be alone in the house in Little Gaddesden and a night's sleep might give me a chance to get things ironed out and put on the line.

Dirty washing. I was a mass of dirty washing – why should I expect Mark to do the laundry for me? I ought never to have come back. There he was standing at the door and there was a thin woman in black standing next to him and as we got nearer I could see it was Mother. 'Come in, dear,' she said, 'I've explained it all to Mark and he quite understands about the baby. He says he'd have done the same in my place.' And she opened her mouth to smile but in place of her teeth . . .

I reared up in the car and blinked ahead at a twisting road. We were following a lorry, and the red light kept winking in and out as we turned the corners.

'All right?' said Terry.

'All right.' After a minute I said: 'I'm sorry about you and Mark, Terry. You know I've always liked you. I'm sorry we can't all be friends.'

'Think nothing of it. There's a lot of life left. In twenty years we shall have forgiven each other for the dirty tricks we played on each other, and we shall have forgiven each other for not having forgiven each other earlier.'

That red eye of that lorry was like Dr Roman's eye when he tried to hypnotize me – only it worked better. It had a nasty dirty wink about it. Roman said: 'It's no good coming to me, my dear. I can't help you now, my dear, it's not psychological, it's in the blood. Child murder, it carries on from generation to generation; if you had one of your own you'd do it in, my dear. You're for it, my dear, didn't you know?'

Suddenly the red eye got bigger and bigger and came up to my side of the car and peered in like an evil face, and then before I could scream we'd overtaken the lorry and it was gone.

'Not long now,' Terry said. I thought even he sounded tired and strung up.

Mark was there waiting at the door again, only this time Mother wasn't with him. He came out, down the path past the stable to the small gate. And he said: 'It's all nonsense, Marnie, all these barriers you're putting up. *Nothing's* in the blood, *nothing's* in the upbringing, *nothing* happened at Sangerford that we can't throw away for ever if you want to *try*, if you've got courage and some *love*. Because they're so much stronger than all these shabby ghosts. If you once find your way through the first thickets, there's nothing then that we can't do together.'

I jerked my head up as the car began to slow. I said: 'There's nobody here, because I sent Mrs Leonard home. But I'll be all right tonight.'

'OK.'

I said: 'I think I'm pretty well all in, Terry. I'd ask you in for a drink but I'm pretty well all in.'

'That's OK.'

I said: 'I'll try somehow to make it up between you and Mark, Terry. It may not be too late.'

'It'll be impossible.'

'Why?'

'Well, my dear, I tell you it'll be impossible.'

The car turned in at the drive, but the gravel crackled in a different way. The house – there was a light in the house.

Terry blew his horn.

It wasn't Mark's house. I said: 'Where are we? This isn't our house.'

'No. I had to call here. I promised. It won't take a minute.'

I looked at him. His face had got a shiny look as if it was damp. It was shiny like a fish, with rain or with sweat. It looked green. He was whistling but there wasn't any sound.

The door of the house opened. A man stood at the door, and there was another one behind him.

Terry said: 'You see, my dear, I'd arranged to take you for a run this evening. You promised to come so I arranged to call in and see these people – for a drink. It's about four hours later than I arranged but that can't be helped, can it?'

'What are you talking about?'

The man came down the steps. The other man followed him. There was a woman at the door now.

The man who was first down the steps was Mr Strutt.

Terry said: 'In a way I'm sorry to do this to you. At the last minute it seems pretty hard to – to carry through. In a way I'd rather it hadn't to be you, my dear. One makes promises to oneself. One pays one's debts, if you see what I mean. But I doubt if you'd understand.'

'I don't understand.'

Even his eyes looked green in the light coming from the house. 'Just work it out. You don't need to look very far. I'm sorry, but really, you know, Mark had it coming to him, didn't he?' He was still talking half to me, half to himself – talking to keep his own thoughts off himself, I think – when Mr Strutt opened the door.

'Good evening, Miss Holland. We'd almost given you up.'

'I telephoned,' Terry said.

'Yes, but it *is* rather late. Do get out, Miss Holland, we want to ask you a few questions. Let me see, you know our Birmingham manager, don't you? Mr George Pringle.'

When that sort of thing happens to you you don't faint. Not if you're my type, you don't. You get slowly out of the car and look at Mr Pringle for the first time for two years, and you're suddenly back in that office and you remember every pimple and blemish and blotch of his face.

And behind you you hear the other car door slam and you know that Terry has got out, and for a moment that swallows everything else, how you've been such a fool as to think he was willing to be a friend to the wife of the man he hated most in the world. Half of your mind thinks that and the other half thinks but maybe it was better that you never suspected he would stoop this low. If you have to live in the world, then you have to have some view of the world that doesn't drip with slime.

And they've not exactly caught you, but they stand one on either side of you and slowly you begin to walk up the steps to the top where Mrs Strutt is waiting. And you think, well, this is the end of everything now, it's out of your hands. This is the end. For a second you think, maybe you could fight, you could still fight; deny everything, how can they force you to admit what you won't admit; just go on stalling till Mark comes. But when the second is gone you know somehow that that isn't the answer any more, that is, if you really are going to make a break with things as they used to be.

And you think – because it's true what people say, that a drowning man lives all his back life in a few seconds, and so a drowning woman has plenty of time to think between steps – and you think anyway whatever happens you can still wait till Mark comes. Everything rests on him.

But by the time you are at the top of the steps – and Mrs Strutt, looking embarrassed and rather sorry for you, has stepped aside to let you go in – I mean you know that really deep down at root it isn't Mark it depends on but you yourself. Because he can only help you to help yourself. If you can't stand him touching you and you still only want to get away from him and you want to go on living a solitary life and codding up a make-believe world with a different name and personality every nine months and rustling bank notes stuffed surreptitiously in your handbag – then he can't help at all. He can only help if all that is over and instead you want at any rate to try to love him and to trust him and to be loved.

And the only way to love and trust now was through this door, among enemies, with a police-sergeant any minute being called at the end of the phone.

I stopped there and looked back, but not at any of the three men. I looked across the garden. The high wind was still blowing here, and a ragged cloud like a broken fish and chip bag drifted just over the trees. The trees were rustling and waving and they smelled of pines. All the garden looked dark and foreign and strange.

Mark had said: 'I want to fight *for* you. We're in this together'; that was something I'd have to hold on to.

I thought, the way to love is through suffering. Who had said that? Did it mean anything or was it just the usual talk?

You know, I thought, this isn't going to be the hardest part, this is the easiest part, going through this door.

I took a deep breath and turned and went in.

WINSTON GRAHAM

Ross Poldark

£6.99

PASSION, TIDE AND TIME –
THE LEGENDARY CORNISH SAGA RETURNS

*Cornwall in the 1780s – when powerful forces of revolution
and reaction are at large in the world.*

Tired from a grim war in America, Ross Poldark returns to his
land and his family. But the joyful homecoming he has
anticipated turns sour, for his father is dead, his estate is
derelict, and the girl he loves is engaged to his cousin.

But his sympathy for the destitute miners and farmers of
the district leads him to rescue a half-starved urchin girl from
a fairground brawl and take her home – an act which alters
the whole course of his life . . .

*The first Poldark
A Hero   A Heritage   A History*

'From the incomparable Winston Graham . . . who has
everything that anyone else has, then a whole lot more'
Guardian

WINSTON GRAHAM

Demelza

£5.99

CORNWALL 1788–1790 . . .

Demelza Carne, the impoverished miner's daughter Ross Poldark rescued from a fairground rabble, is now his wife. But the events of these turbulent years test their marriage and their love.

Demelza's efforts to adapt to the ways of the gentry – and her husband – bring her confusion and heartache, despite her joy in the birth of their first child. Ross begins a bitter struggle for the rights of the mining communities – and sows the seeds of an enduring enmity with powerful George Warleggan.

The second Poldark
A Hero   A Heritage   A History

WINSTON GRAHAM

Jeremy Poldark

£5.99

CORNWALL 1790

Ross Poldark faces the darkest hour of his life. Accused of wrecking two ships, he is to stand trial at the Bodmin Assizes.

Despite their stormy married life, Demelza has tried to rally support for her husband. But there are enemies in plenty who would be happy to see Ross convicted, not least George Warleggan, the powerful banker, whose personal rivalry with Ross grows ever more intense.

The third Poldark
A Hero   A Heritage   A History

WINSTON GRAHAM

Warleggan

£5.99

CORNWALL 1792

Ross plunges into a highly speculative mining venture which threatens not only his family's financial security, but also his turbulent marriage to Demelza.

When Ross and Elizabeth's old attraction rekindles itself, Demelza retaliates by becoming dangerously involved with a handsome Scottish cavalry officer. With bankruptcy an increasingly real possibility, the Poldarks seem to be facing disaster on all fronts . . .

The fourth Poldark
A Hero   A Heritage   A History

All Pan Books are available at your local bookshop or newsagent, or can be ordered direct from the publisher. Indicate the number of copies required and fill in the form below.

Send to: Macmillan General Books C.S.
                Book Service By Post
                PO Box 29, Douglas I-O-M
                IM99 1BQ

or phone: 01624 675137, quoting title, author and credit card number.

or fax: 01624 670923, quoting title, author, and credit card number.

or Internet: http://www.bookpost.co.uk

Please enclose a remittance* to the value of the cover price plus 75 pence per book for post and packing. Overseas customers please allow £1.00 per copy for post and packing.

*Payment may be made in sterling by UK personal cheque, Eurocheque, postal order, sterling draft or international money order, made payable to Book Service By Post.

Alternatively by Access/Visa/MasterCard

Card No.   ☐☐☐☐☐☐☐☐☐☐☐☐☐☐☐☐☐☐

Expiry Date   ☐☐☐☐☐☐☐☐☐☐☐☐☐☐☐☐☐☐

Signature   _____

Applicable only in the UK and BFPO addresses.

While every effort is made to keep prices low, it is sometimes necessary to increase prices at short notice. Pan Books reserve the right to show on covers and charge new retail prices which may differ from those advertised in the text or elsewhere.

NAME AND ADDRESS IN BLOCK CAPITAL LETTERS PLEASE

Name _____

Address _____

_____

_____

_____

                                                8/95

Please allow 28 days for delivery.
Please tick box if you do not wish to receive any additional information. ☐